BRUMBY'S RUN

THE WILD AUSTRALIA STORIES - BOOK 1

JENNIFER SCOULLAR

PILYARA PRESS

Version 1.0
Print: ISBN 978-1-925827-02-6

Pilyara Press
Melbourne

ALSO BY JENNIFER SCOULLAR

Currawong Creek (The Wild Australia Stories - book 2)

Billabong Bend (The Wild Australia Stories - book 3)

Turtle Reef (The Wild Australia Stories - book 4)

Journey's End (The Wild Australia Stories - book 5)

Wasp Season (The Wild Australia Stories - book 6)

Fortune's Son (The Tasmanian Tales - book 1)

The Lost Valley (The Tasmanian Tales - book 2)

The Memory Tree (The Tasmanian Tales - book 3)

DEDICATION

To those who help the brumbies. To those who rescue, train and rehome them. To those who campaign to improve their management in the wild. To those who work to raise their profile as part of Australia's heritage, and also as wonderful riding and companion horses

It lies beyond the Western Pines
Towards the sinking sun,
And not a survey mark defines
The bounds of "Brumby's Run"

Brumby's Run
by Banjo Paterson

PROLOGUE

'Choose, Mrs Kelly,' says the doctor. 'The adoptive couple is here to collect the child.' He leans in close and lowers his voice. 'They're concerned there's a problem.'

Well, wasn't there? If this didn't count as a problem, then nothing ever would. Mary smiles at her sleeping twins. How to decide? There is no way, it's Sophie's choice. She could play eeny, meeny, miny, mo? Or rock-paper-scissors with the doctor? He wins, and Charlene might go. She wins, perhaps Samantha? The doctor puts on a sympathetic expression. 'Of course, if you've changed your mind ...'

'No,' says Mary, with hoarse haste. 'I haven't.' It would be difficult enough raising a single baby. She plucks one, then the other, of her dark-haired daughters from their shared crib, and cradles them in her arms. She inspects their faces. All the clichés make sense to her now. They do have button noses, and rosebud mouths that purse sometimes in sleep. They are utterly perfect, and she can't choose. She can't even tell them apart.

'Mrs Kelly.' Mrs Kelly. Why is he calling her that? There is no Mr Kelly. A sop to his own sense of propriety, perhaps? 'If you need more time, perhaps the couple can come back.'

No, that will prolong the agony. She just requires some sort of a sign, some indication of what to do next. The left-hand twin parts her lips in a delicate yawn. The room grows airless. With infinite care, Mary raises the baby that lies in the crook of her other arm, her right arm, and offers her to the doctor.

'Are you sure?' he asks.

Of course she isn't sure. There is no certainty any more, and there never will be again. The world is a senseless place, filled with random acts of cruelty and prejudice, but she nods anyway. As he receives the right-hand baby from her, she yawns too. A misgiving, cold as death, stalls Mary's heart. The doctor checks the infant's wristband. She wills time to stretch. She counts the seconds it takes for him to cross the floor, to reach the door, to vanish with her baby. She consciously commits each detail of the scene to memory. Mary looks down at the single, sleeping baby in her arms. Is it Charlene or Samantha? What if she's given away the wrong child?

CHAPTER 1

'I'll rub him down myself,' said Sam.

Brodie gave her a lascivious look. 'Sure you don't want a hand?' He chewed on a piece of straw. It dangled limp from the corner of his fat lips.

She slammed the stable door in his face, causing Pharaoh to start. Brodie mooched off. Sam hung up the horse's hay net, stuffed it full of his favourite lucerne, and kept some hay aside to make a wisp. Her deft fingers twisted the leafy stalks into a long, thin rope. Then she gathered the top end into two loops and wound the remaining string back through to form a solid pad of hay. 'Ready, Pharaoh?' The big chestnut lent his body towards hers. 'One, two three …' She began to strap his neck with long, regular slaps. The tempo increased as she found her rhythm. Pharaoh tensed and relaxed, tensed and relaxed, in time with Sam's movements, and she slipped into a kind of meditative trance. The horse was not the only one to benefit from such an isometric workout. By the time she'd worked her way along his back and rump on each side, girl and gelding were both spent.

Sam sighed in satisfaction. Summer was just a week away, and life was good. Her eighteenth birthday and the endless exams of Year Twelve were behind her now. The future stretched invitingly ahead –

a future where her mother wasn't in charge of every aspect of her life. Since Dad had taken up his overseas posting a couple of years ago, it had been just her and Mum, rattling around in their big old house together, getting on each other's nerves. A white Christmas, and a month with her grandparents in France, was just what the doctor ordered. Fingers crossed Dad could talk Mum into going back to Dubai with him. The prospect of coming home alone was too perfect to contemplate. She'd be able to spend each spare minute with Pharaoh, preparing for the summer dressage trials. And maybe, without Mum interfering all the time, she might even find herself a social life.

'Samantha?' Her mother peered over the stable door. Whatever was she doing here?

'Just a minute.' Sam hid the wisp, so Pharaoh wouldn't eat it, and went out into the stable yard. Her mother's always pale complexion had turned ivory, and her eyes were red, like she'd been crying. But that was impossible. She never cried. 'What's wrong, Faith?'

'I wish you wouldn't call me that. It's not natural.'

Sam was ready with a smart remark, then thought better of it.

Her mother seemed genuinely distressed.

'Get cleaned up, Samantha. We need to talk.'

'You can't talk to me when I'm dirty?'

Faith heaved a great sigh. 'Don't be difficult, darling. Get changed and meet me at the car. We'll do lunch.'

Sam was starting to worry. She was already halfway through her mushroom risotto, and Faith had barely said a word. Her salad lay untouched. Sam reached across and stole a cherry tomato and an olive from her mother's plate.

'Mum? You said we needed to talk.'

Faith gave a tremulous sigh and met Sam's gaze. 'There's no easy way to say it, so I'll just say it.' A dramatic pause. 'You mustn't hate me, Samantha.' What on earth was she on about? 'Promise me?'

Sam wanted to argue the absurdity of making a blind promise, but her mother's expression silenced her. 'I promise.'

Faith's clasped hands trembled, just a touch, where they lay on the white, linen table cloth. 'Samantha.' A deep breath. 'Your father and I adopted you as a newborn.' Odd shivers fluttered like moths across Faith's shapely neck. 'We couldn't have children, you see.' Her eyes lost focus for a moment and she corrected herself. '*I* couldn't have children.'

It felt like all the blood had drained from her head and formed a sickening pool in her stomach. Sam's chest grew tight. Why was her mother saying this? Was she sick? Delusional? Sam had known for a long time that something was wrong. She'd found pills in Faith's upstairs bathroom and looked them up on the internet. Anti-depressants. But this? It didn't make any sense.

'I'm sorry for calling you Faith,' Sam said, struggling to understand her mother's words. 'Instead of Mum. Some girls at school were doing it with their mothers. I suppose they thought it sounded more grown up, or something.' Sam gave an encouraging smile. 'Of course you're my mother.'

A brief ripple of relief flitted across Faith's face. She reached for Sam's hand with icy fingers. 'Thank you, darling.' Her voice was taut. 'You're right, I am your mother, in every real sense of the word. Your birth certificate says so, doesn't it?' She paused, and tears tracked down her pale cheeks. 'But I didn't actually give birth to you, I'm afraid.'

Sam withdrew her hand and placed it in her lap. She examined her mother's face. There was no trace of artifice. She tried the adoption hypothesis on for size, dared to examine it. Plenty of times, as a teenager, she'd imagined she didn't belong to her parents, had even hoped that she didn't. But that was just wishful thinking. Wasn't it?

'What do you mean? Where did I come from, then?'

Faith took a very deep breath. 'Your birth mother lived in a small country town, in the north-east of the state. Currajong. She was unmarried, Samantha, and quite poor. She relinquished you as an act of self-sacrifice, to provide you with a better life.' Faith fanned herself with the menu. Beads of sweat appeared on her flawless forehead. 'She was just a girl . . . only seventeen.'

Faith fixed Sam with cool green eyes. Sam had always envied her mother those startling green eyes. Her own were the same dark brown as her father's. Tea arrived, and Faith poured herself a cup, her hand steadier now. 'This is extraordinarily difficult, darling. You have no idea.'

Sam gasped for air. Faith had always skirted around the story of Sam's birth, protesting that it was something she didn't like to talk about. *I can't explain it. Quite an out-of-body experience. It felt like somebody else was giving birth to you.* There was also a lack of physical resemblance between them. It had always bothered Sam, but she'd put it down to taking after her father in a big way. Faith was petite and fair. Sam was tall and leggy, with the slender strength of a natural athlete. Her sable hair always threatened to escape its tie and fall in unruly waves around her shoulders – quite a contrast to Faith's neat blond bob. These differences seemed suddenly imbued with a dreadful significance. Sam fought against a rising suspicion that her mother was telling the truth. 'I had a right to know all this a long time ago,' she said, in a faltering voice.

'Please, Samantha. I'm telling you now, aren't I?'

The ground shifted beneath Sam's feet and a million questions raced through her brain. 'I need to know everything,' she said. 'Times, dates, places . . . people. I can't promise I won't be angry. I deserve to be, if I want to be.' Sam heard the high panic in her voice. 'Who am I?'

Faith looked around uneasily. 'Darling, you're making a scene.'

So that's why Faith had brought her to this popular restaurant for lunch. There'd be less chance of any histrionics. It was like a public dumping. 'I want to go home,' said Sam. 'To talk. But first, answer me this. Why are you telling me now? Why is it suddenly the right time?'

Faith looked unsure again. She clung to the edge of the table, as if it might somehow anchor her to safety. Several times she opened her mouth to speak, then wavered. 'There's more,' she said at last. 'You are . . . you're a twin.'

A twin? Now this was plainly ridiculous. They were back in the territory of delusion. Sam wondered if she was asleep, and began to run through the techniques she used to wake herself from conscious dreaming.

'Apparently,' continued Faith, 'your sister is very ill and wants to see you. Her mother – your birth mother – contacted me.' She spoke too fast, as if the words were loathsome, or poisonous, and she wanted to spit them out before they killed her. 'You don't have to do this, Samantha. We don't even know these people.'

The sharp sting of impending tears stabbed Sam's eyes, her nose, her throat. It was like she was seeing her mother for the first time. 'And whose fault is that?' She grabbed her bag from under the table and ran out the door.

CHAPTER 2

The most important meeting of her life, and she was running late. Faith had offered to come along, but Sam had sensed her reluctance. In the end she'd gone off in a cab by herself, under a gloomy sky. It was probably for the best. This was something she needed to do alone. The car swished through the rainy streets. Sam stared out the window, stomach knotted tight in anticipation. She was about to meet a sister she'd known about for less than twenty-four hours.

The hospital was enormous and confusing, a rabbit warren of corridors and lifts and doorways. Preoccupied people rushed this way and that, everybody certain of where they were going – everybody except her. A fat woman pushed a teenage girl towards her in a wheel-chair. Could that be her mother? Her sister? She turned to watch them pass, and cannoned into an orderly. 'Lost?' he asked. Sam nodded, and he steered her to a reception area.

When she gave her name, the receptionist reached for the phone. 'Samantha Carmichael here to see you.' She gave Sam a warm smile. 'He'll be down in just a moment.' Who would be down? Sam stood, ill at ease, wondering what to do. An escape out the front doors was at the top of her favoured list of options.

A tall Asian man in a suit emerged from a nearby lift and looked in her direction. He beamed when he caught sight of her, and hurried over. Sam stood awkwardly and took a few tentative steps towards him. 'Samantha Carmichael.'

He grasped her extended hand and shook it energetically. 'No need for introductions, Miss Carmichael. I know exactly who you are.' His smile was kind. 'I'm Professor Andrew Sung, head of the acute myeloid leukaemia program, and the diagnostic molecular haematology laboratory. If you'll please come with me.'

Sam followed him back into the lift, up to the tenth floor, and into a large room. It was some sort of lounge, with sofas and low tables and a flat-screen television on the wall. A loud gasp came from the corner, from a woman standing near a coffee machine.

Sam turned and knew she was looking at her birth mother. She blushed with shame to think that she'd wondered about the person pushing the wheelchair. Did she think she wouldn't know her own flesh and blood? Sam had never seen anybody that looked so much like her before. It hurt more than she could have imagined.

Professor Sung took the woman by the hand and led her over to Sam. 'Samantha Carmichael, this is Mary Kelly, your birth mother.'

'Hello.' It was all Sam could manage, a shy hello.

Mary Kelly was an attractive woman, with a high forehead and even features. Sam had calculated her age, from the scant information supplied by Faith. Mary looked much older than her thirty-five years, looked at least as old as Faith, and Faith was almost fifty. Mary's hair, russet and wavy, was streaked with grey. Her eyes were set in dark rings, and fine, vertical wrinkles pinched her lips. The impression was one of tarnished beauty. Her eyes though were Sam's own, and at the moment they were very wide indeed.

'Samantha,' said Mary. The word sounded like a prayer on her lips. 'You're so very lovely . . . and so very kind to come.'

Mary looked at Professor Sung, and Sam saw something pass between them. He gave Mary a tight-lipped nod. 'There's a good chance, yes,' he said.

'A good chance?' said Mary. 'There's more than a good chance. I couldn't tell them apart when they were born, and I doubt if I could now, except for Charlie being so skinny and all.'

Sam pricked up her ears. Her sister's name was Charlie. Sam seized onto this new piece of information, as if her life depended on it. Charlie. That was a boy's name. It must be short for something. Charlotte, perhaps. She explored the word, tried to conjure up an image based on the name.

'This is too perfect,' whispered Mary. A great smile transformed her face. It shed its shadows and creases, its worry and care. It was suddenly clear that she had once been a great beauty.

Sam tore her gaze away from this stranger who was her mother. 'A good chance of what?' she asked.

'We mustn't put the cart before the horse,' said Professor Sung. 'This is a lot for Samantha to take in. However, since time is of the essence…Would you like to meet your sister?'

'I should bring her something,' said Sam, in a sudden panic. 'At least some flowers.'

The professor shook his head. 'Your sister has a suppressed immune system. She can't have flowers, or fruit. Nothing like that.'

Time was of the essence, the doctor had said. How sick was her sister? Was Charlie going to die, before she even got to meet her?

Mary and the doctor were talking to each other in low whispers.

'Is my sister okay?' said Sam in a sudden panic. 'What's wrong with her?'

Mary burst into tears. Professor Sung placed a hand on the woman's shoulder, but she kept on crying. 'Samantha?' He gestured towards the door. 'Let's have a talk?' Sam trailed out of the room after him, leaving Mary behind.

Professor Sung led her to an adjacent waiting room and indicated for her to sit down. He pulled a chair over and sat facing her. His expression was kind, concerned. 'I'm a haematological oncologist, which means I'm a doctor with special training in the diagnosis and treatment of blood diseases, especially blood-cell cancers.'

'Is that what my sister has? Cancer?'

He nodded. 'Yes. It's something called CML – chronic myeloid leukaemia.' There was a practised pause in his spiel. Leukaemia. That was bad. Sam's friend's little sister had died from leukaemia. Sam felt a sudden shiver down her spine.

'When someone has CML, the bone marrow produces too many white blood cells. They interfere with normal blood production and cause anaemia, bleeding and bruising, that sort of thing.'

'Can't you do something for her?' asked Sam. She wanted to say Charlie instead of *her*, but she couldn't find the courage. To say *her* was horrible. She was ashamed to refer to her sister like that.

'Your sister is in what we call the accelerated phase of the illness. She's had the standard treatments, but nothing has worked. It's unfortunate she wasn't diagnosed earlier, but her family live in quite a remote, rural area. Her symptoms weren't recognised until they became debilitating, and by then the disease was advanced."

'Is she going to die?' asked Sam. Her phone rang, Faith's number. Sam turned the phone off mid-ring.

'We're a long way from that point,' said Professor Sung. 'But I'll explain a little more after you've seen your sister.' He stood, and Sam did likewise, following him back to the lounge room.

Mary was clutching her arms nervously, pacing back and forth. 'I'm going to duck out for a cigarette.'

Sam was aghast. 'You're not coming with me?'

Mary shook her head. 'Charlie might want to see you by herself, just to start with. I'll be back in a jiffy.' Before Sam could protest, she hurried off to the lift.

'I'm afraid Mary can barely last twenty minutes between smokes,' said Professor Sung. 'The stress of Charlie's illness doesn't help.' Sam didn't know anybody who smoked cigarettes. Such a stupid thing to do. She felt a sudden burst of anger. It was inconceivable that she was related to that woman. Maybe they had it all wrong. Maybe she shouldn't even be here.

As they walked down the corridor, Professor Sung asked a lot of questions about Sam's health. 'Your sister's ANC count is low, so it's important that you don't have a cold, or anything like that. She's highly vulnerable to infection right now.'

Sam nodded, wondering what he was talking about. 'ANC count?'

'It stands for *absolute neutrophil count*,' he said. 'An estimate of a person's infection-fighting white blood cells.'

They walked into a ward, and stopped at the nurse's station. A middle-aged woman looked up from her notes, and did a double take. She looked from Sam's face to the doctor's, and back to Sam. 'Oh my Lord,' she said. 'Charlie's sister.'

'Do I look like her, then?' asked Sam, excitement mounting in her chest.

'That you do, dear. That you do. I'm Colleen.'

'This is Samantha,' said Professor Sung. 'Could you fix her up with a mask and gown, please?' Colleen took Sam's temperature and asked her to wash her hands. After she'd finished, Sam donned a disposable gown, popped on a mask, and followed the professor into a nearby hospital room.

There was a window, a steel hospital bed, and a figure on the bed. That must be her sister ... that must be Charlie. No matter what happened next, her sister would never be just *she* or *her* again. Sam held her breath as she approached, barely daring to believe she was in the same room as her sister. Tubes sprung from Charlie's chest and left arm, attached to a dangerous looking silver machine. It loomed beside the bed, like a Dalek out of Doctor Who. Charlie's eyes were closed, and she was motionless.

'What does that machine do?' asked Sam. She didn't know why she was whispering.

'That's a leukapheresis machine, filtering out abnormal white blood cells.' The doctor observed her concerned expression. 'It's quite painless.'

A soft toy frog, Kermit green, sat on Charlie's bedside table. There were more frogs on the windowsill, some in zip-lock plastic bags. Ceramic frogs, plush frogs, wooden frogs. Sam dared to focus on the figure in the bed. Charlie wore faded Chinese pyjamas and a colourful scarlet headscarf. A beautiful scarf, vibrant and out of place in the functional sterility of the hospital room. Charlie's eyes opened suddenly and she reached for a remote control, turning off the tiny television mounted on a swinging arm above the bed.

Sam got her first good look at her sister. Why did Colleen say that they looked alike? There wasn't much of a similarity, was there? Maybe Sam couldn't see past Charlie's gaunt eyes and sunken cheeks. Maybe she just didn't want to. It was frightening to imagine herself looking that sick. Then Charlie smiled and the resemblance was plain. 'Take off your mask,' said Charlie. 'Just for a minute, so I can see you.' Sam looked at Professor Sung, who nodded. Sam slipped the mask off. 'You're Samantha,' said Charlie. She swung her legs over the side of the bed, and started to sit up.

'Whoa there,' said Professor Sung. 'Not so fast.'

Sam hurried over and instinctively reached for her sister's back. It was strange being so close to Charlie – like looking into a magic mirror in which your reflection had a mind of its own.

'This is the coolest thing,' said Charlie. She was frail, but her voice sounded strong. 'I've been dying to meet you all my life.'

'You knew about me?'

Charlie nodded. 'I've been wanting to find you for years, but Mum said that wasn't right. She said that it was your decision to make.'

Sam smiled bitterly. Her decision, except that she'd never even heard of Charlie. At least Mary had had the decency to be honest with her daughter. Her own parents had taken it upon themselves to erase Sam's entire history. She was sure that it was only Charlie's illness that had made Faith relent. Otherwise she may have never learned the truth. 'My parents didn't tell me about you. I didn't even know I was adopted. If I'd known …' There was no way to finish the sentence. This was all too new, too much.

'That sucks. We could have had so much fun tricking people. Nobody would have been able to tell us apart,' said Charlie. Sam was unconvinced and it must have shown. 'I haven't always looked this ill,' Charlie said indignantly. She took a photo out of her bed-side drawer and handed it to Sam, who shook her head in disbelief. It was a photo of herself, dressed in jeans and a check shirt. She was riding a horse she didn't recognise, a compact bay with a baldy face. The most amazing thing of all was what she was doing. She was chasing a cow.

'That can't be me,' said Sam, confused. 'I've never even seen that horse, or those clothes . . . or that cow.'

Charlie laughed, a healthy belly laugh that suited her wide smile, but not her skinny frame. 'No, it's not you. It's me, last year before I got sick.' She pulled a few more photos from the drawer – school ones, childhood ones, more on horseback.

Sam stared in disbelief at the images. 'We look the same; exactly the same.'

'That's right,' said Professor Sung. 'You may not have immediately recognised the resemblance, partly because Charlie is so unwell, but partly because it is sometimes difficult for us to see ourselves as others see us. But trust me, the likeness is striking ... and I hope it can be more than that. I hope it can be life-saving.' He took Sam's hand in his. 'Charlie's very best hope of a complete cure is to receive a syngeneic stem-cell transplant. That's a transplant from an identical twin. Very few people have such an option.' He patted her hand gently.

Sam slowly took in his words and their significance. She turned back to her sister, and saw Charlie's brown eyes, so much like her own, so full of hope.

'Perhaps we could talk a little more outside?' said Professor Sung. She couldn't leave yet! She'd just got there and had so many questions, so much she wanted to ask Charlie. But Professor Sung insisted. 'You two can catch up again later,' and with that he whisked her out the door.

Samantha sat next to Mary in a small room off the ward. Professor Sung sat opposite. 'Would you like me to explain things, Mary?'

'Would you?' said Mary. 'I don't have the words.'

Professor Sung gave her a brief smile and turned to Sam. 'As I said, Samantha, Charlie's best hope of recovery is a stem-cell transplant from a close relative. We've already tested your mother. Not a good match, I'm afraid.'

For a moment, Sam thought he meant Faith, and wondered why she would have consented to such a thing. Faith wasn't renowned for her charitable nature. 'If you wouldn't mind, could you stop calling Mary Kelly my mother? It's disconcerting. My mother is Faith Carmichael.'

Professor Sung held up his right hand, like he was going to swear on the Bible. 'You have my word.'

'And if Mary isn't a match, what about me? I could be one, couldn't I?'

Professor Sung gave her a pleased smile. 'You could be, Samantha. You could be a very good match indeed. Would you be willing to undergo some medical checks?'

'Of course,' said Sam. She wasn't about to forgo her lost sister just when she'd found her. 'Ready when you are.'

Mary put a hand over her mouth. Her eyes grew large, creasing her forehead like corrugated cardboard. 'You're an angel.' She moved to embrace her.

Sam dodged away from the woman's outstretched arms. 'I may not be suitable.'

'We're about to find that out,' said the doctor.

Sam spent the rest of the afternoon undergoing a battery of tests, and replaying the scene in Charlie's hospital room, over and over. She hadn't even said hello, or goodbye. She hadn't asked Charlie how she was. She hadn't hugged her or said what a miracle it was to meet her. She'd made a complete hash of it. The desire to see her sister again grew hot and insistent. When the final test was complete, Sam hurried back to the oncology ward, terrified that Charlie might die before she could talk to her properly. Colleen waylaid her with a gown and mask before she rushed into the room.

Charlie was sitting up, and the Dalek was gone. She wore a

different headscarf – emerald-green this time. It perfectly matched her stuffed toy frog.

'Hello, Charlie.' Sam walked over to the bed, and pulled up a chair. It was good to see her sister alone, and without the tubes tying her to the silver machine. 'How do you feel?'

'Not too bad,' said Charlie, with that sunny smile again. How could she look so happy? 'I'm freezing and there's an awful tingling feeling in my mouth, but it's not too bad. How are you, Samantha?'

It was an oddly formal question. 'People call me Sam.'

'Right. Sam. How does it feel, to know you've got a sister?' Charlie looked suddenly unsure. 'Are you okay with that?'

What a question. 'I'm thrilled,' said Sam. 'I always wanted a sister.' Charlie's expression remained unchanged. 'I'm not just saying that. I wanted a sister so badly, it was like . . . like I knew I should have had one.' Yes, that's how it was. Faith had said how lucky Sam was that she didn't have to share anything, when all she really wanted to do was to share everything. And she'd never really talked to Dad about it. How could she? Even before he moved to Dubai for his diplomatic posting, he was never home, and when he was, he was busy. So her desire for a sister had become a private wish, unexpressed though fervent. Something to dream about.

'We always thought you knew,' said Charlie. 'That was the deal when the Carmichaels took you. Mum said they were supposed to tell you.' Charlie swallowed hard and looked lost. 'They were supposed to tell you about us.'

Up until then, it hadn't occurred to Sam that her father was also complicit in the deception. Everyone she trusted had betrayed her. 'Well, they didn't.' Sam looked away trying not to cry. 'Can you tell me about your life?' she said, to change the subject. 'If you feel up to it?'

'I was about to ask you the same question.'

'I asked first,' said Sam. 'Who's the horse in the photo, for starters?'

'That's Tambo,' said Charlie. 'I broke him in myself, when they ran in the brumbies. He's one of the best campdraft horses in the district.'

'He's a brumby?' Sam looked at the photo again. 'He's beautiful.'

'There are lots of beautiful brumbies,' said Charlie. 'People don't realise how good they are.'

'I have a horse too,' said Sam. 'Pharaoh. A five-year-old Warmblood gelding. We do dressage together.'

'Dressage?' said Charlie. 'Now that's some fancy riding. People say twins have a connection. Maybe with us it's horses.'

Maybe. It was unlikely, though, that horses had played as central a role in Charlie's life – or in anybody else's life for that matter – as they had in hers. Horses had rescued Sam from a lonely childhood, a smothering mother, an absent father; they had been her sanctuary and her ticket to freedom. Anything worth knowing, she'd learned from the back of a horse.

Colleen came into the room. 'Time for your shower, Charlie,' she said. 'And it's time for you to go, Samantha. I expect we'll see you tomorrow then?'

Tomorrow? Sam nodded. Tomorrow and every day after that. Nothing mattered more than Charlie. Charlie reached for her hand and squeezed it. 'Will you really come tomorrow?' she asked.

Sam leaned down and kissed her sister's drawn cheek. 'Just try to stop me.' It was a wrench to leave the room. Sam hurried to the lift, faint with emotion. Mary was a little way down the corridor, waving madly. Sam didn't acknowledge her. Instead she slipped down the stairs, taking them two steps at a time, before escaping from the hospital into the rain-drenched afternoon.

CHAPTER 3

How to make her mother understand? 'Even if I'm a perfect match,' said Sam, 'and even if Charlie recovers quickly, she's still going to be in hospital for weeks, maybe months. I can't go anywhere for a while.' Didn't Faith realise how important it was for Sam to spend time with Charlie?

'But I've already bought the tickets,' said Faith, 'and arranged the itinerary. Dad's going to meet us there.' Sam shook her head. 'But you love France, darling, and your grandmother is expecting you.' Faith gave her a particularly intense look. 'She's eighty this year . . . it may be the last time.'

'Don't give me that,' said Sam. 'Mamie will outlive us all. And yes, I do love France, but I can't go now.'

'You're punishing me for protecting you,' said Faith. Sam struggled against a rising tide of resentment. 'I always had your best interests at heart.'

'Maybe you thought you were protecting me, but you weren't. You were lying to me, that's all. You and Dad.' Sam had spoken to her father on the phone earlier in the evening. What she'd hoped for was a proper apology, and some attempt to explain why he'd made a lie of her life. What she got instead was a flat denial of her right even to know. She would have preferred excuses.

'Things would be better all around if it hadn't got out,' he'd said, as if that was that. 'And this whole debacle proves my point.'

Easier for who? *This is about me, not you, Dad,* she'd tried to say. If he'd had his way, she'd probably still be in the dark, dying sister or not. She had to give Faith some credit. At least she'd found courage enough to do the right thing in the end.

'I knew this would happen,' said Faith. 'I knew I'd lose you someday.'

'You're not losing me, Mum. I love you, and I'm your daughter, no matter what. I just can't go to Europe right now, that's all. There's nothing to stop you from going.'

'Maybe I will,' said Faith in an injured voice. 'Don't you go falling for this Mary woman. Remember I'm the one who's loved you all these years.' There was an undercurrent of real anxiety in her mother's voice.

Sam blinked back the start of tears. 'I won't fall for Mary. I don't know if I even like her. But I have to be around to help Charlie recover – and I want to get to know her. It's about time, don't you think?'

Faith eyed Sam suspiciously. It had been an emotional morning for them both. Sam had demanded answers, and for once Faith was well and truly on the back foot. Endometriosis, she'd said. Nobody could imagine how she'd suffered. And a diagnosis of premature ovarian failure at thirty-two. 'You were the answer to all my prayers, Samantha. Daddy's too.' She poured herself a glass of shiraz and wrinkled up her face, like the wine wasn't good enough, but then nothing was ever good enough for Faith. 'I loved you from the very first moment,' Faith said simply. 'I had no idea, actually, that I could love somebody like that.' She took a sip. 'And now you stab me in the heart.'

Sam sighed, frustration and sadness clouding her mind. It was too much to expect, apparently, for her parents to see that this wasn't about them. 'Mum, you know that's not fair. I'm going to bed,' said

Sam, 'and I'm going to the hospital first thing in the morning. And I'm not going to France.' She tried to make the stairs before her mother could play the victim again.

'Fine,' called Faith, raising her voice and following Sam from the room. 'Do as you please.'

CHAPTER 4

They were a match. Genetically identical. Sam sat quite still as Professor Sung told her the marvellous news.

He handed her an information leaflet. 'HLA stands for human leukocyte antigen,' he said. 'It's a marker the immune system uses to recognise which cells belong to your body, and which ones don't. A good HLA match between donor and recipient is vital to the success of a stem-cell transplant.' Sam waited expectantly, encouraged by the broad smile spreading across his face. 'A transplant between identical twins, such as yourself and Charlie, guarantees complete HLA compatibility.'

Sam was hesitant. 'So this means?'

'There's an excellent chance of a complete cure. Really excellent.'

'Does Charlie know?'

'I told Charlie and Mary this morning.' The mere mention of Charlie's name provoked in Sam an unsettling craving. The pull of her sister was strong, and Sam rose to leave. He gestured for her to sit back down. 'I want to be sure you understand the process. For the next few days, starting from today, you'll receive injections to stimulate stem-cell production; to encourage their movement from your bone marrow out into your bloodstream. Meanwhile Charlie will receive high doses of chemotherapy, to destroy her diseased cells and make way for your new ones. If all goes well, we'll harvest your stem cells one day next week in the morning, and transfer them to Charlie that same afternoon. Do you have any questions?'

Only a million, but Sam shook her head. The details didn't matter. The only thing that mattered was Charlie getting well. The universe had narrowed its focus to that one pinpoint of light, that one wish. Professor Sung gave Sam an appointment card. 'You're booked in at the Apheresis Unit at eleven-thirty for your first G-CSF injection today. Will your mother be coming along?'

'I asked you not to call Mary that,' said Sam.

'I don't mean Mary. I mean your adoptive mother.'

For a moment the term made no sense. 'I don't need Faith's permission,' said Sam. 'I'm over eighteen.'

Professor Sung frowned. 'Only just, Samantha.' Of course. He knew how old Charlie was, so he knew how old she was too. How strange. 'The injections have some side effects, and I want somebody with you, to make sure you get home in one piece.'

'I'll be fine …' she began.

'No, no,' he said, holding up his hand. 'I'm the doctor, and I say you need a support person. Either I ring your mother, or Mary can look after you. Take your pick.'

Mary. She was a complete stranger. What use could she be? But things between Faith and Sam had gone from bad to worse lately. 'Fine,' she said, with a little eye roll that masked her apprehension. 'Mary then. Can I see Charlie now?'

Professor Sung nodded. 'Just remember, the chemotherapy will take it out of her. Don't stay too long.'

Colleen ushered Sam into the room, then closed the door. Charlie was connected once again to the ubiquitous battery of machines. A murky-looking fluid flowed through the central line, like a poison aimed straight at her heart. Charlie lay very still, eyes closed, listening to an iPod with headphones, flicking at it with her fingers. Sam watched her sister unawares – curious and guilty all at once. Charlie looked older, smaller, shrunken. Sam could blow her away with one breath; she needed weighing down. A black head-scarf patterned with scarlet salamanders and snakes coiled about her head.

Sam moved to the foot of the bed, into her sister's field of vision, and touched her leg. 'Hello, Charlie.' Charlie took out the earphones and grinned. The transforming effect of her smile was remarkable, like she'd switched on her life force. It shone brightly from her hollow eyes, and Sam answered Charlie's smile with one of her own. 'We're a goer,' she said, giving her sister the thumbs up.

Charlie nodded, face flushed palest pink with pleasure, and shifted position in the bed. It cost her a noticeable effort.

Sam experienced a stab of sadness, mingled with frustration. It was so unfair. She wanted to take off her mask, go for a walk with her sister, run with her, ride with her. They deserved at least that. Her parents had stolen their past, their right to a shared childhood, and now this cancer threatened to steal their hope for a common future. Aggravation must have shown on her face.

Charlie's smile fell flat, and she looked away. 'It's okay if you don't want to do the transplant. You can change your mind.' Her sister's voice was alarmingly weak, but Sam recognised the spiny prickle in the tone. It was too often in her own.

Sam pulled up a chair close to Charlie. 'Just try to stop me.'

Her sister's smile returned and she reached out her hand, bony and pale. An angry rash, like rope burn, extended from wrist to forearm. It disappeared beneath the sleeve of her unflattering flannel nightgown. Her sister deserved better. How far up did the ugly rash go? Did it cover Charlie's thin chest, her breasts? Did it hurt? Sam tried to think of something to say, a message of tenderness, but before she could find the words, Charlie gave her hand the faintest squeeze. The back of Sam's neck tingled.

'Thank the Goddess you're a match.' It was Mary's voice. She rushed to embrace Sam, clearly reaching for some sort of connection with her long-lost daughter. She wouldn't find one. Sam felt nothing for this woman; this woman who'd given her life, then given her away.

Mary turned her attention to Charlie and moved over to the bed without a word. She caressed Charlie's cheek, unwound the serpent headscarf, and pulled out a new one from a plastic bag in the bedside drawer. Sam flinched at the sight of Charlie's naked scalp. With ritual concentration and loving precision, Mary twisted the fresh scarf to shield her daughter's skull. It had a paisley tadpole design, rich teal in colour – almost aquamarine – with long ties and elastic at the nape. It was gorgeous, and a perfect fit.

An unexpected jolt of jealousy left Sam breathless. Was she jealous of Mary for her unspoken bond with Charlie, a bond born of years spent together? A painful stab of insight suggested it might be the other way around. That she might be jealous of Charlie for having had her real mother for her whole life. No, that was absurd. Faith was Sam's real mother. Despite all her flaws, she loved Sam, and Sam loved her. Sam mumbled goodbye and hurried from the room. Charlie's swift, disappointed glance stayed with her for a long, long time.

CHAPTER 5

Drew cantered towards the mob of horses and raised his rifle. A shot punched the frosty air, then another. The herd turned tail and galloped for the ridge line. He glimpsed a flash of hides through the branches: buckskin, grey and the usual bays and browns, perfectly camouflaged, blending with the trees. He'd been right. There was a mob of brumbies roaming Maroong Mountain.

Drew urged Clancy across the creek. Man and horse trotted alongside the rusted barbed wire that marked the boundary between Kilmarnock Station and Balleroo National Park. He spotted the big blue gum on its side, toppled in last week's storm. It had lain low ten metres of fence line, and hoof marks churned up the ground on both sides of the breach. Too late to do much tonight. Best come back on a bike in the morning.

Drew toyed with the idea of telling his father about the mob, but it would just stir up trouble. He and Bill were at odds about the brumbies. To his father they were nothing but pests, eating good grass that should be saved for fattening cattle. Things would be different if Gramps was still alive. He called wild horses the *spirits of the high country*, admiring their beauty and independence. He'd scoffed at Bill for his hostility, saying he had no heart, no feeling for the land. Drew had always marvelled at his grandfather's courage. Nobody else ever dared stand up to his father.

Drew peered through the darkening bush, but the horses were long gone, back up the mountain. Feed was scarce on the higher slopes this summer. They'd be back. But there'd be no more brumby running for Drew, no matter what Bill said. He'd joined his dad on a run last summer. Never again. For years he'd longed to go along, but had stayed away out of deference to his mother's wishes. It was only after she left that he'd joined Bill and the boys on a weekend trip up the mountain.

Mum had always called it cruel, and she was right. Drew hadn't understood, had thought her too sentimental. It wasn't as if they were shooting horses from helicopters, like they did in some parts. His father and the other brumby runners were financial members of the Alpine Feral Horse Management Association. They had permits to remove brumbies from the park. It was all above board, just a sport – a true test of horsemanship, and from all accounts, exciting as hell to boot.

Drew didn't like to think back on the experience. The first unsettling thing had been the dogs. Two of Dad's loudmouthed kelpies came along, as he'd expected. But the other blokes, four contract brumby runners he'd never met before, had brought monsters. Bull Arab hunting dogs, weighing in at fifty kilos each, with heavy heads and muscled bodies; trained to hold wild boars for the bullet. Permits called for the dogs to be muzzled, but who was to see, that high up on the range?

The six of them had headed out from Kilmarnock Station, setting an easy pace up to base camp. They climbed spurs, framed by stringy barks and peppermint gums, stairways to alpine flats where cattle and horses had grazed for generations. The herds of red and white Herefords were gone now – driven off the mountain by reluctant cattlemen when concerns were raised about damage to the high country from hard-hoofed animals. A few mobs of scrubbers evaded the musterers and lived on in this remote place. And so, of course, did the brumbies.

They'd risen at dawn to a cold fire and skins of ice on the water in the billies. Drew watched the men fit heavy-duty motorbike knee-pads beneath their jeans. His dad had thrown him some gear, and he'd copied the others. Leather chaps strapped from crotch to ankle and synthetic rubber gloves completed the outfits. He could barely clamber onto Clancy, stiff-legged and weighed down by his modern brumby-runner's armour. Perversely, they wore no protection at all on their heads – just their customary Akubras. With ropes slung over shoulders and spurs gleaming, the riders were ready.

The dogs ranged ahead of the horses. 'Your horse is everything in this game,' his father told him. 'It needs to stay level-headed, and be able to look after itself as well as its rider. It needs disc brakes, power steering, and it needs to jump like a kangaroo.' The other men rode rangy thoroughbred types with hogged manes – fit and lean and just a bit mad. Their saddles were specially designed with outsized kneepads, grooved at the base. To hold a plunging wild horse, the rider looped the rope around this groove to stop it from slipping.

Drew played with his catching rope while they searched for the brumbies. The aim was to unsling it from shoulder to hand in about two seconds. It needed to be strong enough to snub a wild stallion to a tree, stiff enough to hold the noose in shape, and fine as a lady's finger. Bill had indicated a white and brindle dog, nose to ground, leading the pack. 'That's Bess,' he'd said. 'She's our finder.' Even the other dogs seemed to be watching her. If she took off, so would the riders.

Without warning, Bess flushed a mob of brumbies, and the riders went after them at full tilt, tearing over logs and through trees. Hoofs flung out stones as the horses scattered into the tangled forest. The dogs soon caught up with a small, fat mare – lame and obviously pregnant. She stumbled. A black dog latched onto her head and brought her down. A man leapt from the saddle and snatched a home-made headstall from the bundle on his pommel. The plaited hay band was cheap and hard to break. But it was also thin, like wire, and cut into the mare's skin when she fought it.

The man kicked the dog and made it let go. The mare struggled to her feet. Her left ear was bleeding, almost torn in two. She turned to flee, but was pulled up short, snubbed to the ghost-white trunk of a twisted candlebark by the halter. Fear and pain transformed her into a writhing, rearing, raving thing. The man mounted and waved for Drew to ride on, leaving the horrified mare to fight her invisible demons alone.

Clancy trembled beneath him. Drew hadn't signed up for this. He bit his lip, soothed his horse with uncertain words, and cantered after the others. Similar scenes repeated themselves all that dreadful day, up and down the mountain. The contract runners were suicidal in their determined pursuit of their sport, chasing at breakneck speed through bogs, over rocks and between trees. Never had the old saying *a rider's grave is ever open* made more sense, but adrenalin had got the better of them all. Drew smashed his knees against trees, and didn't even feel it. Only later at home, looking at his purple, swollen legs, had he appreciated the true value of those kneepads.

Drew had finally roped a swift bay colt, elated at first by the capture. The hard nylon catching rope locked onto a large leather eye to prevent the horse from choking, but still the colt laboured to breathe, and struck out with wild, panicked forefeet. It reared over backwards and lay still. One of the other men jumped down, haltered the prone yearling and secured him to a tree. 'He'll be on his feet by the time we get back,' he told Drew. Drew wasn't so sure.

By dusk, six brumbies stood tied to trees. Bill shot dead a young foal, injured by the dogs as it tried to return to its captured mother. His father also shot dead the mob stallion. The big black had turned on Bess and snapped her front leg in a rage as it tried to protect a roped mare. Drew leapt from the saddle and knelt to comfort the whimpering dog. For all he knew, they'd shoot her too. Normal bush rules about fair treatment of animals had for some reason been suspended on this gloomy mountainside.

'I'll take Bess back,' Drew had offered. 'If you don't need me,' he'd added, trying not to sound too keen. There'd been a brief discussion between the men. Finally his father had nodded assent, and helped haul the bitch astride Clancy's saddle. She'd whined and wagged her whip of a tail in thanks. Drew had stroked her head, grateful to the dog for giving him an excuse to escape. On the way down the mountain he passed the bay colt he'd caught. It was standing now, sweating and shivering, forefeet splayed and hanging back on the taut tie rope. Not a bad sort. Maybe Bill would give him a go at breaking it in. Further on, Drew passed the pregnant mare with the ripped ear. She lay dead, head at an impossible angle, neck broken in her furious attempts to free herself.

Drew hadn't stopped when he reached the camp, as his father expected him to. He'd kept right on down the mountain. How naive he'd been, how foolish. It wasn't like Bill to pull any punches, and he hadn't. Drew just didn't think brumby running would have turned out to be so brutal a process. He had a better idea of how the rest of the trip would go now, the idealised scenes wiped from his imagination. Bill and the other men would collect the haltered brumbies and chase them ahead on ropes back to the campsite. There they'd be tied to trees, while the men went and caught more brumbies over the next few days. Bill had said the brumbies were offered food and water, but Drew couldn't imagine those traumatised animals eating or drinking anything. At the end of the weekend, the men would retrieve their Toyotas, fitted with stock crates. They'd use a boat winch to drag the frightened horses onto the trucks, and take them to the stockyards at the showgrounds in town.

When Drew finally caught up with Bill after the weekend, the news was worse than he'd imagined. It turned out that whole group of brumbies had gone to the doggers, even the swift bay colt Drew had his eye on. No, he wouldn't tell his father about the brumbies on Maroong Mountain. Good luck to them.

He whistled up Bess and they headed for home, south across Snake Creek. The dog trotted on ahead of Clancy, nose to ground. Her lamed leg made her useless as a hunting dog, so the contractors had let Drew keep her. Bess was loyal, with a surprisingly gentle nature, and she made a nice change from Dad's hyperactive kelpies and heelers.

Drew passed a sagging bush gate, the back track into Charlie

Kelly's place. For a moment he contemplated making the trip down to the house, to see if she was home. He missed Charlie. She was a headstrong, faithless pain in the arse, but she was also a lot of fun. He missed their bush races, Charlie always cheating, cutting corners to win. He missed her dropping by to demand help with a fence or a calving cow. Missed how she always somehow turned everything into Bill's fault. She wasn't far wrong there. Truth was, Drew was still half in love with Charlie. They'd gone out for a while last year, until he'd discovered the hard way that Charlie preferred rodeo cowboys.

Her mother, Mary, ran a motley, inbred herd of crossbred Angus breeders on Brumby's Run. Her heart had never been in it, and now Charlie and Mary had been gone for weeks. Mysterious, how they'd just disappeared like that, without a word. Max, one of Mary's dodgy mates, was supposed to be looking after the place. Max owned the second-hand dealer's yard at Tallangala, and Drew had seen his wreck of a truck coming and going a few times. But not lately.

Come to think of it, Charlie had been avoiding Drew even before she left, keeping to herself. Maybe Mary was in some sort of trouble with the law? She'd struggled more than once to stay on the right side of it. Bill called her trash. There'd been convictions for drunk driving, some petty fraud, a drug charge. Charlie might come to Drew for help around the farm, but she would never have come to him if her mum was in some kind of a mess. She was too damned proud. If he didn't hear something soon, he'd ride on over to the house. Take a look, keep an eye on things for Charlie till she got back. After all, wasn't that what neighbours were for?

CHAPTER 6

The daily injections Sam received in the week prior to the transplant had left her ill and in pain, with a throbbing deep in her bones, like her core was cracking. Her head ached, her stomach ached, and she vomited up her food. Mary made sure Sam was safely in a cab home after each day, and she often fell asleep in the back-seat, overcome with fatigue.

Faith was there to meet the cab outside the house each afternoon, fussing around Sam and insisting she rest. Sam knew she meant well, but the double dose of mothering from Mary and Faith just added to her exhaustion.

Fearing she had the flu, Sam presented to Professor Sung. 'It's the shots, not a virus,' he told her. 'The side effects will dissipate within a few days of the last dose. You're not infectious, if that's what you're worried about. You're no threat to Charlie.'

A swift flush of shame had burned Sam's cheeks. Charlie. What were a few side effects compared to what her sister was going through? She silently put up with the dizziness, the nausea, the cramping in her limbs in the days that followed. At night, she lay awake and concentrated on mobilising stem cells from the centre of her bones – like a general, rallying her troops. She galvanised them, made them multiply, burgeon, pile up and up on themselves until they spilled through the bone-marrow barrier and crowded into her bloodstream.

If Faith noticed her daughter wandering about the house in the early hours, unable to sleep, she didn't say anything. If she saw Sam in the garden at the compost bin, quietly disposing of her morning bowl of fruit and muesli, she didn't ask. She seemed afraid to mention Charlie or the treatment at all.

Mary, on the other hand, had made an effort to find out about the effects G-CSF injections might have on donors. She knew that they hurt, for one thing. This is going to sting, the nurse had said when she gave Sam the first one. Sting? Biting fire ants swarming over her stomach was more like it. The nurse was cheerful, peremptory, distracted. It was Mary who noticed the tears that Sam tried to squeeze back.

Mary waited for the nurse to leave the room after the injections, then produced a little pot of greenish gold salve. She leaned forward and gently lifted the front of Sam's shirt, reeking of tobacco smoke. Sam screwed up her nose and touched Mary's arm, ready to push her hand away, but Mary shushed her and applied the goo to Sam's burning stomach. It brought instant relief. Sam relaxed back on the hard hospital trolley. 'What is that stuff?'

'Organic aloe and calendula balm,' said Mary, offering Sam the little pot. It looked homemade, and had pretty orange petals floating in it. 'Your mother doesn't make it, then?'

What a question. Faith didn't make anything, except a spectacular entrance. Sam couldn't tell if Mary was being sarcastic. If only she knew more about the woman.

'I'll give Faith the recipe, shall I?' Mary sounded sincere enough.

'Tell me how you made it,' said Sam. A test. For all she knew, Mary had whipped around to the nearest pharmacy and bought the stuff. That's what normal people did.

Mary looked thoughtful, like she was actually trying to remember. 'Pick two cups of marigold petals at noon on a sunny day, so they're not the least bit damp ...'

'Marigolds?' asked Sam.

Mary nodded. 'Calendula, edible marigolds. Our garden at Brumby's Run is full of them.' Sam imagined a picturesque cottage, with a rambling herb garden – chooks and flowers and fruit trees. She wanted to ask Mary about her home, about her life, not about the stupid ointment. 'Put the petals into a small saucepan of sweet almond oil and heat for, oh, an hour or so? Add a cup of fresh aloe vera jelly.' Mary paused, and looked hard at Sam. She seemed to be deciding how detailed the instructions needed to be for her townie daughter. 'You get that by scraping out the inside of the leaves,' said Mary slowly, as if talking to a young child.

'Go on,' said Sam, fascinated.

'Strain it all through a square of cheesecloth, unbleached cheesecloth. Warm the mixture again in a saucepan, with quarter of a cup of melted beeswax, until it's smooth. Tell your mum to pour it into sterilised jars, just like she was bottling fruit – and she can mix in a few petals for colour if she likes before she seals them.' Sam was speechless. 'Would you like me to write it down for her?' asked Mary.

Sam burst out laughing. There was obviously nothing normal about Mary. She'd passed her test with flying colours. 'I'm not laughing at you,' said Sam swiftly, concerned by the hurt on Mary's face. 'It's just funny thinking about Faith bottling fruit, or going to so much trouble over anything, let alone something you could just go out and buy.'

'Oh, but you can't buy this,' said Mary earnestly. 'It can only be made by a mother or a grandmother for their child. There's a slightly different recipe for fathers, but they don't often seem to bother.' Sam smiled, unsure if Mary was making a joke. How could she remain so . . . so heartfelt and preposterous at the same time? 'The magic of a mother's love is the active ingredient,' said Mary. 'That's why it worked so well for you.'

Sam turned the strange little pot of ointment around in her hand, like an object from another world. It promised to be a very steep learning curve indeed with this woman, her birth mother.

Mary was equally attentive to Sam's other ills. Ginger tea for the nausea. Nettle soup for the yawning ache in her bones. Mary could identify the problem with one glance. 'Here, take a couple of these,' she said one day as Sam sat outside Charlie's room, waiting for her sister to wake. Mary offered two little sticky tablets, looking like miniature rum balls. 'They'll help with the headache, sweetie.' Sam's head *was* pounding, too furious for analgesic relief. Mary fetched a plastic cup of water, and Sam swallowed the odd little pills without question.

Mary's treatments had proved at least as effective as conventional remedies. But what she liked most about these odd cures was hearing how Mary made them. Sam never wrote them down, and Mary didn't seem to expect her to. She was a little girl listening to fairy stories. 'I suppose you want the recipe?' Mary asked after Sam had swallowed the pills, and Sam nodded. 'Let me see . . . two tablespoons each of dried valerian, chamomile, peppermint, and rosemary. Then the active ingredient – extract of feverfew.' There was always an active ingredient, usually something rather dark-sounding, like skullcap tincture or devil's shoestring. 'Grind them together.' Mary mimed the actions. 'Blend with enough bloodwood honey to bind. Break off pill-sized pieces and roll into balls. Then store them in a tightly sealed tin, on the sill of an open window overnight.'

'Why do you put them by an open window?'

'So they can absorb lunar peace,' said Mary simply.

Marvellous. Sam imagined the country cottage. She felt she knew it quite well by now. Mary, working the mortar and pestle in a sunny kitchen, fragrant with fresh herbs. Charlie, sitting at the rough-hewn timber table, eating scones with homemade blackberry jam, warm from the wood stove. As Sam's headache lost its grip, she imagined out the window to the herb garden. A mountain beyond. She'd not got so far before. A gum-tree gully, a rough paddock of native grass and bright alpine daisies. Some wide-horned cattle. Herefords, was that what Charlie had said? And a herd of wild horses, escaping up the distant hillside, necks arched, manes and tails streaming in the breeze.

By the time the course of injections was finished, Sam had a complete picture of Brumby's Run in her head. Charlie and Mary hadn't been much help. They couldn't even show her a photo. Mary's phone was ancient, too old to take pictures and Charlie's phone was broken. Mary talked a lot about her herb garden, but that was all, and the intensive chemotherapy had laid Charlie so low she could barely speak. Sam spent every spare minute at the hospital, willing her sister to get well, craving the day when she could talk to Charlie properly.

CHAPTER 7

Charlie looked up as two people entered the room. Mum and Sam? With those ridiculous gowns and masks on, it was never immediately obvious who anybody was. A figure leant over her. 'How are things, sweetie?'

Mum asked the most stupid questions. How did she expect things to be? The deadly routine was killing Charlie. She dreaded waking up just to take a gazillion more pills. If she turned on the TV, she was too weary to keep track of the program. She couldn't see the sun, didn't even have a window. Breakfast had looked crappy, and she wouldn't have eaten it even if she could. She was so tired she'd gone back to sleep, and woke up puking her guts out. Nurses came in and out of her room taking vitals – blood pressure and temperature and a million other things – God knows how many times a day. She felt awful all the time and didn't see anybody except Mum and Sam. Had it only been a week since she'd started on this high-dose chemotherapy treatment? It felt like months. The days were a miserable blur, and she wanted to rip out the central line snaking from her chest, delivering its cell-destroying venom. Rip it out and break its back. Charlie wanted to say all this, but she could hardly speak at all. Her mouth was like sandpaper, and she had ulcers all over her tongue, inside her cheeks, even down her throat.

'I'm fine, Mum,' she said.

Mary placed a few ice chips and a little lozenge in her mouth. 'Peppermint, powdered ginger and violet petals,' she said, for Sam's benefit. Her brand-new sister was quite taken with Mum's mumbo-jumbo. It was a pity Mum couldn't whip up a herbal remedy for leukaemia.

Sam reached for her hand. 'I can't wait for tomorrow.'

Charlie nodded. Tomorrow, the fifth of December, was D-Day, peripheral stem-cell transplant day – the day she'd begin to get her life back.

Sam yawned. It was a bit of an anti-climax really. She was hooked up to the Dalek machine that had so frightened her the day she'd first met Charlie, just ten short days ago. Not that the machine was any fun, but it wasn't all that bad either. Not compared to the horror stories people liked to tell about the alternative – surgical bone-marrow donation. That involved an enormous needle, sucking a litre or more of warm liquid marrow from deep inside your hips. Sam clenched her pelvic floor involuntarily just to think of it.

That same afternoon, Sam's stem cells were transplanted into Charlie. Sam waited anxiously for news. When Professor Sung came to see her, she knew it had gone well – the doctor couldn't stop beaming. The transplant had been textbook perfect. Mary performed some sort of pagan ritual of thanks in the hospital car park, with chalk circles and burning beeswax. Charlie was exhausted, but smiled weakly at Sam when they were finally able to see each other. 'Here's to a shared future,' she said.

The only person who didn't seem overjoyed with the news was Faith. 'I can't understand why you didn't want me there,' she said that evening after Sam arrived home. 'I'd have been your support person. But no, you had to go straight to that Mary woman.' This last remark came with a theatrical flourish.

Sam took a deep breath. 'It was something I needed to do, Mum. Mary was only my support person in hospital. You've been here for me the whole time at home.' And about as supportive as a wet dish-cloth, thought Sam. 'And anyway, it's given me a chance to get to know Mary.'

Faith snorted her displeasure. 'And what's she like then, this Mary?'

Sam wouldn't answer. Couldn't answer. Mary was a contradiction. She'd never met anybody quite like her. Sometimes Mary didn't seem any older than Sam herself. Sometimes she was selfish and childish. Sometimes she was patient and wise. She was far too direct. At times she was just plain rude, especially if she had a complaint about Charlie's care. Sam smiled. Faith would approve of Mary's fearless advocacy on her daughter's behalf. She had scant respect for hospital rules and regulations. She'd been thrown out, more than once, for smoking in the toilets. But when she wasn't with Charlie or Sam, she spent her time reading to children in the paediatric ward, or visiting a growing army of elderly patients who didn't seem to have any family. None who cared, anyway. Mary never seemed to have any money, except to buy cigarettes and Charlie's beautiful scarves. Sam had bailed her out a few times already – ten dollars here, twenty dollars there, but she didn't mind. Although Mary never had enough money, she always had enough time for her daughters.

'She's nothing like you,' Sam said to Faith. 'It's difficult to explain.'

'Hmm,' said Faith sniffily. 'I'll take that as a compliment, shall I?' She swept out of the room and began clattering about in the kitchen. Being at the hospital, although frustrating and worrying, was no hard-ship compared to being at home. Since Faith had revealed the truth about Sam, she had grown brittle, defensive – paranoid, even. And for someone who'd rarely cried before, she was making up for lost time. Despite claiming she wanted to help, Faith had turned the whole thing around so that she was the victim. The victim of an unfeeling, ungrateful daughter, willing to toss her aside after eighteen years of love and self-sacrifice. This dynamic allowed Sam no leeway to ask the questions she most needed answers to.

What Sam wanted most was to sit down for an entire afternoon and hear her mother's side of the story. She fantasised about it, and even wrote a list of questions in her journal. How had Faith found Mary? Had she wanted both girls or not? Why had she wanted a closed adoption, a confidential arrangement allowing for no interaction between birth mothers and their children? Had she ever wondered about Charlie? The list was endless. And of course, the most burning question of all - how could she justify having never told Sam the truth? In Sam's fertile imagination, this illuminating afternoon always ended up with Faith's teary apology. An *I'm sorry* would go a long way to help make this mess right. Of course, Faith didn't really do *sorry*, but for once Sam wouldn't be emotionally blackmailed into taking the blame.

Sam spent more and more of her time at the hospital. She abandoned the few friends she had. She even neglected her horse, Pharaoh, ringing the stables and telling them to turn him out.

'But he's in top condition,' protested her coach. 'You can't spell him now. You'll miss the national squad trials.'

'I won't be trying out for the squad,' said Sam. 'And I'm quitting as coach of the juniors. Just do as I say, please.'

'Fine,' her coach said. He sounded disgusted. 'But I'll have to clear it with your mother first. She pays the bills. It will mean cancelling your training contract and altering Pharaoh's terms of agistment.' He hung silent on the end of the phone for a long time. 'Are you sure you want to do this?' he said at last. 'It's a waste of a fine young horse, at the top of his game.'

'I'm sure.' Sam ended the call. She had no time for Pharaoh right now. She had no time for anybody but Charlie.

CHAPTER 8

Charlie grew stronger each day, and as her strength grew, so did her willingness to talk about life back home in Currajong. She was a born storyteller. 'Brumby's Run is simply the most beautiful place on earth,' she told Sam. 'Just wait until I show you. A thousand wild acres in the shadow of Balleroo Range, half an hour's drive from town. At its highest ridge line, on the edge of the national park, you might as well be on the roof of the world. It's magic. The air is magic. The view is magic.' Charlie's eyes shone with a vitality Sam hadn't seen before. Her voice took on a compelling quality. 'To the north there's Maroong Mountain, a granite monolith like Uluru. Parts of it are covered with cypress pine forests. That sort of disguises it, but it's bigger than Uluru; almost twice as big.' Sam tried to picture it. 'There are rock pools with rare frogs at the top. I love frogs.'

'Who knew?' said Sam with a smile, looking around the amphibian-themed hospital room.

'When it rains, streams spill off the bluff, turning the rock to molten silver, and there are permanent waterfalls as well. Balleroo is an Aboriginal word for *rain god*. I'll take you there in spring when the snows melt. Show you the platypus in Snake Creek, and the lyrebirds at Wagtail Gully, and the Powerful Owl nest in the hollow candlebark above the home dam. God, I miss it.' Telling stories seemed to settle Charlie, helped alleviate what Sam sensed to be a growing homesickness. Sam spent whole afternoons listening to tales of brumbies and musters and rodeos. 'When I was twelve,' said Charlie, 'I got lost chasing steers in the foothills. Had to camp alone overnight near the creek, and I swear I saw a panther come down to drink.'

'A panther?' asked Sam. 'How?'

'Oh, there are panthers in the mountains all right. Some say they're descended from mascots released during World War II by visiting American servicemen.' Charlie smiled. 'Of course, I was just a kid. It might have been a big wild cat. We do get some whoppers around Balleroo.'

'You were allowed to go off by yourself at twelve?' asked Sam.

'Sure. Went on my first muster when I was ten. I was a pretty feral kid.' It was hard to imagine this frail sister as feral. 'Half the time Mum never knew where I was, or what I was doing. Wagged school as often as I went.'

What a life. The thought of that much freedom was intoxicating. Charlie had more independence at ten than Sam did now. Faith had been, and still was, a helicopter mum. Sam's eighteenth birthday had so far made little difference.

Sam was torn between love and frustration every time she thought of Faith. She knew Faith had added Valium to her daily pill cocktail. *To calm my anxiety,* she'd said. Well if that was its purpose, the drug was a dismal failure. Faith, always highly strung, now seemed to live on the rim of hysteria. Sam had been keeping informal track of the stash of tablets in the upstairs bathroom. They were disappearing faster than ever before. Perhaps she should tell her father? But Dad could be so judgemental where Mum was concerned. Best not give him anything that could be used as ammunition.

Sam surprised herself by beginning to cry. Her mask served as a shield, so Charlie didn't immediately notice. Perhaps she could stem the tears in time – she didn't want to explain to her sister, didn't know how to explain.

Charlie extended a fragile arm and took her hand. 'What's wrong?'

Too late. Sam's words came all in a rush. 'Your life sounds so perfect, idyllic …' she said. 'I wish I was you.'

Charlie squeezed her hand with newfound force. 'That's the nicest thing anybody ever said to me.' Her expression grew puzzled. 'And the silliest. I'm half dead. Bald. Stuck in Melbourne for another two months, or even longer. When I do get home, I'm not supposed to have contact with pets. I live on a bloody cattle station, and I'm not supposed to have contact with animals. How's that going to work? Tambo's probably half-starved or cleared off with the brumbies. Mum's broke, and you wish you were me.'

'You've had freedom,' argued Sam. 'An authentic life. I'd forfeit a lot to be able to say that. I've been so protected, it feels like I haven't lived.'

Charlie released Sam's hand. 'I haven't asked you much about yourself. You've been so interested in me. Maybe I've been rude. Truth is, I didn't much feel like hearing about your big house and rich friends and fancy school. I don't blame you or anything; I'm happy for you. But Mum and me, we've had some really tough times. I sometimes wished she'd given me away to the posh family, instead of you.'

'You wouldn't have liked it,' Sam assured her. 'Believe me. My mum would drive you mad.'

'My mum already has,' said Charlie. 'You don't know her.'

A twinge of bitterness caught in Sam's throat. That was hardly her fault.

Charlie continued, oblivious. 'She makes a big show of all her herbal concoctions, but she drinks like a fish, smokes like a chimney and blows what's left over on the pokies. And the men? Damn, there've been that many of them. None of them lasted, of course.' Charlie looked sad and angry at the same time. 'Mum loves me, don't get me wrong, but she's dysfunctional as hell.'

'My mum takes pills,' said Sam, like it was some sort of contest for who had the worst mother. 'That's just as bad. She's kind of clingy and cold at the same time. And Dad doesn't even live with us.'

'So your folks have split up?' asked Charlie.

'No, Dad's an ambassador. He's lived in Dubai for the last three years.'

Charlie whistled approvingly. 'Some cushy job. Why didn't you and your mum go too?'

'It's like living in an oven for eight months of the year, and women don't have much freedom. Mum refuses to live over there, and I can't blame her.' This wasn't the entire truth. Sam had witnessed enough blazing rows between her parents over the years to guess there might be more to the separate living arrangements. 'But Dad went anyway, and sort of forgot about me. We speak on the phone sometimes, but I only see him twice a year.'

'At least you have a dad,' said Charlie. 'Mine was a ratbag. Shot through when Mum was pregnant.' She stopped short.

'Um . . . that ratbag would be my birth father too, remember?' said Sam. They burst out laughing.

'Listen to us,' said Charlie. 'We're a pair of jealous bitches.'

'We should do the prince and the pauper thing,' said Sam. 'We should swap lives.'

Charlie suddenly knelt up on the bed and yanked out the tube attached to her central line. Amber fluid spattered across the white hospital spread. With a deft twist she tossed her headscarf to the floor, exposing an ugly red rash. Her inflamed scalp looked as thin as eggshell. She spread her pale arms high and wide above her head, as if in supplication to some terrible god. The dramatic pose accentuated her wasted frame and gaunt features.

'I think people might spot the difference,' said Charlie. 'Don't you?'

CHAPTER 9

The counselling session was Professor Sung's idea.

Sam wasn't a default pessimist, but her gut told her this wasn't going to work. 'My mother's impossible,' she'd confessed to him on more than one occasion. 'One minute she's obsessed with hearing about everything that's happening at the hospital. Next minute she doesn't want to know, and accuses me of abandoning her if I even mention Charlie.'

Professor Sung had nodded, his eyes wise and understanding.

'There is an implicit tension in the relationship between Mary and Faith,' he said. 'Whether they admit to it or not, adoptive parents often feel secret jealousy, or even anger toward birth parents, and vice versa.'

'There's nothing secret about it with my mum,' said Sam.

'Faith has done all the hard work of parenting, and now worries an interloper might take over your affection. This rarely happens – but the fear is still there. It's quite natural.' Sam had almost argued the point. She was the one who'd done all the hard work. Being Faith's trophy child hadn't been easy. 'I'll schedule a group counselling session,' he'd said.

They'd arrived early. Faith's hair had been done especially for the occasion, cut in an immaculate geometric bob. She wore a plum silk shirt, Donna Karan slacks, and sat in the waiting room with her back to the wall and a good view of the door. Sam sat one seat away. The room was otherwise empty of people, though the air was thick with anticipation.

They heard Mary before they saw her. A little sing-song chant grew louder as she approached. There was a jangle of bangles and there she was, standing larger than life at the doorway, in a flowing white skirt and beaded peasant top. Purple-polished toes poked from fringed leather sandals. She wore flowers in her untidy hair – daisy chains woven into an olive turban headband.

Faith glanced at Sam with a look of horror, then wrinkled her nose as the combined odour of tobacco and incense wafted in. Sam couldn't help but grin. 'Sam,' said Mary, her eyes lighting up. 'I've got something for you.' She produced a jar. 'Lemon bath salts. Wonderfully calming.' Sam acknowledged the gift with a nod, intrigued to see what would happen next. Turning her attention to Faith, Mary enveloped her in a huge hug. Faith recoiled, like the little cat in the old Warner Brothers cartoons, trying to escape Pepé Le Pew's malodorous embrace. 'And for you,' said Mary, when she finally released Faith, 'my famous anti-ageing cream.' Sam gasped out loud. 'For those of us who want to pretend that we didn't have a forest fire of candles on our last birthday cake, eh?' said Mary with a laugh.

Faith's face contorted, like she was struggling with something. In the end she forced a smile and took the proffered jar. 'You're Mary?' she asked, as if she was hoping there'd been some mistake. Mary nodded and beamed. Faith inspected the jar. 'Homemade, then?'

'Of course it's homemade,' said Mary. 'Only the best for my Sam and her family.' Faith visibly flinched at the *my* Sam. Mary couldn't be doing a better job of alienating her if she tried. 'You take two ripe cucumbers, skin and all. Half a ripe avocado, a few leaves of mint, almond oil and a cup of rainwater. Oh, and a good dash of Friar's Balsam.' Faith grimaced. 'Shall I write down the recipe?' asked Mary. 'You could mix some up yourself. That little jar won't last you long.'

Sam began to suspect that Mary's motives were not pure. Faith was fastidious about her appearance and horrified about growing old. She'd had a brow lift, lip lift, eyelid lift and attended quarterly appointments at one of Melbourne's most exclusive aesthetic-surgery clinics. She'd even presented Sam with a rhinoplasty gift certificate for her sixteenth birthday. 'Now you'll be able to do something about that nose,' Faith had said brightly.

'Mum,' she'd said. 'My nose is fine.'

'Well, of course it is, darling. It's beautiful, just like you. But at the moment it turns up at the tip. Weren't you saying that you'd like it a little straighter? A little more classic in profile?'

'No, Mum,' she'd said. 'That was you saying that. Leave my nose alone.'

Faith was forever chasing eternal youth, and she would not react well to the suggestion that she needed wrinkle cream. Not well at all. Sam was gloomier than ever about the forthcoming counselling session.

A smooth-looking woman emerged from a hallway and summoned them into another room, where they seated themselves in a semi-circle on comfortable chairs.

'I'm Sandra,' the woman said with an unctuous smile, and made the introductions. 'I'm here to help you all find a new equilibrium.' Everybody looked blank. 'We'll begin with you, Faith.' Faith blinked. Sandra put on a serious face. 'Adoptive parents often have powerful negative feelings about a child searching for their birth family. We're here to help you work through those feelings.'

Faith bristled. 'Samantha never searched for her birth family.'

'That's because she didn't know she had one,' said Mary. Petals from her wilted headband floated to the floor. 'Sam was supposed to know about me and Charlie all along.'

'We're not here to argue,' said Sandra evenly.

'Why didn't you tell me, Mum?' asked Sam.

'I thought it would be . . . less complicated, and in any case, your father wouldn't allow it.' There was a catch in her throat. 'Victor was adamant, and since he'd arranged the whole thing, well . . . he said it was to be a closed adoption.'

Less complicated. That was a good one. This was about as complicated as it got.

'Where is Victor?' asked Sandra. 'It would have been very useful
for him to come.'

'He's . . . he's overseas,' said Faith.

'There *was* no closed adoption,' said Mary, with a real edge to her
voice.

Sandra rose to her feet, shaking her head and positioning herself
between the two women, who were now glaring at each other in open
hostility. It was the first time Sam had seen Mary drop her serene,
earth-mother persona.

'Adopted children are nearly always hungry to know their own
personal stories,' said Sandra. She smiled encouragement. 'Would I be
right, Samantha? Is that what you want?' Sam nodded. Sandra looked
pleased and resumed her seat. 'Equally, birth parents and adoptive
parents often want to hear from each other. Want to gain a complete
picture of their child. To fill in the blanks, as it were. It's a gift only
you can give each other.' Nobody spoke. 'Right then, let's start with
you, Mary. I'm sure Samantha would like to hear the circumstances
that led to her adoption. Only tell us what you're comfortable with.'

It was pretty much as Faith had said back at that awkward lunch
almost three weeks ago. Mary had been an unmarried teenager, barely
able to provide for one child, let alone two. Sam hung on every scrap
of information. Mary's mother had died in a tractor accident when
Mary was just three, leaving her to be brought up by her father, Jock
Kelly. He'd been a lazy, uninterested parent, by the sound of it, who'd
pulled Mary out of high school to help him run the farm. 'Dad died of
lung cancer the year before the girls were born,' said Mary. 'I worked
Brumby's Run by myself after that . . . but I was never very good at it.'
She shrugged. 'Should have sold the damn place, but I promised Dad
before he died that I'd hang on if I could. So like a sentimental fool, I
kept my word to the old bastard.'

'Tell me about my real father,' said Sam, her breath coming fast.

'It's not a pretty story, my sweet,' said Mary. 'His name was Robert
Smith. Some sort of travelling sales rep. I left messages on his phone

to tell him that I was pregnant, but he never called back. My final message was when you twins were nearly due. Said I'd have to relinquish one baby if I didn't hear from him. Never a word. It did my head in, Sammy, it really did.' How desperate must Mary have been. So young, just seventeen. Sam struggled to put herself in Mary's place. 'The adoption agency found a suitable couple the same day I approached them. All I knew was their name, Mr and Mrs Carmichael, and that they had loads of money.'

'Would you like contact with your birth father, Samantha?' asked Sandra. 'Is that something you'd welcome?' Faith looked horrified.

'Maybe,' said Sam. 'Mary, tell me more about Charlie. What was she like before she got sick?' It was a question that she'd been dying to ask.

'You wouldn't know it to look at Charlie now,' said Mary. 'But she's always been a bit of a devil. Skipping school, running off into the mountains after brumbies. Disappearing for days at a time, to who knows where, with who knows who.' Faith frowned at Mary's words. 'But in spite of that, your sister has a heart of gold.' Mary smiled at Sam. 'Just like you, sweetheart.'

'Samantha recently completed her final school exams,' said Faith, sitting up a little straighter. 'She did very well, I might add, and has been accepted into a Commerce degree at Melbourne University. My daughter always took her education seriously.'

'What choice did I have?' said Sam, suddenly angry. 'You made me study day and night. You wouldn't let me go anywhere except music lessons or the stables. My friends were never good enough. You wouldn't let them come over, wouldn't let me go to their places. I always felt so isolated.' It was Mary's turn to frown.

'You have friends. What about Cate?' said Faith, in a grasping- at- straws kind of voice. 'I always liked Cate.'

'You only liked Cate because she's Randolph Fox's daughter. You used to go on about it all the time, how she was heiress to a media empire. It's just a fluke that I liked her too. Now that she's gone away to that stupid school in Switzerland, I don't have a single friend left in Melbourne.'

'Darling, you know that's not true. And besides, that was a marvellous opportunity for Cate,' said Faith. 'Le Rosey is one of the most exclusive schools in the world. Cate will rub shoulders with the Getty's and Rothschilds.'

'You're such a snob, Mum. I'm surprised you didn't send me off as well. Oh, that's right – it would be too difficult to live your life vicariously through me if I was in Switzerland.' Sam was shocked at herself. Had she really said all that? Had her bitterness finally found so loud a voice?

Sandra said something about one person talking at a time, but nobody paid her any mind.

'Poor darling,' crooned Mary. She reached over and patted Sam's hand. 'When Charlie's right, you come home with us to Brumby's Run. We'll show you how to have some fun.'

Faith rose to her feet. In spite of her petite frame, she seemed to tower over Mary. 'How dare you! You're not fit to look after your own child, let alone mine. What sort of mother lets her child miss school and run wild like that?'

'At least I didn't lock her up like a nun!' retorted Mary. 'If you'd had something else to occupy your time – like a job, maybe – my girl could have had a normal childhood. Sam says you've never worked a day in your life.'

Faith shot Sam a swift, disappointed glance. Mary looked at her too, like she was expecting her to take sides. 'Shut up!' said Sam, her voice rising. She jumped to her feet. 'Shut up both of you! I'm not anybody's child. I'm eighteen, I'm an adult, and I don't have to put up with any of this crap.' With one last contemptuous stare, she marched from the room.

'Goodnight, Charlie. Sleep tight.' Sam tossed her phone onto the bed and stared out the window. It was late, the new moon already high in the sky, but she wasn't tired. Sam had told her sister all about the disastrous counselling session. They'd dissected it between them, word for word. Having Charlie was like having a best friend and a shrink all rolled into one. They shared everything about their lives. Well, perhaps not everything. There was one topic Sam had steered clear of: boys. She had the impression that Charlie knew quite a lot about boys. Sam had never even had a date. The very idea would have sent Faith into a tailspin. It was a prime example of just how cosseted she'd been. So Sam quickly shut down any talk of Charlie's love life, whenever it raised its embarrassing head.

The phone rang. Dad. 'How's tricks, Sammy?'

'Charlie's getting better every day.'

'Good, good.' The pause that followed seemed interminable. 'Are you okay?' he said at last.

'No, I'm not,' she said. 'And neither is Mum.'

'Well, there's not much I can do from over here, Sammy. We'll thrash things out at Mamie's.'

'No we won't. I already said, I'm not coming to France.' There was another long silence on the end of the line. 'Dad, why didn't you tell me about Mary . . . about Charlie?'

'It's complicated, sweetheart. There are things you don't know.'

'Obviously.'

This time the silence lasted so long that she thought he might have hung up.

'Your mother isn't answering her phone.'

'She's had a rough day.'

'Well, just tell her I rang. Tell her I love her.'

'Okay.'

'Thanks, Sammy. Love you too. You know that.'

'Bye, Dad.' The end of the call came as a physical jolt. She tasted tears although she didn't know she was crying.

Sam slipped out to the landing at the top of the staircase. Classical music played – a sad flute solo – and a light shone from the lounge room. Sam padded downstairs. Faith stood staring out the window at the dark garden, a near empty wineglass in her hand. 'Mum?' Faith started. 'Dad's been trying to call you.'

'Has he?' Sam followed her mother into the kitchen. Faith opened the fridge and reached for a bottle of Shiraz. Her glass knocked against the bench and broke into three pieces. Faith tried to put them back together with shaking hands.

'Don't, Mum,' whispered Sam. 'You can't fix it.' She eased the broken glass from her mother's grasp, cutting herself in the process. Blood dripped from her finger, mixing with the spilt red wine. It hurt more than she expected it to.

CHAPTER 10

In an hour Faith would be gone – flown to Paris. Sam concentrated on the road, on finding the airport turnoff, steeling herself against her mother's constant stream of words. 'You mustn't move those two into our house while I'm away,' said Faith, her voice taut with anxiety. 'This is so hard for me, Sam. I can't have Mary taking over my home as well as my daughter.'

Sam's grip tightened on the wheel until her knuckles were white. Careful now. Faith would soon be in France. A long month away, breathing space for them both. 'Why would you think I'd do that, Mum?' she said. 'I never said anything about them moving in.'

'I've done my research. Charlene won't be able to return to that backwater with her mother, not for ages. They'll need ongoing treatment in the city, and they'll be looking for somewhere to stay. Don't tell me Mary Kelly can afford to pay for accommodation here in town?'

'I don't know if she can afford to or not. It's none of my business, and even less of yours.'

'As soon as they know I'm gone they'll work on you,' said Faith. 'That Mary is a gold-digger, you can see it a mile off. She'll try to take advantage, and with you so naïve …' Faith shook her head in disgust.

'I wish you'd change your mind and come with me. We could take a later flight?'

'For the umpteenth time, Mum, I'm not coming.' Faith let out a great sigh.

Sam repeated the secret mantra beneath her breath – jabberwocky, jabberwocky, jabberwocky – a psychological ploy she used to trigger a calm response in the face of extreme provocation. 'You're right about Charlie not being able to go home. She needs to stay in Melbourne for a couple of months. But don't worry, the Leukaemia Foundation are putting her up in an apartment. Mary's already there.'

'She is?' asked Faith. 'You've seen it?'

Thank God. The airport was in sight. Not long now. 'Yes,' said Sam. 'I've seen it.'

'Where is it?'

'In East Melbourne somewhere.'

'What's it like?' asked Faith.

'Nice,' said Sam warily. 'Room for one patient and one carer. There's a rooftop gym, and a pool. Even an organic grocery store nearby.' She was about to say what a fan Mary was of organic produce, but bit her lip in time.

'Why on earth didn't you tell me? Don't I deserve to know anything?'

Past long-term parking, swinging around towards the international terminal. 'You get upset when I mention Mary,' said Sam. 'I didn't want to upset you.'

'Why?' demanded Faith.

'What a stupid question!' said Sam. 'I didn't want to upset you because I love you.'

'You do?' Faith's face softened and she reached a hand out to stroke Sam's arm.

'Yes, I do love you,' and then, under her breath, 'God knows why,' But Faith didn't hear. 'I'll see you off Mum, then I'm going out to the stables. It's been ages since I saw Pharaoh.'

For some reason, her mother seemed in a sudden hurry. 'No need, just let me out here.' Sam swung into the passenger drop off lane and helped Faith with her bags. 'I'll be fine,' said Faith, taking charge of her monogrammed Louis Vuitton luggage. 'Call you when I get to Mamie's — and have a lovely Christmas, darling.' Sam embraced her in a mighty hug, like the bear hugs she used to give when she was small. Faith's face lit up in a smile. 'You'll crush my suit,' she complained, but they both knew she didn't mean it. They both knew this was the very best possible note on which to say goodbye.

Sam watched her mother stride off on her ridiculous heels, holding her breath until Faith disappeared into the crowd. Sam tossed her keys in the air and caught them with a deft flourish. Finally she could start living her life, her way. She couldn't wait to tell Pharaoh.

'That horse?' said Brodie. 'That horse ain't here.'

'I can see that for myself.' She'd checked his stable, yard and all the private turn-out paddocks. No sign of Pharaoh. Sam waited in vain for an explanation. She'd have to spell it out. 'So, where is he?'

A slow, sleazy smile spread across Brodie's pinched features. 'Dunno, Miss. All I know is that horse is gone. Some bloke loaded it onto a float yesterday and took off. Ain't seen it since.'

'That's not possible.' Why was she wasting her time, talking to this creep? He probably couldn't tell one horse from another, and there were half a dozen chestnuts at the stables. Perhaps Pharaoh was in the wrong loose box? Sam turned to go.

'Sal says your mum sold that horse.'

Sam stopped short. She swung around, her stomach coiled in nasty knots. 'What did you say?'

Brodie's face creased into a malicious grin. 'Nothing.'

'You said Pharaoh's been sold.'

'Did I, Miss?'

He deserved a good slapping. Instead Sam sought out Sally, the stable manager. She was in the office, on the phone, a mug of coffee in hand. Her cheerful face fell when Sam came in. 'I have to go,' said Sally, ending the call in obvious haste. Her expression toughened. It looked like she was preparing for a fight. 'I'm sorry, Sam.'

So, it was true. 'Where is he?' Sam's voice broke with emotion, with rage and grief and disbelief.

'Pharaoh's gone to Andrew Wolf,' said Sally. 'He was most impressed with him. You should be proud.'

Sam wanted to scream, accuse, demand to know how Sally could have done it. How she could send Pharaoh away, cast him into the unknown, without Sam's affection and protection. How Sally could face work and phone calls and coffee, all the while knowing that this moment must come. The moment when she'd have to confess the terrible thing she'd done.

'Get me his number,' said Sam, her voice hard. Sally looked unsure for a moment, then handed Sam her phone. Sam scrolled through the numbers, found Andrew's and rang it. The conversation did not go well.

'Sold by mistake, you say? I don't think so. I have the signed transfer papers.'

'My mother signed those. She doesn't own Pharaoh. I do.'

'According to the papers,' said Andrew in an infuriatingly pompous tone, 'Faith Carmichael was the horse's registered owner. She told me about how you'd lost interest. It happens all the time,' he said, as if he understood everything. 'You girls discover boys and, well, horses take a back seat, don't they?' Sam tried to speak, but Andrew talked over her. 'Shame to see Pharaoh going to waste like that.' There was a long silence. Sam got the dreadful feeling that there was no point trying to defend herself against Faith's wicked allegations. 'Are you saying this isn't your mother's signature on the transfer?'

Sally sipped her coffee while Sam explained that Faith was Pharaoh's owner in name only. 'I haven't lost interest. That's ridiculous. I broke him in myself when I was fifteen, and I've been the only one ever to ride him.'

'That's not quite true,' said Sally in the background. 'Rachael worked him sometimes.'

Sam ignored her. 'Please, that horse is my life! You have to send him home. You just have to.' Her voice was a stammer. 'I didn't even get to say goodbye.' But it was no use. Andrew just kept repeating that

Faith had signed the transfer, rubbing it in again and again. Rubbing in her mother's wicked betrayal. Sam threw down the phone and fled. She had to talk to Charlie.

Charlie rewound her outlandish scarf, a colourful cane toad print this time. 'Mothers are like that,' she said, sagely. 'They rip out your heart one minute, and then expect you to keep right on loving them the next. If she's anything like my mum, she'll twist this around until it's all your fault.'

'Mary does that too?'

Charlie nodded, swung her legs off the bed and stood up. She still looked so frail. If only they could leave the damned hospital and go to a bar or something. Drown their sorrows, make a plan to get Pharaoh home. But it was clear from one glance that Charlie's recovery was going to be long and slow.

'Can't you just buy him back?' asked Charlie. 'Isn't your family loaded?'

'I've tried,' said Sam. 'The buyer won't budge. And anyway, there's a limit of ten thousand on my credit card. That's not nearly enough.'

Charlie whistled. The sound was surprisingly strong and melodious. 'How much is Pharaoh worth, then?'

'A lot more than that. It's ironic, isn't it? I spend all year training him, and now he's worth so much, I can't afford him.'

Charlie pulled a tissue from a frog-shaped box, gently lifted her sister's mask, and wiped the tears from her face. The gesture was as sweet as it was unexpected.

'I'm going to miss him so much.' Sam's words erupted in short gasps, like she'd been winded. 'He was all I'd ever wanted. How will I live without him?' Charlie murmured soft words of consolation, but her expression of sympathy only provoked in Sam a further flood of self-pity. 'There's nothing left,' she managed, between sobs. 'Dad's away, and he's always been too busy for me anyway. I don't have any proper friends. Except for Cate, and she's gone too. Pharaoh was it . . .

all I had. There's nothing left for me here in Melbourne. Nothing at all.'

Charlie reached out, stroked Sam's hair and shushed her. 'There are lots of horses back home in Currajong.' She said it in an odd tone, as if the remark was imbued with some secret significance.

Sam blew her nose behind her mask, a great honking blow. 'So?'

'So, you go home to Currajong for Christmas. Home to Brumby's Run.' Charlie slipped from bed and fetched a box from the cupboard. Beneath some action shots of Charlie campdrafting lay a battered stockman's hat. Charlie handed it to Sam. 'For you. My lucky Akubra. Try it on.' Sam did as she was asked, catching her reflection in the mirror. She looked just like the girl in the photographs. 'You already said that there's nothing for you here,' said Charlie. 'The house back home is empty, and the stock need checking. Mum asked Max to look in on the place, but he's a dodgy old bastard. You'd be doing me a favour.' Charlie pointed to the horse in the pictures. 'Tambo could use some TLC.' Sam took a long look at the photos.

'Well?' asked Charlie, with a broad smile. 'What do you say?'

CHAPTER 11

Bill pushed aside the half-finished plate of bacon and eggs. 'Mary Kelly is a failed hippy, not a farmer. She's got no bloody idea.'

'Fair call,' said Drew, 'but why should her stock suffer for it?' He could feel the hot rush of blood to his temples, something that was happening all too often lately. 'We can't just let them starve.'

'They'll manage until the autumn break,' said Bill, with a dismissive wave of his hand. 'And anyway, what exactly do you propose that I do about it?'

'It's your fault in the first place,' said Drew angrily. 'You've leased every bit of good land she has for a song, pushed her cattle into that rocky top corner. That's mongrel country. Not enough grass up there for goats.'

'Nobody put a gun to Mary's head to make her sign that lease.' Bill gulped the last of his tea, and wiped his mouth with the back of his hand. 'If she's overstocked, that's her problem.' He stood up and stalked away, thereby declaring the subject closed.

Drew started to clear away the dishes. Mai, their housekeeper, appeared from the kitchen. 'I do that,' she said. He nodded. 'I decorate?' she asked. 'Mrs Chandler always have me decorate on Christmas Eve.'

Christmas Eve. If Mum was here the place would be groaning with ornaments and lights and the biggest cypress pine Bill could find. There'd be the smell of roasting pork and homemade plum pudding. Chocolates and lollies and bonbons. Extravagantly wrapped gifts spilling from under the fragrant tree. Melinda, Steph and Mum, arguing and giggling, a joyous confusion of perfumed hair, pretty clothes and flashing, Santa Claus earrings. His sisters could always make Dad smile. But Mum was spending Christmas in Sydney this year, with her new bloke and the girls. She'd asked Drew to join them, but he wouldn't leave Dad on his own. He was beginning to regret the decision. Without Mum's festive energy, the day would be just a poor copy of Christmas.

Drew looked at Mai's expectant face. 'Decorate if you want,' he said.

'No tree?' she asked.

'No, Mai,' he said, and grabbed his hat from a peg by the door. 'No tree.'

After breakfast, Drew finished bolting the new rails on the round yard, then he and Bess took a run into town. The day was stinking hot, the bitumen on the road already sticky. He picked up fuel and a few things at the produce store: oats, layer pellets, dog kibble. Lunchtime found him at the pub, asking questions.

'Mary Kelly?' said Kevin, behind the bar. He wore a hat sprouting Christmas reindeer antlers. They waved when he shook his head. 'Who knows where she is?'

'In jail?' suggested Harry, the town mechanic.

'Best place for her,' said a dour-looking man.

Drew sighed and ordered the mixed grill. Mary was unpopular amongst some of the older cattlemen, who judged any unmarried mother harshly. She'd been just a teenager when she inherited Brumby's Run following her father's early death. Jock Kelly had been a lazy drunk, who'd neglected his land. For years Jock's lower pastures had acted as a weed reservoir. They'd infected neighbouring properties with a flourishing cornucopia of invasive species, infestations that Mary in turn had also mainly ignored. Waterways choked with willow and Cape broom. Purple paddocks of Patterson's curse. Bridal creeper, blackberries and boxthorn. Horehound, periwinkle and ragwort. Brumby's Run seemed to spontaneously generate every noxious weed known to man.

The Department of Environment had issued Mary with a string of infringement notices, none of which she'd complied with. Fines accumulated, totalling thousands of dollars, but you had to hand it to Mary – she'd argued no capacity to pay, and requested that her fines be converted to community service in lieu. Mary never paid a cent. But she did establish a glorious herb garden for the old folks at the Tallangala nursing home. In desperation, neighbours slashed and sprayed Mary's paddocks themselves. Bill became the main catalyst for the intervention. By the time he'd finished, Brumby's Run was as clear of invasive weeds as his own Kilmarnock Station. The whole exercise had not won Mary any friends.

There was a long list of other grievances. Common boundary fences weren't maintained. Mary ran up accounts all over town, and came up with bizarre excuses not to pay. *A baby magpie has flown into my house, and I have to stay home to feed it.* Or *all names are put into a hat. If I pull out yours, you get paid. If not, I'm afraid you must stay in the hat until next week.* Drew's personal favourite was when Mary argued she suffered from multiple-personality disorder, and the contract for sale of goods had been made with a personality that she wouldn't be seeing for a while.

By contrast, the local alternative life-stylers loved Mary, and frequently sought her out for her encyclopaedic knowledge of herbal remedies. Even the odd station-owner's wife had been known to surreptitiously pay her a visit. Still, it was unlikely that Mary earned much money that way, and she certainly didn't make a living from beef. Drew couldn't remember the last time he'd seen a pen of Kelly cattle go through the sale yards. Whatever could have happened to her and Charlie?

Bess howled from the pub verandah. Drew wrapped up a burnt

sausage for her in a paper serviette that was covered in pictures of snowy pine trees and gold angels. 'Merry Christmas,' he said to nobody in particular, and finished his beer.

Outside, Bess swallowed the snag in one gulp. He secured her in the back of the ute, then headed out of town. It was time to get some answers.

The rusty wire gate of Brumby's Run hung off its hinge. Drew dragged it open, and drove up the rutted track to the house. A car was parked next to the house. Not Mary's car, but a late-model Volkswagen. It looked like a shiny blue Christmas beetle.

Drew parked the ute and lifted Bess down from the tray. Nose to ground, she trotted to the front door, scratched at it and disappeared inside.

'Hello,' said a girl's voice. 'You're a big girl. Where did you come from?'

It was Charlie's voice – and then again, it wasn't. Drew nudged his way inside. Charlie kneeled by the stove, hugging Bess tight. When she looked up, when she looked straight at him, he couldn't pick at first what was so different about her. Then it hit him. Everything . . . and nothing. Her hair was the same rich brown, with the same slight wave. Yet it was a shorter cut, layered and stylish; fashionable, even. Her figure boasted the same full breasts and slim waist, the same long legs. But her clothes were all wrong: tailored shirt, tapered pants, riding boots. Where were the worn jeans and faded T-shirt? One thing was certain, though. This new Charlie looked a million dollars.

'Where the bloody hell have you been?' Drew asked.

She looked uncertain, bewildered. Charlie was many things, but uncertain had never been one of them. 'You might have me confused with my sister,' she said in a hesitant voice. Her pretty mouth moved in an unusual way, rounding out each vowel with particular care, and clipping the consonants. It was Drew's turn for confusion. Charlie gave Bess one last hug and stood up. She extended a slim arm. 'I'm

Samantha.' Drew just stared, open-mouthed. She let her arm fall to her side. 'Charlie's sister. We're twins.'

'What are you playing at now, Charlie?' he said, shaking his head. 'Gone and got yourself a makeover?' He walked around her, nodding approval. 'It sure does suit you.'

'I'm not Charlie Kelly,' she said firmly and with great poise. 'My name is Samantha Carmichael.' A hesitation, like nerves had the better of her, then she flushed like a schoolgirl. It was absolutely charming. 'People call me Sam for short.'

This gorgeous girl might be the spitting image of Charlie, but she sure as hell didn't act like her. Argue with Charlie, and she was likely to jump on you like a wildcat. Drew shook his head. It was such an absurd story though. A pile of luggage lay on the kitchen floor. Expensive-looking luggage. Could she be telling the truth?

'Now that I've introduced myself,' said the girl, 'just who, exactly, might you be?'

She had perfectly even white teeth. Charlie had a little gap. Drew took off his hat and slapped at a fly on the table. 'You're fair dinkum,' he said at last.

She nodded. 'I'm fair dinkum.'

The phrase sounded foreign on her tongue. No doubt about it, this girl was not Charlie. 'Okay, I'll bite. Where is she?' Drew was intrigued, fascinated by this non-Charlie. So beautiful, so classy. He couldn't take his eyes off her. 'And where did you spring from?'

'My sister wants her whereabouts to remain confidential for the time being,' she said with preposterous formality. 'Her mother, Mary Kelly has expressed a similar wish.'

Drew raised his eyebrows, and moved closer to Sam. He looked furtively around, as if he thought someone might be listening, then leaned in close. 'They're in jail, aren't they?'

'Of course they're not! Now, would you please leave?' The girl who wasn't Charlie escaped out the door, marched past the house and started up the hill. Drew followed as if drawn on a string, with Bess bounding after.

Sam stopped by the closed gate of the dam paddock. She turned around and tossed her head, seeming surprised and annoyed all at once to see him there. They locked gaze. She had Charlie's eyes – eyes that burned right into you. 'Who are you?' she asked again.

'Apologies, m'lady.' Drew bowed low. 'Your neighbour, Andrew Douglas Chandler, at your service.' She scowled, but there was the hint of a smile behind it. 'You may call me Drew.'

She played along, and offered her hand. 'A pleasure, sir.' Drew kissed it instead of shaking it, noticing the manicured nails and smooth fingers. This was no Charlie. They turned at the sound of a piercing neigh. A bay horse with a white face cantered down the hill towards them.

'Tambo!' said Sam with a delighted smile. Drew looked at her quizzically. 'I recognise him from a photo Charlie showed me.' The horse skidded to a halt at the gate. 'He's so thin,' she gasped. It was true. His neck was skinny, like a snake. Each rib stood out in stark relief, and his rump was hollow and bony. 'The poor thing.' Sam took off her belt, put it round the horse's neck, and opened the gate. 'Come on, Tambo.' He snatched hungrily at the fresh grass outside the fence. Sam put her nose to him, breathing in his warm, equine smell, like it was an expensive perfume. Then with some urging, she persuaded Tambo to follow them back down to the house.

Sam turned him into the overgrown garden, rubbed his ears fondly, then fossicked around in the tumble-down hay shed. Drew trailed after her. Nothing but a few spoilt bales of coarse grass hay. She squealed as two big rats scuttled off, then kicked the mouldy hay and fixed Drew with those liquid amber eyes. 'Where can I find some fodder?'

'No worries,' said Drew. He whistled Bess, and lifted her into the tray of the ute. 'I'll rustle you up a few bales from home.'

'Are those oats?' asked Sam, spying the sacks in the back.

Drew nodded. He backed the ute up to the cavernous shed. 'Consider it a Christmas present.' He turfed a bag to the ground.

'Thank you,' she said, 'but won't the rats get it there?' Sam used a broken broom to dust off some forty-four gallon drums along the back wall. 'What about putting it in one of these?' Drew hopped out, heaved the heavy sack onto his broad shoulders, and deposited it into the nearest bin. He could feel her eyes upon him as his muscles strained with the load. 'Thanks,' she said. 'That's very generous of you.' He was a sucker for flattery, especially from a beautiful girl. 'I'll need some chaff too,' she said, '… and maybe linseed?'

'I'll see what I can do.' It gave him an excuse to come back, after all. 'You staying on for a bit, then?'

She nodded. 'For several weeks. I'll be running the farm.' He looked down at his boots, in an attempt to hide his amusement. She was too damned cute. 'Did I say something funny?' He shook his head. 'Is Brumby's Run not a farm? Or is the joke that I will be in charge?'

It was a bit of both, really. Why the hell couldn't he stop smiling? Maybe better to change the subject. 'There's never much in Mary's fridge at the best of times. How about I bring back some steaks, along with the chaff?' She considered the matter for the longest time. It annoyed him, how he was hanging on her decision.

'I'd like that,' she said at last, her eyes meeting his. He took off down the track, feeling like he'd won the lottery, and wondering why.

Sam watched Drew's utility spin its wheels, take off down the drive and disappear. She'd never met anyone like Drew Chandler before. He was good looking, no doubt about it. Tall and broad-shouldered with smiling green eyes and a square, determined jaw. There was a suggestion of lean muscle through his torso where it met his narrow hips. But it was more than that. His body would be the envy of any fake tanned Toorak gym junkie, yet he carried himself without a hint of vanity. Drew moved with natural animal grace, like a splendid wild colt, unconscious of his own beauty.

Sam turned back to face the house. No beauty there. It was nothing like she'd imagined. No pretty portico, no shuttered timber casements, no bullnose verandah. Just a tumble-down shack of weathered timber and rusted roofing iron. Torn fly screens flapped against dirty windows. Piles of junk lay strewn alongside the drive: wheel rims, rusty tools and rotting posts. Tambo picked his way around old fencing coils, snatching at tall grass growing through the wires. It was a depressing sight.

She went back inside and explored the house, still thinking of Drew. A tiny entrance hall, lined with chipboard shelves that overflowed with books. A tiny kitchen with a peeling linoleum floor, grimy walls and an ancient stove without a range hood. The filthy fireplace in the lounge room was clogged with ash. Sam opened the window wide, and screamed when a large black crow appeared from nowhere and landed on the sill. It only flapped off with the greatest reluctance when she shoved it with a worn out broom. She opened the fridge and gagged. It had been turned off, but left closed. The interior, together with a few items of unidentifiable food, was a mass of stinking green mould. Quickly she slammed the door shut, feeling the tingle of tears. What a dump. Her bags still lay in the corner of the room. She could still leave, if she wanted to. But maybe the bedrooms would be better.

She moved gingerly down the hall. The first room on the left must have been Charlie's. A single iron bed beneath the window. Bare mattress. Shabby wardrobe. A low timber-pattern laminate dressing table, with a cracked mirror and gold plastic handles. Sam thought of her own bedroom back in Melbourne, furnished in French provincial style to remind her of Mamie. Sheets of fine Irish linen. Goose down pillows in French lace slips graced the ornate lime-washed bed. Her lovely oaken armoire, carved with roses and boasting hammered brass handles. Her burnt-oak commode, of graceful serpentine design. On her walls, prints of roosters. She liked roosters.

Not as much as Charlie liked frogs, though. Her dusty bedroom was full of frogs: figurines, toys, pictures. And cowboys. Posters of nameless cowboys, brooding at the camera or riding bucking horses. She took a closer look. One image was particularly arresting: an Ashton Kutcher lookalike, astride an enormous bull in what looked like mid-flight. In the corner was an autograph. *To Chaz. Forever Spike xx.* The cowboy seemed to be, unaccountably, looking straight at the camera – posing for the shot instead of concentrating on his perilous ride. He seemed to be looking straight into her eyes.

Sam reread the dedication. Was this rodeo rider cowboy Charlie's boyfriend? She hadn't mentioned him, or Drew either. The only local Charlie had mentioned was an awful man named Bill, who owned Kilmarnock Station, the property next door. Apparently he'd bribed Mary to lease him most of Brumby's Run. Charlie was still furious about it. Said her mother didn't have a clue. Said it didn't leave them enough land for their own stock. The lease was due to expire, though. Charlie hoped that with Mary off in Melbourne, distracted, out of contact, they could get their land back. It was Sam's job to inform this Bill character that the current contract would not be renewed, and he'd need to muster his cattle off Brumby's Run by new year. Maybe Drew could give her some advice.

Sam dumped her bags in the next room along the corridor, clearly Mary's room, on the only bed that was made up, and went off to investigate the bathroom. It wasn't too bad, by comparison to the rest of the house. The toilet, however, was unusable. Was there an outside loo? There was, in an alcove off the back porch. Spiderwebs festooned the ceiling, and squares of newspaper hanging from a nail made a sorry excuse for toilet paper, but it was cleaner than the one inside.

She sat down, wary of creepy crawlies. When she pressed the flush button, nothing happened. Sam groaned. The toilet could wait. Her first priority was to clean that kitchen.

Heading back inside, she turned on the sink taps. Nothing. Great. Grabbing two large pots, she went outside and filled one from the galvanised-iron rainwater tank behind the house. The water teemed with mosquito larvae. Sam made a face and went back inside. She flicked a light switch. No electricity. She tried calling Charlie. No reception. What was she going to do? Sam thought for a moment, then rummaged around in the kitchen cupboards until she found a strainer. She took it outside and tried pouring the water through its fine wire mesh into an empty pot beneath. It worked. The strained water was free of wrigglers, a small victory. Back in the kitchen, she put the pots on the stove, and turned it on. It took a minute to confirm that nothing was happening. Of course not. The stove was electric. Determined to remain positive, she found a plug, emptied the pot into the sink, dusted off a bottle of detergent, and started washing dishes in cold water.

Through the cobwebbed window, the sun was sinking below the timbered ridge-line. It burnished the forest a dramatic red and gold. There was a special quality to the light up here in the mountains. The beauty and serenity of the scene buoyed Sam's spirits. It didn't matter that she'd forgone the comforts of her old life. In this untamed place she'd gained much more than she'd lost; she'd gained her freedom.

The crunch of wheels on gravel. Drew? She ran outside to see a twin-cab four-wheel drive. A substantial middle-aged man, with square shoulders, got out and started towards her, holding a document wallet. 'Where's your mother?' he asked in a terse voice. Sam remained silent. 'Never mind. Just make sure she signs these.' He handed her the wallet. Sam took it, still staring. This must be Bill. She should say who she was, but he was so stern, and her story so unlikely. She dreaded going through the absurd spiel all over again, so instead she just nodded. Bill seemed satisfied. 'I saw Bushy today. He's got a yarding of brumbies. Wants you to turn up eight o'clock sharp, Monday. Otherwise he'll get somebody else.' With that, he left.

Sam opened the folder. A lease for land, signed by William Chandler. Chandler. Drew's last name was Chandler. There was such a lot she didn't know about this place.

Sam and Drew sat out the back on kitchen chairs. It was almost dark, and a welcome breeze had chased away the oppressive heat of the day. Steaks sizzled on the barbecue. Drew cut slabs of white bread, and spread them thickly with butter. Faith didn't allow real butter in the house. Said it hardened your arteries and made you fat. Sam tried a piece of the bread. Delicious. Drew turned the steaks, his sleeves rolled up over muscled forearms, and handed Sam a can from the esky in the back of the ute. Beer.

'I'm not a huge fan of beer.' She handed it back. 'Do you have anything else?'

He cracked the can himself, and gave her an amused look, his white teeth bright in the dusk. 'Sorry, m'lady.' Then he lit the kerosene lamp and hung it from the clothesline. The white- hot mantle burned with unexpected brilliance.

'Thanks for all this,' she said.

He flashed that smile again. 'Keep the barbie until you've sorted out your power problems. At least you'll be able to cook.'

'Won't your father mind?'

Drew shot her a curious look. She pulled out the lease document from her bag and handed it over. He glanced at it, gave it back, and slipped the steaks onto odd plates she'd found in the kitchen – not her mother's fashionably mismatched antiques, but cheap ceramics, cracked and chipped.

'Mary won't sign the lease,' said Sam. 'Not this time.'

'Fair enough.' He slapped the meat between slices of buttered bread 'Sauce?'

'Who's Bushy?' Sam cut the fat off her steak and gave it to Bess.

'Town horse breaker,' he said, between mouthfuls. 'Works at the racecourse. Top bloke, is Bushy.' Drew certainly didn't waste words. 'Your dad told me to be there at eight o'clock sharp, Monday morning.'

'Dad thought you were Charlie?' She nodded. Drew whistled. 'Probably no point denying it. He'd have thought you were pulling some sort of scam.' Drew absentmindedly traced two fingers along the steel frame of his chair. Sam wondered how they would feel on her skin instead. 'Shame though. Your sister's been aching to get that job. It'll kill her to miss out.' He threw Bess some gristle. 'Tell you what,' he said. 'Why don't I ride over in the morning and give you a tour of Brumby's? You do ride, don't you?'

She nodded and told him about Pharaoh. Drew sat quietly as she spoke, his dark eyes gleaming in the kerosene light. She liked how he listened – really listened, nodding encouragement every now and then. 'He was sold by mistake,' she finished.

'Tough break.' He put a consoling hand on her arm. Every nerve of her skin felt exposed where he touched her. When he pulled his hand away, she wished he hadn't.

'Think I'll take you up on that beer after all,' she said.

After dinner, he helped pack up the few dishes, and handed her the kerosene lamp. 'Good night, Sam,' he said, drawing close. 'Will you be okay here, on your own? It's a tough way to spend Christmas Eve.'

She bit her lip, tempted to say, 'No, stay here with me.' But she barely knew him – and surely he had plans. Instead she said, 'Good night, Drew. Merry Christmas,' and watched his tail lights retreat down the hill, growing smaller and smaller until they vanished.

There was no moon, but stars shone large in the night sky, in a way they never did in Melbourne. Sam made her way through the dark house to Mary's room. She lay down and turned out the lamp. How odd, to curl up in the bed of her birth mother for the very first time. The pillow still smelt of rosemary and thyme.

Frogs croaked a loud chorus outside. For how many years had Charlie drifted off to this frog-song lullaby? Sam's heart ached with the shapeless loss of what she'd never known, and despite the beer buzz it took a long time for sleep to come. When she finally closed her eyes, Drew's face and the sound of his voice stayed with her. This was going to be a most unusual Christmas.

CHAPTER 12

Drew chained Bess up by the back door. 'Bit far for you, old girl.' He fondled her ears and offered a lamb shank. The dog whined and gave the bone a half-hearted lick. Poor compensation for missing a day out on the range.

They'd made a perfunctory exchange of gifts that morning – him, Mai and Dad. It was a dismal scene. Mai had escaped afterwards to spend the day with relatives in Wodonga. Bill was off to Christmas lunch at neighbouring Brigalow Station. He'd expected Drew to tag along. 'It's a fine thing,' Bill grumbled, 'when your own children can't be bothered with you on Christmas.' Drew had excused himself from the breakfast table, his appetite suddenly gone.

Sam was towelling her hair dry by the water tank when he arrived, Tambo by her side. Singlet top, denim shorts showing off long, shapely legs. Pale legs. Her complexion was like alabaster, her arms, her graceful neck. All white. Drew tried to recall Charlie's nut-brown tan, and failed. Even Sam's voice didn't sound so different this morning. He was getting used to this gorgeous new Charlie. 'Merry Christmas,' said Drew, swinging down from the saddle. Well, well, well - very nice. She'd lit right up at the sight of him.

'Merry Christmas!' Sam came running and hurried straight past him. It seemed his horse was the attraction. 'What's her name?' she asked, stroking the red-roan mare's nose.

'Chiquita.'

Sam ran her hand appreciatively down her shoulder. 'Quarter horse?'

Drew nodded. 'Dad's a fan.' He combed a burr from Chiquita's chestnut mane with his fingers. 'I don't go along with him there. Give me an Aussie stock horse every time.' The mare stamped her foot, as if in disagreement. 'Charlie used to back me on this one. To hear her tell it, riding quarter horses was tantamount to treason. Un-Australian, she used to say.'

Sam gave him a strange look. 'Charlie's not dead.'

'So you said.'

'Then perhaps you could stop referring to her in the past tense.'

'Did I?' He tied Chiquita to the fence. 'Have you had breakfast?'

'I didn't feel like stale Froot Loops without milk,' she said. 'You?'

'I had a dingo's breakfast.'

'What's that?' she asked.

'A yawn, a piss and a good look around.' Sam made a face at him as an impatient Tambo shoved her in the back with his nose. 'He's keen to get going,' said Drew. 'Been shut up in that dustbowl of a paddock for too long.'

Sam looked doubtfully at the gelding's scrawny frame. 'Do you think he's up to it?'

'My oath,' said Drew. 'A brumby like him will run all day on a sniff of feed.'

'He's not shod.'

'His feet are neat and hard. He won't be needing shoes – not out here in the bush.'

Sam looked doubtful. 'If you say so,' she said. 'Give me a minute to change.'

'Righto.'

Ten minutes later she emerged looking like a magazine model, wearing jodhpurs, an ivory shirt, gleaming boots, and carrying a stock saddle. Drew whistled in admiration. She sure was something to see.

Beneath the hint of a blush she looked a little lost. 'I found this inside.' She heaved the saddle onto a rail. 'Is it Tambo's? Will it do, Drew, do you think?'

He nodded, liking the way his name sounded on her tongue. 'Want some help?' She had the surcingle back to front, and the breastplate upside down. 'Thought you knew about horses,' he teased. 'Or do you just dress the part?'

Sam put her hands on her hips. 'I've never used this kind of saddle. I use a straight-flapped dressage one back home.' She frowned. 'Or at least I used to, when I still had a horse to ride.'

Drew came over, deftly fitted the surcingle and breastplate, then slapped the pommel. 'This here's a handmade Tony Gifford Jubilee Poley,' he said. 'Specially made for campdrafting. The flap's shorter than usual, cut a little more forward. You can shorten up your stirrups and get your leg right on the horse.' He pointed to the kneepad. 'See this angle? Your thigh fits snugly, but you can still get up out of the saddle. Charlie won this little beauty at the King of the Mountains festival last year. It's the town's annual big bash.'

'I'm very honoured to use it, then.' She pulled a black riding helmet from a bag at her feet. Jesus. She'd cop a serve if anybody around here saw her wearing that. Still, she might need it. Tambo had a cold back. Sam strapped on the helmet and mounted. The horse took off, pigrooting down the driveway. She rode well, sitting out the half-hearted bucking display with ease.

Drew swung into the saddle and they headed up the hill at a brisk canter. When they came to the dam paddock, Drew reined his horse in. 'Tambo's a champion at opening gates. Just push him forward, use your legs.' Sam did as he said, leant forward and unlatched the gate. 'Now back up, swing his quarters around. No, hang onto the gate. Back up again, and there, you're done.' Sam's horse stood facing him on the other side of the closed gate.

Sam grinned. 'Tambo just executed a perfect turn on the forehand.'

'A what?'

'A turn on the forehand. The basis of all lateral work in dressage. The horse's inside leg steps under his body. It encourages correct engagement.'

'What, like this?' Drew moved Chiquita up to the gate, performed the same deft manoeuvre, and joined Sam on the other side.

'Just like that,' said Sam, smiling. 'Charlie warned me that Tambo would seem green compared to the horses I'm used to.' She leant forward and patted his neck. 'I must remember to tell her it's not true.' They started up the hill, walking fast on a loose rein, without breaking into a jog. 'You know what we're doing now?'

'As far as I can tell, nothing,' said Drew.

'We're doing an extended walk. *The horse covers as much ground as possible without haste, and without losing the regularity of his steps,*' she recited. *'The rider allows the horse to stretch out his head and neck without losing contact with the mouth.'*

'Tambo's a good walker, I'll give you that,' said Drew, mystified, 'but we're still just bloody walking.'

'There's walking, and then there's walking,' said Sam. 'Look.' She turned around, and pointed to their hoof prints in the dusty track. 'In the extended walk, the hind feet touch the ground clearly in front of the footprints of the forefeet.' He nodded. It was as she said. Sam forged on uphill, a smug smile on her face. Lesson one. With this girl, straightforward things could quickly get complicated. It certainly made things interesting.

The sun rose ever higher into a sky of flawless blue. Drew and Sam followed the winding creek upstream. Grassy clearings opened up around each bend. Three grey kangaroos stood like statues, before bounding away at the riders' approach. Sam cantered forward, then lost them in the forest of peppermint gums.

'Did you see that?'

'Roos,' said Drew. 'So what?' A small mob of fat Herefords, red and white, calves and cows, raised their heads from the tall grass, then trotted away from the riders. Tambo pricked up his ears and sidled sideways, impatient with the bit.

'They're just how I imagined them,' said Sam. 'I thought you said Brumby's Run was short of feed?'

'Those cows are in good nick, I'll give you that,' said Drew. He swatted a stinging fly from his arm. 'Trouble is, they're not yours. They're Dad's. He leases these creek flats. It'll be a different story higher up.'

The track led upwards through a ragged thicket of tea-tree to a rusted gate. In sharp contrast to the lush country they'd just ridden through, the land beyond the gate was starved-looking land, bare of grass. Grey clay showed between patches of woody scrub. Even unpalatable stringybarks told the tale of hungry stock – their trunks chewed and ragged, some ringbarked completely.

A sorry herd of black baldies picked their way across the barren hillside. The rotting carcasses of a cow and calf stank out the air. Drew frowned. He trotted up the hill to take a closer look at the herd. The cattle were no more than skin and bone.

'They're starving,' said Sam, staring open-mouthed at the walking skeletons.

Drew sized up the herd. 'Get behind them,' he said. 'We're going to push the mob further up the hill.'

Sam did as he asked, a distressed look on her face, and the herd made its faltering way towards the ridge top. It was painful to watch. Drew rested them frequently, allowing the weakened cattle time to catch their breaths. It was more than an hour before they saw the northern boundary fence — the fence that separated Kelly land from Balleroo National Park. In stark contrast to Brumby's Run, the park boasted sunburned seed heads, swaying above a carpet of summer pasture. A bare strip ran the length of the fence, where famished stock had pushed their heads through, wrapping hungry tongues around each precious leaf or blade of grass within reach. It was a sorry sight.

Drew swung forward at a canter, scouting the boundary, searching for something. There, by that patch of black cypress pine – a crude bush gate, just wire and droppers, fastened to a tree with baling twine.

Drew slashed the hay band, dragged the gate wide and urged Sam to help press the stock through. The starving animals rushed the opening, bellowing low, propping a few metres into the park and snatching at the grass with desperate urgency.

'Won't they run away?' asked Sam.

'Run?' Drew snorted. 'Take a look at them.' They sat on their horses and watched the cows for a while. 'We'll move them to your lower paddocks once Dad gets his cattle out. In the meantime, they could use a good feed, don't you think?' Sam nodded, open-mouthed, still staring at the skeletal beasts. 'Come on,' said Drew. 'Let's pick up the rest of them.'

That morning Sam got a crash course in mustering. She was a dead-set natural. Of course, it helped that she was riding a top stock horse. Tambo could have just about done the job on his own. But not all the cattle were as poor as that first lot, and more than once Drew wished he'd brought a stockwhip. His dad said riding out without your whip was as bad as riding out without your pants. One mob of lively steers really gave them a run for their money. Tambo may have been thin, but he was keen as mustard, eagerly running down each breaking beast, swinging it hard back to the herd. At first Sam sat straight in her saddle, glued to it, body swaying in graceful time with Tambo's props and turns. Sexy? Yes. Gorgeous? Undoubtedly, but perhaps not the best seat for running rough stock through the bush.

Drew reined left, gathered a cow and young calf from their tea-tree hide, and steered them towards the herd. Sam galloped Tambo across the facing gully. That was better. Her legs had slid forward into traditional stockman position. Lying flat over Tambo's wither, she drew level with a beast and expertly shouldered it back into the mob, like she'd done it all her life – just as Charlie would have done.

He cantered over. 'We'll make a cowgirl out of you yet.'

Sam's face shone with excitement and triumph. She leaned over and stroked the horse's neck. Her breasts swung down a fraction, changing the contours of her buttoned shirt in a fascinating way, sending a shiver of desire right through him. Watch it, boy, he told himself.

'It was all Tambo,' she said, but he could tell she didn't mean it. There was pride behind her words, a small conceit. He nodded approval and urged his mare after the mob, guiding them uphill towards a second gate in the boundary fence.

By noon, maybe fifty cows and calves were feasting on the national park side of the fence. It was good to see the hungry cattle filling their bellies, but there were so few of them. How many were there meant to be? Whatever the number, they'd been left to fend for themselves for far too long. Guilt made him shift uneasily in the saddle. How could he have known that the Kellys would just take off like that, without a word of where they were going or when they'd be back? He watched Sam follow an inquisitive calf up the faint, rocky track. She knew where her sister was – knew, but for some reason wasn't telling. It was most mysterious.

Drew trotted after Sam. 'Come on,' he called. 'I want to show you something.' He took the lead, winding his way through the stringy-bark and tea-tree, pushing his mare up the stony slope. The muffled thud of Tambo's unshod hoofs sounded close behind him. The approaching horses flushed out a bold daytime fox, sleek and fat as butter. It darted downhill.

'Foxes and dingoes will be having a field day,' said Drew. 'There's good pickings for scavengers at Brumby's.' He reined Chiquita in, regretting his words as soon as they were uttered. The path widened, and the horses walked two abreast. Sam didn't look at him, staring straight ahead between Tambo's pricked ears. 'I'll tell you something you don't know about foxes,' he said.

'How about I tell you something you don't know about them instead?' said Sam. 'Where are there more foxes, do you think? Per square kilometre, I mean. Here? Or in Melbourne?'

'Here,' he said. 'They're bloody everywhere. What would a self-respecting fox be doing in town anyway?'

'Wrong. Urban environments are full of garbage. Highly beneficial for foxes. Towns support population densities up to ten times greater than rural areas.'

'Is that so?' said Drew. 'Well, since you're such an expert, perhaps you can explain this. Out bush a while back, I saw this pretty little vixen tearing bark off a tree with her teeth. Should have shot her, I suppose, but instead I just watched, quiet like, so as not to scare her. She carried a mouthful of bark down to the creek, and backed into the water, until all I could see was her black nose, and the strips of bark between her teeth. She stayed stock still for a few minutes, then dropped the bark and let it drift off downstream. Jumping back onto the bank, she gave herself a bit of a shake and trotted off, happy as Larry.'

'That's the strangest thing,' said Sam. 'I can't imagine why a fox would behave in such an odd way.'

'Thought a smart girl like you could figure something like that out.'

She cracked a smile, the kind that set a bloke dreaming. 'Do *you* know?'

Drew nodded. 'That little fox was getting rid of fleas. See, as she backs into the creek, they jump forward, to get out of the water. Eventually they all jump onto the piece of bark between her teeth, and she lets it float off, so the fleas get a chance for a bit of white-water rafting.'

'No.' Sam laughed. 'I don't believe that for a minute.'

Drew tipped his hat. 'True story.' Then he cantered off, with Sam chasing close behind.

Their path intersected with the old stock route used in years gone by to bring the mountain cattle home. Almost there. An ancient hut appeared through a curtain of gum leaves. It had a rusted tin roof, corrugated-iron rainwater tank, a crumbling chimney at one end, and a rough porch at the other. 'Dead Man's Hut,' said Drew. A creek bubbled from beneath rocks nearby, spilling past the ramshackle building into a chain of clear pools.

Sam and Drew tethered their horses to a rail of the bush timber yard. Sam loosened Tambo's girth, then pulled the saddle off altogether. 'It's hot,' she said. 'Might take him for a swim.'

Now that was a tantalising prospect. Sam sat down on a split log bench near the door. Drew hesitated for just a moment before unsaddling his own horse. How could he resist? He pulled a water bottle from the saddlebag and sat down close beside her.

'Drink?' She took a swig. Water trickled down her neck and delicate cleavage. His groin ached at the brief pressure of her thigh against his.

'Why is it called Dead Man's Hut?' she asked.

'You don't want to know.'

'Looks like it's straight out of *The Man From Snowy River* movie,' said Sam, in a delighted voice. 'And I'm Jessica Harrison.' She ran her fingers along the warm grain of the timber seat. 'I'm rebellious and reckless.' And sexy and gorgeous, thought Drew. Don't forget gorgeous. He had a mind to say it out loud.

Sam stood up and struggled with the rusty lock. Drew pressed close to her warm body, reached around, pulled back the bolt and pushed the door open. Inside was a rickety bunk with worn horsehair mattresses, a dusty table and a blackened fire-place. A bridle, green with age, hung on a nail, and a few rusted tins of bully beef stood along a splintered plank shelf.

'It's charming,' said Sam.

Drew saw nothing charming about the gloomy interior. He saw only isolation and loneliness.

'Imagine living up here, waking up to that.' Sam pointed down the valley, past the ridge of candlebark and wattle, to the rolling hills below. A glittering stream meandered through the river flats in great loops. The sun caught it, transforming the winding watercourse into a chain of shining, silver crescents. 'Well?' asked Sam.

'It's nice,' he admitted, feeling foolish. It wasn't his custom to reflect on the scenery.

'Nice?' scoffed Sam. 'It's more than nice. It's stunning!' She heaved a great sigh. 'You're so lucky to live here.'

Lucky? This place was home, and he loved it, but he'd never thought of himself as lucky to be here. Quite the contrary. It was duty that bound him to these mountains. His two older sisters were long gone, drawn to Sydney like moths to lamps, building careers, hunting for husbands, escaping the tyranny of their critical father. Even his mother was gone. Last year when Mum left to visit her plugged-in Sydney daughters, she'd never come back. A long-distance divorce, and his father hadn't seemed to flinch.

And him? Well, his heart wasn't in the cattle business. Horses were his passion, especially Australian stock horses; a beautiful breed of tough, intelligent animals exemplified by the Walers – station-bred horses turned war horses, renowned as the finest cavalry mounts in the world. Drew's dream was to build up a quality herd of studbook mares, purchase a stallion or two with Abbey heritage and found his own line of stock horses. A line with particular emphasis on temperament, to suit a wide range of riders, of varying abilities. He wanted to run treks into the spectacular high country, showcasing the versatility and kind nature of his horses. Drew had saved up to buy Clancy as a colt for just such a purpose – the foundation stallion for his future herd.

Bill, however, had no patience for his son's dreams. *Kilmarnock is a cattle station, always has been and always will be*, he'd said.

Drew came home one day to find Clancy gelded.

I won't have any ill-bred stallion running around, harassing my mares. And that was that. Things at home would be run Bill's way, or no way at all. Plenty of times Drew had wanted to chuck it in. Station hands talked about the money to be made in the mines out west. But paternal expectation is a powerful thing, and Drew was the only son .. . There was just so much a man could take though, and Drew's patience was wearing thin.

Sam removed her helmet, looked at him and smiled. 'Don't you ever take off that cowboy hat?'

He shrugged one shoulder. Truth was, he rarely did. 'It's not a cowboy hat. It's a stockman's hat.' His dad was the cowboy hat fan. Big and black, ten-gallon style with a high crown, pencil-rolled brim and studded, buckled band.

'It looks like a cowboy hat to me.' Sam reached up, snatched it from his head and tossed it onto the grass. She laughed and crouched down to retrieve it, dark hair parting at the nape. He wanted to kiss the pale skin of her neck.

'How pretty.' She picked up the curled crescent of a gum leaf. A small green frog sat in its centre, no more than three centimetres long. Contrasting black stripes extended from its nostrils, right over its eyes and head like a costume mask. Its back was striped a stylish emerald and brown. Tiny discs decorated its digits and webbed toes. Sam jumped as a surprisingly loud series of low whistling notes burst from the tiny amphibian. 'Do you know what species it is?'

'Of course.' Drew leaned in close for a better look, close enough to feel the light heat of Sam's body, and to catch a scent of her perfume; strange and exotic and marvellous. 'It's a species of frog.'

Sam laughed. 'I bet Charlie would know.'

'I bet she would, at that.' It had been the first mention of Charlie for a while. 'Do you have a boyfriend?' asked Drew suddenly. 'Back in . . . back in wherever you come from?'

She met his gaze. 'No.' Her reply came swift, bold and unequivocal

Hallelujah. 'Come on.' He took hold of Sam's right hand, helping her to her feet. 'Your sister would never forgive us if we let anything happen to that frog.' He didn't let go of her hand as he led her to the ferny creek behind the hut. Truth was, he didn't want to ever let it go.

'Goodbye, Mr Frog,' said Sam, setting it free. The little creature launched itself into a pool, paddled away to a clump of reeds, and sat watching them.

'You're left-handed,' said Drew. 'Like Charlie.'

'Of course,' said Sam. 'We're identical – physically, anyway.'

It was just too intriguing. She looked at him with those tawny eyes of hers, like tiger eyes, and the desire to touch her overwhelmed his caution. On an impulse he spread his arms in invitation, and willed her to him. It worked. She moved into his embrace like it was the most natural thing in the world, her body soft and warm in his arms. He folded her in, lowering his head to her lovely mouth for a kiss. But her response was stiff, uncertain. Resistant. Then it dawned. Perhaps she hadn't done this before? After all, this girl was no Charlie. She had class. You wouldn't find her behind the chutes at a rodeo, beneath some hotshot bull rider. His kiss turned from ardent and probing, to tentative and tender. He drew back and Sam pressed in against him, her eyes locked on his.

'I've never met anybody like you before,' he said softly.

'Of course you have,' Sam said, smiling. 'What about my sister?'

Drew shook his head. 'Charlie's not like you. She's feral – crazy even.'

Sam pulled away and gave him a penetrating look. 'She doesn't seem crazy to me.'

'Well, she is – and she likes rodeo cowboys way too much.' Why were they talking about Charlie? He wanted to talk about Sam. 'Why didn't she ever mention you?'

'I don't know,' said Sam. 'Why didn't she ever mention you?'

'She didn't?'

'No. But she mentioned your dad. He's a complete bastard, apparently.'

Chiquita whinnied loudly. Drew and Sam looked around to where she and Tambo were tethered beside the yard. The roan mare stood at attention, head high, ears pricked towards the gully. It was then they heard it. A close, trumpeting neigh. Chiquita shivered in her skin, pawed the ground and raised her tail.

A buckskin horse emerged from the stringybark trees. He marched with arched neck and a bold, high-stepping gait, right up to the restive mare. Could it be Jarrang? Chiquita reared and squealed; the high, insistent squeal of a mare in season. Drew leapt up and darted for her head. Too late.

The brumby stallion laid his ears flat back as Chiquita's reins snapped. His head snaked to her flank, biting hard. Drew yelled and tried to force himself between the horses. The buckskin lunged straight at him, all bared teeth, slashing hoofs and wild, rolling eyes. The bugger. Drew ducked beneath the rail, and watched as the stallion half drove, half cajoled his mare across the clearing. The pair disappeared at a gallop into the trees. Tambo neighed and danced at the end of his reins.

'Damn!' Drew glanced at Sam, standing wide-eyed by the yard. Then he swung bareback onto Tambo, and took off after Chiquita.

The horses headed straight up the hill. The buckskin knew what he was doing. He kept to the trees, staying between Drew and the mare, lashing out with both hind feet whenever Drew came too close. It was all Drew could do to keep pace with him. When they reached the ridge's rocky spine, Chiquita faltered. It was a precipitous place, and treacherous underfoot. She swung back around into the open. Drew rode at right angles to intercept her, pushing Tambo into her shoulder and grabbing her trailing reins. The buckskin wheeled, but Drew had hold of her now. He spun Tambo around, drew his horses to a halt and faced the stallion. Drew was certain of it now. This was Jarrang, Charlie's orphan foal, all grown up.

Jarrang retreated in a series of small, defiant rears, right back to the escarpment. Tambo and Chiquita stood with heaving sides, but the brumby stallion seemed unfazed by the uphill gallop. He'd matured into a striking horse, about fifteen hands, with the deep chest, short back and good length of rein so typical of early Walers. The type of horse that might even impress Drew's father – if his father didn't know Jarrang was a brumby, that was. What Drew needed was a rope. Jarrang reared again and boxed the air, as if reading Drew's mind. Drew leaned down to stroke Chiquita's damp neck. 'Come on, girl. Let's get you home.'

They turned to go. The buckskin screamed with anger. In a surprise move he thundered back and shot past so close that Drew could have touched him. Startled, Chiquita rose high on hind legs, and Drew impulsively wound her reins around his hand. Bad move. Tambo leapt forward. Chiquita hung back and wrenched Drew to the ground. Even then he didn't drop the reins, but Jarrang was determined to have his mare. He galloped straight for Drew, ears flattened, forcing him to dive for cover. Swiftly the stallion urged Chiquita on, nipping at her wither. With a dreadful, sinking feeling, Drew watched the horses scramble up the scree and vanish behind a rocky overhang.

For a moment he feared he'd lose Tambo as well, but the bay seemed to understand the stallion would not welcome his company.

He stopped short at the base of the stony slope and played hard to get for a few precious minutes, before allowing Drew to mount. There was no point giving chase. Those horses were long gone. Drew spat on the ground in disgust, and headed back to the hut. His dad would be furious. Merry Christmas, indeed.

CHAPTER 13

Eight o'clock, Monday morning. 'So, you're Charlie.'

Sam nodded uncertainly, as if she didn't believe it herself. Don't say a word. Her voice would give her away more than anything. She'd been practising talking like Charlie – trying to speak from the back of her tongue and limiting lip movement a little. And she needed to speed up her speech, and run the words together a bit more. It was like giving herself elocution lessons in reverse. Thank goodness Bushy didn't seem to expect her to talk.

Sam had never met an Aboriginal person before. Bushy wore a funny, old fashioned hat – an iron-grey fedora, like Indiana Jones might wear – along with moleskin trousers, an ancient tweed jacket and a black tie. Quite an eccentric look.

He extended his hand and she shook it, limp-wristed, willing her own hand not to shake. His grasp was firm and Sam wished she'd applied more pressure. Bushy scrutinised her, hawk eyes peering from a weathered, leather-skinned face. As with an old saddle, it was impossible to guess his age. Fifty? Seventy?

'You're a bit pasty for a country girl,' he said. There was no answer to that. This was never going to work. Why on earth had she thought she might pass for her sister? 'You've a way with horses though,' he said. 'That's what they say.' Bushy gestured for her to follow him. 'We'll soon see if it's true.'

In the corner of the showgrounds stood a stockyard, and in the corner of the stockyard stood a frightened palomino colt with a flame-shaped star. His eyes were wary, his head held high, forefeet balanced in readiness to flee left or right as circumstance demanded. 'There's a little brumby for you,' said Bushy. 'Straight off the mountain. Passive trapped, so he's not been hurt.' He picked up a rope, and they climbed through the rails into the yard. 'That colt is as frightened as you'd be if you were stuck in a room with some fella from outer space. That fella might be friendly, or he might want to have you for supper.'

Sam jumped as a noose snaked out from Bushy's hands and landed neatly over the horse's head. The colt screamed and reared, battling the pull on his neck. 'Leave it loose to start with. Prove you mean no harm.' Bushy handed Sam the rope. 'I want you to halter-break that brumby.' He took a pouch of tobacco and papers from his pocket, and proceeded to roll a smoke. 'You've got half an hour. Do that, and the job's yours – and you get to name the colt.'

Sam felt sick. She'd be exposed for the fraud she was. But before giving up she considered her task. Hadn't she broken in Pharaoh herself? However there'd been a team of trainers on call, and he'd arrived at the stables as a well-behaved youngster, with perfect ground manners. A far cry from this wild, fearful creature. Still, the basic principles were the same, and she was wearing Charlie's lucky hat to boot. How difficult could it be? Sam cautiously shortened the rope. She'd never used a rope on a horse before, but the stiff noose held its shape, and the large leather eye seemed designed to prevent choking. The palomino fought against the slightest pressure. Sam kept up a firm, light contact, letting the stout rails do the work of containment for her. Dust choked her throat and her pulse was racing. The line lightly slipped and slid along the horse's flanks and over his rump as he twisted and turned. After a minute or two he seized upon a new way to escape his captor, plunging round and round the yard with wide, rolling eyes, searching the rails for any weakness. But no matter how he tried, he couldn't evade Sam's quiet touch. His first terror gone, the colt lowered his head and turned to face her.

'Good,' called Bushy from outside the yard. 'You're halfway there.'

Sam spat the dirt from her mouth and checked her watch. She'd better be. Only fifteen minutes left. Sam controlled her anxiety, allowing the golden colt to settle down, to appreciate that the rope around his neck was no threat. What now? She played it by ear, swinging the rope softly, slow and rhythmic, so it brushed his muzzle, his cheek, then up to his ear. He flinched, but didn't move, watching her. She crooned a sing-song stream of reassuring words. 'There's a boy, stand up, I just want to pat you.'

'Pat him?' yelled Bushy from the side. He roared with laughter. 'That's a new one.'

Sam ignored him. She forgot about the time. Each nerve tingled in tempo with the palomino's racing heart. She steadied her breathing, and the colt steadied his. Then he relaxed his jaw and yawned. Sam smiled and moved right up to his shoulder, crooning all the while, unable to believe her luck. He examined her with his velvet muzzle, taking her in, the taste and smell of her. She looped the rope into a rough halter and slipped it over his nose, stroking his shivering neck all the while.

'You still gotta lead him,' called Bushy.

Sam backed up, in line with the colt's forefeet, and flicked the rope end. He moved smartly around the yard at a trot. Sam relaxed her body and the brumby dropped back to a walk. With infinite patience Sam approached his shoulder, coiling the rope as she went, keeping pace with him. Soon she had the colt following her around the perimeter of the yard, just as calm as could be.

She glanced up at Bushy, heart banging with pride. He nodded. 'You'll do. Turn him loose.'

Sam punched the air, letting out a whoop of excitement. The brumby reared, causing the halter to tighten on his nose. He thrashed violently from side to side. Sam dropped the rope and ran for the rails. Bushy slipped into the yard, picked up the line and urged the horse into a canter. When he slackened the rope, the colt turned to face him, and Bushy released him with one expert flick of his wrist.

'It's wise not to get ahead of yourself with any horse,' he said, chuckling. 'Especially a wild brumby.'

'Do I still get the job?' asked Sam, breathless.

Bushy took an extra long look at her, as if he was contemplating a difficult question. 'You do,' he said at last. 'Come back after lunch.' The palomino pranced and neighed. 'You got a name for him?'

'Phoenix,' she said without hesitation. 'I'll call him Phoenix.'

Sam climbed up on the rails, and watched the young brumby buck his way around the yard. 'It's a new start for us both,' she whispered.

Sam sat in her car and tried calling Charlie again. Her phone had been dropping out badly ever since she'd arrived. Maybe there'd be better reception out here at the showgrounds. Even when she did manage to get through, all calls went through the hospital switch-board. A conspiracy of nurses seemed determined to thwart any attempt to talk to Charlie. Her sister was either asleep, or having tests, or having showers or having lunch. Didn't they realise these calls were important? Charlie must be going insane, wondering how things were going. 'One moment please,' said a voice, and then, miracle of miracles, she was through.

'Sam?' Charlie sounded excited, and much stronger than Sam remembered. 'Tell me absolutely everything.'

Sam launched into a report of her four days so far at Brumby's Run, guided by Charlie's enthusiastic inquisition. But an odd thing was happening. As she told her story, she found herself editing the account in little ways. Or maybe they weren't so little. Bill, for instance. He'd mistaken her for Charlie and she'd let the impression stand. How could she explain that? How could she convey, on a shaky phone line, how difficult it was to swear that you weren't who somebody assumed you were? But she hadn't deliberately misled Bill – not like she'd done with Bushy. When Sam got to that part, she told Charlie that she'd taken the job with Bushy in order to hold it for her when she came home. This was true, after all. Totally true . . . and Charlie had been thrilled to hear it. Any misunderstandings could be cleared up later. And then there was Drew. She mentioned how helpful he'd been – but not the toe-curling kiss they'd shared. She tried to talk casually about him, sure Charlie would be able to see through her nonchalance. But her sister was caught up in her own problems.

'Remember, don't tell anybody I'm sick,' said Charlie. 'They feel sorry enough for me around Currajong already. You should hear them. Poor little Charlie, having a mother like that. A drunk. A druggie. Running around with all those men. No wonder she turned out like she did. Sanctimonious jerks. I couldn't stand any more pity! And anyway, Bushy might think I won't be up for the job.'

'Don't worry,' said Sam, feeling faint. 'Nobody knows.'

'What about Drew? What have you told him?'

'That you're away on confidential business,' said Sam. Charlie thought that was funny. She laughed, loud and strong. There was something about the laugh that Sam hadn't heard before, a disturbing quality. It took her a while to pick it. Charlie's laugh was sounding too much like her own.

'He must be mad with curiosity,' said Charlie finally, a note of immense satisfaction in her voice.

Now it was Sam's turn to ask questions. It turned out that her sister's recovery was proceeding beautifully. She'd be home in a couple of months, touch wood. 'You've saved my life, you know that?' said Charlie, just before the line dropped out for good.

Sam went over the conversation in her head. Her gaze wandered to the imposing blue peaks of the Balleroo Range, to the clear azure sky, to the beautiful brumby dancing in the stockyard. A satin bowerbird, in splendid blue-black plumage, swooped on spilled oats outside Bushy's feed shed. Its odd creaking cry sounded like the opening of a long locked door. 'No, Charlie,' said Sam, as she started the car. 'I think it's you who's saved mine.'

CHAPTER 14

Bill tossed the last hay bale down. Drew fielded it and stacked it on the tray of the truck. Monday afternoon, and he still hadn't told his father they were losing the lease for Brumby's Run. The opportunity was staring at him over breakfast. Bill had been on the phone to Tom about stocking rates for next year, but Drew hadn't mustered up the courage. What was worse, his father was talking about buying in more cattle.

'I want you to inspect those Benambra weaners for me next week,' Bill said as he dusted off his hands. 'Make sure they bring in the bloody lot, so they can't hide the tail.' The *tail* was the inevitable percentage of poorer calves in any yarding. Bill had been caught out last year, buying a motley, weedy mob based on an unrepresentative sample of yarded stock. It was Drew who'd warned Bill against them, so there was a certain irony in Bill's words of caution. 'And don't act too keen. Buying paddock mobs is like playing poker, and you've never been much good at poker.' Bill walked away whistling, looking pleased with himself.

'Yeah, yeah,' muttered Drew to himself. Gloom gathered over him like his own, personal cloud. Why shouldn't Dad look pleased? He'd had a win, no doubt about it. Thanks to the recently elected state government, cattle were going back into Balleroo National Park –as a trial to start with. A phone call that morning confirmed the stock would mainly come from Kilmarnock. It didn't hurt that Bill and the new environment minister were old school mates. So now Bill had plans to move the cows and calves from Brumby's up into the park, and put a few hundred new weaners onto Mary's land. Drew needed to tell his father to back off before things got out of hand — and he needed to do it soon.

Drew was ready to jump in the cab when Bess began to bark. Sam's bright-blue beetle was scooting up the drive. From his vantage point at the hay shed, he watched his father stride down to meet her. After a minute or two Bill raised his voice and Sam retreated to her car. With a dismissive wave of his hand, Bill marched back to the house. Drew headed down the hill at a run. Charging around the corner of the verandah, he cannoned headlong into his father coming the other way. Too late - the beetle was heading off. Drew mumbled an apology to his father and tried to appear offhand.

'The Kellys are back,' said Bill. 'Hate to think how they got their hands on a car like that.' He shook his head. 'The girl, Charlie — she was just here.' Bill gave Drew a shrewd look. 'Don't you go getting keen on her again, son. She's not for you.' Drew took a long, steadying breath. Just ignore him, don't give him the satisfaction. 'Know what she said?' Bill gave a hollow laugh. 'She said Mary won't renew the lease.'

Drew put on a look of suitable surprise. 'Well that scotches the cattle buying trip then.'

'It bloody well doesn't!' barked Bill. 'Mary will come round. You're still going, right after you round up those damned horses and get Chiquita back for me. I'm not losing my top mare to some mongrel stallion, not like Don Campbell did at Jindabyne.' Yes. The little issue of Dad's mare. 'I'm sending Ted to repair the yards up at Dead Man's Hut. Then I want those brumbies run in.'

'What do I do with them?'

'Shoot them, dog them, I don't care – just get Chiquita back.' Bill walked off, still looking pleased with himself. Drew remembered the horror of running the brumbies last year on Maroong Mountain. One thing was certain. This time things would be done differently.

The sun blazed low in the western sky when Drew set off for Brumby's Run. He'd packed a box with Christmas leftovers: cold meat, salad, half a pavlova, mince pies and fresh fruit. A bottle of wine sat on ice in the esky.

This was Drew's second try today. The first time, he'd gone by just on spec and Sam hadn't been home. He'd hightailed it out of there, scared she'd catch him on his way out and think him desperate. This time he'd had enough sense to try her mobile and score himself a proper invitation. Sam was waiting for him outside the house wearing Charlie's clothes: jeans, plaid shirt and an Akubra. She looked tired and happy, her skin flushed, her face sunburned - even prettier than he remembered. Bess scrambled off the tray to meet her before Drew had a chance to lift the dog down.

Sam had put up a card table under the peppercorn tree out back, set with plates and cutlery. Charlie's pet crow cawed from a low branch, causing Sam to jump in fright. 'That's Condor,' said Drew, throwing the friendly bird a piece of ham. 'Charlie hand-raised him when Dad shot his parents. Poor little fella must be missing her something shocking.'

'I had no idea,' said Sam. 'And to think I've been chasing him off.' Sam held out a piece of bread by way of apology. The big black bird received it with great dignity. 'Condor - that's an unusual name.'

'You know what a nature nut Charlie is,' said Drew. 'Condor's named after those big American vultures, cause he's a bit of a scavenger. And by the way, don't let Charlie hear you calling Condor a crow. He's an Australian raven, apparently, although I'll be buggered if I can tell the difference.'

Drew produced the wine and poured it into tumblers that had once been jam jars. 'A toast,' he said. 'To bringing Chiquita home.' They clinked glasses, and locked eyes. Hers sparkled in the twilight, and he wanted to pull her into his arms again, but dressed like that, with her sister's Akubra and all – the resemblance to Charlie was too disconcerting.

'Don't you ever take off that cowboy hat?' he asked. She smiled, tossed it off, and they tucked into the food. He told Sam about the plans to retrieve Chiquita.

Can I help?' she asked. 'After all, I'm a professional brumby breaker now.'

Drew went to speak and stopped himself. He'd better watch it; he'd almost called her Charlie. 'You fooled Bushy?' He supposed it wouldn't have been that hard. Bushy had never met Charlie. He'd only recently arrived as a replacement for the last horse breaker, a man whose penchant for hard liquor had got the better of him. Bushy had settled on Charlie for the job by word of mouth alone, for she had a formidable local reputation as a horsewoman.

Sam's tone was instantly defensive. 'You said yourself that it would kill Charlie to lose that job.'

'Maybe so, but you can't go around town masquerading as your sister forever.' She didn't respond. The truth was, Sam probably could get away with it if she kept to herself, at least for a while. The resemblance was striking, and for the past few years the Kellys had been on the outer. Mary's unconventional lifestyle and erratic behaviour had seen her marginalised from the mainstream Currajong community. Over time she'd been frozen out of the Parents and Friends Association, the garden group, the picnic race committee. Unfortunately, this prejudice had extended to Charlie.

It had started with a few girls at pony club, deriding her and her brumby mounts with vicious barbs. *Trust a feral to ride a feral* or *Since when were donkeys allowed at rallies?* or *Is Charlie wearing those clothes for a bet?* It didn't matter to hot-headed Charlie that the bullies were in the minority. One cruel remark was enough to set her off. She was kicked out of the club after terrifying one of her tormentors with a stockwhip. Things grew worse as she got older. The insults became more personal, and were no longer confined to the horse she happened to be riding. *Why does Charlie look so confused? Oh, that's right*

— *it's Father's Day* or *You must have been born on the highway because that's where most accidents happen.*

Charlie always gave as good as she got. *It's a shame to ruin such beautiful blonde hair, by dyeing your roots black* and *If the zombie apocalypse comes, you'll be safe – they eat brains.* When the others pushed her too far, she just jumped them. Drew had no doubt they were jealous of this stunning girl who could ride the pants off the best of them. No wonder Charlie had grown up to be a loner. Horses and the bush became her closest companions. Romantically, she favoured the kind of superficial relationships she could find with the travelling picnic race jockeys, or cowboys on the rodeo circuit. Drew had found that out the hard way.

'What happens when Charlie comes back?' he asked. The uncomfortable silence grew, and it soon became obvious that Sam did not intend to respond to his question. For some foolish reason he felt compelled to point out a few more home truths. 'And you've got other things to worry about besides Charlie. No electricity means no running water, no flushing toilets.'

'Anything else?' Sam's tight lips belied the cool tone of her voice.

'No fridge, no lights, no way to cook, or to charge your phone. Does the landline work?'

Sam shook her head. 'Cut off too, just like the power. I paid the bills and tried to reconnect, but I need Mary's passwords, and she's forgotten them . . . but it's fine, Drew.' There was something about the way Sam said his name that made it sound important. 'I can manage.'

She was pretty resourceful for a city girl, he had to give her that. Drew fondled Bess's floppy ears, and questions crowded back in. Where the hell were Mary and Charlie? And why wouldn't Sam say? She really was the most fascinating girl, tough and naive at the same time – a beautiful contradiction.

Drew couldn't resist any longer. Should he try to kiss her again? What if she pulled away? He took off his hat, reached across slowly, watching her, and smoothed the tangled hair back from her dirty face. He'd been thinking about doing that all day. Their faces were almost close enough to touch – but something was holding him back. Sam broke eye contact and the moment passed.

'Admit it, Sam,' he said. 'You need me. Tomorrow I'll rig you up a generator.' She really did have the cutest nose. 'If you run it for a few hours in the evening, at least you'll be able to cook and have a shower.' The corners of her mouth turned down. 'What's wrong?'

'I didn't think I'd have to cook. I thought you were going to bring me dinner every night,' she said with a straight face.

'That could be arranged, m'lady,' he said. 'Very easily. But you'll still need a shower.'

Sam fingered her top button. 'I could skinny-dip in the dam.'

Drew reached for the bottle of wine, not trusting himself to look at her. 'You're a tease, Samantha. You know that?' He topped up her glass, trying not to imagine her naked. 'Perhaps you're more like your sister than I thought. And if you think a dip in the dam will get you clean, then you're not accounting for the mud. And then there's the whopping great water bugs. They bite something shocking. The mozzies will eat you alive, and a big yabby could nip your toe clean off. Not to mention the snakes.'

'What do you mean, more like my sister?' asked Sam, suddenly serious.

'I just meant she could be a flirt too. All girls can be. Sometimes I think they can't help it.' Sam moved away and started picking strawberries off the pavlova. Terrific, now he'd offended her. Perhaps if he changed the subject. 'So you talked to Dad?'

Sam nodded and ate the last strawberry. 'I told him we're not renewing the lease, and that his cattle have to be out by the end of the week.'

'It's not that simple,' said Drew. 'He won't listen to you. It has to come from Mary.'

Sam shrugged. 'Without a lease his cattle are trespassing. I'll call the police if I have to.'

'What,' said Drew, 'with your stock wandering loose all over the national park? That could backfire badly.'

'I don't know,' said Sam. 'Maybe I'll just chase them out myself. Can't you talk to him?'

'Won't do any good,' said Drew. 'He doesn't listen to me either — never has. As I said, you'll need Mary. Could you get her to ring my dad?' Sam shuffled her feet and avoided his gaze. 'Or doesn't Mary know? Is ending the lease something you and Charlie have cooked up between you?'

Sam turned on him. 'That's none of your business, and don't you dare tell your father.' He made a show of packing up the picnic. 'What on earth was I thinking? You're the last person I should be talking to about this.'

Drew stood up. 'Fair enough.' He put on his hat. 'I'll be around tomorrow with the generator.'

'Don't bother,' said Sam, glaring. 'I don't need your help.' She was holding onto Bess like she meant to confiscate her.

Drew nodded, almost said something, then changed his mind. He'd royally stuffed this one up. Drew whistled and Bess wriggled from Sam's arms. Then he tipped his hat and left.

CHAPTER 15

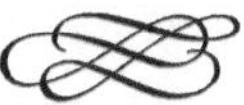

Friday already and Drew still hadn't been back. Each day after work as Sam tidied the yard, or washed the windows, or cleared out the hay shed, she listened for the sound of his wheels on the drive. At night she lay in Mary's bed and wondered if Drew was wondering about her. How did these things work? She'd regretted her harsh words just as soon as they were out, but it seemed the damage was done. It had been a stupid idea to discuss the lease with Drew in the first place. He was Bill's son, after all. She'd given Charlie a solemn oath to get back Brumby's Run. Yet if Bill found out that Mary didn't want it back, he'd never move his stock.

Sam stroked Tambo's nose as she fed him a carrot. 'Well, boy, it looks like it'll be just you and me seeing in the new year together.'

Her first week of working for Bushy had passed much too quickly. Each morning she rose at the clear light of dawn, and made coffee and instant porridge on a portable butane cooker she'd bought from the produce store in town. 'No point trying to put that on the account,' the man had told her. 'Your mum's three months' late on payments as it is.'

'No worries, George.' She'd learned his name from Bushy, who, oddly enough, didn't seem to turn a hair when she asked him such questions. What's the butcher's name again, Bushy? I forgot. Where's Duffers Lane? Who can I get some lucerne hay from?

'Can I have a copy of that overdue account please?' she'd asked George. He'd narrowed his eyes and complied. 'I'll fix that up for you now if you like?' Sam had said, to his obvious surprise and pleasure. She'd done the same all over town, paying off accounts at the grocer, the butcher, the service station. Who'd have thought that you could buy petrol on account? But Mary had managed it.

'You and your mum must have come into a bit of money, then?' said Harry at the service station as he checked her oil and water. It was a remark she'd heard all too often this past week, and the townsfolk's curiosity made her wary. Sam avoided people as much as possible. It wasn't hard. She loved her work, and she loved being home at Brumby's Run, cleaning up the house or weeding the garden in preparation for Mary and Charlie's return. She was far too busy to feel lonely.

Every day after breakfast Sam washed the dishes outside at the tank, tossed Tambo a few biscuits of hay and headed for the racetrack. The historic course at Currajong doubled as the showgrounds and was picture perfect, nestled at the edge of the forest on the outskirts of town. There were usually a few trainers and gallopers on the track when she arrived. She'd learned to slip into the jockey rooms to grab a quick shower and leave her phone charging, hidden behind a bench. Then she joined Bushy for a cup of tea and hot, buttered raisin toast before they started the day's work.

Close to forty brumbies stood in the stockyards: weanlings, yearlings, two-year-olds and a few mature mares. These horses, along with many others, had been trapped high in the range as part of a concerted federal push to remove them from national parks. Most went for slaughter, but a rescue organisation, the Brumby Coalition, had selected the most promising horses for rehoming. A wealthy sponsor had engaged Bushy to assess the brumbies, and teach them a few ground manners prior to their auction at the picnic race-day in a month's time. Ryan, a serious, bespectacled young man from the organisation, visited occasionally to ensure the horses were progressing well. They had lessons in leading, tying up and standing quietly for grooming; lessons in picking up feet for the farrier, and loading into floats. All the essentials for any self-respecting horse. Sam had soon found her favourites among them: the greedy, taffy gelding with the wall eye who seemed determined to eat her hair, the sweet chestnut filly who tried so hard to please – and then, of course, there was Phoenix.

Bushy had assigned the palomino colt to her as a personal project. It was a relief to know that Phoenix wouldn't go through the sales next month along with all the other brumbies. 'You started him,' said Bushy, lips clinging to the inevitable roll-your-own. 'Now you better finish him.' Each morning he coached her. Working with the colt generated in Sam a fierce, possessive pride, akin to that first thrill of working with Pharaoh. Sometimes she felt disloyal, as the pain of losing Pharaoh lost some of its bite.

Phoenix raised his head, and nickered at her approach. 'Hello, gorgeous,' she said. 'Was that welcome for me, or for this bucket of feed?' Sam slipped into the yard beside him. The colt nosed the fingers of her extended hand, snuffling low. She reached out and buried her hand in his snowy mane, stroking his neck, his nose. The strength of their connection was palpable. Phoenix lowered his head, blinking evenly as she emptied chaff and oats into the old tyre feeder. Long pale lashes framed his big amber eyes. She liked how his ears swivelled independently of each other, simultaneously keeping track of her and any movement outside the yard. Tracing the muscular definition of his graceful neck, she admired the range of colours in his sleek summer coat. Silver, blonde and chestnut – combining to create the illusion of spun silk. She couldn't wait for the day she would ride him.

Sam picked up a comb and tamed his mane, no longer a tangle of knots and twigs. Instead it tapered neatly down his neck, like a fashion accessory, designed to lift and float, to add beauty and symmetry to his outline.

Grabbing a handful of hay, she wove a wisp. Fingers flew in practised precision. She could almost have been back at the stables in Melbourne, about to put Pharaoh through his paces. Caught in this pleasant dream she leaned back and thumped the wisp down on the colt's neck.

Phoenix exploded in a flailing flurry of hooves, climbing the air. Sam ducked under the rail as he tore to the far side of the yard and stood watching her, all rolling eyes and stamping forefeet.

'What the hell did you do there?'

Bushy's voice. A cold nose nuzzled the back of her hand. Bess? She turned to see Bushy shaking his head, with Drew grinning beside him. Sam showed Bushy the wisp and tried to explain. 'It's a massage pad made by plaiting hay. You slap it along a horse's neck, shoulders and rump to tone his muscles.'

'Well, that's a damn fool idea,' said Bushy. 'Phoenix? He ain't no tame city pony. You belt him with that, he'll more than likely belt you back.'

'I wasn't belting him!' protested Sam.

'Sure seemed like it to me.' Bushy indicated the outraged colt. 'And to him too, by the looks of it.' He picked the wisp up off the dusty ground and grunted. 'Waste of good hay.' Phoenix snorted in loud agreement. 'You get that fella back and groom him up proper.' With that, Bushy walked off in disgust.

Drew shuffled his feet and tipped his hat forward a little. He was trying unsuccessfully to hide the broad smile on his face. 'Morning.' Why did he have to be here, of all people? To see her dressed down like a foolish schoolgirl. Still, in spite of her embarrassment, she was glad to see him. 'Good morning,' said Sam, and went to retrieve the fractious colt.

Drew eyed Phoenix approvingly. 'He's a nice sort.'

'Come to check up on me?' she asked. At least he'd stopped smiling – almost.

'Dad sent me over with a couple of two-year-olds for Bushy to break. You did know he works for Dad too, didn't you?'

Sam spun around. Phoenix half-reared at her swift movement, as if he thought she might give him another thumping. 'Well, of course I didn't,' she said in a loud stage whisper, looking around to make sure Bushy was out of earshot. 'How was I supposed to know that?'

Drew shrugged. Whose side was he really on? If Bushy worked for Bill, and she worked for Bushy, then it meant she was indirectly working for Bill herself. It was an unsettling thought. Phoenix decided Sam's fit of madness had passed, and returned to his feed bin at a high-stepping trot. He sent her flying with a cross toss of his head, and she landed seat first in the dust. Drew helped her up, holding her hand a little longer than necessary. A sudden panic gripped her. She had to do something or say something, right now, to show him she was still interested. She couldn't bear for the moment to be lost.

'I'm sorry about the other night, Drew. You were right about Mary,' said Sam. 'She does mean to renew the lease. It's Charlie who doesn't want to.' *Don't forget to send the contract to me, will you, sweetheart?* Mary had said before Sam left. *It's very important, I'll post the signed documents back for you to give to Bill.* But Sam hadn't given them to Bill. Instead, she'd burned them on the barbeque.

'No worries.' Drew trailed a hand idly along the fence. It felt like he was trailing his fingers up and down her spine. He looked thoughtful, as if he was trying to make up his mind about something. 'I'm having a shot at catching Chiquita tomorrow,' he said at last. 'Going to run the brumbies into the yards up at Dead Man's Hut.' He drew a line in the dust with his boot. 'Sure could use some help.'

'Really?' asked Sam. 'You mean me?'

Drew leaned against the top rail and watched two horses go around the track. 'Dad won't be causing you any problems for a while. Came off his bike yesterday and smashed his leg. Nasty break. It'll lay him up for ages.'

'I'm sorry,' said Sam, although she wasn't. She had no sympathy for Bill.

She must have sounded as false as she felt, because Drew held up his hand. 'I never agreed with him leasing your land in the first place. Fact is, nobody will make a decent go of Brumby's until our cattle are gone. Dad knows that.'

Phoenix was watching the gallopers too. Nerves twitched beneath his satin coat.

'It's New Year's Eve,' Sam said, 'and the lease ends today. I sent your dad a text last night. Told him to move his stock out by tomorrow, or I will.' It had been an empty threat. Her beginner mustering skills would never stretch to moving hundreds of cattle by herself.

Drew raised his brows. 'Then I suppose you'll be needing some help.'

This was too perfect. Without thinking, Sam threw her arms around Drew's neck in a swift, grateful hug.

Phoenix approached the rails, allowing Drew to stroke his muzzle. The colt reached over, snatched the hat from his head and cantered off, thrashing it from side to side like a terrier shakes a rat. 'Cheeky bugger,' said Drew with a laugh. Sam ducked into the yard, played a short game of tug of war, then came back with the hat, complete with teeth marks. Drew looked at it ruefully. 'It's had a hell of a hiding.' He shook it a few times. 'You know, Dad's old school. Can't abide texts. You should hear him. *If something's worth knowing, it's worth saying face to face.* He could go forever without checking his phone. You sure you sent it?' Sam nodded. 'I reckon that's fair notice then.' Drew slapped the hat back onto his head. 'Tell you what, I'll make sure he gets the message – after we've moved the cattle, that is.'

'Deal,' she said, smiling. Why had she ever doubted him?

'Let me take you out tonight,' he said. 'There's a few parties on.'

For a moment Sam was tempted. A night out with Drew was more than she'd hoped for. But then reality set in. 'Do you really think that's a good idea? Who would I go as? Myself or Charlie? I might be able to fool the traders in town, but I'd never fool friends, people I'm supposed to know.'

'Why are you pretending to be Charlie anyway?'

'I don't know. I didn't set out to,' she said. 'I just went along with everybody. It was so much easier than having to explain.'

'In the short term, maybe. But not in the long run.' Drew gave her a knowing, sideways glance. 'I think it's more than that. I think you're enjoying yourself.'

'That's ridiculous,' said Sam. 'You think I enjoy having to watch every word? Enjoy not even being able to go out on New Year's Eve in case I give myself away?'

'Yep,' said Drew, with an infuriating smile. 'Admit it. It's exciting, isn't it? Fooling everybody? There's the thrill of not being found out, of living a double life. It's like being undercover, or a spy or something. My guess is your old life was kind of tame.'

Why did he always have to do that? Call her out, embarrass her just when things were going well? Still, she'd learned her lesson. No more hasty words this time. She wanted Drew to help muster the cattle out, didn't she? So she mustn't put him off. But a nagging internal voice challenged her to be honest with herself. Sam examined the dusty ground for answers. Who was she kidding? She wanted a lot more than that.

Bushy appeared from around the corner, halters in hand. 'Hey, Drew. You going to stand yakking to Charlie all day, or come help unload those horses?'

'I'll be over later with that generator,' Drew said in a low voice. 'We'll see in the new year together, eh? I've got some ideas you might be interested in.' She nodded, feeling her flesh goosebump in anticipation.

'Come on, fella,' called Bushy. 'Any slower, you'd be in reverse.' Drew tipped his hat to her, a delightfully old-fashioned gesture.

'Until tonight, m'lady.'

Sam waved goodbye to Bushy.

'See you next year,' he said, and laughed at his own joke. For once, Sam was leaving work on time. All week she'd stayed long past knock-off. There was always plenty to do and see. She might give a nervous yearling some extra handling, or head over to watch the thoroughbreds on their evening gallops. Not tonight though.

As Sam reached the car her phone chimed - a message from Faith. She hadn't forgiven her mother for Pharaoh, not by a long shot. How could she? How could she ever pardon such a base betrayal? She'd sent Faith a brief text on Christmas Day, but that was all. By contrast, Faith had bombarded her with phone calls. When they went unanswered, Faith wrote text messages as long as her arm. These missives were full of apologies. Good, so they should be . . . but the apologies were weak and full of excuses. Sam read her mother's latest offering.

I'm sorry, Samantha. It was wicked of me to sell Pharaoh. Faith should have stopped right there. Sam could have almost accepted such a simple, heartfelt admission of guilt. *But you were always so busy with Charlene,* she continued foolishly. *So busy with Charlene, and that Mary woman. You certainly had no time for me. You had no time for Pharaoh. You'd absolutely deserted us, Samantha. I honestly thought the horse would be better off with Wolfe.* Sam deleted the message.

These sorts of stupid, selfish rationalisations only served to harden Sam's heart. 'Get Pharaoh back,' Sam had said bluntly on the one and only occasion she'd answered Faith's call. 'Then we'll talk.' Faith responded with a message avalanche, detailing the extraordinary lengths she'd gone to, trying to do just that. But apparently Wolfe wouldn't budge. *He's set on a berth in the Olympic squad, and he thinks Pharaoh is the horse to take him there. It's such a compliment to your train-ing, Samantha.*

That was true. A wonderful compliment with a poison arrow at its heart. So her family communications had been confined to Dad and Mamie. She'd spoken to her father a couple of times, and he'd been surprisingly supportive. He'd asked after Charlie, and had even been solicitous about Mary. He'd promised to give her a generous monthly allowance while she was in Currajong. But he still refused to discuss the adoption. That talk would have to wait until they stood face to face.

Sam stopped at the little Currajong supermarket on the way home for supplies. It wasn't a supermarket in the normal sense of the word at all. No endless, gleaming aisles and self-checkout lanes. It was a traditional general store, doubling as the post office. Its old-world charm would have been more appealing if Sam didn't always have to be so careful. Every time she went to town, every time somebody looked at her with recognition in their eyes . . . every time somebody called her Charlie, Sam's heart was thumping in her throat.

'What are you up to tonight, Charlie?' asked Marjorie, the kindly middle-aged woman at the checkout. Sam had learned her name from the tag on her ample bosom.

'Staying home.'

'That doesn't sound much like you. Is your mother back?'

'Not yet. She's still working in Melbourne.' This was her new line. She hoped the idea of Mary working didn't sound too preposterous, and it helped explain where the money had come from to pay off the bills. The money that had actually come from Sam's own dwindling bank account.

Sam wandered down one aisle and back up the other. She bought cheese, a jar of olives and another of sun-dried tomatoes. A tub of French onion dip. Crackers. Some cherries and grapes. There wasn't much vegetarian fare on offer, but a diet of barbecued meat had begun to pall. She walked out with her purchases and felt the first plop of fat, summer rain. To the east, dark clouds boiled higher and higher, warning of an approaching storm. Looked like they'd be eating inside tonight. On an impulse, Sam dashed back inside. Braving Marjorie's curious stare, she bought a box of tea-light candles, a pair of plastic wine glasses and a bag of ice. Then she headed for home, nervous anticipation churning her stomach. Sam thought of her sister, still languishing at the hospital in Melbourne. She must call later in the evening to cheer Charlie up and wish her a happy new year.

Raindrops ran down the windows and drummed on the tin roof as Sam did a final check. Everything was ready for Drew's arrival. The formerly filthy kitchen shone with shabby chic and smelt of lavender. Sam placed the last marigold into the jug-cum-vase that adorned the tiny table. A faded sky-blue curtain, washed and line-dried, stood in for a regular table cloth. The antipasto platter spilled over with the last of the season's sweet cherry tomatoes, and looked suitably festive. A jam jar of billy buttons and silver snow daisies sat on the sill. Sam peered past it to see Drew pull up and lift Bess from the tray of his ute. Finally! She dashed outside, heedless of the pouring rain, or of seeming too eager.

'Hello.' Sam raised her voice above the noise of rolling thunder. 'Why do you always lift Bess down like that? She must weigh a tonne.'

'She's got a bung leg,' he said.

The massive dog ran over and buried her wet nose affectionately between Sam's knees. Drew heaved something that looked like a motor off the tray. The power of him showed in his upper arms, as they strained with the load. Drew stashed it on the narrow verandah, then squatted down to make an adjustment. His sodden shirt was translucent, the colour of flesh. The crouch accentuated the length of his back and the strength of his thighs. Sam knelt down beside him, shivering. Heat radiated through his wet clothes. He smelt of horses, earth and saddle leather. She moved closer until their bodies touched. The motor thing must be the generator. Sam almost regretted that candlelight might not be the only light tonight.

Drew dashed back to the cab and emerged with a white paper parcel and a wine bottle. Fish and chips and champagne. Bess shook herself in a rainbow of spray. The pair ran inside laughing, leaving soggy Bess complaining on the porch.

'It's the cleanest I've ever seen this kitchen,' Drew said, an expression of wonder on his face. Sam just smiled, suddenly shy. Drew looked her coolly up and down, and she felt her pulse quicken. 'Will I set up the generator?'

'Let's eat first.' Dusk was gathering around them, reaching dark fingers through the window. Time for the candles. Her arm stretched for the matchbox on the table.

'Allow me.' Drew covered her hand with his own, and extracted the box from her curled palm. Round the kitchen he went, lighting the tea lights, one by one, until the room was bathed in a soft, romantic glow. The act seemed imbued with special significance. It was a ritual, and he the high priest.

Drew pursed his lips and blew out the match. Seconds ticked by. She waited with bated breath. Then his arms were round her, sure and hard, the most natural thing in the world. Drew lowered his mouth to hers, and she parted her lips to taste him. The kiss was so sensuous and slow that Sam wished it might never end. Was this love? This dizzy warmth, this flush of desire, this feeling that her body knew exactly what it was doing?

Drew pulled away first. 'Jesus,' he said. 'That was a bombshell kiss.' He reached up to gently run his knuckles down her cheek. 'You don't know your own strength. Or was it beginner's luck?'

'All beginners need to practise,' she said, and tugged him back to her, amazed by her own boldness.

Bess ruined the mood. The dog's determined scratching had finally paid off, and she burst into the kitchen through the flimsy screen door. Bess and Drew dived as one for the parcel of fish and chips on the table, and he rescued it just in time. The aroma of wet dog replaced the fragrance of lavender. 'Bad dog,' said Sam, but her tone was not scolding. She sank to her knees and hugged the happy hound.

Drew laughed. 'Yeah, that's the way to tell her off.' He reached for Bess's collar.

'Let her stay,' said Sam. 'It's her new year's eve too.' Bess barked in approval.

'I thought three was a crowd?' said Drew, but Bess was already following Sam to the esky, smiling and waving her whip of a tail.

'Does she like bacon?'

Bess whined in assent and swallowed two rashers in one gulp, before Drew's withering stare sent her slinking into the corner. The big dog squeezed behind a bucket, designed to catch drips from the leaky roof, then curled up tight as if she hoped she might become invisible.

'Come on. Let's eat,' said Drew, 'before she cons you into feeding her our dinner, as well as our breakfast.' Sam gave him a searching look. Breakfast? Was that a statement of intent, a circuitous request? An offer?

Drew didn't appear to appreciate the significance of his remark. He went about dividing the portions of battered fish and steamed dim sims. He made two mounds of lukewarm soggy chips. Sam poured the sparkling wine into the new glasses, and proposed a toast to the new year. They each took a sip.

'I've got another one,' Drew said. 'To us.' He leant across and kissed her again.

The last thing she felt like doing now was eating. Nonetheless Sam tried a chip. It wasn't until the food hit her palate that she realised how hungry she really was. Fresh air and hard work had piqued her appetite. The chip was warm and creamy on the inside. Salty. Yummy. The fish tasted even more delectable. A search of the pantry turned up a bottle of white vinegar and some soy sauce for the dim sims. It was, quite simply, the most delicious meal of her life.

Drew topped up her glass. 'So what's the plan?'

'Plan?' What exactly was he asking her? 'For tomorrow? Is that what you mean?'

'I meant your long-term plan. The big picture.'

'I don't suppose I have one,' she said.

'Are you staying on?'

Did he want her to, was that it? Was he asking her to stay? 'Maybe.' She didn't mention the commerce degree awaiting her in Melbourne.

'When will Charlie be back?'

Why were they suddenly talking about Charlie? This wasn't what she'd expected, an inquisition. It caught her off guard. 'A couple of months . . . when she's well.'

'So, she's sick?'

Damn, there was no denying it now. The implication of her words had been plain. Sam nodded miserably. Her first real slip. 'Where's the shame in that?' asked Drew, sounding puzzled. 'Why all the secrecy?'

'Charlie doesn't want people feeling sorry for her.' Sam was just making it worse. The charm of the evening was fast evaporating. She was stuffing it all up. 'I'm sorry. I'd rather not talk about my sister.'

But Drew wasn't about to let it drop. 'That's Charlie for you. Too much pride in one direction, and not enough in another.'

Sam experienced a tight twinge of envy. She hated to hear Drew talking about Charlie with such easy familiarity. Talking like he knew Charlie better than she did. Confirming all she'd missed, these past eighteen years. And she hated to think of Charlie, alone with Drew, so many times. A sharp gust of wind blew out the tea lights on the table, and the marigolds had closed their bright petals.

'Exactly how well do you know my sister?'

'Charlie and me? We go way, way back.'

That was the wrong answer. A loud clap of thunder made Sam jump. Bess whined in fear and came to lay her head in Sam's lap, but Drew remained unphased. 'I've got an idea to run past you,' he said. 'A way to make a living from this place, until you can afford to restock.'

A business proposition, now? What was this evening really about? She poured herself the last of the wine. What she wanted most was a big tub of chocolate ice-cream and a spoon.

'Trail rides,' said Drew. She rewarded him with a blank look. 'Trail rides,' he repeated, as if she hadn't heard him the first time. 'There's a string of ten horses and ponies going at Gidgee. The bloke's been keen to sell them for a while, with no luck. He plans to put them through the Currajong horse sale. I'll bet if you made him an offer, you'd get the lot for a song.'

'Why would I want to do that, exactly?'

'Hang on,' said Drew. He disappeared outside and returned with dripping hair and a six-pack of beer. The romantic mood was fast disappearing. 'Want one?' Sam shook her head. Clearly Drew did not intend for this to be a dry argument. 'Your mum will be skint when she gets back, that's a given.' Sam hesitated, then nodded. How strange to hear Mary referred to as her mother. 'She relies on Dad's lease fees and not much else. Without them, she'll need some sort of replacement income.'

'What about the cattle? Can't she just sell some?' asked Sam. 'Isn't that how it works?'

Drew snorted and shook his head. 'There's maybe fifty head, all skin and bone. It'll be six months before those calves are fit for sale, and you can't put cows that poor straight back in calf.' Drew stood up and began to pace around. 'Want to know what I'd do?' Perhaps she'd have that beer after all. 'I'd cull the bulls and chopper cows. Wean the calves. Winter down any cows you want to keep. Then buy new bulls and restock slowly. Problem is, it all takes money. That's where the trail rides come in.'

'Chopper cows?' asked Sam.

'Old, sick, infertile. Bad mothers. Cows that have twins and can't raise them both. Cows that don't have a calf each year.'

'And what, they're killed?'

A draught extinguished more candles, casting Drew into shadow. 'Well . . . yes,' he said. 'There's no retirement home for cows.'

'No, I suppose not.' Bad mothers. There was no equivalent penalty for bad mothers in the human world. Absurdly, Sam imagined Mary and Faith as cows. Would they qualify as choppers? Forfeit their lives for terrible parenting? It was unfair to kill a cow because she couldn't get pregnant. Faith couldn't get pregnant. Mary couldn't raise both twins. Sam's head swam with conflicting emotions. It hadn't occurred to her that she might be required to make decisions about the practical operation of Brumby's Run.

'I want to keep all the cows for the time being,' she said. 'Give them another chance.'

Drew's expression grew soft. 'We've a way to go before we make a farmer out of you. Tell you what, you keep the cows. But you'll have to cull the bulls. That herd is inbred enough as it is.'

'Deal,' said Sam.

Drew pulled her to him. 'What is this?' he asked, with the hint of a smile. 'Feminism for cows?'

'Maybe.' She certainly didn't have the heart to steal their calves away, and then send those poor, starved creatures to be slaughtered. Not yet, not after all they'd endured. She pictured her cows wandering lush paddocks in spring, growing fat, new calves gambolling at their feet. 'Maybe I'm just not cut out for the cattle business.' The idea of running trail rides certainly seemed a far gentler way to earn a crust.

'You're a hypocrite, Sam. You know that, don't you?' said Drew. He threw an olive in the air and caught it in his mouth. 'I didn't see you turn your nose up at my steaks.'

'It's true, I do eat meat. I try to eat free range though, no intensive pork or chicken or grain-fed beef. It's not the death of an animal that I object to, as long as it's humane. We all have to die sometime. My problem is with a life of suffering.' She cracked open the beer. 'I don't think I'd normally have a problem with selling cattle. Those ones of your dad's, for example – they looked completely content. Death isn't so bad, is it? Not after a happy life.' It mattered that he understood her. 'Our cows have suffered so much,' she said. 'I want them to have some happiness.'

Drew relit a candle. 'Fair enough,' he said, with a decisive nod. 'We'll have them knee-deep in clover, literally. Dad's been saving your eastern flats for winter feed. All sown down to rye and clover. We'll move the poorer cows in there and they'll be happy as free-range pigs in mud,' he said, 'I guarantee it.'

'Perfect.' She wanted to add, *enough with the talk*. Wasn't he ever going to kiss her again? On an impulse Sam laid her hand on his chest, feeling the firm muscles beneath. She slipped her fingers between a button, felt the warmth of his skin, the beat of his heart. He fixed her with eyes intense with desire, and one by one undid her own buttons, big fingers fumbling a little. She smiled encouragement, the blood rushing in her ears. He leant in close, landing a flurry of tiny, whispery kisses over her face and neck. Now his tongue was in her ear, his hands running over her bra, the swell of her breasts, pausing on a hardening nipple, stroking her sensitive belly. Sam's legs went weak, and her skin burned beneath his touch. A delicious feeling swelled deep between her thighs, a sensation of exquisite sweetness. She sighed as his hands encircled her waist.

With a loud whoosh, the storm sent a whipping surge of wind through the kitchen, extinguishing every candle. The sudden darkness was complete. So was the silence. 'Come to bed,' whispered Drew, taking hold of her hand. She quivered with the anticipation of his touch in the dark.

But as Drew urged Sam to her feet, the dull throb of a motor sounded in the distance. Gradually the noise grew louder and louder. A car was coming, its headlights visible now through the window, brightening the room enough for Sam to find the torch in the cutlery drawer. She hurriedly buttoned up her shirt as Bess launched herself out the back door, baying like the Hound of the Baskervilles with Drew hot on her heels. Sam checked the time on her phone. Ten to twelve. Friends of Charlie's, maybe, come to ring in the new year? Should she hide? Too late. She heard a heavy thud outside and shrank back from a shadowy male form that loomed in the door. Not Drew. Taller and fair-haired, but with the same thin-hipped, broad-shouldered silhouette.

Torchlight lit the man's face, making it ghostly, like a Halloween mask. Sam shivered in spite of the warm night air and fumbled for matches. She lit a candle while the stranger watched. He looked puzzlingly familiar. Had she seen him in town, perhaps? No, Sam felt sure she'd have remembered a face so striking.

There was a mathematical formula for beauty, or so she'd read. The golden ratio. The divine proportion. Something about the distance between mouth and nose, the width of the lips, the height of the cheek. In this man's handsome face, the formula was made flesh. His blue eyes held her own with a disturbing intensity, supremely confident, a little arrogant, like those of a young lion. Currajong certainly knew how to grow good-looking men.

'Chaz,' he said. 'Long time no see.'

She had it. The poster cowboy. Drew pushed past him. 'Hey, man,' said the cowboy, extending his hands with palms upheld. 'It was an accident.'

'What was an accident?' asked Sam.

'The bastard tripped me.' In the faint candlelight she could see mud caking the front of Drew's shirt and smudging his nose.

The cowboy surveyed the candle-filled kitchen with the manner of a man who'd been drinking, but was not yet drunk. 'Very romantic.' He flicked the useless light switch and clicked his tongue. 'Or did your mum just not pay the bill?'

Drew shouldered the stranger. 'Get out, Spike.'

'I'd say that's Charlie's call, wouldn't you?' He had the kind of eyes that ran up and down a woman's body like a searchlight. Drew waited, looking at Sam expectantly – waiting for her to back him up.

'Yes,' she said at last. There was a simmering tension between the two men that she couldn't read. 'Would you go, please?'

Spike pricked up his ears. 'Since when did you start bunging on a voice, Chaz?' He came closer, examining her with curious eyes. It was like a physical touch. She felt vulnerable, exposed, but deliciously so. It was no use, she couldn't fool him.

'You've confused me for my sister,' she said, hearing her voice falter. 'I'm Samantha. Charlie is away.' Now for the disbelief, the doubt, the astonishment. Comprehension was the last thing she expected, but there it was, plain on his face.

'My mistake.' He spoke in a low, modulated tone, at times a half-drawl. No two ways about it, Spike's voice was very sexy – and not just his voice.

'Completely understandable,' she said. 'Charlie and I are identical twins.'

Spike shot Drew a look. 'Man, what a beautiful dream.' Drew sprang forward and Sam instinctively moved between the two men. 'You're not going to kick me out, are you, Samantha?' Spike checked his phone. 'Not at five minutes to midnight, in the rain, on New Year's Eve?' He took off his hat and put it on the table, as if it might anchor him to the room.

'That's exactly what she's going to do,' said Drew. He rammed the hat back onto Spike's head and gave him a helpful push.

'Okay, okay,' said Spike. 'No need to shove.' He removed his hat, inspected its shape, and replaced it with a flourish. 'If you want, Samantha, I'll come over tomorrow and set that generator up for you. No point just having it sit there for clumsy folk to trip over, now is there?'

'Get out,' snarled Drew. Bess growled in low agreement.

Spike gave Sam a dazzling smile. 'Do me and yourself a favour, will you, sweetness? Dump this clown.'

Then he was gone. The headlights retreated down the hill, and the tiny kitchen was theirs once again. But the mood was spoiled, the air heavy with Drew's anger.

'You don't like him?' asked Sam.

'Spike's a jerk.' Drew arched his back, hands clasped behind his head 'You told him your name. Why him?'

Sam shrugged. 'He already knew I wasn't Charlie.' She checked the time. Five past twelve. 'Happy New Year.'

'Happy New Year.' A single candle flickered on the table. Sam tried her best to suppress a yawn, suddenly overcome with fatigue.

'You're tired,' said Drew. 'I'd better go.' He gave her a chaste kiss on the cheek. 'See you first thing in the morning.'

She nodded, feeling crushed. If only Spike hadn't arrived. Now everything was somehow changed.

He whistled Bess and the pair disappeared out the door, braving the storm.

Sam swapped the half-full bucket beneath the leak for an empty one. The anticlimax was almost unbearable. What had she done wrong?

She tipped the water into the sink and washed up the few dishes, mind still too busy for sleep. She wiped down the benches, covered the remainder of the cheese platter with cling wrap, and put it on ice in the esky. Lightning lit up the sky and the trees outside the window. It lit up Tambo's dark form in the yard above the house.

For the first time since being at Brumby's Run, Sam was genuinely lonely. She picked up the candle and headed for the bedroom, replaying every detail of the evening over and over in her mind. She thought of Drew, and then of Spike – of the overt hostility between them. What was it, she wondered, that they weren't telling her? It was only in the wee small hours of dawn, as she finally drifted off to sleep, that she remembered she hadn't rung Charlie.

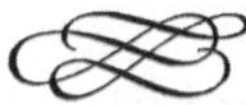

CHAPTER 16

Charlie scoffed the rubbery scrambled eggs, the tough toast, the cold tea. In the process of tearing the top from a tiny container of long-life orange juice, she managed to tip the lot down her front. Not a very auspicious start to the new year. She swore and dabbed at the spill with the scrap of paper napkin provided. Being no bigger than a postage stamp, it wasn't much use. She wiped the stain with the sheet instead. What she wouldn't do for a real breakfast right now. Charlie's head sank back onto her pillow, eyes closed, and let her imagination take flight. Fried eggs on slabs of thick white toast, smothered in butter. Rashers of juicy bacon. Tomato halves, grilled until their skins turned black. Pan-fried field mushrooms.

The ringing phone jolted her back to reality. Charlie snatched it up. 'Sam?' she said. 'At last! It seems like ages since we've talked.'

'Not so long,' said Sam. There was a defensive note to her sister's voice. 'Happy New Year. I did try to call last night. Couldn't get through, though.'

Charlie didn't challenge the remark. Mobile phone reception was unreliable in Currajong, but it still sounded like an excuse. The possibility that she was being lied to unsettled her, even if it was only a little white lie. Sam was supposed to be her window on the world back home, yet in the last eight days they'd hardly spoken.

'Happy New Year to you, too,' said Charlie. 'How are things? How's Tambo?'

'Tambo's fine,' said Sam. 'I'm riding him up to Dead Man's Hut today to help Drew run in some brumbies. A wild stallion stole one of Bill's mares.'

Charlie squeezed her eyes and held the phone away from her head. She could still hear the small, indistinct prattle of Sam's voice, but thankfully could no longer make out the words. They conjured up far too clear an image of all she was missing. Charlie took a deep breath and returned the phone to her ear before Sam realised she'd been away.

'. . . decide what to do with them once we get Chiquita back. What do you think?'

'So, you're yarding the Maroong Mountain mob?' asked Charlie.

'Yes,' said Sam. 'I suppose they're the ones.'

'Big buckskin stallion? Cocky as all hell?'

'Yes,' said Sam. 'It sounds like him.'

'That's Jarrang,' said Charlie. 'I love that horse. You let him go, Sam.'

'Drew might have other ideas. His father doesn't want us to release them.'

'I don't give a damn what Bill wants,' said Charlie, her voice rising. 'Just let him go, along with a couple of mares for company. Otherwise he'll keep on stealing station horses.'

'I'll try,' said Sam. 'More importantly, how are you doing?'

'I'm getting out next week. Moving into the apartment with Mum.' Professor Sung had told them last night. Apparently her recovery was progressing perfectly. Charlie was sceptical by nature, but it was true that her appetite had returned with a vengeance, and she was feeling stronger every day. 'Your stem cells really packed a punch, Sam.'

'That's fantastic! How long before ...' Charlie heard a man's voice in the background. 'Sorry,' said Sam. 'Got to go. Drew's here. I'll call you tonight and let you know how we went.'

Charlie's mouth went dry. No, Sam couldn't go yet. Their phone call had just started. 'Remember what I told you,' said Charlie. 'Look after Jarrang. We're old friends.'

'I'll remember,' said Sam, and then she was gone. Charlie hurled the phone to the floor. What she wouldn't give to be home right now, joining the hunt for Bill's lost mare, galloping the wild slopes of the Balleroo Range. Silent tears flooded her face. She used the sheet to mop them away, then extracted the set of painted pagan prayer beads from her drawer. Sitting cross-legged on the bed, she worked to clear her mind of envy and longing, like her mother had taught her, then repeated the familiar chant.

My blood, my bone, my body, is healing now, healing now. The goddess force is in me. She heals me now, heals me now. Strength of day, strength of night, give me strength beyond my sight.

The prayer's comforting words worked, as they always did, to soothe away the anxiety and unravel the taut threads of her nerves. Get well. That's what she needed to do now. Get well and return to Brumby's Run. Get well and reclaim her life.

CHAPTER 17

A flock of crimson rosellas exploded from the trees into a sky of perfect blue. Clancy pawed the ground as Drew swung into the saddle. 'Wear that riding helmet or you're not coming,' he said over his shoulder. Sam had taken to wearing Charlie's lucky hat recently.

'Won't the others think it's a bit strange?'

'Who cares what they think? Put it on or stay here.'

Sam looked like she was about to argue. Then she apparently thought better of it, threw Tambo's reins over the fence, and ran back for her helmet.

Drew wasn't quite sure how to act around Sam today. There had really been something between them last night – hell, they were about sixty seconds away from consummating that something. But then Spike had shown up. Talk about déjà vu hitting Drew over the head with a mallet. It might be with a different girl, but it was close to the bone. Sam and Charlie, Charlie and Sam – it was all too weird to be falling in love with Charlie's twin, especially when Sam wouldn't tell him what was really going on. And look at what happened when Drew fell in love with Charlie herself – not exactly a ringing endorsement for either girl. He pushed his feelings to the back of his mind and tried to concentrate on the task at hand. Once they got going, he'd be right.

Sam came back with her helmet, and there was a noticeable tremble in her legs as she mounted. Tambo had broken into a sweat. The horse sensed Sam's excitement, sidling sideways and playing with the bit. Although still early, the day was already uncomfortably warm. A shimmering haze rose above the purple peaks of the range, adding a silvery surrealism to the scene.

Since meeting Sam, Drew was seeing the world with fresh eyes. He paid attention now. He paid attention to the sound of the creek on its way down the mountain, to the subtle fragrance of the bush, to the pictures in the clouds. What would a stranger make of this view? He guessed they'd be pretty impressed. But most of all, he paid attention to Sam. Her laugh, her frown, her childlike wonder in the world. He loved just watching her ride. The way her hips swayed in time with her horse. The way her slim arms reached down occasionally to hug Tambo's neck. He imagined those arms wrapped around him instead. Her very presence heightened his senses, making life infinitely more exciting.

'Ready?' asked Drew. Sam had Charlie's stockwhip on the saddle. 'You know how to use that thing?'

'No, but I'll learn.' Sam adjusted her stirrups. 'Charlie said to let the brumby stallion go.'

'Did she now?' Drew grinned. 'That's cause her and Jarrang, they're old mates. Charlie raised him from a baby after he was separated from his mother during a storm. She couldn't have been more than twelve years old. I weaned one of our foals and lent her the brood mare, hoping it might adopt the little colt. Nothing doing. Instead it tried to kick his head in. So Charlie milked that damn mare like a dairy cow, morning and night for months, and bottle-raised Jarrang.' Drew slapped a fly off his thigh with his hat. 'That little colt was a good sort. I said she should geld him and keep him for herself. But Charlie hasn't got a practical bone in her body. Said he wouldn't be happy in captivity.' Drew didn't put the rest of his thought into words; didn't say that Jarrang would be a lot happier in Charlie's paddock than in the knackers' yard. If the federal government had its way, a knackers' yard was where all the park brumbies would end up.

'So what do we do?' asked Sam.

'Tell you what,' said Drew. 'If we run in Jarrang, you can have him. Let him go if you want, or keep him for when Charlie comes home.' Sam nodded. 'Come on,' he said. 'We've got horses to catch.'

They cantered up the hill, past the dam, heading for the northern boundary of Brumby's Run. Drew had constructed 200-metre-long wings – ring-lock wire fencing, disguised with hessian chaff bags – to funnel the brumbies into the yards at Dead Man's Hut. He was pleased with the job. It helped that Chiquita was no wild horse. Since Christmas he'd left the big yard open and generously supplied with salt licks and hay. Hoof prints and vanishing feed told Drew she'd led the mob inside more than once. They'd be less wary now. Still, if he missed them the first time, they'd be on to him. You only got one chance with brumbies.

When they reached the old stock route, they saw five riders approaching at a spanking trot, stock whips slung by their side. Two eager blue cattle dogs trotted behind. Drew reined Clancy in and waited.

'Who are they?' asked Sam.

'That's Tom Ward, our head stockman. Bushmen don't come any better than Tom. The other four are contract brumby runners.'

'Why's that one got a rifle?' asked Sam. Drew thought back to his own disastrous experience running brumbies the previous year, and prayed she wouldn't wind up just as disillusioned.

'If a horse breaks a leg, we'll have to shoot it,' he said honestly. 'It's the kindest thing.' Sam stared in open astonishment and his stomach lurched with doubt. There was fear and apprehension in her large eyes now, and he was the one who'd put it there. Drew suddenly wished he hadn't brought her along.

'G'day Tom,' said Drew, as the lead rider reached them. Tom pulled up his horse and leaned his elbow on the horn of the saddle while he rolled a smoke. A crashing sound in the scrub provoked the two heelers into a mad flurry of barking. A small mob of fat black baldies, tails held high, broke from a stand of tea-tree and lumbered into the bush. Tom silenced the dogs with a word and stared at Drew. They were Kelly cattle. He must have missed them when he mustered the herd home to Brumby's Run. Their presence would not go unreported.

'Those brumbies aren't too far away,' said Tom. 'Spotted them yesterday, in the clearing below Waratah Spring. Me and the boys will circle round and try to get above them.' He nodded towards Sam. 'You and the girl hold down the flank. We'll make plenty of noise for you.'

'Righto,' said Drew. Tom and the others veered left off the track, heading uphill through the trees, while Drew and Sam rode on to the hut. The brumbies had been there, and recently. Hay was trampled all about. So far, so good. The new wing fences hadn't spooked them.

Drew led Sam to a position fifty metres along the northern wing. 'Tambo knows what to do. Just stay put and stand your ground.' He pulled the stockwhip from her saddle and offered it. Sam took the coiled lash, holding it as cautiously as she might a snake. 'You'll hear the horses coming a mile off. Don't let them past.' Sam nodded, face flushed with either excitement or fear. 'You okay?' He put his hand on her arm.

'I'm okay,' she said, and inexpertly brandished the whip. It slithered across Tambo's wither, making him shiver. Drew gave what he hoped was an encouraging smile, then rode down around the yards and hut, and back along the southern edge of the trap.

It was a waiting game. He could just make out Tambo further up the mountain, tucked amongst a patch of snow gums. Far enough back to escape detection unless the brumbies headed straight for him. An hour passed. Little pestering flies crowded the corners of his lips and eyes. The sun swung higher and higher. He cleared his mind, allowed the silence to seep in, a kind of meditation. Another hour passed. Clancy stamped his feet, weary of the morning vigil. Their plan required the patience of an ambush predator. Tambo remained motionless, statue-still on the hill above the yards. The sun grew fierce. Drew had backed Clancy beneath the shade of a black wattle.

The horse dozed sporadically, resting a hind foot. Drew's left foot insisted on going to sleep.

He felt them before he heard them. A certain low vibration, travelling through Clancy's body into his own, alerting them both. In the distance came the faint cries of men and the drumming of hoofs. Careful now. Don't show yourself without cause. Let the mob momentum carry the horses right through to the yards. The noise grew louder. A volley of whip cracks told him they'd tried to make a break. Drew didn't breathe until he was sure they were still on track. Then, bursting over the brow of the ridge, he saw them.

An avalanche of horses in full flight, flanked either side by riders, was heading straight for the trap. There was Chiquita in the lead, and Jarrang bringing up the rear, galloping dangerously close to the lower hessian fence. Dust plumed in their wake, and hammering hoofs dislodged rocks that rattled and rolled down the mountainside. Clancy trembled beneath him. Drew didn't need Sam's *looking through another's eyes* strategy to appreciate the spectacle. By anyone's yardstick it was a magnificent sight.

The mob thundered closer. In another minute they'd be past him. Tom trailed close to Jarrang. The stallion's pace lacked the panicked quality of the other brumbies. Instead, he moved with a watchful, confident grace. If any horse broke rank, it would be him.

As the mob drew close, Clancy's excitement got the better of him. He raised his head and let out a long, trumpeting neigh. The sound quivered right through his body, through the saddle, through Drew. Without missing a beat, Jarrang veered into the hessian wing, tearing it apart at a join only metres from them. Clancy leapt forward and flung himself into the stallion's shoulder. For one bone-jarring moment it seemed all three of them might come crashing to earth. But as Drew recovered his balance, he plied the stockwhip with all his might and sent Jarrang hurtling back down the hill after the herd, with Tom hard on his heels.

The horses approached the open gate and the riders slackened their headlong pursuit. Nobody wanted Bill's mare to hit the yard at a dangerous gallop. With perfect timing, first Chiquita, and then the brumbies surged in at a slow canter. They milled around, shapes blurred by dust, in search of an escape route. But the trap was already sprung, the slip rails in place.

Drew glanced around for Sam. There she was, trotting back down the hill. Somehow she'd swapped her helmet for Charlie's hat. Sam joined him by the yards. They dismounted and surveyed their catch. Twelve horses in all. Jarrang kept a close eye on the humans, like he was assessing what danger they might pose. His mares and youngsters had arranged themselves facing the other way at the back of the yard. They presented a solid row of round rumps. When Sam moved around the yard, the brumbies quietly rearranged themselves, maintaining the maximum possible amount of distance from her.

The two heelers emerged from the bush, wild-eyed and panting. They trotted up to Drew, tails wagging, and he leant down to pat the spent animals. Dogs were worth their weight in gold on a mountain muster. Where thick trees or scrub might turn a rider, dogs could run right through and set a breaking beast back on course.

Tom led his horse over. The gelding was lathered in sweat and caked with dust. 'We had a bugger of a job finding them. You did well to hold that buckskin.' Drew nodded in recognition of the compliment. Tom didn't give them lightly. 'We'll leave the mob overnight to settle down. Cut Chiquita out, will you, and yard her separately. The trucks will be here in the morning.'

Drew nodded again. 'How about I pick Chiquita up this evening,' said Drew, 'along with one of those brumbies? That'll leave ten horses, two trucks' worth. Save you making an extra trip.' Behind Tom's back, Sam pressed her palms together and mouthed a thank you.

'Good idea,' said Tom. 'Want a hand?'

'We'll be right,' said Drew. 'I'll drop the brumby off at the showgrounds after I've taken Chiquita home.'

Tom nodded. 'There's a nice young grey in that lot,' he said. 'A decent size and all. I reckon she'd suit the stock contractors. That stallion too.' He glanced at Sam. 'Charlie.' The barest acknowledgement, then he led his horse off towards the troughs.

'Stock contractors?' asked Sam.

'They supply bulls and bucking horses for rodeos.' Drew didn't like the look on Sam's face. 'Don't worry. I promised you Jarrang, didn't I?'

'What about that grey Tom's talking about?'

'The Brumby Coalition buys any likely youngsters. She'll be fine. Anyway, rodeo horses have a good enough life. Only work for maybe eight seconds a day, two days a week. There are worse gigs.'

Sam looked unpersuaded. 'You said the Brumby Coalition takes the young ones. What happens to the rest?'

'They'll go through the feature horse sale, next picnic race day. The sale I told you about last night – the one where you might be able to pick up that string of good trail horses, if you have a mind to.'

'Will any of these brumbies go for slaughter?'

Jesus. He really didn't want to get into this with her. 'I don't know,' he said. Sam turned and moved off along the rails. Drew followed her, getting his first good look at the captured horses, standing well back so as not to stress them. He spotted the young grey straight away. Tom was right. The mare was no average brumby. Sired by Jarrang, to go by her presence, and the unusual stripes on her hoofs. But she wasn't out of any of these mares. Way too tall for one thing. A three-year-old, he guessed, from Jarrang's first crop of foals. Powerful body, well balanced with great bone. Clean legs. An elegant head, slightly convex in profile, and the most magnificent full mane and tail he'd ever seen. Who might her mother be?

'She's stunning,' said Sam, eyes filled with admiration. 'Can I have her too?'

'You're joking, right?' She didn't look like she was joking. 'Contract runners get to keep the brumbies as part payment for their work,' he explained. 'They'll want them auctioned off at the highest price. It's going to be hard enough explaining when Jarrang goes missing.'

'I'll buy her at the sale then,' said Sam.

'If you want. She's a nice type of filly.' Sam's expression brightened. Drew took another look at the grey. Very nice indeed. Maybe he'd buy her himself as a present for Sam. Chiquita pricked up her ears as Sam offered a handful of hay through the rails. Jarrang bared his teeth, warning the mare not to approach the humans. 'Stay away,' said Drew. 'Just let them settle.'

The other men didn't stick around for long. A shared thermos of tea, a brief rest for the dogs and they were gone. In spite of Drew's admonitions, Sam remained glued to the rails, watching the brumbies. Jarrang watched back. Occasionally he rolled his eyes, or laid back his ears at her. 'I reckon that stallion's the only one in Currajong who can tell straight off that you're not Charlie,' said Drew. Sam smiled at him. She looked extraordinarily beautiful, face flushed pink with happiness, glossy hair escaping from a careless knot at the nape of her neck. 'Come on,' he said, giving himself a swift kick. 'It's time to cut out some horses.'

It didn't prove too difficult to separate Jarrang and Chiquita from the mob. Chiquita had greedy eyes for the bucket of oats, and Jarrang had greedy eyes for Chiquita. When the mare finally slipped past her jealous keeper into the side yard, eager for a treat, he followed in an attempt to retrieve her. Drew stood guard between the two horses and the gate, stockwhip in hand, while Sam secured the sliprails. 'Nothing to it,' she said with a triumphant grin.

They fed the stock and filled the troughs. 'I want to stay here while you get the truck,' said Sam, still staring at the horses.

'They won't disappear, you know, if you take your eyes off them,' he said. Sam didn't answer, didn't even look around. The brumbies had apparently hypnotised her. With the exception of Jarrang, the horses paid no attention to Sam, as if by determinedly ignoring their captor she might go away. A dun foal, the baby of the group, occasionally peeked at the humans from between its mother's legs. The others stood with backs turned, deceptively quiet in the fierce noon-day heat. They could have been a string of riding school horses on a lunchtime break. Only Jarrang remained vigilant.

Drew untied Clancy and swung into the saddle. 'You sure you'll be okay out here by yourself?' She didn't seem to hear him. 'Sam?' At last she turned around.

'What about Jarrang?' she asked.

'I'll pick him up in the truck this arvo, along with Tambo and

Chiquita, drop him off at your place on the way through. Got your phone?'

Sam nodded. 'What will you tell Tom?'

'That I lost him. He'll think I'm a fool, but what can he do?'

'I can't thank you enough,' said Sam. 'Just wait until I tell Charlie.'

Drew wheeled Clancy around. 'Don't thank me too soon,' he said, pointing to Jarrang. 'That one's trouble on four legs. You might be cursing me before too long.'

CHAPTER 18

Sam waited at the yards for Drew. It was hot, too hot. The glare of the sun made her squint. She fanned herself with Charlie's hat. Its broad-brimmed protection hadn't been enough, and a deep flush of heat warned that her nose and cheeks would be painfully red and sunburned by morning. Why hadn't she bothered with sunscreen? Back home, she wouldn't even walk down the street without following her mother's carefully prescribed skincare regime. Yet out here in the bush? In the sun, with the flies and the dust and the heat? Out here it didn't seem important.

At least the heat helped take her mind off Drew. She had no idea what had happened between them. Last night they'd been – well, she'd been – she didn't really know, but she'd been ready to do just about anything for him. And now, while Drew wasn't cold, he was treating her with a certain distance. If only she had someone to talk to about it. Maybe Charlie could help? On second thoughts, maybe not. Sam had the feeling there was history between Drew and Charlie, and she wasn't sure she wanted to know what it was.

She turned back to the horses. Eleven brumbies in all. Jarrang, six mares, three yearlings and the foal. Most were bays, very cob in type, with lightly feathered legs and lots of white markings. Superior height and conformation set Jarrang and the young grey well and truly apart from the rest. The pair were in top condition. From a distance they'd all looked well, with shiny summer coats and fat bellies. But on closer inspection, the others weren't so good. Skinny necks, prominent ribs, jutting hip bones. Their fat bellies more indicative of pregnancy or a load of worms than anything else.

Bushy had dispelled Sam's romantic notions about brumbies. 'It's a hard life, especially for a mare,' he'd told her. 'Pregnant, back to back, when you're no more than a baby yourself. There's droughts and freezing winters. Parasites. Wild dogs take foals and injury's a death sentence. To top it off, them brumby-runner fellas are out to get you.'

Sam came from a world where horses lived in pine-lined loose boxes and sheltered day yards. They ate nutritionally balanced pellet and grain mixes, wore satin hoods and rugs, and travelled in padded floats, with bandaged legs and sheepskin boots. An image of Pharaoh came to mind. What would he make of this harsh, magnificent place? Sweat dripped from her nose. It was so hot that even the ants had gone to ground. Defeated by the sun, she sought out the shade of the hut's little verandah. The plastic water bottle in her saddlebag was warm, its contents unappetising. The creek presented a far more inviting option. Sam checked her phone. Hours yet before Drew would return with the truck.

She slipped from her shirt and jeans, and left them on the porch. Dressed only in bra, panties and riding boots, Sam made her way to the creek. Giant tree-fern fronds filtered the sunshine here, in this cool haven from the dust and flies. Soon her boots lay discarded on the bank. Smooth pebbles and damp river sand lodged between her toes. The stream, when it hit her feet, was painfully cold. She let out an involuntary squeal. Hard to believe that the heat of the air and the cool of the water could exist in such delicious proximity. Soon she was numb to her knees, her thighs, her sensitive waist. Fallen logs, woven together, had created a natural dam. When she stood in the deepest part of the creek, the water reached her breasts. The icy shock made her think of Drew; of his hands, and the charge that had spread through her body at his touch. Enough of that she told herself.

Sam paused mid-stream. The trick was not to imagine the biting creatures that Drew had so kindly alerted her to: the water bugs and yabbies; the snakes? But the creek was clear as glass, transparent as the water in her swimming pool back home in Toorak. Surely she'd spot any danger? Sam ducked down and let her hair fan out on the water. Heaven. She could linger in this shady sanctuary forever.

It was then she saw it — the striped, bronze reptilian head, barely wider than its dark copper body. It slid from the bracken towards the creek, forked tongue flicking in and out, tasting the air. Tasting her? Keep still, wasn't that the advice? She hardly dared to breathe. The snake stopped, frozen like Sam herself, and the pair were locked in a deadly standoff. An intricate pattern of pale cream scales striped its gleaming length. The creature had been hand-painted by a grand master. Was she safe in the water? She didn't know, didn't know enough about snakes, didn't know enough about living in the bush. She should be in Le Midi, relaxing at her grandmother's elegant villa at Provence. Such a safe place, filled with history and art. She tried to imagine it — no yarding of untamed horses, no confusing romantic notions ... no snakes.

But her imagination reached only as far as Brumby's Run. The idea of this wilderness had consumed memories of gentler places. Her calves ached, yet her thighs were numb. For how long could she stand so still? She guessed the patient reptile could outwait her. They stared at each other. Its eyes were twin yellow globes. They blazed with a sort of fire, beautiful and mesmerising. Like being lost staring into flames. She understood how helpless the snake's prey might feel, caught in that hypnotic gaze.

Was that an engine? Surely Drew couldn't be back with the truck yet? Or had fright made her lose track of time? Sam wanted to call out, wanted to scream for help. But that might antagonise the snake. It lay wound in elegant coils on the bank, still intent upon her, to judge by its stare. The sound of the motor grew louder and louder, then stopped. Perhaps she should make a run for it? Or should she just stay still, and wait for Drew to come and find her? The snake raised its head and Sam let out an involuntary scream. It flared its neck a fraction, looked left, looked right, then slid into the pool. Barely breaking the surface tension, it glided towards her in a serpentine pattern, the first quarter of its metre-long body rearing from the water.

A figure appeared at the periphery of her vision. 'Don't move,' said an unfamiliar male voice. For some unlikely reason the voice had a German accent. She couldn't have moved even if she'd wanted too — frozen as she was, legs dead from cold, with the snake closing in. If she took her eyes off it for even a second, she knew it would strike.

'Don't scare her. She won't hurt you if you stay still.' Who was that? And how the hell did he know? The snake lowered its head, so the full length of its bronze body sailed on the surface.

Only centimetres away now, it paused. 'Hold your nerve,' said the voice. The snake reached out with infinite slowness. Sam willed herself to stone, felt the fleeting tickle of a forked tongue on her goose-fleshed arm. She flinched and the snake vanished into the reeds. Sam remembered to breathe again, relief flooding her body and leaving her limp with shock.

A man dressed in khaki stood on the bank. Mid-twenties, slim and athletic-looking, with close-cropped blond hair and serious grey eyes. 'You've had a close encounter with Austrelaps ramsayi. Gravid, I'd guess, by her girth. A rare privilege.' Sam staggered from the pool, all too conscious that she wore only underwear. Her nipples pushed, embarrassingly erect, against the translucent wet cotton of her bra. She wrapped her arms around her chest, convulsed with violent shivers. 'So it wasn't dangerous?' she asked, teeth chattering from more than cold.

'On the contrary.' His tone was clipped and formal, such a contrast to the usual Aussie country drawl. 'Alpine copper-heads are extremely dangerous. Quite capable of inflicting fatal bites.'

'Then why did you say it wouldn't hurt me?' she asked, incredulous.

'They're shy, not usually aggressive,' he answered calmly. 'Bites are uncommon.'

'Uncommon?' repeated Sam. She'd meant the word to drip with

sarcasm, but the stranger either misunderstood or deliberately over-looked her intent.

'Yes, quite uncommon. Even on land, a snake can only strike a distance of half its body length. A snake in water does not have a solid surface to thrust against, so its striking ability while swimming is quite limited. You were probably in no danger.'

She wanted to scream, shout at this idiot, whose only advice during an encounter with a deadly snake was not to scare it. But confronting a strange man while so scantily clad was not ideal. 'Do you mind if I get dressed?'

'Of course not. That would seem prudent.'

Jesus, he really was Mr Literal. The afternoon heat swiftly chased away the chill from her frozen legs. She hurried back, grabbed her clothes and dressed in the privacy of the hut. Why she should be so modest about putting clothes back on was a mystery to her.

'Whose horses?' he asked, when she emerged.

Sam didn't answer. She wasn't quite sure who they actually belonged to, and anyway, shouldn't she be the one asking the ques-tions here?

'Who exactly are you?' she demanded.

The man extended his arm. 'Balleroo park ranger Karl Richter, at your service.' She shook his hand, which was smooth with a gentle grip. 'These are feral horses, then?'

She didn't like the way he said feral horses. The term stripped them of their dignity. 'They're brumbies, with a few saddle horses among them.'

The man looked suddenly stern. 'I suppose you know that a permit is required to remove feral horses from the park?'

She shrugged. 'Sorry, I don't know anything about that. You'll have to talk to Drew Chandler.'

'Chandler.' The ranger rolled the name around on his tongue. 'He owns Kilmarnock Station, right?'

Sam nodded. 'Drew and his dad, Bill.'

'This area is not part of the grazing trial,' said Karl. 'Cattle have been roaming illegally here for weeks. Once I identify their owner, somebody's in a lot of trouble.' He frowned. 'I'm new and don't know the locals yet, but I've been briefed that either the Chandlers or the Kellys are the most likely culprits. Your surname isn't Chandler, is it? Or Kelly, perhaps?'

Sam didn't know what to say, mind spinning through the possible responses, weighing them up. Karl was new here and didn't know folks – that's what he'd said. She could take advantage of that igno-rance. 'My name's Samantha Carmichael and I live in Melbourne,' she said. 'I'm just visiting Currajong.'

Karl gave her a searching look, then walked over to the yards and peered through the rails at Chiquita. Jarrang took offence. The stal-lion laid his ears flat back and, accompanied by a series of ferocious snorts, thundered to the fence. The ranger leaped back. Something in his manner told Sam that Karl knew nothing about horses. 'Christ almighty,' he said. 'You could have warned me.'

'Like you warned me about your deadly snake?' asked Sam.

Karl laughed. 'Touché, Miss Carmichael. I suppose that vicious brute is one of the brumbies?'

Sam ignored his stupid comment. All this talk of permits had her worried. Had Drew run this roundup by the book or not? Could Karl confiscate the mob if their paperwork wasn't in order? What would happen to the horses then? 'No,' she said, quickly. 'That's Jarrang. He's mine, along with the baldie-faced bay. And the golden chestnut mare belongs to the Chandlers.' Karl looked around vaguely. It was obvious that he couldn't identify the particular horses by reference to their coat colours, and anybody with any horse sense would guess Jarrang was no stockhorse. Karl didn't have a clue. Sam almost claimed the grey filly as well, but Drew had been so insistent she must go with the others.

The ranger approached the yards again, wary this time. 'That's ten ferals then. I'll be checking someone holds a valid licence to remove them. Don't misunderstand me, you're doing a good job here, getting rid of them I mean. There's a plan to eliminate wild horses from the park all together. Management's considering an aerial cull.'

'What?' said Sam, with a growing sense of horror. 'You don't mean shoot them?'

Karl nodded. 'It's not an ideal solution, if you ask me,' he said. 'A public relations disaster waiting to happen. But one way or another, the brumbies have to go.' Jarrang reared. Karl backed off with such haste that he stumbled over a grassy tussock and almost fell. 'Well,' he said, regaining his balance. 'If you see the Chandlers or Mary Kelly, let them know I want a word.' He handed Sam his card. 'Now you're dressed, you have a pocket to put it in. How very convenient.' What a nerve. 'Well, it's been a pleasure to meet you, Miss Carmichael. You look quite fetching in your underwear, by the way.' She wanted to slap him. Instead she just watched him climb in his jeep and head off in a cloud of dust.

The scorching sun was already sinking low in the western sky before the truck bumped back up the track. Sam's heart lifted at the sight of it. Drew's face grinned at her from the cab. He'd brought a hamper of choice sandwiches and pastries prepared by Mai, which Sam wolfed down, along with a bottle of warm lemonade.

They loaded Tambo first, then Chiquita. 'How are we going to do this?' asked Sam, pointing to the stallion, who was climbing the rails.

'Why don't you just let him go?' suggested Drew. 'Save yourself a world of strife.' Sam shook her head. She told Drew of Karl's visit, and of the proposal to cull the brumbies. She left out the bit about the snake and being caught in her undies. 'I heard they'd hired a new ranger,' he said. 'The last bloke was a lazy so-and-so, never gave us any trouble.'

'This one seems keen,' said Sam.

'That's a problem then. Okay, let's get Jarrang loaded. We can't have him being used for target practice, can we?' Sam was prepared for a long and difficult fight to get the stallion on the truck. But Jarrang ascended the ramp with surprising alacrity, and began to preen Chiquita's neck. 'He'd follow that mare anywhere,' said Drew. 'And remember, Jarrang was hand raised. He doesn't have the same fear or respect for all things human as a normal, wild-born brumby does.'

Tambo took advantage of Chiquita's close proximity to sniff her flanks, then her tail. He tilted his head up and curled his lip, savouring the mare's scent. The stock crate rattled and shook as a jealous Jarrang made a concerted effort to attack him through the steel partition. Tambo snapped back.

'Tambo's a gelding,' said Sam. 'Why is he interested in Chiquita?'

Drew double-checked the tail gate and grinned 'He can dream, can't he?'

'Will those two fight,' asked Sam, 'when we get them home?'

'Probably,' said Drew. 'Although Jarrang won't be so full of himself without his mares. They'll have nothing to argue about.'

An orange sunset streaked the sky by the time they unloaded the horses at Brumby's Run. The air was still oppressively hot. What Sam wouldn't do for air-conditioning ... Drew helped her settle Jarrang and Tambo in adjoining yards. Then he reloaded Chiquita. 'Time to say goodbye to your girlfriend.' The stallion reared. Drew climbed into the cab of the truck and set off down the track. Chiquita and Jarrang exchanged frantic neighs until the truck was out of earshot. Then, just as Drew had predicted, the buckskin fell quiet. More than that, he was positively lounging – head low, ears relaxed, resting a back foot. No male posturing at all.

Tambo boldly touched his nose to Jarrang's. With rivalries apparently forgotten, the stallion pricked his ears in polite acknowledgement, then resumed his nap. Sam burst out laughing, in spite of her exhaustion and headache and sunburn. For some unaccountable reason, she was reminded of New Year's Eve. Maybe men were like that too? Only at each other's throats when you added a girl to the mix? Perhaps Spike and Drew would have behaved like old mates as well, if they'd met down the pub that night, instead of in Sam's kitchen.

CHAPTER 19

This was Sam's first picnic race day. The quiet, almost deserted racecourse where she worked each day with Bushy and the brumbies, had been transformed into a vibrant festival of colour and crowds. She looked warily around, keeping her hat pulled down firmly over her eyes. Such a public outing was fraught with risk. Which identity was she supposed to claim?

'Here you go,' said Drew. 'One roast beef roll and a coke.'

It had been three weeks since New Year's Eve, and there'd been a certain tension between them ever since. Sam had no idea what to do about it. The odd glance, the odd brush of the hand or leg told her that the story wasn't over. Drew remained attentive and helpful, but that was all. Sam was utterly bewildered. Had she done something to make him back off?

In his father's absence, Drew had organised the removal of Kilmarnock cattle from Brumby's Run. They'd spent last weekend mustering the Kelly herd home, watching the cows and calves reclaim the rich pastures and shady creek flats that belonged to them. He'd cut out the bulls, trucked them to the Wodonga saleyards and returned with a cheque made out to *M. Kelly*. Sam had proudly deposited it into Mary's account the next morning. The rush of pleasure and pride provoked by that achievement was in no way proportionate to the small sum involved.

To say thank you, Sam had cooked dinner for Drew. If she was honest with herself, she'd hoped for a repeat of New Year's Eve, minus the interruption. She'd found instructions for preparing a Sunday roast in a dusty cookbook, and had spent an afternoon struggling to understand the mysteries of Mary's ancient oven. The bottom rack seemed barely to warm food at all. The top rack burned everything to cinders. With a great deal of trial and error, she'd turned out a passable meal with all the trimmings. Drew had been full of praise, devoured several helpings, then finished off the tiny tub of toffee ice-cream that barely fitted in her miniscule freezer. He'd complimented her on dessert, as if she'd made it herself. Afterwards they'd played poker for matchsticks, drunk cider until midnight — and still nothing.

She'd been weak with anticipation when, at the end of the evening, Drew had finally gathered her into his arms by the door. But a brief, almost perfunctory, kiss on the lips was all that followed. Then he was gone into the bright night. She'd wandered across to visit Tambo and Jarrang, her mind in turmoil. The stallion had half-reared at her approach, a *levade* equal in elegance to any performed at the Spanish Riding School in Vienna. The moon's orb loomed low on the horizon. Stars pricked the roof of the sky, dazzling in their brilliance, and a warm wind played through the trees. It had been a night tailor-made for romance. What a waste.

'Do you want to watch this?' asked Drew, dragging her thoughts back to the present. He pointed to a sheep-dog display going on in the arena. Sam surreptitiously studied his handsome face in profile. What on earth was she doing wrong?

'Let's eat lunch in the stands,' she suggested. Sam loved the Federation timber and cast-iron grandstand, so full of old-world bush charm. Together they climbed the wooden stairs beneath the broad verandah, weaving their way through the throng to a space near the top. 'Now,' said Sam, as she gazed across the track to the forested mountainside beyond. 'Can we go through the plan one more time?'

'There's not much to it,' said Drew, downing half a hot dog in one bite. 'We meet the bloke before the sale starts and make an offer. Don't worry, I'll suss out the auctioneer on the price first.'

'When do I get to see these horses I'm supposed to be buying?' asked Sam.

'The truck from Gidgee isn't here yet. But like I said,' Drew swallowed the other half of the hot dog, 'I've already checked them out.' Sam couldn't quite believe it. In the space of a month she'd be going from completely horseless, to buying ten in one fell swoop.

Charlie had loved the idea of setting up a trail-riding business. 'Fantastic,' she'd said. 'I know every inch of Balleroo. We could do a ride to Maroong Mountain, with the best view in Victoria. Bluff Falls could be another. What about platypus-watching at Snake Creek Billabong? Or brumby-spotting? Maybe an eco-ride, visiting endangered alpine bogs.'

Sam was pleased to hear the newfound strength and enthusiasm in her sister's voice, but she couldn't help wondering how practical the plan really was. When would Charlie realistically be fit enough to conduct these rides? She'd need a lot of help, and for an extended period. You couldn't run such an operation by yourself. There were costs too, for insurance and registration fees. Permits to ride in the national park. So many rules and regulations to comply with. Would they need to provide food for clients? What about toilets? First aid? Riding equipment? And the most important question of all — what would happen when Sam took up her university course in Melbourne in a month's time? The prospect of leaving Brumby's Run, of leaving Drew, was gut-wrenching.

Drew had dismissed Sam's fears out of hand. 'You can count on me,' he'd said. 'Tom's got Kilmarnock running like clockwork. It's so much easier with Dad away. He makes such a big production of everything. I reckon Tom will manage fine without me for a bit.'

'For a bit?' she'd said. 'We're going to need help for more than a bit.' But that wasn't quite true. It wouldn't be *we*. Soon it would be Charlie alone who'd need Drew's help.

'For longer then,' Drew had responded. 'Let's just concentrate on getting our hands on those horses.' Sam's imagination took flight.

Drew and Charlie, working side by side, building up the business. Riding the wild slopes of Balleroo without her. Sam suddenly lost her appetite. 'You've got a bit of gravy on you,' said Drew. He reached out his hand, dabbing gently at her chin with a paper serviette. Sam shivered, but just as soon as his hand touched her skin, it was gone again.

Drew turned away to hide his frustration. It was maddening. He'd simply reached out to wipe Sam's chin, and had almost wiped away his resolve instead. His resolve not to fall for her. The moment he'd touched her, Drew knew he was in trouble. It had taken all his determination to keep his distance from Sam over these past weeks. She hadn't made it easy. She'd been giving him every come-on signal in the book. The flick of her head, the intense eye contact, the half-smile that promised something good, something wonderful. It took a monumental effort to resist. Then Drew thought back to New Year's Eve, and it was suddenly easy.

That night when Spike had shown up. The night when Drew had remembered why he didn't want to mess with the Kelly girls – or the Carmichael girls, or whatever they were called. Not again, mate, he'd told himself. He'd seen it too many times before, the way girls looked at that puffed-up narcissist. He'd seen it with Charlie. It was the same way Sam had looked at Spike that evening. He'd been about to take her to bed, and next thing she's making goo-goo eyes at Captain Fantastic. And then there was the knowledge that Sam was hiding something from him – like the real reason she was at Brumby's Run, and where exactly her sister and mother might be. It was enough to make a bloke seriously gun shy.

A piercing double whistle blasted him out of his reverie. Speak of the devil. Spike bounded up the grandstand, two stairs at a time, a broad grin on his stupid face. Drew groaned. He'd thought Spike was safely away on the rodeo circuit.

'You two kids having fun?' Spike punched him lightly in the arm.

Drew gave him a sour smile, his hand clenching into a fist. 'Hear you're after Terry Mitchell's horses,' said Spike. 'What's up with that?'

Sam opened her mouth to speak, but Drew's black expression warned her off.

'Don't all talk at once,' said Spike, plonking himself down and lighting a cigarette with maddening slowness. The cold shoulder didn't seem to worry him one bit. He seemed perfectly happy just to sit and stare at Sam.

'Those horses are for Brumby's Run,' said Sam at last. 'We're thinking of branching out into trail rides.'

'We?' asked Spike. 'I do so hope you're talking business partners only.' A loudspeaker announced the next race, the Currajong Ladies Bracelet. Spike blew a series of expert smoke rings. 'And it doesn't hurt that four of Terry's mares are registered Australian stock horses now, does it?' Spike moved closer to Sam. She crossed her legs as he lowered his voice and stage-whispered in her ear. 'Drew wanted a stock-horse stud for Christmas, but Daddy wouldn't buy him one.' He tapped the side of his nose with his forefinger. 'Looks like you're going to be Santa Claus instead.'

'Shove off, Spike,' said Drew roughly, pulling Sam to her feet. 'Or better still, we will.' He bustled her down the steps, out into the throng and over to a grassy spectator mound. Time to change the subject. 'See there?' said Drew, pointing to where transports were pulling up at the stock pens behind the racecourse. 'Your horses have arrived.'

The Mitchell horses milled about the yard. Six mares: two chestnuts, two creams, a brown and a black. Two solid taffy geldings with flaxen manes and tails, and a pair of skewbald ponies with the longest blond forelocks and eyelashes Sam had ever seen. 'They're gorgeous,' she said to Drew, pleasantly surprised. The label of *trail horse* had conjured up an image of worn-out riding-school hacks. One of the ponies came up to the rails and explored Sam's outstretched hand with its warm, whiffling muzzle.

'Knew you'd like them,' said Drew. He was looking pretty smug. 'Those two mares in the corner?' He pointed to the pair of classy chestnuts with white stars. 'They're in foal to Condamine Joe.' She looked blank. 'That stallion is a legend, and he carries a double Abbey cross in his pedigree.' To judge by the excitement on his face, this was something very special indeed. However Spike's words still echoed disturbingly in her ear.

'What use will broodmares be in a trail-riding operation?' she asked. Drew wasn't listening. Instead he was up and over the rail, talking to a stout, elderly man in a blue singlet. Why hadn't they thought this through more carefully? She didn't even know by what name she should introduce herself.

Sam climbed over the fence, and with an apologetic smile to the man, pulled Drew aside. 'Who does he think I am?' she whispered.

'Does it matter?' asked Drew.

'Of course it matters. I'm not committing fraud by signing my sister's name on any transfer papers.' Sam could hear the rising irritation in her voice. 'And what about the cost? What's he asking?'

'You won't believe this.' Drew glanced around as if somebody might be eavesdropping. 'Three thousand bucks for the lot, including all their gear. The sentimental old codger has a mind to keep the string together.'

Sam did some quick thinking. It would leave her with almost no savings, but she couldn't argue with that price. And Bushy paid her a modest wage in cash each week. If it came to the crunch she could always ask her father for money. Equine buying and selling certainly was a different proposition back home in Melbourne. Trials, guarantees, insurance, exhaustive vet checks. That would have been the deal when Andrew bought Pharaoh, but here in Currajong she was contemplating buying ten horses without ever having seen them under saddle. A pig in a poke, as Bushy would say. All she had was Drew's vague assurance that he'd checked them out. It was madness.

Sam looked from the lovely herd to Drew's expectant face, and then back to the herd. She imagined the horses grazing in the paddocks of Brumby's Run. She imagined Jarrang's excitement when he laid eyes on those pretty mares. She drew a huge breath and nodded. 'Let's do it.'

Terry Mitchell heard her and looked hopeful. 'We have a deal then?

Good on yer. You'll never find a finer string at the price. Just promise me they'll get a good home.'

'Of course,' Sam reassured him. 'Will you take a cheque?' She was half-afraid Mary's reputation had preceded her, but Terry just nodded and smiled expansively. She wrote out the cheque, then took possession of the sheaf of transfer papers and service certificates. Sam signed her name as Samantha Carmichael, but Terry didn't bat an eyelid, and continued to happily call her Charlie.

One of the friendly ponies laid its head on Terry's arm. He hugged its neck, burying his face in its bushy mane. Was this tough-looking man crying? 'You be good then, Topsy.' He turned to go, his face crumpled and red.

'Wait,' said Sam. She could see how much these horses meant to the man. 'You can't leave yet. Not before I know a bit about each of them.' She dug around in her bag for a pen and notepad.

A grin cracked Terry's face. 'Well, you've met Topsy, and that,' he said, pointing to the matching skewbald pony, 'is his mate Turvy.' For half an hour Sam listened to Terry talking about his horses like they were best friends. 'Those cream mares, they're wild-caught brumbies. Quietest, most well-mannered horses you could find. And see that liver chestnut by the trough? That's Flicka. She's due in the middle of March. It's her first foal, so she'll bear extra watching. And Jet,' he called to the black mare, who disengaged herself from the herd and walked straight to him. 'Jet, here,' he said, stroking her cheek. 'Jet loves to be at the front of the ride. She'll jog and fuss otherwise, so you may as well let her have her way.'

Sam carefully recorded all he told her. When he was finally ready to leave, he shook Sam's hand, an expression of immense gratitude on his face. 'You treat 'em right, and they'll do the same to you. I reckon they couldn't be in safer hands.' The old man hobbled from the yard without a backward glance.

'That was a good thing you did,' said Drew.

'It was practical, that's all,' said Sam. 'How else would I know that Ruby only stands for the farrier if she gets liquorice?'

Drew's laugh lit up his handsome face and Sam's misgivings fell away. Everything would be okay. She and Drew would make this trail-riding operation a success. His enthusiasm for the deal was infectious. 'Come on,' he said, giving Topsy a final scratch behind the ears. 'The auction's about to start.'

A stand was set up in front of the campdrafting ring where the feature sale was to be held. The sign above it read *National Brumby Association*. Sam browsed the posters and other paraphernalia on display. 'There's a brumby studbook?' she asked the round woman behind the trestle-table counter. 'I had no idea.'

The woman nodded. 'Established in 2007 to promote the Australian Heritage Brumby as a recognised breed.' She introduced herself as Margot, and handed Sam a brochure. *The Australian Brumby Horse Register*, read Sam, *brings to owners the formalisation of the Brumby as a unique breed. It will help to preserve the bloodlines and the heritage of this unique animal, that has developed through natural selection in the wild for more than a century.*

'Do you have a particular interest in brumbies?' asked Margot. 'Or perhaps you own one?'

Sam considered the questions. Two months ago she barely knew what a brumby was. She knew nothing of the world of wild horses. But now? She'd spent the past month working with over forty of them. She supposed that counted as a special interest.

Did she own one? Come to think of it, she actually owned more than one. There was Tambo — technically Charlie's, but as good as hers. And Jarrang? She smiled to herself. Could anybody really own Jarrang? Then there were Terry Mitchell's creamy brumby mares - *her* creamy brumby mares now. She even had the transfer papers in the name of Samantha Carmichael to prove it. After what had happened with Pharaoh, that was a very reassuring thing. And what about Phoenix? Sam had decided some time ago that, sooner or later, the golden colt would be hers. And then there was that graceful grey from Jarrang's mob – she wanted her too. 'Yes,' she answered at last. 'Yes to both questions.'

'You'll want to join then.' Margot handed her a membership form. 'And register your horse.' A registration form landed in her hand. Sam must have looked unsure, for Margot went into a promotional spiel, worthy of the finest infomercial host. 'The National Brumby Association accepts all authentic brumbies into the register, and welcomes anyone interested in preserving our brumby heritage to become a member. All horses that can be verified as coming from a wild herd are eligible. Progeny from authenticated brumbies can also join, and there's an appendix register for part-bred brumbies.' She paused for breath. 'If your brumby isn't registered, please consider joining.'

What could she say to that? Apart from, 'Can I have some more registration forms please?'

Margot beamed. The loudspeaker announced the sale was about to begin. 'Come and see me afterwards if you've got any questions,' said Margot. Sam thanked her and went to find Drew.

Drew and Sam sat on one of the giant hay bales surrounding the campdrafting arena. The auctioneer knocked down the last of Bushy's horses to a local family, and the pretty yearling pranced from the ring. There'd been a surprisingly strong demand for the ground-broken young brumbies, even from interstate. Sam would miss working with them, and was very glad Bushy had held Phoenix over. There was no way she could have afforded to buy the colt now, not after paying for the Mitchell string.

'Want a beer?' asked Drew.

Sam nodded. He jumped down and wandered off towards the bar. The loudspeaker crackled back to life: 'Next we offer a yarding of ten wild brumbies, captured three weeks ago straight off Maroong Mountain.' Jarrang's mob. She looked around for Drew. He wouldn't want to miss this.

Sam felt the weight of somebody scaling the bale behind her, then two hands covered her eyes. She yelped. 'Drew, so help me …!' But it wasn't Drew. It was Spike.

'Disappointed?' he asked, flashing a winning smile.

'Annoyed is more like it,' Sam said. 'Now shush. I want to see what happens.' The elegant grey mare trotted into the ring. No – it was more like she floated in. Sam had seen that graceful gait before. She racked her brain to think where it had been. National dressage championships, Sydney equestrian centre, Horsley Park. A charismatic, dappled stallion, the first Andalusian she'd ever seen in the flesh, performing the passage – a high-school movement consisting of an elevated and extremely powerful trot. How was it that this brumby mare, straight off the mountain, moved with the same degree of collection and impulsion as had that exotic stallion from Spain? It was like she was dancing on air. An appreciative murmur rose from the crowd and the bidding commenced.

Ryan, the young welfare officer from the Brumby Coalition, made a bid. Sam did sums in her head for the umpteenth time. She couldn't possibly afford to buy again today. No matter. If the mare fell to Ryan she would be in charge of its basic education anyway. Plenty of time to save up for the mare, and for Phoenix as well. Now a rough-looking man to her left raised the bid. Sam peered around Spike, looking for Drew. Her shoulder inadvertently pressed against the bull rider and he responded with a subtle pressure of his own.

Sam moved away a fraction.

Ryan raised the offer, and the other bidder followed suit. A stray kelpie suddenly slipped between the rails and darted for the mare's heels. She exploded in a frenzy of bucking, hurling herself skywards with stiffened legs, spinning like a whirling dervish. The crowd cheered as she turned on the red dog and pursued him from the ring with flattened ears and bared teeth.

'Wayne won't let her go now,' said Spike, leaning close.

'Who's Wayne?'

Spike pointed at the rough man to her left. 'Wayne Clarke from Clarke and Sons. Rodeo contractors. That mare? She's got a mean buck.'

Sam's heart fell. Ryan had to buy her. The magnificent mare had to stay at the racecourse, safe with Bushy, safe with her. She couldn't go to some rodeo. Drew would help. Sam stood up and looked over the crowd milling below the stand. She spotted him wending his way back with drinks in hand. Sam waved both arms in the air. Great, Drew had seen her. He smiled and waved, but he was coming so slowly.

Sam jumped up and down, screaming his name. 'Drew, hurry up!' Some people nearby glared in her direction, but Sam didn't care. 'Quickly!' Couldn't he hear the auctioneer's voice over the loud-speaker. *'Wayne Clarke can see the potential in this young brumby as a bucking horse. He normally gets what he wants, and he wants this grey brumby. Do I hear a new bid?'* Sam already knew the answer; knew that Ryan was on a tight budget and couldn't compete with the cashed-up contractor.

The penny must have dropped for Drew. Too late, he came sprinting towards the stand. A brief scattering of applause, and the mare was knocked down to Wayne Clarke.

Sam sank back down onto the bench and buried her head in her hands.

'Not to worry, princess,' said Spike. 'A good bucking animal's worth its weight in gold to those guys. I've seen horses get a lot worse treatment in show-jumping rings. And don't even get me started on jumps races.' He moved sideways to let Drew through, then moved back before Drew was properly past, jostling him.

Drew shoved back, his face darkening. 'Don't tell me Wayne got his hands on that grey?' He handed Sam the beer. She took the can and nodded dumbly.

'I tried to tell her the horse'll be okay . . . ' Spike started.

'Shut up, Spike.' Drew took Sam's hand, tugged her from her seat and out of the stand.

'Sorry, Sam, but that bloke really rubs me the wrong way.' Drew took a swig of beer. 'And I'm sorry about that mare.' He took off his hat and wiped his brow with the back of his hand. 'I should have been here, should have bid on her myself — they usually leave the best horses until last. But for once, even though it kills me to admit it, I have to agree with Spike. Those rodeo blokes do the right thing by their stock.'

Sam couldn't agree. To her rodeos were blatant exhibitions of animal abuse that had no more place in a civilised society than cock-fighting or bear-baiting. It made her sick to the stomach, thinking of that lovely filly being forced to buck. And to think that she'd been involved in the horse's capture, that she was responsible for delivering her from a life of freedom to one of torment.

The auctioneer announced the next entry. The bay brumby with the inquisitive dun foal trotted into the ring. Sam turned to watch. Thank God Ryan was back in full swing. Bushy stood beside him as he bid against a thin man in a baseball cap. After the mother and foal were knocked down to him, Ryan spotted Sam by the rails and he and Bushy came over to say hello. Another horse entered the arena, an older roan mare this time. 'You'd better get back over there,' said Sam. 'The next brumby's out.'

Ryan made a show of turning his pants pockets inside out. 'I'm done for the day,' he said. 'It's a shame I lost the grey filly. What a beauty.'

'Drew says she'll be okay,' said Sam, doubtfully. 'So does Spike.' She was trying to convince herself as much as Ryan.

Bushy looked grave. 'Normally I'd agree with them fellas,' he said. 'But there's something about that horse.' He shook his head. 'I reckon rodeo will turn that one bad.' Nobody spoke for a bit, depressed by Bushy's gloomy prediction.

'On a brighter note,' said Ryan. 'You guys will have six new ones to work with on Monday.'

'Only six?' asked Sam. 'What will happen to the rest?' She pointed to the roan brumby, standing alert and uncertain in the middle of the arena. 'What will happen to her?'

'We can't save them all,' said Ryan and he turned away.

His words gave her a chill. When the sale was over, Sam returned to Margot at the stall.

'What got you into this brumby thing?' asked Sam.

'I suppose the original inspiration was an author, Elyne Mitchell. Like so many other girls of my generation, I was raised on the Silver Brumby books. When my husband and I bought our first brumbies, the meat truck pulled up behind us. They took the ones that we didn't take. I was horrified.'

Sam looked over at the chain-smoking man with the baseball cap who had just bought the nervous roan mare, and an awful realisation hit her. Mr Baseball Cap was the knackery man.

CHAPTER 20

It took only a week of working alongside Sam each day to completely destroy Drew's resolve. She was drop-dead gorgeous and his body had a mind of its own. At times his longing for her was so powerful that it felt like an illness.

They spent their days testing out the new horses, extending the yards, fixing up the sheds and disposing of truckloads of rubbish. The old place had never looked so good. Sam was always tantalisingly near; standing at the opposite end of a saw plank, or a two-man post hole digger. Having a crack at hoof trimming, bent down right in front of him while he steadied the head of a fractious horse. She was a fast learner, a quick thinker and never shirked a task, however difficult or unpleasant. The more he got to know her, the more he grew to love her. To hell with guarding his heart. It was time to take a risk.

On Saturday he took Sam on a ride, right to the rim of the range. To gaze out from Ram's Head Rock was like being suspended in space. It felt good, sharing that dramatic view with her. To the south the ridges were clothed with virgin forest, as far as the eye could see. To the west a jagged wall of granite cliffs rose like battlements. To the north a silver streamer hung down the cliff. It broke into rainbows of spray on the rocks below, filling a chain of deep reflective pools. A primeval scene. They could have been the last people on earth.

'Stay with me,' he said. 'Stay with me tonight at Dead Man's Hut.' His invitation echoed around the range. Sam studied his face for the longest time. He dreaded seeing reticence or refusal in her eyes. When she finally smiled her assent, he'd wanted to sing.

Dusk was falling fast by the time they reached the hut. Drew couldn't ever remember being so happy. He sat on the ground before the campfire, propped against his saddle, Sam's back between his knees. 'So what do you think of the Mitchell string now?' He lightly combed her silky hair between work-roughened fingers. 'Will they do?'

'They'll more than do,' she said. 'And that ride we took today? Seriously, it's stunning, absolutely magical. People will beat a path to our door for an experience like that.' Drew, leaned forward, gently turned her head, and kissed her, a proper kiss this time, a deeply sexual kiss. She could not have mistaken its meaning, and still her response was warm and eager, a consent not only with her lips, but with her entire body. Easy now. Don't push it.

The two creamy brumby mares nickered in their yard. Drew tore himself away from the kiss and jumped to his feet. 'Relax,' said Sam. 'Jarrang's safely back home at Brumby's Run. He won't be stealing any mares away from you tonight.'

That was true. The brumbies were gone from Maroong Mountain, for now at least, though it wouldn't take long for a new mob to claim Jarrang's deserted territory. Drew wandered over to the yards where the mares stood with high heads and pricked ears, transfixed by some invisible presence in the gloom. An uncertain moon rose behind the peak. It hesitated for a few moments, then throwing caution to the high winds, launched its round orb skywards. Soft light lit the night and gilded the cream mares in polished silver. A snowy owl silhouetted on a twisted branch hooted gently as Drew peered into the dark. Black limbs of trees gleamed pale against the sky, and the ground was striped and patterned in moon shadow.

Drew loved night-time in the mountains. Life seemed less complicated, reduced to its essentials, stripped bare of daytime cares. Its sheer simplicity sometimes scared him.

The deep-throated lowing of cattle echoed through the ghost gums. So that's what had disturbed the mares. Most likely Kilmarnock cattle, part of the trial grazing deal his father had wangled with his government mates. Although there were, he knew, wild bands of scrubbers roaming the range, elusive as phantoms. They bore no brands, endured no whips or dogs. They grew old and died in the shadow of Maroong Mountain instead of in the shadow of the slaughterhouse. Drew's grandfather had believed that bad luck would befall any man who tried to muster in the scrubber herd. Even Drew's practical father had not dared to test the theory. So they had remained for generations as free and untamed as Balleroo itself.

Drew threw the mares a few biscuits of hay, then hurried back to the warmth of the fire, to the warmth of Sam. Drew's body thrummed in anticipation, his every nerve ending alive. He wanted so very much to sleep with Sam, to hold her all night in his arms, to make love to her. He imagined her sweet, soft body cradled naked beside him, and desire welled up in a physical way. But he wanted something else much, much more. He wanted to know who she really was, and how she came to be here with him on this star-studded night, on this magic mountain.

'I'm shivering,' she said on his return. 'Let's light a fire in the hut.'

Drew shovelled up the hot embers and took them inside. With the help of some extra logs, the hut's long-abandoned fireplace soon blazed bright. For the first time in years its cheerful radiance lit up the cracks and crevices in the rough-hewn timber walls. A light that would leave no shelter, Drew hoped, for dark secrets to hide. He buried a few spuds in the coals, found the chops in his saddle bag, and poured cups of black tea from the billy hanging over the fire. Sam lit a candle and dragged the wooden bench over. They sat side by side, staring into the flames, waiting for their dinner to cook.

She laid her head on his shoulder. Drew turned her face and kissed her. He could feel the sudden quiver of her breath, like the heart of a startled bird. He traced her moist lips with his finger. 'Sam?' he said quietly. 'Tell me about you and Charlie. I can't go on with . . . with us, until you level with me.'

A long silence followed his question. She lifted her head and looked at him, boring in with those beautiful brown eyes. 'Is that why you pulled away?' she asked. 'You did — you know you did. After New Year's Eve, after Spike's visit, you seemed ...' She paused, as if struggling to find the words. 'You seemed almost frightened of me.'

It was his turn to struggle. How to explain? That Spike's appearance had stirred up painful memories? That he'd suddenly realised how little he really knew about Sam and her life? She seemed so fresh, so innocent, so guileless. And yet he'd learned in life that things were rarely what they seemed. Sam was, after all, Charlie's sister. He took her delicate hand in his and pressed it to his lips. 'I suppose I was,' he said. 'Frightened of being in the dark. You still haven't really told me what's going on. Where Charlie and Mary are, for instance, and how come nobody's ever heard of you before? Where you come from, and ... and how long you'll stay.'

Sam looked away. 'You're right, Drew. I owe you an explanation.' Over a dinner of lamb chops and roast spuds, washed down with billy tea, Sam told him everything. She told him about her solitary childhood, her absent father and controlling mother. About Pharaoh, and how horses had rescued her from a terrible loneliness. About how she'd discovered the reality of her adoption, and of her sister, in almost the same breath. Of Charlie's deadly battle with cancer, and of the procedure that had transformed both their lives.

'Jesus, Sam. That's some story.' Drew sat awhile, trying to digest all he'd been told. 'Come to think of it,' he said, 'Charlie did get pretty skinny last year. Although she's such a tomboy, it was hard to tell. It's not like she wears tight, sexy clothes.' Something in Sam's expression warned him to change tack. 'Will she be all right?' he asked. 'When does she come home?'

'Professor Sung predicts a full recovery, thank God.' Sam sipped her tea. 'As to when Charlie will be home? I don't know. In a month maybe,' she said, sounding oddly unenthusiastic about the prospect.

Drew reached for a log to add to the fire. Sam stopped his arm, with her hand on his. 'Your turn,' she said.

'My turn?' He grabbed the log, tossed it into the hearth, and lit a candle.

'Your turn to tell me about you,' she said.

'What do you want to know?'

'You're being coy,' she said, with a laugh. 'Just start at the start.'

'It's weird.' Drew shook his head, as if in disbelief. 'But thanks to some strange twist of fate, you and I have a lot in common.'

'We do?' She sounded sceptical. 'Certainly not the circumstances of our lives. Me in Melbourne and you …' She swept her arm around. 'You out here.'

He poured himself another mug of tea and stood with his back to Sam, facing the flames. 'I've never told anybody this before,' he said. 'but I'm adopted too.'

'You're kidding me.' Sam sat open-mouthed.

'After my sister Melinda, Mum couldn't have more kids. They wanted a boy. Well, Dad did anyway. My aunt worked for an adoption agency in Wodonga, and kept her eye out. I was born to a teenage mother, just like you were. She wasn't seventeen, though – she was only fifteen, and her parents insisted she adopt me out. The family moved interstate afterwards. To make a fresh start for their daughter, I guess. I've only ever received two letters from my mother. One on my eighteenth birthday, and again last year on my twenty- first. She loves me, she says, but she's married now with two children, a girl and a boy. Her husband doesn't know she had another baby and she wants to keep it that way.'

'What about you?' asked Sam. 'Do you want to keep it that way?'

'Absolutely,' he said. 'She was just a kid. Who can blame her for wanting to live her life?'

'Don't you want to meet your brother and sister?'

'Not now. It might spoil things for her … for them. She promised to tell them when they grow up. Then if we get curious we can arrange to meet up. But right now? It's not that big a deal.' Sam looked astonished. 'I reckon it's different for me,' he said. 'I always knew.

Can't ever remember not knowing. Mum and Dad were up front right from the start.'

Sam stood up and slipped her slim arm round his waist. 'That's it,' she said. 'You knew, so you don't have a trust issue with your parents.'

He cupped her chin in his hand and kissed her, savouring her sweetness. 'No, I don't,' he said. 'Not with my parents.'

Sam cocked her head and regarded him curiously. 'With who then?'

He laughed, trying to keep it light, hoping he didn't sound bitter. 'If you must know, I've had the odd girlfriend or two that I couldn't trust.' Sam opened her mouth to speak. 'I'm definitely not going there tonight though,' he said, holding up his hand. 'What is this? Truth or dare?'

'If you won't tell the truth,' she said, 'perhaps you'd rather a dare?'

'Dare me to make a bed for you,' he said, and pulled a rubber mat from his saddle bags.

'It's like the Tardis in there,' she said, laughing.

'May I present to you the Thermarest 2000, a self-inflating double mattress.' He pulled out its plug, and the core immediately began to plump up.

'You certainly came prepared,' she said.

'Would you rather sleep on those filthy horsehair mattresses?' Drew pointed to the single bunks and went over for a closer look. He peeled the pock-marked surface layer of timber from a bedpost, and held it up triumphantly. 'Borers, m'lady,' he announced. 'I'm afraid occupational health and safety regulations preclude me from allowing you to use these bunks.'

'Kind sir,' she said in mock seriousness. 'I'm a law-abiding girl who wouldn't dream of flaunting regulations.' She stared down at the partly-inflated rubber bed. 'The Thermarest it is, then.'

Drew was down on his knees in a second, blowing great lungfuls of air through the plug to speed up the process. When he'd finished he reached for Sam's hand, anticipation shivering through his veins. She let him pull her down, and he kissed her gently, his lips exploring the contours of her face.

A sudden series of loud thumps and bumps sounded from the roof, accompanied by a blood-curdling screech. Sam rocketed into his arms. He stroked strands of hair from her face, ignoring the excited clenching in his abdomen. 'Possums,' he said, mouthing a silent prayer to the helpful little marsupials. 'Just possums.'

'It sounds more like World War Three.' Sam sat up and looked doubtfully at the roof. 'What are they doing?'

'Mating,' he answered. 'Are you cold?' She nodded, wide-eyed and trembling slightly – whether from nerves or cold, Drew couldn't tell. He stood up, stoked the fire, and fetched some blankets from a pile in the corner. The rooftop hissing and screaming reached fever pitch.

'Truth or dare?' whispered Sam, wrapping a cover around herself. 'And you won't like the dare, so you'd better take truth.'

'Okay, hit me,' he said, settling back down with her on the mattress. 'Truth.'

'Why is this called Dead Man's Hut?'

'You really want to know the story?' She nodded solemnly. 'Okay,' he said. 'I just don't want to scare you.'

'You won't scare me,' she insisted, and moved closer, nestling into his shoulder.

'Once upon a time,' he said, like he was telling her a bedtime story, 'there was a man who packed up his belongings and went to live in a hut he built in the bush.'

Sam stared up at him. 'You mean this hut?'

Drew nodded. 'He was a cattle duffer, by all accounts. Nicked cleanskin calves and grazed his stolen mob around Snake Creek.'

'What was his name?'

'Nobody remembers,' said Drew. 'But he earned himself the nickname Brumby Jack. In fact, they named your place after him. Jack claimed to be the son of Mad Dog Morgan, the bushranger, although nobody knows for sure whether he was telling the truth.' Drew brushed a strand of hair from her face. 'A man alone in the bush for too long can grow a bit peculiar. His imagination plays tricks on him. That's what happened to Jack. He stopped coming into town for supplies, stopped dropping by musterers' camps for a chat. Instead he spent each day riding the range. Rain or shine, even in the winter snows.'

'Why?' asked Sam.

'He was searching for a horse. Jack used to talk about a wild, white stallion, telling anyone who'd listen. He said it led a herd of magic mountain brumbies: brumbies that became invisible when you chased them, brumbies that could fly. Jack became completely obsessed with catching this enchanted stallion, but of course it only existed in his imagination. One day his horse stumbled into Currajong, caked in sweat and bloodied from the spur. They sent riders up to check on the old man.'

'And?' asked Sam, staring at him with rapt attention.

'They found Jack lying out in the yard, a catching rope still clutched in his dead hand. One end was snubbed to a post. The noose end had snapped, like it wasn't strong enough to stand the strain. The churned-up ground told of a terrible fight. Jack's skull was crushed. But this was the strangest thing . . . the gate was shut tight, bound securely with ropes, yet the yard was empty. Whatever killed him had jumped eight-foot rails from a standing start.'

'Or simply flown away,' said Sam, with a faraway look in her eye.

'Don't you start believing in magical brumbies.' His fingers reached for the buttons of her shirt. 'How about believing in me instead?' Was that a shadow or the first flush of arousal darkening her pale skin? He stretched out beside her and they kissed – ardent, but not urgent. They had all night, and he dared not rush a single, extraordinary moment. The smell of perfume and leather, her body soft and fresh, the firelight bright on her face. She closed her eyes and he willed her to open them, willed her to look at him. Drew nipped Sam's ear and her lids flickered back up. Long lashes framing almond eyes, and real desire there. Drew leaned across and blew out the candle. His lips found the hollow of her neck in the dark, and he knew he would remember the curve of her throat and the taste of her skin for all of his life.

Early morning light filtered through the tiny hut window. Sam stretched and opened her eyes, feeling Drew's sleeping warmth beside her. A possessive arm lay flung over her naked body. It was no dream. She kissed his arm and placed the palm of her hand over his heart. Drew stirred and pulled her close, his eyes still shut, an expression of supreme contentment on his face. She took a deep breath and snuggled further under the covers, moulding her body to his. They were as one. It was hard to tell where her skin ended and his began. Drew looked like she felt: deeply happy.

Later, over mugs of breakfast tea and toast cooked on green twigs before the fire, Drew told her that he loved her.

Sam felt tears come into her eyes – tears of joy, tears of wonder. It was overwhelming. Was she supposed to say it back to him? Was that how it worked? The problem was that she couldn't. Not because she didn't love him. She thought that she probably did, but how to be sure? How to define these new feelings? Mouthing *I love you* seemed just too corny, seemed to trivialise the potent emotions he'd awakened in her.

'It's just the beginning ...' said Drew as he rolled up their bed, 'and I'm already so crazy in love with you. I swear, nothing's even come close to this.' He dropped the bed and took her by the waist, kissing her roughly before waltzing her around the hut. His raw energy overcame her in a heady rush. She could feel her body's automatic response and gasped for air. Like on her first abseil, or a rollercoaster ride; the simultaneous thrill and terror of being out of control.

Drew swept her up in another long, sweet kiss that left her dizzy. When he let go she sank down on the old bunk, and shook her head to clear it. He fished around in his magic pudding of a saddle bag and pulled out a little box.

'For you.' He tossed it onto her lap. 'Bought it in Wodonga last week. It's set up and ready to go.' He'd bought her a present? That meant he'd been thinking about her all along. She opened the box. - a new smart phone.

'Thank you,' said Sam, kissing him. 'I love it.' The present could have been a dish mop for all she cared, and she would have said the same thing. It was most definitely the thought that counted.

'You never seem able to get reception with your old one,' he said.

'You'll be able to ring Charlie whenever you want with that. Or your mother.' He laughed at her bemused expression. 'You've got two of those to keep happy, remember?'

Sam made a face. He pulled her in and clasped his strong hands behind her back. 'I don't suppose Charlie's ever got any credit to ring you. How do you think they're managing for money?'

'That's the peculiar thing,' she said. 'They're doing just fine, apparently. Somebody's been making deposits into Mary's bank account. Generous deposits too. According to Charlie, they've never been better off.'

'So Mary's got an anonymous benefactor,' said Drew.

'Looks that way.'

'I bet there's a story there. No wonder she hasn't made a fuss about Dad's money.'

Sam nodded. 'Just as well for us.' She played with her new phone. 'Thank you,' she said again, hugging him. 'You're very thoughtful.'

He nodded. 'I am, aren't I?'

Sam wriggled free and punched him playfully. 'Let's go, you big egomaniac. I can't wait to get home and have a long, long talk to Charlie.'

CHAPTER 21

Mary had met a man. Well, of course she had — she always did. Charlie shaded her eyes from the afternoon sun, and watched from the window as her mother climbed into his battered old Buick. It was disgusting to see her giggling like a girl, flirting and simpering with pony-tailed Carlos. They'd met at the hospital and bonded over cigarettes smoked outside on the street. It was a perfect match. Two ageing hippies, behaving like teenagers, not realising how pathetic and embarrassing they were.

The car drove off. It grew smaller and smaller, turned left around a corner and vanished. Charlie grabbed her giant soft-toy frog and collapsed on the bed in tears. She'd imagined that life in this East Melbourne apartment would have been a big improvement on the hospital. No more gowns or masks or over-the-top hand-washing. No more endless waiting: for engraftment, for blood-cell counts to return to safe levels, for side effects to lessen. But she'd been wrong. This lonely hole in the wall was worse than a prison.

Who would have thought she'd miss the nurses and doctors at that bloody hospital? She even missed Colleen, bossing her around, fussing like a mother hen. Here in the apartment she saw nobody but her mother. Oh, and Carlos of course. She knew the drill. She should, after all these years. Carlos trying to be friends, laying it on with a trowel for her mother's benefit. How many times had she been through this? It could be worse, she supposed. Carlos was a dork and a massive pothead, but aside from that he was inoffensive enough. Some of her mum's past boyfriends had not been so harmless. A suggestive comment here, a hand on her thigh there - gifts of money or alcohol behind her mother's back.

Charlie's phone rang and she lunged for it. 'Sam?'

No, just her mother, asking how she was and whether she needed anything. Charlie braced against the surge of disappointment. 'Crikey, Mum, you just left. What could have possibly changed?' Charlie threw down her phone and it slid under the bed. Good riddance.

She put on the kettle in the kitchenette, and searched through the tea bags in the pantry. Just as she thought – every herbal concoction under the sun when what she really wanted was an old-fashioned cup of plain black tea. No, what she really wanted was a beer. Well, why not? Mum probably wouldn't be back for hours. She'd gone ostensibly to buy a secondhand laptop from some dodgy friend of Carlos. A present, Mary had told her, so Charlie could keep in touch with friends and download music and movies — that sort of thing. First, she didn't have any friends. And second? It was more than likely that the pair would end up in a bar, forget all about the computer, and not return until late at night. City living wasn't good for her mother Charlie had decided. Too much temptation.

On impulse Charlie found her wallet, slipped out the door and descended the steps to the lobby. Though well enough to leave the hospital, her recovery was far from over. Some days she still felt too weak to do much more than sleep, sit up, and walk a bit around the apartment. Her only outings so far had been back to the hospital for tests.

According to Professor Sung it could take six months before she was ready to resume normal activities. 'During this period your white blood-cell count may be too low to provide normal protection against the viruses and bacteria encountered in everyday life,' he'd explained. 'You must therefore restrict contact with the general public. Crowded movie theatres, supermarkets, department stores – these are places you must avoid during your recuperation. Often patients like to wear protective masks when venturing outside the home.'

Stuff that. Charlie emerged from the double doors onto the street. At first the rush of human traffic made her dizzy and a little afraid. There was nobody to lean on. But bit by bit she found her land legs. The late-afternoon sun shone mellow and bright. It relieved the constant chill that still plagued her bones. Her reflection in the mirror of a shop window was frightening in its frailty. Look straight ahead, aim for that bottle shop on the corner, she told herself.

The attendant peered at her. 'I *am* eighteen,' she said.

'I'll need some ID, love.' Charlie fished around in the wallet for her learner's permit. This would be her first legal purchase of alcohol. It was wonderful to be treated as a normal person again. She bought a six-pack of beer, headed for a park beyond the bottle shop and removed her shoes. The grass was soft between her toes. She lay down and buried her face in the soil. It had no fragrance. Chemo had destroyed her sense of smell, perhaps. Or was it the city smog that had rendered the natural world odourless? Whatever the case, this artificial patch of green, surrounded by countless square hectares of concrete, had no discernible scent at all.

Charlie approached a stunted Eucalyptus ficofolia, a red flowering gum tree in sparse bloom, its trunk ridged and deformed by a tight cement collar around its base. Charlie stroked its rough bark and plucked a leaf. The scent of eucalyptus was faint and far away. 'Like your home forest,' she whispered. Charlie settled down, beer in hand, with her back propped against the sad gum tree. It must have been peak hour, to judge by the increasing flow of pedestrians on the street. 'Well,' she said companionably, draining the first beer and opening another. 'You might be a sorry excuse for a ficofolia, but you look a damn sight happier than those buggers.' She toasted the tree.

Shadows lengthened. Occasionally Charlie moved around the trunk to a new spot, seeking out the low slanting rays of the descending sun as it swung westwards. It would be lost below the city sky-line well before it set. She removed her head scarf, exposing her fuzzy scalp, and swigged the beer. Passers-by cast disapproving glances her way. She smiled and raised her bottle. 'Cheers,' she shouted, enjoying herself for the first time in a long time.

Charlie cracked another beer. 'Where are your birds?' she called. 'What sort of a park are you without any birds?' How long had it been since she'd seen a bird? Charlie didn't count flying rats like Indian mynahs and sparrows and pigeons. The city was infested with them. She meant real birds.

As if summoned by her thoughts, a ragged black raven alighted on a rubbish bin just metres away. Charlie knelt up with a sharp, excited sigh, and it responded with an almost human sounding *aarr, aarr, aarrrr*, the last note long and drawn-out. 'Hello, Mr Raven. You remind me of a very good friend.' The bird hopped to the ground, walked closer, and inspected her with striking ivory eyes. It looked so much like Condor. For a moment Charlie believed that by some miracle he had found her, but when she reached out a hand, the raven flew away.

Charlie hurled the bottle after it and stumbled to her feet. 'It's easy enough for him,' she complained to the tree. 'He can just fly away whenever he likes, back to the bush.' She gave the tree trunk a swift hug. 'Not so simple for us now, is it?'

'Are you all right?' asked a dreadlocked young man who'd stopped to watch her.

Charlie grabbed the three remaining beers of her six-pack. 'No,' she said. 'I'm not.'

The man walked over, retrieved her scarf from where it lay on the grass, and handed it to her. Then he picked up the scattered empty bottles and threw them in the bin.

'You know what?' said Charlie, rewinding her scarf and giving him the once over. 'You're pretty hot. Want to go for a drink?'

It was after nine o'clock when she finally arrived home. Mary was furious.

'Where in heaven's name have you been?' she demanded. 'I've been worried sick!'

Charlie wondered for how long her mother had even been home. Not long, she thought. There was only one butt in the ashtray. 'I've been for a drink,' said Charlie, 'with an ever so nice young man. It was fun.'

'You're drunk,' said Mary.

Charlie ignored the comment, although there was plenty of truth in it. 'Did you get my laptop?'

'No.' Mary sounded suddenly cagey. 'Something came up. Carlos will bring it round tomorrow.' Charlie knew exactly what had come up. She could smell the pot on her mother's clothes. Mary lit a cigarette, stood back and took a long look at her. 'You're not supposed to go out yet. You know your cell counts are still low. Did you kiss him? What if you catch an infection?'

'No, Mum, I didn't kiss him. I only just met him. Who do you think I am - you?'

Mary frowned, purse-lipped. She was such a hypocrite. About men, about everything. How could her mother have the nerve to lecture her about health when she smoked a pack a day, and the rest?

'Suit yourself,' said Mary, looking wounded. 'Next time, although I hope there won't be a next time, take your phone with you.' Charlie looked around for it. 'It was under your bed,' said Mary, taking it from her pocket. 'Sam's been ringing. We had a lovely chat, although she was worried about where you were, of course. She said she'd ring back later.'

Charlie snatched the handset from her mother's hand, just as it rang. She marched off to the bedroom with the hard kernel of a headache germinating within her skull. She'd had some monsters lately, and all that beer could only make matters worse. She really was an idiot. Charlie checked the caller display. 'Hi Sam, how're things?' she asked. 'No, I'm fine. Surely I can go out once in a while without everybody making a big production out of it? Tell me about Brumby's Run. I've been dying to hear.'

She listened to her sister's excited stories of life back home; of working with Bushy and the six mares from Jarrang's mob that had been purchased by the Brumby Coalition, of trying out the Mitchell horses, a different one each evening.

'Drew was right,' said Sam. 'They're all great rides, quiet and responsive.' She was positively gushing. 'The two ponies are a little stubborn at times, but that's safer for kids than being too speedy.' The beer buzz was like a haze in Charlie's brain, a dense swirl of confusion. Sam kept talking. 'Jarrang and Tambo are terrific, although Jarrang is obsessed with the new mares.' The pounding in Charlie's head made it hard to hear. 'You should see him prancing about, so full of himself, showing off.'

A swift shaft of jealousy pierced through the pain. It left Charlie breathless at all she was missing. Her sister's voice faded to a drone. Only the most significant, most important phrases penetrated the white noise. Drew had given her a phone . . . Drew had trucked over hay . . . Drew had reinforced and extended Jarrang's yard . . . Drew had taken her to Bluff Falls . . . Drew this, Drew that. There were too many sentences starting with Drew. She tried to focus, tried to inject some clarity into her thinking . . . The two of us, overnight at Dead Man's Hut. What was Sam saying?

'Drew told me he loved me, and I think I love him too.' Sam fell silent.

As her sister's words sank in, Charlie wailed out loud. 'You can't!' she said, tongue struggling to translate her fear into speech. 'That's my life, not yours. I caught Tambo. I trained him. I raised Jarrang on a bottle. That job with Bushy and the brumbies? That's my job, not yours.'

She heard Sam's sudden, sharp intake of breath. 'But this was all your idea. I've just been trying to help.'

Trying to help? What a cruel joke! How was stealing somebody's life helping them? Well, Sam wasn't the only one who could be cruel. 'Haven't you got enough already?' Charlie spat. 'With your fancy clothes and overseas holidays and university courses? Do you need to take what little I've got as well? Even my boyfriend?'

'Boyfriend?' came the uncertain response. 'How do you mean?'

'Do I need to spell it out?' Charlie knew she was out of control, but fuelled by envy and anger, goaded by alcohol and the skull-splitting ache in her head, she couldn't help herself. 'Bloody hell,' she said with a hollow laugh. 'What a complete bastard. Drew does one twin, then the other. He's living every bloke's fantasy.'

'But how is that possible?' said Sam. 'You never even mentioned him.'

'Would it have made a difference? Everything of mine seems to be fair game for you.'

'Of course it would have made a difference,' pleaded Sam. 'I had no idea, and I'm so, so terribly sorry. Charlie, please calm down. Please? When will you and Mary be coming home?'

'Are you sure you still want me to?' Charlie's voice cracked as she started to cry. 'Maybe you won't want your invalid sister hanging round, cramping your style.'

'Don't say that!' said Sam. Was she crying too? It was hard to tell, so hard to make sense of things with this terrible hammer in her head. 'I'm doing all this for you, for Mary. I can't wait until you're home, you must know that. Charlie, I love you, you're my long-lost sister. I'll never ever let anything come between us, I promise — least of all a man.'

So good to hear those words. So comforting. Sam loved her. Why had she ever doubted it? 'Love you too,' said Charlie. 'But I've got such a splitting headache.'

'Why don't you go lie down?' suggested Sam in a soothing voice. 'Have one of Mary's famous sleeping tonics. Chamomile tea with rose hip and valerian — is that it?'

'And a little milk and honey,' mumbled Charlie. Maybe that was what she needed.

'That's right. Hop into bed, and I'll ring you in the morning.'

'Promise?' said Charlie.

'I promise. Now go get some rest. I love you, Charlie. Don't you ever forget that.'

'I won't,' whispered Charlie. 'Love you too.'

She dropped the phone as her mother came in with toasted cheese sandwiches and a pot of tea. Mary put the tray down, pulled a fresh nightie from a drawer, and tossed it to Charlie.

'Pop into bed, sweetheart.' She turned on the little television. 'There's a documentary about the Spanish Riding School of Vienna. Your sister's been there, hasn't she? Want to watch it?'

Charlie nodded and sipped her hot drink. Aah, Mum's tea always did the trick. Charlie closed her eyes and imagined herself home in the kitchen at Brumby's Run. The pulsing pain in her skull eased, but her head was still spinning, making her dizzy. Eight Lipizzaner horses performed in an elegant indoor school hung with crystal chandeliers. Fairy-tale horses, the last word in animal grace. Charlie's lids grew heavy. She struggled to hold her eyes open. Sam would like this show. How was her sister going, she wondered? She tried to remember when they'd last talked. It had been a while, hadn't it? Perhaps she'd better ring Sam in the morning. And as the splendid snow-white stallions danced across the screen, Charlie fell into blissful, oblivious sleep.

CHAPTER 22

Drew escaped out the front door of the rehab centre at a run. He didn't envy the nursing staff left behind. They were locked, so to speak, in the lion's den. Bill was finally out of the full leg cast that had so infuriated him, but it didn't mean he was free and clear, not by a long shot. 'There are complications,' the surgeon had told Drew. 'Fractures of the tibia can be tricky, and I'm afraid your father's attitude has not helped matters. He's been on his feet against all medical advice. The pressure it put on the cast has compromised circulation in Bill's lower leg. On top of that he has nerve damage that hasn't healed.' The surgeon shook his head. 'Your father needs daily physiotherapy to restore a full range of ankle and knee movement, and the muscle strength lost in traction. If he went home now it would be in a wheel-chair.' Dad was spitting chips, but no amount of complaining was going to fix his leg. He wouldn't be physically involved in the property management side of things for months.

It was hard to feel too sorry for his father. Life had been sweet at Kilmarnock in Bill's absence. Tom had the place running like clock-work, and Drew didn't interfere. They were all happier without the old man breathing down their necks about each little thing, micromanaging his way through everybody's day. And Bill's absence allowed Drew to spend most of his time next door at Brumby's Run.

There was just one cloud on the horizon. Sam. Here it was, Valentine's Day of all days, and there'd been no repeat of the blissful night they'd shared together at the hut. That was more than a fortnight ago now, a fortnight fraught with frustration. It was the most confusing thing. One day they were in love, or so he'd believed. They'd shared the stories of their lives, shared their secrets, shared their bed. Twenty-four hours later, Sam was behaving like it had never happened.

'What's up, Sam?' he'd asked, the first time she ducked away from him. She wouldn't answer. Instead she studiously ignored him, or laughed off his questions. Sometimes she stared at him, as if she expected him to know. But he didn't, and it was killing him – being so close, within arm's reach, but not being able to hold her. Not even being able to touch her.

'This isn't a game, Sam,' he'd said. Was that what she thought it was? 'What the hell's going on?' But she wouldn't say. He wanted to grab her and kiss her til her breath came ragged, until she spat out the problem. Once he'd even caught her looking at him with a certain grim resentment, though it might have been his imagination. It was driving him nuts.

On the surface Sam was still friendly enough, keen for him to help set up the trekking business. Together they'd planned a variety of trips for the trail riders, ranging from two hours up to an overnighter at Dead Man's Hut.

'I can drive up the day before and drop off the camping equipment, stock the hut with hay and food, that sort of thing,' Sam had said. 'That's if I can borrow your four-wheel drive.' He'd nodded. Didn't she realise? What was his was hers. 'Then I can tell them the story of how the hut got its name. We can sit around the camp fire swapping ghost stories. It will be magic.' Drew had nodded, though the only magic he wanted to create at that damned hut was with her. He'd spent sleepless nights trying to figure the whole thing out, and had come to the conclusion that he'd simply moved too fast. It was the only possible explanation. Sam's first time, and he'd barged ahead like a bull at a gate. She'd seemed as eager as him, but maybe he'd been wrong. Maybe she needed time to come to terms with it.

His own first sexual experience had been very different — a dangerous liaison in his fifteenth summer with a woman from the local takeaway shop. She was ten years older, and separated from her violent, jealous partner. Looking back, Drew wondered how he'd survived the affair. He'd plummeted head over heels, and would have risked everything for Darlene Darcy. Correction, he did risk everything for Darlene. He nicked station vehicles in the dead of night to drive, unlicensed, into town. Then he crept from her door before dawn, drove home like a madman and climbed back in his window before his parents woke up. He'd risked his father's wrath by stealing whole days with his lover, when he was meant to be fencing or checking on calving cows. He'd risked becoming the target of her estranged husband; a stupid, stalking brute of a man, who randomly and frequently turned up at Darlene's caravan. It had been the most exciting time of his life. Only a return to St Leonards, his Wodonga boarding school, had succeeded in tearing him away. Drew had maintained his passion through sexy texts, professing undying love with his thumb, sending messages through the ether from his dorm room in the early hours.

The crunch had finally come in the form of a newspaper cutting from the Currajong Gazette, sent to him by his sister with a note that read simply, *A wake up call. That could have been you. Love Melinda.* It seemed there'd been a shooting.

'A 33-year-old man is in a serious condition after being shot twice in the back with a rifle on the main street of Currajong. Shane Darcy of nearby Tallangala has been charged with the attempted murder of Kevin 'Bomber' Wilson. It is believed the victim was confronted after being discovered sharing a caravan with the accused man's estranged wife.'

It was funny, looking back. He'd been gutted about Darlene seeing another man. And he'd been mortified that Melinda apparently knew all about his clandestine relationship. But thanks to the folly of youth, he didn't appreciate that he'd literally dodged a bullet. Later on he heard the news that Bomber Wilson was wheelchair-bound for life, a paraplegic. It was only then that the penny finally dropped, and he realised how fortunate he'd been.

He wasn't going to make the same mistake twice. After that disastrous debut he'd been careful to only date girls without prior attachments. There'd been quite a string. Drew liked women and they liked him. Getting them wasn't the problem — it was keeping them. 'The right girl will come along, soon enough,' said his mother. 'Don't be so impatient for it to happen.'

There was a time last year when he'd hoped Charlie might be that girl. They'd grown up neighbours. He'd helped her with the occasional orphan baby, like Jarrang, for instance. But with him off at boarding school and his family holding the Kellys in such low regard, he'd generally had little to do with the pretty tomboy next door. That all changed when he completed his senior year at St Leonards and returned home to be groomed for his career at Kilmarnock.

The first time Charlie had really registered on his radar, Bill had stormed into the kitchen screaming something about goats in the garden. 'I've got an appointment this morning with my accountant.' His face was like a thundercloud. 'Those vermin better be gone by the time I get back from Wodonga,' he'd said, 'or goddam it, I'll use my rifle.'

Drew had wandered outside to find his mother armed with a broom, pursuing a legion of little angora goats around the garden. 'My roses,' she'd wailed, as the mini mops on legs stripped leaves and blooms from stalks with relentless efficiency. 'Drew, do something!'

Drew had unchained Jock, expecting it would be an easy matter for the kelpie to round up the goats and yard them. But he hadn't counted on one thing. Goats don't herd, not like sheep do. The cute creatures had shot off in singles and pairs, at odd angles, in all directions. He'd grabbed a broom and leaped into the fray. The two of them dashed around like mad things, their shouting adding to Jock's excited barking and the goats' indignant bleating. It had taken forever to collect a group in the corner of the chicken yard. But even then they wouldn't stay put. They seemed to have no respect for humans, no fear at all – charging scornfully past all attempts to block them.

It had soon become obvious that this strategy wasn't going to work. Drew had been loath to bring out the big guns. Dad's tough heelers were liable to make mincemeat out of the petite little goats. But if he didn't do something soon, his mother was liable to make mincemeat out of him.

Suddenly a new sound had joined the general cacophony — the sound of pealing laughter. Drew had turned to see a tall, dark-haired young woman watching them, splitting her sides with mirth. She'd looked familiar somehow. But how could he have overlooked such a beauty? Tanned skin like dark honey. Chestnut hair cut like a pixie's, long on top and short around the back and sides. It had emphasised the length of her graceful neck and her almond-shaped eyes. The most mesmerising eyes — like pale, luminous amber, daring you to look away. Could this be the rude, skinny kid from next door, all grown up? The next minute he lay sprawled on the grass, butted from behind by a small sharp-horned goat that packed a big punch.

'Are you hurt?' the girl asked, rushing over.

'Nah, I'm good,' he'd said, picking himself off the ground. But Drew had soon realised that her professed concern was not for him, but for the goat.

'Hammerhead, you naughty boy.' The wayward goats had lined up to be petted and fussed over by this gorgeous girl. Drew had wanted to get in the queue. Then, like she was some sort of modern day Pied Piper, the animals had followed her meekly home.

After that day, Drew and Charlie had become friends. Her mother, Mary, was always coming up with one mad scheme after another. Like all its predecessors, the angora goat stud didn't last long. Mary couldn't afford the shearer. Then the goats got out and chewed their way through a local blueberry crop. The grower had kept the flock as compensation. Two years later he'd established a thriving mohair operation with Mary's goats.

'How come he could make it work, and we couldn't?' Charlie had asked Drew.

He didn't have the heart to tell her. And anyway, he knew that deep down, Charlie already knew the answer. That her mother never put a sustained effort into anything. That she spent too much time drinking and smoking and fooling around with men. That she'd never make a success at anything unless she changed . . . and that she'd never change. Mary just lurched from one disaster to another, all at her daughter's expense.

From what Drew could figure out, the pair had scraped by for the last few years on little more than his dad's lease fees. Why Bill wanted the extra land in the first place was a mystery. Kilmarnock always turned a substantial profit. Drew had walked in on a couple of blazing rows between his parents on just that subject. Mum accusing Dad of wanting to help Mary – although why that should be a problem, Drew still didn't understand. Mum's favourite preacher at church was always urging the congregation to help their neighbours.

The issue had coincided with the collapse of his parent's marriage. Their relationship had always been adversarial. There'd been fighting for as long as Drew could remember. Mum had been feeling increasingly isolated in far-flung Currajong, and Drew supposed that his sisters' move to Sydney was the final straw. She'd left Drew and Bill to battle it out on their own.

Charlie had always had a way with animals, with horses in particular. When Mary sold their horses to pay the rates, Drew had helped Charlie run in a few brumbies and let her keep Tambo for herself. He'd soon spotted Charlie's talent for riding in general, and camp-drafting in particular. Before long she was winning events. She and Tambo caught lifts with Drew and his horse truck to the local competitions. It was a crazy time, a happy time, and he'd fallen hard for Charlie.

But it had been a ruinous romance. Charlie could no more stick with one man than her mother could. Drew had given Charlie a great deal of leeway, suffering a flood of snide remarks and vicious rumours along the way. He'd endured all the gossip that the town could throw at him, and still he'd stuck by Charlie. Stuck by her for months. And then, he'd discovered Charlie and Spike together on the ground, behind the chutes after the Walawai rodeo. More than together …and it was clear it wasn't the first time.

But even this final humiliation hadn't been enough to end his friendship with Charlie. She'd had a tough life, he knew that. Abandoned by her father, neglected by her mother, ostracised by her peers in the town. Of course, Charlie could be her own worst enemy, lashing out at those who tried to help or befriend her. *I'll get you before you get me* seemed to be her chief philosophy. There'd been a couple of other girlfriends since the breakup, but none with Charlie's vitality and spirit – poor carbon copies at best.

Until a miracle had come along. Sam. All of Charlie's beauty, all of her sparkling energy, minus the chip on her shoulder – and with a phenomenal personality of her own. Sam was a girl in a million. If he could just figure out how to get their romance back on track …

Drew pulled off the road into a truck stop, where a cheerful Italian woman was selling flowers from a stall beside a caravan. What were Sam's favourites, he wondered? He picked up an arrangement of natives – scarlet waratahs, flanked by kangaroo paws and bull-rushes. They would have been Charlie's pick, but Sam wasn't Charlie. Drew grabbed a big bunch of red roses as well.

'You want both?' asked the woman. Drew nodded. 'Your sweetheart, she's a lucky girl.'

He gave her a rueful grin and wished Sam agreed with her. Drew drove on, anxious to swing by Brumby's on his way home. He was hanging out to see Sam. A day apart from that girl felt like a week. The Currajong Festival was on this weekend. Was Sam the kind of girl to be impressed by a King of the Mountains title? He wasn't sure, but it was worth a shot. There was one thing he was sure about, however. Nothing and nobody would make him give up on Sam now.

Sam was in the hay shed when Bess bounded in and Drew's head appeared around the door. 'Afternoon,' he said, proffering the bunches of flowers. 'Here I am, reporting for duty.' Sam took them from him, stammered her thanks, then put them aside. He ducked inside, put his hands around her waist and bent his head to hers. The kiss was long enough to stir the butterflies in Sam's stomach, and short enough to leave her hungry for more.

'Don't.' She half-heartedly squirmed from his grasp. 'I'm busy. Thanks to you and your crazy schemes there are about a dozen horses to feed.'

'I'm here to help, aren't I?' He looked briefly irritated. 'Crikey, Sam. You sure do run hot and cold.'

What could she say? He was right, of course. Ever since her sister's surprise phone revelation, Sam was about as confused as a person could be. Drew hadn't changed – keen as ever, helpful, devoted even. He found any excuse to come around. Resisting him took all of her willpower, leaving her frustrated and miserable. Damn Charlie! She'd ruined everything and made Sam's life a misery. The strangest thing was that Drew barely ever mentioned her. When he did, there was no trace of anything but friendly concern in his voice. He was so cavalier that Sam almost doubted Charlie's assertion that Drew was her boyfriend before she left for Melbourne.

Sam had spent a lot of time thinking of ways to suss out the truth of her sister's story. She just couldn't bring herself to ask the question outright. She'd ploughed through all sorts of scenarios, ways to casually raise the topic. She stopped to watch Drew swing a bail over a rail. He moved with an easy grace. She loved the sure sweep of his arm, the angle of his hips. She loved everything about him.

Why on earth couldn't she just come right out with it? Were you sleeping with my sister? If I wasn't here, would you two still be together? Is it me you want, or her? These were the questions she needed to ask, but she was scared she wouldn't like the answers. Scared of looking like a fool. Scared to ruin such a good thing – although it had already been ruined, she thought bitterly.

Her phone rang. Mary. Sam sighed and picked up. 'Hi, Mary . . . Yep, I'm fine, things are good here . . . So Charlie's doing well? . . . When are you coming home? . . . I will. Goodbye, Mary.'

'What's up?' asked Drew. 'How's Charlie?'

Here was her chance. Sam's heart beat faster. She inspected Drew's expression, ready for any trace of deceit. 'What did Mary think,' she asked, 'about you dating Charlie?' There, she'd said it. She wanted to see shock on his face. She wanted him to say that he'd never been with Charlie, and why ever would she think such a stupid thing? She wanted it not to be true — but Drew didn't deny it. He didn't bat an eyelid. He just answered the question, as if it hadn't been laden with hidden meaning.

'Mary hated it when me and Charlie hooked up,' said Drew. 'Beats me why.' He smiled, his green eyes full of humour. He had the most gorgeous smile. 'Bit of a laugh, Mary not approving of me. I reckon it should have been the other way round.'

Sam gulped hard. So Charlie was telling the truth. She was disgusted with herself. What sort of a person hopes to discredit their own sister? If only there was some way to fall out of love with Drew. It really would be so much easier.

CHAPTER 23

Brumbies, Sam had come to understand, were different from other horses in a few fundamental respects. Bushy said it was because they were raised the way horses were meant to be raised, in a herd dynamic, within a settled social structure of equine law and order. Foals stayed with their mothers for a year or more, learning brumby lore, growing up with a firm sense of their own place in the world. 'Those poor little tame horses, I feel downright sorry for them fellas,' said Bushy. 'All that early weaning and not enough mothering – it's a crime.' Sam had learned about attachment disorder in humans. About how the strength of the parent-baby bond affected the emotional health of the child, right through to adulthood. Perhaps it was the same for horses? Perhaps it was the same for her.

A lot of the pampered mounts she'd known back at the Melbourne stables were terribly temperamental – flighty or bossy or downright vicious. By contrast, the wild-caught brumbies were extraordinarily grounded and level-headed. They swiftly embraced their position in the new pecking order. Bushy taught her how to tune into this natural aptitude, how to show leadership but never domination, how to earn the animals' respect. Brumbies treated this way, even high-spirited colts like Phoenix, displayed a touching innocence and willingness to trust. They bonded closely to humans in a way rarely achieved by domestic horses.

Sam rode Phoenix once more around the yard. He was a dream ride: intelligent, spirited and responsive. Pure fire and air. Bushy stood beside the rails, observing the pair with his usual critical eye.

'That'll do,' he said, and Sam brought the colt to a halt. Bushy ran a hand down Phoenix's shoulder and grunted approval. 'You be here by six o'clock sharp tomorrow.' Sam nodded. Tomorrow was the first day of the annual Currajong Festival. It was exciting to be helping with the brumby demonstrations. 'They're trucking in a dozen new horses for the Brumby Catch,' said Bushy. 'I've got a fella coming both days to lend us a hand.'

She dismounted and rubbed the colt's golden neck. 'Do you think he's ready?'

'My oath,' said Bushy. 'He's a smart youngster, that one.'

Sam kissed Phoenix on the nose, and the colt tossed his head at her impertinence. 'Did you say somebody's helping us out tomorrow?'

'Yep. I reckon you already know him. Spike Morgan.'

'Why do we need help?' she said, trying not to squirm. 'What's wrong with me?'

'There ain't nothing wrong with you, girl. You got a hell of a gift with them brumbies.'

'Then why do you want Spike?'

Bushy climbed through the slip rails and took the colt's reins. 'There's a couple of long days ahead of us,' he said simply. 'I could use a top horseman.' For some unaccountable reason he chuckled. 'Go home, Charlie,' he said, and with that he led Phoenix from the yard.

Sam rummaged through the pantry for something to eat. She opened a tin of spaghetti and ate it standing up, cold from the can. Ugh … she threw the empty tin into the sink and dragged herself back outside. There were still so many jobs to do after she'd already worked a full day at the racecourse. Normally she didn't mind. Normally she willingly launched into the feeding and watering: admiring Jarrang's arrogant displays, laughing at Topsy and Turvy's antics, fussing over the pregnant mares.

Evenings used to be her favourite time. When the sun sank low behind the mountain, she'd finish up, wash her hands and cook a simple meal. An omelette or chicken breast, with fresh salad greens and sweet cherry tomatoes picked from Mary's overgrown garden. She'd fill up a glass from the jug of tank water in the fridge; the sweetest, purest water she'd ever tasted – once the wrigglers were strained out, of course. Then she'd eat at the table under the peppercorn tree, sharing her meal with Condor and the occasional bold currawong.

Or Drew would come around and barbecue some steaks. She stopped herself from smiling at the recollection. Ever since that dreadful phone call with Charlie, Drew's absence in the evenings was like a physical ache. It left her empty, hollowed out. But there was no getting around it. Drew had betrayed Charlie, and by extension Sam herself. He'd admitted it, and hadn't even have the good grace to be ashamed. This was an unfathomable, unbearable fact, and the implications were clear. It meant the death of their relationship. What did Drew think about her pulling back from him? She'd never explained herself. Most probably he'd figured out the truth for himself. How could he have slept with her when he was going out with Charlie? It was a bastard act. It would have been easier if she could have made a clean break of it, excised Drew from her life, but she was still bound to him in so many ways. Without his help there could be no future trail-riding business. She couldn't do it alone. Her impulsive purchase of the Mitchell string would turn into one huge folly, a white elephant, a financial albatross around all their necks. She tried to imagine what Mary might say, returning home with a sick daughter to face no lease income, and the added cost of a dozen extra horses to feed.

Sam gulped down a glass of water, headed for the haystack and heaved a bale onto the rusted wheelbarrow. She looked miserably at its flat tyre, then staggered up the hill towards the dam paddock, casting Drew firmly from her mind. She had more pressing problems. Like how on earth she was going to manage things tomorrow, with Bushy calling her Charlie, and Spike calling her Sam? What a mess she'd made of things. Why the hell had she allowed people to believe she was Charlie in the first place? She was an idiot, plain and simple.

Sam tossed biscuits of hay over the fence at regular intervals, and watched the two ponies boss all the bigger horses out of the way. She turned and trundled back down to the hay shed for a second bale. If only she could get Charlie's voice out of her head. *That's my life, not yours!* Drew had accused her of much the same thing. Accused her of being seduced by the adventure of living a double life – of living Charlie's life. Was he right?

Sam hurled the bale onto the wheelbarrow with such force that it tipped over. She could agonise over motives, or she could concentrate on coming up with a plan to fix things. Because like it or not, she was living in a house of cards, and tomorrow was tumbledown day. Then and there she made a resolution to put things straight, no matter what the cost. Because the truth was, Charlie didn't know the half of it. If her sister was upset now, how would she react to the news that Sam had been impersonating her all over town, however innocently it had begun? Sam grimaced. It didn't bear thinking about.

As Sam hauled the hay back into the barrow, she heard a car pull up in the drive. Please no, not Drew. She couldn't bear the prospect of all those *I told you sos*. What right did Drew have to be so sanctimonious? His deception had been far more deliberate, and far more cruel.

'Charlie? Sam? Jesus Christ, which one are you, darlin'?' Spike strolled around the corner, lithe and languorous, like a well-fed tiger. Sam let out a great, relieved sigh. Spike was one of the few people in Currajong with whom she'd been honest, right from the start.

And what was better, he didn't seem to be the type to moralise. 'I'm

Sam!' she yelled. 'Samantha Carmichael. Any resemblance to Charlene Kelly is purely coincidental.'

'That's not what I hear,' said Spike. He smiled seductively. 'Shove over.' Tossing the bale to the ground, he wheeled the empty barrow down to his truck and inflated the tyre using a portable air compressor he found in the tray. 'How's that?' Sam nodded approval. The wheelbarrow now moved with ease.

'Allow me, princess,' said Spike, marching the hay up the hill. 'I heard Charlie bought Terry Mitchell's horses,' he said, as they fed out the second bale. 'Drew's idea?'

'It was me,' she said, in compliance with her new policy of full disclosure. 'Me who bought them, and I signed my true name, but Terry kept on calling me Charlie and I didn't correct the mistake. So shoot me.' She heard the defiant note in her voice. Why was she angry with Spike? None of this was his fault. 'I've left a great many misunderstandings uncorrected,' she said, trying to sound more contrite.

Spike whistled, smooth and low. 'So I figured.' He cast his eyes over her and the horses. 'Not a bad-looking bunch,' he said. 'Now you've got them, what in the world are you gonna do with them?'

Sam ignored the question. 'I gather we'll be working together tomorrow.'

Spike nodded his head, an amused glint in his intense blue eyes. Sam had never seen eyes quite like them before. The colour of cornflowers, with a luminous quality that made you feel like an animal transfixed by headlights. Electric blue. Bedroom blue.

'Don't worry,' he said, and crossed his heart. 'I won't give the game away.'

She held up her palm. 'No, I'm coming clean about everything tomorrow. I'll explain to Bushy, and anybody else that wants to hear, who I am and how things got so out of hand.'

'That'll be a real shame,' said Spike. 'Folks around town are fans of the new Charlie,' he said. 'She's polite, friendly, reliable. She pays her debts. There's been quite a turn-around in public opinion.' He lit a cigarette. 'I wonder if they'll like Charlie's sister as much. Especially when they find out she's been playing them for fools.'

Sam was stunned. She hadn't thought this through. Of course people would feel tricked – betrayed, even. She didn't want that. She liked the people of Currajong, and apparently they liked her too. Marjorie at the general store had popped a few extra rolls and a jar of homemade blackberry jam into Sam's order last week. 'I always make too much anyway,' she'd said, laughing, dismissing Sam's protests. And there'd been two extra bags of oats in the delivery from the produce store. When she'd told George, he'd simply said, 'Don't worry about it. Just keep on doing a good job with those brumbies. I've got a soft spot for the mad buggers.' Harry at the mechanic's shop had repaired a punctured tyre, then refused payment. 'In appreciation for fixing that account up, love, and for giving my young bloke a lift when he missed the bus on Tuesday.' Dozens of little kindnesses, adding up to a community-wide spirit of acceptance. For the very first time Sam felt like she really belonged somewhere. It was a precious thing, something to be protected and treasured, not deliberately cast aside.

Things had been so perfect. Her time in Currajong, in spite of all the difficulties, had been quite simply the happiest time of her life. Free of Mum and all her dreadful expectations. Free of the pressures of school. Living in the true knowledge of who she really was, and where she came from. Perversely, it felt more authentic being Charlie than it had ever felt being herself. Resentment rippled out across the pond of her thoughts. Resentment for her mother, her father, for Mary. And there was no point denying it - a swelling wave of resentment against her sister. Charlie had accused her of stealing a life. What if it was the other way round? What if Charlie had stolen hers? Maybe she was the one who'd been meant to grow up in this beautiful place. Maybe Charlie had been supposed to live with Faith, and because of some stupid mistake when they were babies, they'd been switched. Currajong, Brumby's Run, the horses . . . Drew. Maybe they were all really meant to belong to her?

'I'll help you finish your chores,' said Spike. 'Then I'll take you for a slap-up meal at the pub.'

The matter was apparently settled. Sam hadn't eaten in town before. She'd not wanted to raise suspicions, but anger made her bold

– reckless, even. She wanted to step out with this gorgeous cowboy, wanted to talk and laugh and drink, to socialise. She wanted to have some fun, without always wondering if she'd give the game away. Tonight she'd be whoever the hell she wanted to be. And for one honest, shameful moment Sam wished that Charlie might never come home.

CHAPTER 24

Spike was in one hell of a hurry. He unzipped the swag. 'Take off your boots and get in.' His voice was low and urgent. Sam did as she was told and lay very still. Though wrapped tight in the sleeping bag, she still felt exposed, like the eyes of the world were upon her. Judging from the sound of shouting voices, they soon would be.

This certainly was a crazy competition. Part of the Currajong Festival, it was like some kind of fast-forward day on the farm. 'In the Station Team Muster,' boomed the announcer, 'a team of two people are required to light a fire, boil a billy, cook an egg and eat it, ram in a steel post and take it out again, split wood, tie a sheep, move a hay bale on a bike, and scull a warm beer, all in six minutes flat. Rafferty's Rules apply, which means they are subject to change at any time and the judges' decision is final.'

Sam held her breath, closed her eyes and waited for the swift kick that she knew was coming. Spike would be on the bike, winding his way back through the poles towards her. The shouting grew louder and finally she felt his toe in her ribs. 'Wake up, princess!'

Sam scrambled from the bag, pulled on her boots and used the kindling and newspaper in their box to light a fire. Yes, it flared with the first match. Sam grabbed the billy and plonked it over the flames, almost extinguishing them in the process. She nursed the fire back to life and cracked the egg into the pan.

Sam glanced up. Spike had reached the fence with the hay bale still safely on the motor bike, and was now tying the legs of a ram he'd caught. Close behind him, Drew and another man leaped into the yard and grabbed a sheep each. The fire was going well now. Sam fanned it with her hat. The egg turned white around the edges and the billy began to steam. Spike said the time-saving trick was to roll up the swag once things were cooking. Sam did just that, strapping it together carefully, keeping an eye on the flames at the same time. A quick look at the other teams showed the wisdom of this strategy. Their swags still lay stretched out on the ground while the cooks fussed over their fires.

Spike sped back, skidded his bike to a halt, almost running over the campfire in the process, then attacked the pile of firewood with an axe. He split the timber in a few sure strokes, then rammed the metal post in like a mad man, until it was in the ground up to the white line. The arena rang to the sound of axes and rammers. All the while, officials wandered about, observing the mayhem with clip-boards and serious expressions.

The third team was out of contention. Their sheep had freed itself from the tie and somehow escaped the yard altogether. Sam sneaked a peek next door, where Drew was yanking his steel picket from the ground in one powerful movement. Cords of muscle stood out on his neck and his shirt pulled tightly across his broad back. He was on his bike a few seconds ahead of Spike. She caught herself in a silent cheer. Wait, who was she barracking for, anyway?

Sam lifted the corner of her egg under the watchful gaze of a judge. Good enough. She scraped it onto the slice of bread, and downed the lot in three gulps just as Spike arrived back from untying their sheep. Drew was already sculling the beer, but his cook hadn't finished rolling up their swag yet. Spike drained the content of his can, hurled it to the dust and punched the air in victory. The crowd cheered, and some triumphant country anthem burst from the loud-speakers. After a brief conference, the officials gave the nod, and declared Team Morgan the winner, while a man with an extinguisher wandered about, dousing the camp fires.

'Congratulations,' said Drew graciously as Sam left the arena. His knock-out smile grabbed at her insides. 'I needed you with me.' Sam braced against a swift stab of shame, trying to tell herself that she had nothing to feel guilty about. Drew shot Spike a poisonous glare, then tipped his hat to Sam. 'If you'll excuse me, I'm on next in the whip crack.'

He disappeared into the crowd, one that seemed far too big for sleepy little Currajong. Sam watched him go and couldn't stop her heart from sinking. Why on earth had she teamed up with Spike? For a bit of fun, like he'd said? That was part of it, but not all of it. A piece of her wanted Drew to feel as jealous and lost as she did.

The King of the Mountains Stockman's Challenge was the Melbourne Cup of bush riding, a weekend-long celebration of traditional skills fast disappearing from an increasingly urbanised world. It was uniquely Australian, and the showcase event of the Currajong Festival. Sam could barely wait for it to start. She'd slipped away early that morning to watch the vet, skills and gear checks that were designed to weed out pretenders. Just as well, as the challenge was potentially perilous. A copy of each entrant's ambulance subscription was a compulsory requirement. There was no doubt about it. When it came to a test of superb all-round horsemanship, the Stockman's Challenge was second to none. Bush men and women competed in six gruelling preliminary events, set to challenge even the most talented riders and their horses. The top ten gained a place in the two final events, the Brumby Catch and the Stock Saddle Buckjump. Spike and Drew were top contenders.

All day the pair had behaved like it was a two-horse race; a head-to-head challenge just between them. Spike had issued his own private challenge to Sam. He'd dared her to go on a date with him if he was crowned King of the Mountain. A proper date. Spike uttered the word *proper* in a slow, sexy drawl with an eyebrow raised. The proposition sounded downright dangerous, and left Sam in little doubt about its implications, but she didn't give herself room to think about that. Spike was more than an instrument of revenge. He was a giddy diversion from her disenchantment with Drew. She was living a modern day fairy-tale – a knight jousting for his lady's hand. It was a wild, romantic notion, and as foreign to the old Sam as it could have possibly been.

Sam had spent most of the day helping Bushy out with the brumby demonstrations on the main arena. But it was hard to concentrate on her work with so many marvellous things going on all around her. She couldn't resist ducking off, and the event which really grabbed her attention was the bareback obstacle course. Competitors not only competed without saddles, but collected extra points if they rode just in halters. Horse and rider teams backed over bridges, jumped hedges, wound their way through hanging obstacles and negotiated tyres and gates – all against the clock. They finished with a thirty-second freestyle opportunity to impress the judges.

She'd been lucky enough to arrive in time to see Drew compete. At an invisible signal Clancy had lain down, flat out on the ground, and allowed Drew to crack a stockwhip over his body. This showed more than good training. It was a remarkable trust exercise for both horse and man. However the most spectacular performance of all was Spike's. Exercising perfect control, he cantered his rangy, coffin-headed chestnut around the course without saddle, bridle or halter – revving a chainsaw in one hand. Spike pipped Drew at the post on points. So did Spike's best mate, a pinch-faced, red-headed stockman named Rowdy. Sam frowned as Rowdy spurred his horse past her, hands harsh on the bit. The three of them would go into the next event neck and neck on the scoreboard.

The elegance and discipline of high-school riding seemed a world away from this rough and ready country carnival. Yet it was impossible for Sam not to connect the two. In the course of the practical events, these stock horses routinely performed flying changes, roll backs, spins and stops that would be the envy of any national dressage-squad hopefuls. And just like in dressage, competition was designed to display the horse's athleticism and ability, while exhibiting the rider's horsemanship. It was a reminder to Sam that modern high-school riding had its practical origins in the ancient cavalry. The same skills that lent a horse grace in the ménage also allowed it to twist from the course of a slashing sabre or maintain the precision of a cavalry charge. Leaps into the air, like the capriole, could have cleared entire lines of enemy infantry at once, while momentary halts, like the levante, perfectly positioned riders for well-aimed sword strokes or musket shots.

An announcement blared from the loudspeaker. 'In a few minutes there'll be a brumby handling display in the main arena for all those interested, proudly sponsored by the Brumby Coalition of Victoria.'

Sam raced back to the yards. Spike was already lunging Allawarra, a pretty piebald filly, in running reins and a roller. They were the picture of calm control. Hard to imagine it was only a few weeks since this young horse had first laid eyes on a human being.

'Sorry,' Sam told Bushy breathlessly. 'Everything's just so interesting. Spike was fabulous in the bareback obstacle – you should have seen him.'

'Spike's a bloody good horseman, all right,' he said. 'Now will you get Phoenix ready? Or is that too much trouble?' Sam apologised again. She saddled the colt and mounted, waiting in the wings with bated breath for Spike to finish his mouthing demonstration. It took her right back to her days of performing with Pharaoh in the dressage arena, the heart in her mouth excitement, just before she acknowledged the judges and commenced her round.

'In you go,' said Bushy, as *The Man From Snowy River* theme music started up. Sam took a deep breath, urging Phoenix forward, cantering around the arena and putting him through his paces. She could hear the appreciative oohs and aahs of the crowd. The beautiful golden colt had a special presence, a certain charisma. Phoenix made Sam feel like a star herself, making it easy for her to throw caution to the wind. He made her reckless. Spike and Drew were both watching from the rails, standing opposite each other.

'This stylish little colt was wild caught off the mountain not two months ago,' said the announcer. 'He's a fine example of the temperament and versatility of some of these brumbies. Let's give him and the little lady a hand.'

Phoenix bowed low, then cantered out to an enthusiastic burst of applause. Now Spike drove Bushy's old Holden ute into the ring. The audience wouldn't believe this next stunt. Sam had barely believed it herself when she'd seen it that morning in rehearsal.

Bushy clambered bareback onto Banjo, his black brumby stallion, and they made their entrance. The announcer cranked back into gear. 'Bushy Nandawarra caught this brumby as a ten-year-old stallion, after it had spent years sneaking into his paddocks to get his stock horse mares pregnant.' There was loud laughter from the crowd.

'So what you're seeing here today is a horse that spent the first decade of his life untouched by human hands. He's a real tribute to the disposition of these brumbies, ladies and gentlemen. Banjo is a registered sire with the Brumby Studbook. Those foals by Bushy's stock horse mares, incidentally, are all appendix-registered brumbies now. And I might add they're fetching good prices, and competing nationally in campdrafts and barrel races.'

Banjo had an extensive repertoire of tricks. He could count, play fetch, and answer questions by nodding or shaking his head. He lay down on command, sat up like a dog, and amused children by pulling the saddle cloth off with his teeth every time Bushy turned his back to fetch the saddle. He reared on cue, and even balanced on a tractor tyre while wielding a stock whip held in his mouth. The most amazing trick of all was when Banjo casually jumped onto the tray of the ute, and stood there calmly while Spike drove a lap of honour around the arena. 'This bloke will put float companies out of business!' the announcer said. Bushy and Banjo galloped from the ring to the sound of thunderous applause. It really was an astonishing act.

Next a clown with a performing mule entered the ring to the laughter of children. 'Go on with you,' Bushy said, as Sam looked longingly across the showgrounds. 'I won't need you for a while.' Sam thanked him and dashed off. Past the yabby-burger stand. Through a throng of tiny boys wearing too-big cowboy hats. They already had the swagger. There was still so much on: a tent-pegging display by the

Australian Light Horse Association, a shoeing competition, the cross-country obstacle course. She couldn't possibly see it all. Sam settled down to watch Drew in the Patterson Packhorse, part of the Stockman's Challenge. 'This challenge,' said the announcer, 'shows our younger generation how things were done before the tray-back truck.'

Drew had to load up a packhorse, ensuring the packs were evenly balanced, lead it from Clancy through an obstacle course, maintaining the balance of the load, and then unsaddle – all in a fifteen-minute time limit. He completed the event with ease, and Sam felt a surge of pride.

Spike was next in the line of competitors. He saw Sam at the ropes, dismounted in a single leap and was suddenly beside her. 'A kiss for luck,' he said. Before she knew it his lips had found hers, eager and insistent. When she pulled away Drew stood nearby, watching, face black as thunder. Spike grinned, saluted him and swung back on his horse.

She burned with embarrassment, unable to stand the accusation in Drew's eyes, and slipped off into the crowd. She was playing with fire. The two men were still behaving like personal rivals. It was a competition within a competition, and if she was honest with herself, it was flattering to think she might be the prize. Problem was, she couldn't decide who she wanted to win. Her head was with Spike . . . but her heart was with Drew.

Next up was the stock-handling challenge. Sam watched a man and dog briefly chase some cows around the arena. What was the point of it? A middle-aged woman sitting beside her must have noticed Sam's confused expression. She introduced herself.

'I'm Faye. Is this your first Stockman's Challenge?' she asked. 'You look a bit puzzled.'

'I am,' Sam admitted.

'Shall I explain the rules?'

'Please.'

A new challenger, Rowdy, entered the ring, and Faye talked Sam through the round. 'He leads his horse in and ties it up. Then the five-minute time limit starts.'

'Five minutes for what?' asked Sam.

'He walks over to the yard – that's called the camp – and is scored on cutting out three unmarked steers on foot. If he lets out more than three, or any marked ones, he's eliminated.' Sam noticed that some of the cattle had different coloured splashes of paint on their shoulders or rumps. 'Then he mounts up and signals for his working dog to be released. The rider and dog have to move the steers through the gate and into that little yard.'

A red heeler loped from the pen, eyes trained on the cattle. At a nod from Rowdy, it sank low to the ground and a rough dance commenced between the man and beasts in the arena, all to the staccato beat of a cracking stockwhip. After a few minutes a bell rang, signalling that the competitor had failed to complete the course in his allotted time. Sam flinched when Rowdy surreptitiously kicked his dog.

'Thanks,' said Sam. 'It's much more fun to watch when you know what's going on.'

Faye smiled and patted her hand. 'You look so much like Charlie Kelly, dear. You must be related.'

A shiver ran up Sam's spine. What was she doing, admitting to some random stranger this was her first challenge? Admitting she didn't even know the rules? There seemed nothing for it but to fess up. 'I'm Samantha, Charlie's sister.'

'Lovely to meet you, Samantha,' said Faye. 'I heard you were in town.' She had? Faye pointed to Spike, leading Bailey into the ring. 'That's my son over there.'

Great. Spike had told his mother who she was, after promising to keep her secret. Who else had he told?

'Spike and Charlie used to be … very close.' Faye reached out to pat her hand, but Sam subtly moved it away. Unbelievable. Spike too? Did she have to get everything second hand from her sister? Sam felt the press of people around her like a threat. It had been foolish to come here today.

She excused herself and returned to the yards. Bushy was mixing up feeds. 'I'll do that,' said Sam and snatched his bucket. What on earth had she been thinking? Best stay close to her brumbies and avoid the crowds.

It was harder to avoid Spike, who came strutting over with his self-importance and tight jeans. 'I'm leading on points, honey.' She ignored him, and readied Allawarra for the three o'clock show. Spike broke into a passable rendition of *The Winner Takes It All*.

'Don't you go writing off the competition yet,' said Bushy. 'Drew'll give you a run for your money.'

'I'm ten points ahead of Chandler.' Spike threw Sam his most devastating smile. 'Ready for that date? I've got tickets for Lee Kernaghan tomorrow night.'

'You told your mother,' she hissed beneath her breath, flashing furious eyes at him.

'Told her what?' he asked in a loud voice, sounding genuinely puzzled. Sam shushed him. He shrugged his shoulders and led the filly onto the arena.

When her turn came to ride Phoenix, she pleaded illness. 'I'm dizzy and have a stomach ache. And a headache,' she added for good measure.

Bushy gave her the once-over and looked unconvinced. 'Spike better do it then. Go home and come back in the morning. You're no use to me sick.' He took the reins from her and led Phoenix to the gate.

When Spike finished the mouthing display, he had a quick word to Bushy and sprang onto the golden colt. Sam felt a pang of guilt and stopped to watch. It was clear Phoenix resented the unfamiliar rider. He fought Spike's hands, tossing his head and clenching his jaw to avoid the action of the bit. Their work out may have looked smooth enough to the uninitiated, but to anybody with a modicum of horse sense the tussle between horse and rider was obvious. Phoenix refused to bow on exit, tensing his neck, instead of yielding and flex-ing. When Spike persisted, the colt reared in defiance; a dramatic exit, but not at all what Bushy had intended. Sam rushed over to the sweat-ing, agitated colt, and stroked his neck while Spike dismounted.

'What did you mean,' he asked, 'when you said I told my mother?'

Sam looked around to ensure Bushy wasn't in earshot. 'About me. You told your mother about me.'

'I didn't, I swear.' Spike kicked the dust. 'I didn't tell anybody.'

'Will you get that ute in the ring?' yelled Bushy as he rode past on Banjo.

Spike nodded and extracted a set of car keys from his pocket. 'If my mum knows something, she didn't hear it from me.'

Now Sam was more confused than ever. If Spike was telling the truth, it meant other people in Currajong knew who she was. And if that was true, why hadn't they called her on it? A wave of paranoia washed over her. The crowd applauded Banjo, who was responding to questions with graceful nods or shakes of his head. If only her own questions could be so easily answered. She remembered the poster of Spike on Charlie's bedroom wall, signed with love. Sam breathed deeply and steadied her nerves. What great taste in men she and Charlie had. Go home, Bushy had told her. It was the best advice she'd had in a very long time.

CHAPTER 25

Sunday morning. The snorting, wide-eyed colts for the Brumby Catch made their hesitating way out of the truck and down the cattle ramp. They'd been brought in from Balleroo last spring, turned out into good paddocks and left alone until today. All were fat and fit, perfect for the event to be held later on that day. They clustered at the far end of the yard in the characteristic way of wild horses, presenting a solid row of rumps to onlookers. A call was made over the loudspeaker for the top ten finalists to draw their brumby.

Sam sipped her coffee, bleary-eyed, and watched Drew stride across the arena to the judges. Spike strolled after him. It would take more than one coffee to get her started this morning. She'd spent a sleepless night. How to sleep with so much riding on today's outcome? Drew may be out of bounds, but the truth was she was still in love with him. She'd hated seeing the hurt and anger on his face when Spike kissed her. Did she really want to pursue this thing with Spike? It would be a rebound fling, entered into for all the wrong reasons. But then maybe that was just what she needed.

The announcer was explaining the rules of the Brumby Catch over the loudspeaker. They seemed designed to make success impossible. A brumby colt would be turned loose into the arena from the bucking chutes. The mounted competitor was required to halter the colt and have it leading within two minutes. Two minutes. Impossible. Sam turned to help Bushy with the morning's demonstration. 'Is the catch hard on the brumbies?' she asked.

'It's a darn sight harder on the catcher,' he said. 'I've seen colts break a man's leg with a well-aimed double-barrelled kick, then be back with their heads down, eating hay, just as soon as they're back in the yards.' Bushy bridled Banjo. 'See that bay over there?' He pointed to a neat little horse ridden by a teenage girl. 'One of last year's Brumby Catch colts. I broke him in no worries. Top pony club horse, that one. You couldn't do that with a traumatised horse.'

'So they won't go for meat?'

'Not this lot,' said Bushy. 'All of them fifteen colts already have buyers waiting.' Sam walked back around to get a better look at them. None of the colts were a patch on either Jarrang or Phoenix. What fine studs those two would make.

After the demonstration Sam raced to find a good seat, for the Brumby Catch was about to begin. There was a real buzz of excitement in the stands. The first colt had a surprising turn of speed and outran Rowdy. His brief time was up without him even getting close with the halter.

The second colt demonstrated what Bushy had said about the event being tough on the catcher. The big chestnut considered offence to be the best form of defence, and spent the time doing handstands, his hind feet lashing out with such ferocity that he was soon back in the yards. The competitor was allowed a reserve draw. His second brumby wasn't much better, flattening ears and snapping at the unlucky rider's horse, who was understandably loath to get too close. The challenger exited the ring for the second time with no score.

Drew was up next. His colt was fast, but Clancy was faster, maintaining pace with the brumby, shoulder to shoulder. Within the allotted time and to Sam's utter astonishment, Drew managed to drop the halter over the colt's head and lead it in triumph around the arena. It was a peerless display of horsemanship – or so she thought.

Then it was Spike's turn. He'd drawn a tough black with a wicked temper. Sam now appreciated that Bailey, Spike's ugly, square-headed horse, was miles better than he looked. He dodged a barrage of nasty kicks and courageously remained neck and neck with the surly brumby. Spike had the black haltered and led off the arena with time to spare. No other contestants completed the challenge. Spike and Drew had rocketed to the top of the points table.

The grey brumby huddled at the far end of the stock contractor's yard. Sam dreaded the prospect of seeing the mare buck, and her nerves were raw. Drew slipped in beside her at the rails, and she jumped like a startled colt. 'That horse is named Demon now,' he said. 'Rowdy's drawn her in the buckjump. Already got herself a reputation, apparently.'

'Demon?' Sam shook her head. 'Can't we do something? She looks so miserable.' The other horses appeared relaxed enough, resting hind feet, nibbling at hay, pretty much ignoring the spectators. By contrast the grey was the picture of tension: erect ears, high arched crest, muscles taut in neck and jaw.

'No, *we* can't,' said Drew. 'Why don't you ask Spike to help you?' He marched off towards the bucking chutes. It didn't matter. Sam wasn't barracking for him anymore, or for Spike either, for that matter. She was barracking for Demon.

Sam hoisted herself up and perched on a top rail, with a good view of the horses being run into the laneway. 'Riders must use the same saddles they've used during previous challenge events,' boomed the announcer. 'Riders must stay on for eight seconds and crack their stockwhip at least once.' Eight seconds? That wasn't long. Maybe this wouldn't be so bad after all. 'Judges award equal points for riding skill, and for degree of difficulty of the bronc.'

It jarred to hear the lovely brumby being referred to as a bronc. The grey didn't belong here. A month ago she'd been living wild and free on the range. Then by some random twist of fate she'd ended up a bucking horse. She might have escaped, or gone to Ryan. She might have been gently tamed and found a loving owner. Was the mare's story so different to Sam's own? Mary had sent her away from where she belonged, away to live with Faith. It had changed who she was. Yes, she and the brumby mare were common victims of a haphazard, indifferent universe. The futility of it all sickened her.

Sam had never seen a saddle-bronc competition before. The first horse to enter the chute was liver chestnut with a wild eye. Drew appeared, carrying a simple hackamore that bore a broad leather noseband and rope lead. He climbed the rail and slipped the head-gear onto the gelding. Next came his saddle, fitted with a curious back cinch. A leather strap lined with sheepskin was fitted around the horse's ticklish flanks. Drew lowered himself into the saddle, wearing nothing on his head but a stockman's hat.

Sam closed her eyes at the foolish irony of it all. Riders of the little motorbikes in the novelty Stockman's Muster had all worn safety helmets. So had the cross-country competitors. But in this most dangerous challenge of all? Of course not. They wouldn't want to spoil their macho image, would they? Someone handed Drew his stockwhip and he signalled for the gate. Sam was sick with fright.

The gelding's mouth yawned wide, and he exploded from the chute in a bone-jarring succession of high, stiff-legged leaps. It was a primal scene – man against beast. Eight seconds suddenly seemed like a very long time indeed. Drew clutched the rope in his left hand, raised the stockwhip high in his right, and the arena rang with whip cracks. In spite of her fear, Sam found herself cheering along with the crowd. Drew seemed to retain his balance by magic, adjusting his body as if he could anticipate his mount's every move. It was an amazing display of horsemanship. Sam felt sure she'd have been unseated by the first buck. A horn sounded and the pickup rider sprang into action, cantering beside the bucking horse, allowing Drew to grab his saddle and jump clear. Sam felt weak with relief and pride.

Surprisingly, the gelding continued to buck after Drew stood safely back on the ground. The pickup rider caught the horse's rope rein, leant down and released the flank strap. Only then did the gelding calm down. So, it wasn't the rider that the bucking horses objected to. It was the flank strap.

'And he's made eight seconds, so let's have a big hand for Drew Chandler riding Nightstalker.' Sam joined in the applause. A gust of unseasonably cold wind caught up willy willies of dust and chased them across the arena, causing people to grab their hats. Sam shivered, buttoning her shirt right up to the neck, and pulling her cuffs over her hands. Spike sat on the rails of chute number two, above a powerful paint horse with a hogged mane. The loudspeaker crackled so much that Sam missed the beginning of the announcement. All she caught was, '... Spike Morgan riding Switchblade.'

Spike tossed away his cigarette, settled in the saddle and fixed his stirrups firm under the arch of his heels. The horse reared and launched itself at the fence, knocking a man off the walkway. Spike kept his seat. At a nod the gate swung wide. For a few moments Switchblade stalled and just stood there, to the amusement of the audience. Then he dropped his head to the ground and erupted from the chute. The horse didn't so much buck as do full handstands, flinging his hind legs above his head past the vertical axis. He bucked so hard and high, it was a miracle he didn't flip right over.

Spike was unbalanced and in trouble from the start. He managed one crack of his whip before Switchblade spun like a top and pitched him over his left flank. As Spike's right foot flew over the saddle, its spur somehow caught on the cantle, leaving him hanging head down, while the horse bucked and plunged. There was a loud gasp from the crowd. Sam grimaced and held her breath as Switchblade cannoned into the fence. Spike wrapped his arms around a post and hung on with grim strength. He jerked his leg free and collapsed to the dust, while the pickup man reached for the horse's rope.

Spike was okay, but he hadn't made his ride. Sam thought it through. He and Drew had been top of the leader board, equal on points, and the buckjump was the last event. That meant the Challenge was now a dead rubber. Drew had won — he was King of the Mountain. Sam sighed. She'd been kidding herself, thinking that she didn't mind who won. The rush of pride and relief she felt at the result told her that.

The loudspeaker crackled into action. 'What a terrific bucking horse this big paint is. Unfortunately Spike hasn't stayed aboard for his full eight seconds. Let's give a big hand for Switchblade.' The crowd whooped and cheered. Spike staggered to his feet and limped from the arena for a medical check. Sam could see her grey mare in chute three, with red-headed Rowdy already in the saddle.

'Next up is Demon, nicknamed The Four-legged Fury.' Demon. Sam wanted to shoot whoever had given the lovely brumby such an awful name. 'Demon has just been bucking for a few weeks, but already this mighty mare has a fearsome reputation. Some horses buck hard and some buck fast, ladies and gentlemen – and Demon does both. Fact is, nobody has so far scored a ride on her.' The mare flung her head around. Sam winced as it slammed into the steel pipe of the chute. 'This horse hasn't come through the Born to Buck program like many others here. She's a genuine brumby. Let's see if Rowdy Clarke can take on Demon today and win.'

The mare reared sideways and Rowdy leaped onto the fence to avoid being crushed. With ears flattened and teeth bared she lunged at him. Men scattered and Rowdy dodged. Easy now, Sam whispered. Take it easy. Back in the saddle, Rowdy gave the signal. Horse and rider exploded from the chute to the deafening strains of *We are the Champions*.

The mare sprang skywards like a spring released. Back arched like a cat, stiff-legged and finishing with a wicked twist. She was a fearful sight. But when she crashed back to earth, Rowdy was still in the saddle. He cracked his whip and spurred in time with her bucks, raking her from shoulder to flank. She foamed at the mouth and launched herself back into the air, screaming. Sam had never heard a horse make such a noise before and was unaware they could. It was a bloodcurdling, devilish sound that set Sam's teeth on edge.

Lightning cracked above the arena, and thunder rumbled in the throat of the darkening sky. The mare ducked and dived. She swiv-elled and spun. She ruined Rowdy's rhythm, sunfished right, then left, always landing with unforgiving, bone-jarring force. The heavens opened to lashing torrents of rain, turning the dusty arena into an instant mud pit. Rowdy was flying high out of the saddle and in trouble. Sound the horn, for God's sake! This was killing them both. Rowdy collided with the ground and lay winded where he fell. 'And The Four-legged Fury remains unridden,' boomed the announcer over the storm. 'Give this great bucking horse a big hand, ladies and gentlemen. And another one for our courageous cowboy.'

The crowd applauded as a pickup man closed in on the brumby mare. He took hold of her trailing rope, leaned down and released the flank strap. Sam breathed a sigh of relief, and shielded her face from the blinding rain. She could barely see now. Jumping off the rail, she sought shelter beneath the cattle ramp, a position that offered a good view of proceedings. Water and bulldust mixed to muck in her eyes. She wiped it away and turned her attention back to the arena. Rowdy still lay, a soggy heap on the ground near the fence, only a metre or two away. He groaned, looked around for his hat and waved the stockwhip to show that he was okay. The crowd cheered encouragement.

Sam frowned and focused her attention back on the brumby mare. Something wasn't right. It showed in the white of her eye, the angle of her ears, the set of her jaw. A chill ran down Sam's spine and she shrank back from the fence. The mare suddenly whirled and let fly with both hind feet, connecting hard with the tender flank of the pickup horse. It reeled and staggered, losing its footing on the slick surface. The pickup man dropped the halter rope and jumped clear of his horse as it skidded sideways and landed in the mud. In the driving rain it was every man for himself, as the crowd dashed for cover. Nobody seemed to be taking much notice of the mare any more.

The grey spun round and advanced on Rowdy in a series of half rears. He lurched to his feet and cracked the whip in the mare's face. It was then that Demon attacked. She charged at the man with striking hoofs, eyes blazing with hatred, and knocked him to the ground. Rowdy ducked and rolled, but the mare was too fast. Taking aim, she slammed the full force of both forefeet into the back of his head. Was it Sam's imagination, or did she hear the sickening crunch of bone?

The mare snorted, seemingly satisfied with the job, and cantered to the exit. A boy opened the gate and she trotted to join the other horses. It was only now that people seemed to realise the gravity of what had happened. An army of people converged on the fallen man. Two ambulance officers waved them away and knelt to examine Rowdy. Two women ran over with a canvas tarpaulin and held it like an umbrella over the paramedics while they worked. Sam watched, unable to move, horrified and fascinated all at once. Somehow she knew already that Rowdy was dead.

Sam sat in Drew's truck, his oilskin around her shoulders. 'It wasn't the mare's fault,' she said, eyes blurry with tears. 'They drove her to it, they drove her mad.'

Drew shook his head. 'Maybe,' he said. 'But everybody saw what happened.' He handed Sam a coffee. 'That was no accident. '

'It was self-defence, that's what it was,' protested Sam. Drew didn't comment. 'What will happen now?' Her hands were shivering too hard to hold her coffee, so she put it down on the dashboard.

'I spoke to Wayne Clarke,' he said. 'The man's absolutely gutted. Rowdy was his nephew.'

'No,' she said. Could it get any worse?

He nodded. 'They thought they were onto a winner with that mare. She bucked like bloody Curio.'

'Curio?' asked Sam tearfully.

'A legendary grey bucking mare. She featured at the Marrabel Rodeo, way back in the fifties. Unridden for eight years. They say she only worked for five minutes in her whole life. Got those cowboys off with just one buck.' Rain was sneaking in on an angle through a narrow crack at the top of the window. Drew wound it up all the way. 'A horse like that would be worth a fortune these days.'

'Well, our grey isn't Curio,' said Sam, 'and five minutes more of that kind of work would be enough to kill her.' She reached for the coffee and took a trembling sip. 'I asked you what's going to happen.' Drew avoided looking at her. 'Just tell me!' she shouted, furiously wiping away tears.

'She's going to the knackery in the morning.'

Sam slammed her coffee onto the dashboard and ran from the car into the pouring rain. Drew sprinted after, both of them slipping in the mud. He caught her in a fierce embrace. They stood that way, still as statues, for the longest time. Water streamed from their conjoined bodies in rivulets, like flooded creeks off Maroong Mountain.

Was it dark enough yet? Drew pulled the curtains apart and gazed into the night as he heated the milk. Damn — he snatched the saucepan from the stove just as it boiled over. Sam sat slumped on the frayed couch in front of a cheap bar radiator, inconsolable, wrapped in a blanket. Her bare shoulder poked out, pale and smooth, bisected by a black bra strap. He couldn't stop looking at it, fought against kissing it.

'I helped catch her,' Sam managed between shuddering sobs. 'She was beautiful and free and happy, and what did I do? I helped hunt her down, helped sell her to the rodeo, helped send her to the slaughterhouse. They should shoot me too.'

Drew concentrated on the task at hand, tipping milk from the saucepan into two cracked mugs, splashing plenty onto the bench. Bess wagged her tail and lapped up the warm liquid trickling to the floor. Drew stirred in spoonfuls of Milo and some extra sugar to boot, then handed a mug to Sam. She shook her head and turned from him. He put down the cup, pulled her around, forced her to face him.

'Listen to me — they won't kill that horse,' he said with more determination in his voice than he felt.

She blinked back tears. 'Why? What do you mean?'

'Stop crying, drink this, and I'll tell you.' He shoved the Milo into her now compliant hands. 'Drink it.'

Sam took a big gulp, then another. 'Why won't they kill her?' she asked in a voice raw with weeping.

'Because I won't let them. Finish that drink and get into some dry clothes.' He wet his lips with his tongue. 'We're going to steal her back.' Sam's eyes grew large and her mouth fell open. In an instant she was in his arms, soft lips pressed against his. Drew felt a familiar ache in his groin as his fingers traced the soft hollow of her hip. He forced himself to pull away. 'Do you want to do this, or not?'

She granted him one more melting kiss, then ran from the room to get changed. Drew drained his mug of Milo, wanting something stronger. He searched the kitchen cabinets for liquor. Nothing. A framed picture of Charlie riding Tambo lay face down in the cupboard. He examined the girl in the photograph, marvelling at how much she looked like Sam. Hadn't the picture been displayed on the sill last time he'd been here? Why had Sam put it away like that? He slammed the cupboard door shut when he heard Sam in the hall.

'I'm ready,' she announced, a shining, expectant smile on her face. 'What next?'

Good question. Bess shoved her nose between them. He put down a blanket and chained the dog to the table leg. 'You stay here, girl.' He offered Sam an oilskin coat. 'Wear this. It's my sister's.' Sam pulled it on. Drew struggled to open the door against the driving rain. 'Come on,' he said. 'We've got some horse rustling to do.'

It was past midnight when the cattle truck laboured through the rain, back up the rutted track to Brumby's Run. What little gravel there might once have been had been washed away in this deluge. The road ran like a river. Drew tried to angle the truck towards the cattle ramp, and almost lost control as the wheels skidded sideways in the mud. He braked and swore. 'If I try to get any closer, we'll slide down the hill and roll.'

'Well, we'll just have to unload her here then,' said Sam. Sure. Just slip a halter on the mad bugger and lead her down the ramp. 'I'm naming her Whirlwind,' said Sam happily, her face alight in the dim dashboard glow.

The truck shook as the mare reared and kicked. Drew figured the name suited her. Lunatic would have suited her better. What a nightmare it had been, trying to load that horse in the rain and dark. She'd been conveniently yarded on her own, right next to the loading ramp, ready for the doggers to pick up in the morning. And he'd taken his dad's two heelers along for good measure. Those dogs were tough enough to tackle wild scrubber bulls straight from the bush. *How hard could one brumby mare be?* he'd thought. He'd thought wrong.

Jasper whined and wagged his tail. Sam stroked him where he lay on the floor at her feet. 'Will he be okay?' she asked.

'I reckon she's broken his leg,' said Drew grimly.

'It wasn't her fault,' said Sam. 'She was scared.' Scared? They were the ones who should be scared. Whirlwind plunged about in the back and the whole truck rattled.

'Let's get her out, then,' he said, not quite knowing how this was going to work. They climbed from the cabin, shielding their faces from the blast of wind and rain. Drew slipped on a head torch, but its beam was swallowed by the rain a few feet from his face. Why the dickens couldn't the weather give them a break? With a spiteful crack of thunder, the wind redoubled its fury. The one saving grace was that the storm had covered their tracks back at the racecourse.

Drew assessed the situation. It was just as he feared; the truck was a good ten metres short of the yard. There was only one option, one he'd prepared for as a last resort. Drew grabbed his catching ropes and climbed up on the truck. He could hardly see. Just as well she was pale grey and not black. He considered himself a good aim, but it was extraordinarily difficult to throw the noose over a moving, snaking target in the dark and the storm. It didn't help that the horse seemed intent on killing him at the same time.

It was only when Jarrang caught wind of his daughter, and announced his pleasure with a trumpeting neigh that Drew got his chance. Whirlwind froze at the sound. Drew seized the opportunity to cast one, then two ropes over her head. Moments later she erupted in a rearing fury, but by then it was too late. He had her. Drew pulled the Lewis winch out from under Sam's feet, and heaved the chainsaw from the rear of the cabin. Opening the gate, he anchored the winch's snatch block to a large strainer post at the back of the yard.

Sam appeared beside him. 'What are you doing?' she asked anxiously.

'Yarding your horse for you.' He retrieved a length of chain from the floor of the truck and fixed it to the ropes around Whirlwind's neck. Then he attached the winch cable to the chain and started the saw. Its savage snarl joined the roar of wind through the forest. Sam pulled at his sleeve. Drew turned off the saw and handed Sam a torch. 'Point it here, will you.' Why on earth hadn't he taken the bar off at home? Fitting the adapter in the dark was just about impossible. 'Hold these, put them in your pockets or something.' He handed Sam an assortment of washers and nuts. Finally it was done. The chainsaw's power block was bolted fast to the winch.

The penny must have finally dropped for Sam. 'You can't!' she yelled urgently, struggling to compete with the screaming wind. 'She hasn't even got a halter on. She'll choke to death.'

'Got any better ideas?' he snapped, regretting his words as soon as they were uttered. 'Look,' he said, in what he hoped was a more conciliatory voice. 'We can't get the truck close enough to unload her straight through the gate. If we unload her out here without the winch, we'll never hold her. She'll go bush, and the first bugger to find that mare will either give her a bullet or run her in for the doggers. Wayne's bound to post a reward.' She might have been crying again, but it could have just been the rain. He tried to sound more encouraging. 'Those ropes have got big leather eyes so they can't pull too tight, you know that. It might not be pretty, but I guarantee I'll get that horse into the yard, safe and sound.' Sam turned, and stared at the truck. 'I can let her go instead if you want,' he said.

'No,' she said at last. She turned to face him. 'What do you want me to do?'

'Just close the gate once she's through.'

Sam nodded. Drew fired up the chainsaw motor and the winch ground into action. When it had taken up most of the slack in the cable, he lowered the ramp. Whirlwind was huddled at the back of the truck. She didn't react when the ropes first grew taut, but as the pressure increased, she began to fight. The indifferent, galvanised cable maintained its inexorable pull. It tightened around the mare's throat, dragging her, choking the fight from her. She took a step forward, then another, her exhaustion showing. Jarrang neighed again and Whirlwind finally capitulated. She stumbled into the yard.

Sam yelled with delight and rushed to close the gate. Drew heaved a great sigh of relief. He ran to shut off the motor and release the catching ropes from the winch cable. Drew shone the torch into the yard. Whirlwind stood drooping and defeated in the corner. The two nooses had loosened, now the strain was off. It would be safe to leave them on overnight.

'She's shivering,' said Sam, wiping streams of water from her eyes. 'She needs a rug.'

Drew shook his head. 'That horse doesn't need a rug. She needs some peace.' And so do I, he thought, feeling a little sick at what he'd done. He pulled Sam into the truck cabin out of the rain. 'Leave her alone until morning,' he said. 'Promise me?'

Sam nodded. 'I can't believe we did it. Thank you.' She softly kissed his wet cheek.

Drew's skin tingled where Sam's lips had touched it. 'I can't believe it either. Now let's just hope we don't get caught.' There was no way to hide the horse. By a stroke of good fortune, the yards at Brumby's Run were set well back, not visible from the house. But if anybody bothered to come looking, they'd find her. No point worrying about that now, though. It was done, the die already cast. 'I'm going to pack up the winch,' he said. 'Then can we please go inside and get dry for the second time tonight?'

'Of course, your Majesty, Mr King of the Mountain. Yes, we can.' Sam threw her arms around his neck and kissed him properly this time. She radiated warmth and happiness right through her soggy clothes, and he remembered why he'd embarked on this ridiculous escapade in the first place. Maybe she was finally ready to try again with him.

Drew extracted himself reluctantly from her arms and jumped out to get the winch. A soft nose nuzzled his hand. 'Bess? What are you doing out here?' Hadn't he left her in the kitchen? Drew stowed the gear back in the truck, hopped in and started the engine, trying not to step on Jasper in the process. The back wheels spun wildly for a few moments, then somehow gained traction. Thank goodness it was a downhill run to the house.

Drew rounded the hay shed, then slammed on the brakes. The headlights' beam revealed a car parked in the drive. Sam glanced up at him, an expression of horror on her face. Drew put his finger to her lips and shushed her with a whisper. He killed the lights and slipped from the cabin.

It was difficult to see in the dark, but he didn't think he recognised the car. One of those generic Japanese things, a Honda or Suzuki or something. Bess stood on the porch, tail aloft and waving. Why wasn't she barking? The dog ran right up to the back door, and with one scratch of the paw, she was in. Drew jumped back in the truck and parked it out of sight behind the hayshed. 'There's somebody in the house,' he whispered to Sam. 'Stay here.'

'I'm coming with you,' said Sam firmly. She jammed her hat further down on her head and hopped out.

'At least let me go first.' She fell in behind him, and they approached the rear windows. There was a lull in the storm. The shadow of a figure showed through the kitchen blind. They moved around to the front porch. But as Drew reached for the handle, the door opened. It was Charlie.

CHAPTER 27

Sam didn't know what to think. Competing emotions made her dizzy. She should be very happy, and she was — in a way. Thankful, certainly, to see Charlie looking so much stronger, although she still had a kind of frail, elfin beauty about her; still looked wrong somehow outside of a hospital setting. Her eyes had grown elegant brows and lovely long lashes. Her hair was an inch or more in length now over her head. If you didn't know she'd been bald, it might have looked like she had a stylish crop, one designed to bring classic definition to her features. It was a great comfort to see this beautiful, healthy version of her sister. But with a jolt, Sam recognised that happiness wasn't on the top of her emotional scoreboard. Disappointment, jealousy, guilt, resentment – these were the clear winners. Charlie's face had filled out, and their resemblance was more disconcerting than ever. Sam was looking into a distorted mirror.

'Aren't you going to say anything?' said Charlie.

Sam pushed past Drew and briefly embraced her sister, feeling meat on her bones for the first time. 'This is such a surprise,' said Sam, meaning *why didn't you ring first?* Charlie started to softly sob. Sam gathered her up in sodden arms, filled with a sudden, fierce, protective love that hunted away all her negative feelings. 'Tell me what's wrong.'

'I got so fed up in Melbourne,' said Charlie, sniffing back tears. 'Honestly, I couldn't stand it for one more minute. What's the point of beating cancer if that shitty city is just going to kill me anyway?' Sam stayed silent and let Charlie talk. 'I've had some terrible fights with Mum. She never gets off my back: don't do this, don't do that. And she's got this new boyfriend. They get stoned all the time.'

Sam couldn't reconcile Charlie's portrait of Mary with that of the woman she'd known in Melbourne. The woman always by her daughter's side, who bought her beautiful headscarves that she clearly could not afford. The woman who concocted homemade herbal remedies, with mother's love as the main ingredient. Sam stroked Charlie's hair. It had the silky-smooth texture of a Siamese cat. She made soothing noises, holding her sister close.

'Come on, you two,' said Drew, 'Get inside. I'll light the fire.' Sam sat Charlie down in the kitchen. Drew caught Sam's eye. Get into dry clothes,' he said. 'You'll be no good to anybody with pneumonia.' Drew was right, she was shaking; whether from cold or emotion, she couldn't tell. Sam ran to the bedroom, threw off her wet things, climbed into pyjamas and tore back down the hall with a mohair rug.

Charlie was sitting at the kitchen table. Drew had a blaze going in the hearth, but she was still shivering. Sam put the blanket round her sister's shoulders. 'Does Mary know you're here?'

Charlie shook her head. 'I finally spat the dummy, and Mum said that if I'd made up my mind, she'd drive me home. She just had to say goodbye to Carlos first . . . she'd only be an hour.' Charlie's eyes blazed with a furious indignation that had chased away any hint of tears. 'Five hours later,' she held up the fingers of a hand for emphasis, 'and she's still not back. Nice one, Mum. So,' she shrugged, 'I drove myself. Mum probably doesn't even know I'm gone.'

So Charlie had driven alone for seven hours, in shocking weather without a licence. Sam was aghast. She'd left her phone behind that morning. Where was it? There, behind the bread. She quickly checked it – five missed calls from Mary and a dozen messages.

'Oh, I think she knows,' said Sam, still reeling from Charlie's sudden appearance. Drew held up the kettle behind Charlie's back, and she nodded for him to put it on.

'I'm a good driver,' protested Charlie, 'and I didn't see one single copper.'

'Thank goodness for that,' said Sam. Charlie yawned. 'Now let's get you something to eat, and then get you to bed.' Sam winced — she was sounding like her mother. 'We'll talk more about it in the morning.'

'I'm not sleepy yet,' said Charlie, like a petulant child. She stood up and looked into the little lounge room. 'The house looks so beautiful and clean. I've never seen it like this.'

Sam swelled with unexpected pride. 'Sleep in Mary's room,' she said. 'You might be more comfortable.'

'No,' said Charlie. 'I've been dreaming of my old bed, my old room.'

Drew placed mugs of tea in front of them. Sam slipped down the hallway and quickly inspected Charlie's bedroom. The posters on the wall, the frogs, the cast-iron bed frame – these were the only original things about it. Sam had bought a new mattress, new bedding, new curtains. She'd painted the grimy walls, and scattered bright rugs over the stained carpet. Charlie's frog collection was displayed on shelves made from bricks and planks, and brightened up with pretty throws. Drew had donated the simple colonial wardrobe with the lovely etched-glass mirror that now stood in the corner. It had been languishing in a Kilmarnock shed for a decade, apparently, ever since his mother refurbished the bedrooms.

Sam had used the old dressing table and wardrobe for firewood. She switched on the antique lamp that stood on the two-drawer timber bedside table, both pieces she'd found at Tallangala's sprawling secondhand-dealer's yard. She smoothed the bedspread, accented with gum-leaf motifs in rich red and green. Frogs featured in the pattern and were embroidered on the pillow cases. What if Charlie didn't like it? It seemed insane to her now, to have tampered with the bedroom without permission.

Charlie appeared in the doorway and Sam held her breath. A stunned look grew on her sister's face as she gazed around. 'It's gorgeous.' Charlie walked about the room, feeling textures, opening drawers. She bounced on the bed, grinning broadly. 'It's like I'm on one of those home makeover shows.'

Sam heaved a relieved sigh. 'I'm glad you like it.' She sat down on the bed beside her sister. 'Are you really well enough to be here? Shouldn't you be near your doctor?'

'I told you, I can't stay in bloody Melbourne. It's driving me insane.'

Drew stuck his head around the corner. 'Supper's up.'

Charlie looked curiously from Drew to Sam. 'Has Drew been . . . helpful?' Sam nodded and smiled, a little too brightly. What was Charlie implying? And for that matter, why weren't Drew and Charlie acting like a couple, if that's what they'd been? She stood up and opened the curtain. Was her face flushed with guilt? Perhaps the cold air by the window would help.

'Sammy?' Charlie hadn't called her that before. Something in the tenderness of her sister's voice broke her heart.

'Let's have that supper,' Sam said briskly, hurrying from the room. In the kitchen they found plates of toasted sandwiches oozing melted cheese, and mugs of Milo.

'Whose car?' asked Drew.

'Mine,' said Charlie. 'Something peculiar's been happening. Somebody's sending me and Mum money. Lots of money. Then this car arrives, registered in my name, with an unsigned *Get Well Soon* card taped to the windscreen.'

'That's crazy,' said Sam, hot cheese squishing out of the corner of her mouth. 'Any idea who?'

'Nope. Mum reckons it must be one of her old lovers made good. Maybe even my dad.' That would be my dad too, thought Sam. It was odd and kind of exciting. A mystery father, showering gifts on Charlie. With a twinge of envy she realised that if this anonymous benefactor was her real father, he may not even know that a second daughter existed.

'Fair dinkum?' said Drew. 'That's some story. You sure Mary didn't just harvest a dope crop or something?'

'No,' said Charlie. 'I'm not sure. Anything's possible with Mum.'

'Why would you say something like that?' asked Sam.

'A few years ago, Drew and I were mustering calves out of the Snake Creek flats,' said Charlie. 'We came across this bloody huge cannabis plantation, half in Brumby's, half in the park. Mum had a real champion of a boyfriend back then. What was his name?'

'Clint,' said Drew, taking the last sandwich.

'Yeah, Clint. What a lowlife. Anyway, Drew and me ripped up the lot and burned it.'

Drew laughed. 'Took us two whole days.'

'We had to stand upwind or get stoned ourselves,' said Charlie. 'You should have seen Clint's face when he discovered the crop was gone. He blamed this mate of his. They got in a fight, Clint got arrested and we never heard from him again.'

Sam was staggered. She wanted to say something, to defend Mary, to demand evidence that she was complicit in Clint's scheme. But what right did she have to even hold an opinion on the past? The story was an unwelcome reminder that she was an outsider here at Brumby's Run. Drew, Charlie, the bush, the town – they shared a history from which she was forever excluded. It was too painful to contemplate.

'If you don't mind, I'm going to bed,' said Sam. 'It's been a big day.' Charlie raised her exquisite new eyebrows, requesting an explanation. 'Drew will fill you in,' said Sam. Of course he would. No doubt they had lots to catch up on. She gave Charlie a hug, and hurried down the hall to her room. No, it was Mary's room. She was just visiting. For the first time in a long time she thought about Faith, about Dad and her grandparents. She thought about university. She'd deferred her course, but now she wasn't so sure that had been a good idea.

Sam could hear low voices in the kitchen still, murmuring, reconnecting. She squeezed her eyes shut and shoved her head beneath the pillow. Sam drifted into troubled sleep, confused about Charlie, desolate about Drew, and trying without success to block out the looming memory of Rowdy Clarke's face.

CHAPTER 28

Charlie had slept on and off for almost twenty-four hours. Each time she'd woken, the sweet, familiar sounds of the bush had lulled her back to sleep. The laughing call of a kookaburra, the distant bellow of a bull, the high roar of wind through the forest — and best of all the dusk to dawn chorus of frogs in the dam. On the second day she'd risen early, rested and restored, just in time to see Sam off to work. Charlie stood out on the porch. She munched a piece of toast and waved goodbye, looking longingly after her sister's car. There'll be time enough, Sam had said, for you to take back the job with Bushy. You're not strong enough yet for a full day's work. Sam was right, although Charlie hated to admit it. Even showering left her spent. She turned back to face the house. The homestead had been transformed, inside and out; gardens weeded, rubbish gone – the front door even sported a fresh coat of paint. It looked fantastic, but the place no longer felt like her own. What on earth was she supposed to do all day? Everything was already done. A sudden movement up at the yards caught her eye and she went to investigate.

The lovely grey mare was not friendly at first. She'd rushed at Charlie with ears pinned back, and threatened her with wicked hoofs. Charlie had studiously ignored her. She'd armed herself with a bag of sliced fruit and a book, put a plastic picnic chair in the middle of the yard, and calmly sat down to read. It hadn't taken long for Whirlwind's curiosity to overcome her caution. Soon she was snuffling the chair, snuffling Charlie, nibbling at the fruit. Charlie had slipped her a piece of apple, and popped another piece absentmindedly into her own mouth. 'Listen to this.'

She read to Whirlwind every day for a week. On the eighth day she tried something different. The mare was standing beside her with twitching ears, while Charlie read to her from Edward Abbey's *Desert Solitaire*.

'Am I boring you?' she asked after a while. The answer, apparently, was yes. Whirlwind's head had drooped. A hind hoof was at rest. Her bottom lip quivered and her eyes were half-closed.

'Let's do something else,' said Charlie. The mare woke with a start and followed her over to the gate. Charlie opened it. 'Come on, then.' She began walking up the hill to the dam. 'Field observation time. You can be my assistant.' Whirlwind stood stock still for a few moments, as though she couldn't quite believe her luck. Then she'd ducked her head and pounded out of the yard, catching up with Charlie and bucking around her in wild, joyful circles. Charlie took her cue from the dappled horse, racing as fast as she could – chasing Whirlwind, and being chased in turn. Her weakened legs seemed to draw strength from the mare's playful exuberance. Vigour returned to her wasted muscles, and she pulled off her top to run in her bra, the sun kissing her skin. When her energy was finally spent, Charlie flopped down in a patch of everlastings. Whirlwind snorted twice and began to graze nearby, occasionally checking in with Charlie, nibbling at her clothes or hair.

Little by little, day by day, the friendship between the girl and the rogue mare grew. Charlie knew about horses. She knew more about horses than she knew about people. And she knew it was only through such a friendship that the damaged mare might heal. A sort of natural wisdom guided her. Wisdom gained during endless days spent riding in the ranges. Like all children, Charlie had had her heroes – role models, people she admired. But unlike most children, they weren't sports stars or pop singers. They were scientists like Jane Goodall and Dian Fossey – pioneering naturalists who immersed themselves in the society of the animals they studied. For them, it was the chimpanzees and gorillas of the central African jungle. But for Charlie, it was the wild horses of Maroong Mountain.

Charlie had learned the hard way that happiness wasn't to be found in the loneliness and exclusion of the schoolyard. Happiness was to be found instead, in the acceptance of the herd. Ever so slowly, with infinite care, she'd insinuated herself into the secret life of the wild horses on the mountain. Charlie may not have been at school, but she was getting an education. She learned the brumbies' waterhole rituals. She won the forbearance of their wise old stallion. She won the friendship of their lead mare, Jarrang's mother. Charlie grew fluent in the language of their bodies and, one by one, the brumbies allowed her to slip onto their backs.

It was through this unique brand of liberty training that Charlie hoped to win over the traumatised mare. No saddles, no bridles, no ropes or round yards. But Charlie wouldn't tell Sam — not yet. This was just between her and Whirlwind.

CHAPTER 29

Charlie wasn't the only one who'd come home. Bill was back too. Back with a nurse, not fully recovered, not able to physically run the property himself. But he was back, and back with a vengeance. He'd never been so impossible, so full of bile. For Drew there was no more time spent next door at Brumby's Run. In the week since Charlie's return, he'd hardly seen Sam. When he phoned, she'd seemed distant. When he dropped by, she was always busy, and Charlie was always there.

Drew remembered Sam's kiss the night they stole Whirlwind. She'd been happy, ready to start off where they'd left off – he was sure of it. What they really needed was some clear air. If Charlie hadn't turned up like she did, who knows what would have happened? Somebody was always getting in their way. Like Bill, for instance. Hijacking every minute of every day. So far Drew had put off telling his father about the expired lease. Why invite trouble? But sooner or later it was bound to come out.

'Mr Bill, he want to see you,' said Mai, as Drew came in for breakfast.

Drew nodded and sat down. 'Those eggs look good.' He grabbed a piece of toast. 'Any chance you could rustle up a few mushrooms to go with them?'

'Mr Bill, he wants to see you now.' Drew took a closer look at Mai. Her eyes were red, and her apron was all bunched up in her hands.

'All right, Mai.' He put down the toast and stood up. She gestured down the hall. Voices sounded from the study. Drew gave her a reassuring smile. 'I'll see what he wants.'

Bill glared at Drew as he entered the room. 'About time.' Tom stood by the door, an expression of pure exasperation on his face. Bill was waving a newspaper about – the latest *Stock and Station*. 'What the hell happened to that Benambra mob I told you to buy? Bob Hunter's got them.' Bill stormed back and forth, as much as a man could storm when sitting in a wheelchair. He rolled over to his desk and searched the drawers, tossing papers and pens aside as he went. Lena, his nurse, gathered the scattered things off the floor.

'And where's the new lease that Kelly woman signed?' He became more and more agitated every second. 'Tom said they turned our cattle out and locked the gates?' Bill shook his head. 'Unbelievable.' He started searching the desk, all over again.

'Dad, stop. Mary never signed the renewal.'

'Makes no difference.' Bill slammed shut the drawer. 'A clause in the agreement states that when the lease expires, it converts to a periodic tenancy. While Mary accepts those lease payments, the contract renews itself automatically each month. She had no legal right to turf out our cattle. I want them back in there first thing tomorrow.'

'Dad.' Drew raised his voice a notch. 'Will you just listen for once? This isn't about the law — it's about what's right. The Kellys need that land for themselves.'

'Mary needs it? What for?' argued Bill, his voice rising. 'That wormy, inbred mob of hers are no better than scrubbers. They're a waste of good feed.' He was shouting now. 'And they'll never earn her an income. I just about keep that woman!' A purple vein throbbed at Bill's temple and Drew began to fear his father might have a heart attack. 'Sucking me dry all these months, without a word? I should brief my solicitor, take her to the cleaners.'

'You mean she's been collecting agistment fees all along?' asked Drew.

'Damn straight,' said Bill.

It hadn't occurred to Drew that his father might keep right on paying Mary, without a signed copy of the renewal in his hand. He was always so tight-fisted.

'Where's Mary?' barked Bill. 'Get her over here. I'll soon sort this out.' He rose from his chair and his face suddenly distorted in pain. Lena sprang forward.

'Mr Chandler. Please don't put weight on that leg. It won't heal right.'

'Stop bloody mothering me!' he yelled, sinking back down. Lena tried to put the rug back onto his knee, and Bill flung it aside, clouting her hard on the leg in the process. She squealed and jumped back. 'And Tom, what's happening with the stock up in the park? You been keeping an eye on them?'

Tom nodded. 'I wish we'd fitted those GPS collars though, Bill. Right now we're in direct breach of our agreement with the state government.'

'Tracking devices for cows,' scoffed Bill. 'What a load of nonsense.'

Drew wasn't listening. He was watching Lena's face. The woman looked absolutely terrified. Somewhere inside him a slow fuse began to burn.

'You imbecile!' Bill was screaming at Tom now, accusing him of not knowing one end of a cow from the other. Lena caught Drew's eye, shrugged and looked helpless. Drew cursed beneath his breath. It was about time someone stood up to his father.

'Tom,' said Drew in a low growl. The two men went on arguing. 'Tom!' Tom stopped in mid-sentence and stared at him, disbelief written all over his face. 'Leave us, please, Tom. I want a private word with Dad.' Tom opened his mouth to speak. 'Leave us, Tom.'

The head stockman shut his mouth and left the room.

Bill looked at Drew like he'd gone mad. 'I'm not finished . . .'

'Oh, you're finished all right,' said Drew, his voice full of controlled fury. 'You're finished fuming and bitching and throwing your weight around. You're finished bullying Mai and Lena. You're finished talking to the most respected head stockman in Currajong like he's a first-year jackaroo.' Drew marched forward and stabbed his father in the chest with a finger. 'And you're finished treating me like a damned slave. If you want to move our cattle back onto Brumby's Run, do it yourself. But if that's your decision, I won't be here to see it.'

Lena cowered in the corner. Bill sat speechless, his eyes popping out of his head. That only happened when he was seriously, seriously angry. Up until now Drew had feared this bug-eyed father, but not today. Today Bill just looked like a sad old man, struggling to keep hold of his shrinking world.

'You have no right —' Bill started.

'It's you who have no right,' said Drew. 'No right to run my life, or anybody else's. You'll drive me off, Dad, just like you did Mum and the girls. I love you, you old bastard, and I don't want to leave Kilmarnock. But if you take back Brumby's Run from the Kellys, I swear, I'm gone, Dad. Gone for good.' He took one last satisfied look at his father's stunned expression, then strode from the room and slammed the door behind him.

Drew took a big breath. His heart was beating like a bongo drum, but he felt like a million dollars. He should have done this years ago, should have taken back the power. Lobbed the ball into dad's court. Stay or go, it was all the same to him now. Not that he'd go too far if it came to that. Not too far from Sam. His gut told him Dad wouldn't call him on this one, but just in case, he'd better head over to Brumby's when Sam got home from work and warn her.

CHAPTER 30

Every morning after Sam went to work with Bushy, Charlie worked with Whirlwind. At first she'd struggled with the exertion, dead tired by lunchtime, crawling wearily into bed for an afternoon sleep. But as each day passed and Whirlwind grew calmer, Charlie grew stronger. She'd started working Tambo too, and today, in this first sparkling week of autumn, Charlie felt ready at last to ride into Balleroo.

Balleroo — the very word was music. Charlie could hardly believe it; she and Tambo together again, sweeping up a grassy slope into the mountains. She could breathe. She was free. Free of doctors, free of walls, free of well-meaning people asking her *Are you okay, Charlie?* in that pointed, exaggerated way, that invited her to respond that indeed, she was not. Charlie was free of everything but the rhythm of Tambo's hoofs on the earth. How good it felt to be physical again. For months her body had seemed like a hostile alien – holding her hostage, attacking her from deep down in her bones, producing nothing but pain. To survive, she'd cultivated such a deliberate disconnect between mind and body that she'd feared it was permanent. But Tambo's world was an intensely physical one, and it required Charlie to be physical as well. Her body moved in time with Tambo's, synchronised to the tempo of his breathing. Her pelvis, her thighs, her heels and hands all spoke to him. She could smell their sweat, their combined heat.

The wasted muscles of her core went to work, keeping her slim frame balanced, bringing it to equilibrium. Tendons tightened in her lower back, her upper leg, all the way down to her toes. Charlie revelled in the sensation. Back in the hospital, she used to wonder if she even had muscles any more. Her fingers played with the reins, keeping delicate contact with Tambo's mouth.

Charlie focused on the mountain, hyper-alert. A rider had to concentrate, lose herself in the present, had to see and hear and smell whatever her horse did. 'Lose myself to find myself,' she whispered. Tambo's ears flickered back at the sound of her voice. Charlie leant down, buried her face in his mane and wrapped her arms around his neck. Tambo stopped and politely waited for Charlie to behave. She laughed and sat upright, breathing in the bush.

A magpie carolled overhead. An old man kangaroo bounded across their path. The soft patter of gumnuts on the ground revealed a feeding flock of red-headed gang-gang cockatoos in the tree tops, and a daytime dingo howled. The fragrance of peppermint gums was sweet and strong. Charlie smiled to think of what Professor Sung would say if he saw her now. *Restrict physical activity,* he'd said. *Avoid animals for fear of infection,* he'd said. What would be the point of living? There was more to a person than blood cells and bones.

Charlie gulped great lungfuls of scented air, and cantered to the top of a ridge clothed with alpine heath and everlastings. Where was that patch of snow gums? They couldn't be far now. There they were, trunks resplendent in splashes of salmon, apricot and peach. How long was it since she'd been to Corroboree Bog? She cast her mind back, past the transplant, past her failed treatments, past the dreadful, desperate days spent hiding her illness from her mother. It had been early spring, just after snow melt. She'd packed a lunch and spent the day taking field notes. It had been an unusually successful breeding season for the frogs in the bog, and she'd found lots of fertile egg clutches. With any luck, she'd find an abundance of healthy young froglings emerging from the ponds.

Ever since she was old enough to ride into the mountains, Charlie had considered herself the keeper of the Balleroo bogs. There was something so hauntingly beautiful and fragile about these primitive wetlands, remnants of the last ice age. Most people couldn't see it. Most people were blind. When the mobile library came to Currajong, Charlie lost herself in private study, in books, in the internet's infinite cloud of knowledge. She became an expert about local landforms, especially the sub-alpine bogs. 'You should study science at university,' the librarian had urged her. 'You're a natural. Not many students engage in all this extra research.' Charlie just smiled. She never studied at school. How could she? She was hardly ever there. It would have been different if they'd taught interesting subjects – like ecology, for instance.

She'd learned at the library that Balleroo's bogs were formed during the Palaeozoic Age, five hundred million years ago. Cradled beneath granite and sandstone peaks, sculpted by glaciers, eroded by rain and snow – each bog had adapted to the particular combination of its own topography and microclimate. Charlie knew each one by the names she'd given them long ago. There was Tree Frog Tarn, Barking Marsh and Bullfrog Bog. She'd found a colony of rare water skinks at Pobblebonk Pond, and even rarer growling grass frogs at Parrot Pools. Her favourite amphibians were the pretty, spotted tree frogs, miniature cousins of the green tree frogs that were popular as pets. Corroboree Bog was a haven for these unique little animals, and she couldn't wait to discover how successful the summer hatchings had been.

Charlie dismounted, aching and stiff from the ride. She tethered Tambo to a tree and walked down through the snow gums. Turning left through paddocks of purple eyebrights and starbursts of hoary sunrays, she reached the fence dating back to the old mountain leases. The hardwood strainer posts were rotten with age; the barbed wire rusted and broken.

Charlie had started down the hill along the old stock route when something made her pause. A prickle along the nape of her neck, like she was being watched. Slowly, very slowly, she turned around.

Only twenty metres away, across the grassy clearing, stood a great red-and-white bull. Charlie gulped the air to calm herself. A skinny black cow with a late calf marched to stand beside it. The cow mooed uneasily. Charlie recognised her by her bright-pink ear tag. That was a Kelly cow. What the hell were Kelly cattle doing way out here in the park? Or any cattle, for that matter?

The big bull pawed the ground and tossed his head. Charlie retreated a few steps. There was something unusual about him; something she couldn't immediately put her finger on. And then it struck her. He had horns. Bill ran poll Herefords, which were hornless. This wasn't one of Bill's bulls. This animal's massive horns curved forward, long and upswept with pointed tips.

The bull snorted, flared his nostrils and trotted a circle around the cow. His hide bore battle scars in place of tags or brands. Charlie's heart lurched when she recognised just what she faced. A wild scrubber bull. He lowered his head to the ground, bellowed, and charged at a candlebark tree. His cow lowed in admiration at the display of strength. Bulging muscles strained against the resistance of the trunk as he scraped his horns from side to side, shredding bark to sawdust. It looked for all the world like he was sharpening his horns.

Charlie glanced around, hoping for her own tree, but she'd left the sheltering forest behind. The old, grassy stock route led down a wide slope to the wetlands, two hundred metres below. She was caught out in the open, with no shelter apart from the rickety fence. Charlie walked backwards down the hill, unwilling to turn around. She sensed that only eye contact was keeping the animal at bay, and it would run her down if she turned tail and made a break.

The bull bellowed a challenge, made a run at her, then stopped to uproot a young wattle. The tree lay over his horns like an Olympic victory garland while he tore at the ground with first one forefoot and then the other, sending clods of clay and clouds of dust sailing over his back and past his flanks. A rumbling battle cry rose in his throat, ending in a deafening roar. This was a bull with something to prove.

Charlie maintained her slow and steady retreat, keeping the tumble-down fence between her and the bull wherever she could.

Until the bull charged. He moved with a cumbersome, rolling gait, but Charlie wasn't fooled. She knew full well the deceptive speed of such a lumbering stride. She turned and sprinted down the hill, hampered by shaky legs and weak muscles, heart hammering in her chest. She tried to judge the proximity of the animal from the sound of his thundering hoofs and rumbling breath. Her own lungs burned now, and it was harder and harder to keep her balance amongst the tussocks of snow grass. Any moment now he'd shove her in the back and trample her to earth. What would it feel like, she wondered? She'd almost lost her life at that hospital in Melbourne. Far better to die on this wild mountain.

Unexpectedly a shot rang out, then another, and another. A bawl of pain and the earth shuddered. Charlie fell down in fright, squeezed her eyes shut and waited. All she could hear was the rush of blood through her body, the thump of her beating heart. Seconds felt like minutes.

Then a quiet voice. 'You're safe. Take my hand.'

Charlie dared to believe she'd survived. She rolled over and there was a man, tall and blond. He wore the khaki uniform of a park ranger, and carried a bolt-action rifle. With a start, she turned to see the bull lying quite dead where he'd speared into the ground, surrounded by blood and churned earth. The man took her by the wrist, helped her gently to her feet and dusted her off.

'It's becoming a habit, saving your life,' he said. 'But at least you've got your clothes on this time.' As far as Charlie could tell, she'd never met this man before. A combination of confusion and shock caused her to wobble violently and collapse back to earth. The man seemed to consider this for a moment, then joined her on the ground. He sat with arms wrapped around his knees, hands clasped. 'Excuse me for being personal,' he said, 'but that's a charming haircut.' He had a faint accent — German, maybe?

Charlie perked up and managed a smile. She wasn't going to die after all. This deluded stranger had seen to that. 'Thanks,' she said. 'If it hadn't been for you ...' That awful possibility didn't bear thinking about. Charlie took a closer look at her saviour. She still couldn't place him. 'Who are you? Have we met?'

'Am I really that forgettable?'

'No,' said Charlie. 'You're not. That's why it's so strange that I don't remember.'

He smiled. 'All right, I'll introduce myself again if I must. Karl Richter.' He extended his arm. She propped herself up shakily on one elbow and shook his hand.

'And who exactly do you think I am?' she asked.

'You're Samantha Carmichael. From Melbourne. Just visiting . . . although it's been a very long visit.'

'Oh, I get it,' she said, laughing. 'You've got me mixed up with my sister. She's Samantha.' Charlie nodded, pleased she'd resolved things in her own mind, if not in his. 'I'm Charlie. How exactly did you meet Sam?' She wanted to add, and why didn't she have her clothes on? No, she'd better direct that intriguing question to her sister. Not that she'd blame Sam. Charlie took a closer look at her mysterious saviour. He was pretty cute – slim, with long muscled legs and intelligent grey eyes. Mary insisted grey eyes were associated with water and wisdom. Their bearers might appear mild-mannered, she said, but in fact they possessed a hidden strength – the inexorable power of water; able in time to wear away even the hardest rock. Maybe Mum was right. Whatever the case, this man's quiet confidence was oddly alluring.

'Look,' said Karl. 'I'd love for us to have a good, long chat about how we met, and who we know, and who you might actually be. But it's not really the time.' He stood up, reached for her, and for a second time she took his hand. She'd always been a sucker for a man in uniform. This time she managed to remain on her feet. 'You okay to walk?' She nodded. 'Let's go then,' he said. 'Samantha, or Charlie, or whoever you are.'

'Where are we going?' she asked.

'To look at a bog.'

'You're kidding me.'

'I know sphagnum bogs don't get good press,' he said,' but they're really quite fascinating. Vital habitats filtering water into mountain catchments. Whole communities of flora and fauna depend on them – the whole ecosystem depends on them.'

'But . . . ' began Charlie.

He held up his hand. 'Considering that I keep saving your life, could you humour me, please?'

Charlie began to hop with excitement, trying to get a word in. 'You don't understand,' she said. 'I love bogs, particularly that bog.' She pointed down the hill. 'They're one of my very favourite places. Along with their frogs and lizards and snakes and things.'

Karl looked at her sideways. 'You've either hit your head or you're teasing me,' he said. 'Last time we met you didn't seem so keen on reptiles.'

'I told you,' said Charlie. 'That must have been my sister, Sam. Did she have a posh voice?'

'I suppose she did,' he conceded.

'Then she didn't sound like me exactly, did she?' It was surprisingly hard work, convincing him that she wasn't her sister. Had it been this difficult for Sam? Had people mistaken her as well?

'Maybe not. You just look so much alike.'

Charlie groaned. 'Never mind,' she said. 'Let's go.'

He nodded, apparently happy with that, and they walked down the hill to Corroboree Bog. Or at least to what had once been Corroboree Bog. Charlie sensed trouble even before she reached the wetlands. The slope had been eroded by the hoofs of cattle, exposing the fragile peaty soil to the elements. The expected summer carpet of marsh marigolds and orange everlastings was nowhere to be seen. Clumps of silver alpine daisies were grazed down to the ground. She glanced across at Karl. He wore a grim expression on his face.

When they reached the bog, what had once been a chain of pristine pools was little more than a wallow. The greenhood orchids were gone; the moss beds trampled. In some places pug holes had run together, creating little downhill channels, draining dry whole parts of the marsh. Karl began to take photographs.

'Look,' said Charlie. She bent down to where a small green frog was struggling to escape from a fresh cow pat. It had a broken leg. 'What are cattle doing back in the park?' she asked, as she went to rescue it.

'Wait,' said Karl. He took photos from every angle of the frogling trapped in the dung. 'There's a trial on,' he said. 'To test whether cattle reduce the risk of bushfires. Although so far, published and peer-reviewed research shows no statistically significant difference between grazed and ungrazed areas.' He spoke like she imagined a professor might speak, and his voice was strangely compelling. Karl pointed to the tiny injured frog that Charlie was releasing into one of the few undamaged ponds. '*Litoria spenceri* - the spotted tree frog,' he said. 'Critically endangered.'

Charlie was stunned. She'd never met anyone who even knew the common name of a frog, let alone somebody who could identify one by its Latin name out in the field, and who also knew its conservation status.

'My mission is to protect the habitat of your little frog friend . . .' He was on a mission? Like James Bond? Fantastic. She didn't know people actually had missions in real life. 'With the help of your keen eyes and these photos,' he patted the camera. 'I hope to get this grazing trial suspended.'

You had to love this bloke. 'I bloody well hope so,' she said.

'It's not just cattle, although they're the obvious culprits here.' Karl gestured to the looming mountain peaks. 'Balleroo is infested with feral pigs, deer, horses - we need to get rid of the lot.'

Charlie went quiet. All of a sudden she wasn't quite so gung-ho for Karl's mission. He went on taking measurements, pictures, water samples. He wandered off to the far side of the wetlands, talking into his iPhone. Charlie squatted down on a trampled bed of cushion plants, took an exercise book from her back pack, and started making her own notes and drawings. After a while Karl returned, a puzzled look on his face. 'What are you doing?'

'Writing a report,' she said.

'Who for?'

'Just for me.' Charlie looked up as he squatted beside her, his face close to hers, his expression more bewildered than ever. Karl wasn't the sort of man she normally went for, but she did love the accent, and he was handsome in a clean-cut sort of way. Of course, saving lives and knowing about frogs made him sexy even without all the other stuff.

'How did you get here in the first place?' he asked. 'I could see no car. Do you know that fire trail is closed to the public?'

'I rode here,' she said. 'My horse is tethered on the hill above the wetlands.' He looked surprised – displeased, even. 'Don't worry. He's more than thirty metres away from any watercourse, and I don't need a permit to ride in this area, do I?'

'No,' he said. 'You don't.' He gazed at her with a clear-eyed intensity that she supposed he usually reserved for endangered species. 'Just who exactly are you?'

'I told you. Charlie.'

'Charlie Carmichael?' he asked.

Charlie Carmichael. She might have been, if things had been just a bit different.

'I'm Charlie Kelly,' she said. 'Charlie Kelly from Brumby's Run.'

CHAPTER 31

Sam gave up, slipped from the yard, and returned to the house through the afternoon shadows. She and Whirlwind were at an impasse. Maybe it was time to ask Bushy for help.

Now Charlie was back, the time was fast approaching when she'd have to come clean with Bushy — come clean with the whole town, for that matter. It was a terrifying prospect, one she hoped could be put off for a few more days. Charlie had said she didn't want to go into Currajong yet, didn't want the curious eyes of the townsfolk upon her. That gave Sam a little breathing space; some time to figure out just how to go about her impossible confession.

Bushy, she'd decided, would be the easiest person to tell. Perhaps she'd start with him. She trusted Bushy. The morning after they'd taken the mare (she didn't use the word stolen, even to herself), Bushy had given his statement to the police, with Sam hovering nervously in the background. 'Kids,' he'd said, with a snort of derision. 'A bunch of them opened the gate. Saw them myself, I did.' He'd glanced at Sam and winked. 'Probably dared each other to get in the yard with that damned man-killer, and then turned tail and ran.' He spat a wad of tobacco at the ground. 'Bloody kids.'

'Bloody kids,' the sergeant had agreed, shaking his head in disgust. 'Wayne said the horse was branded?'

'That's right,' said Bushy. 'UV on the near shoulder, and a 9 on the off.'

'Well,' said the sergeant, with a quick look around, like he hoped that Whirlwind might just trot past or something. 'I suppose it'll be long gone by now.'

Bushy nodded sagely. 'Long, long gone.'

Sam had let out a sigh of relief, loud enough to draw the sergeant's attention. For a moment she was a rabbit in the spotlights, then he gave a wave and left.

'You may have bitten off more than you can chew with that mare,' said Bushy after the sergeant was gone. 'And if I were you, I'd alter those brands.'

Sam felt herself flush firehouse red. 'How do you mean?'

'It doesn't take much to change a 9 into an 8, or a U into an O, or a V into a diamond.' Sam opened her mouth to deny it, but what was the point? 'Let me know if you need me,' Bushy had said.

She needed him now. Whirlwind was eating well, and at least the mare wasn't actively trying to kill people any more. But that was the extent of her improvement. She was still fearful and hyper vigilant, and wouldn't let Sam anywhere near her. None of the standard tactics had worked. Sam free-lunged Whirlwind round her yard each evening, waiting for that precise moment when the mare would drop her head, relax her jaw – grow calm enough for an approach. That moment never came. It seemed that Whirlwind would rather drop from exhaustion than allow a human to lay a hand on her.

Condor trotted along at Sam's feet on her way down to the house. The big bird was missing Charlie, who still wasn't back from Balleroo. Sam tried her phone - turned off. What was Charlie thinking, going off on her own like that? Sam was sick of feeling responsible for her sister. Sick of cooking her nourishing meals, monitoring her medication, worrying about her. Why couldn't Charlie have just listened to the doctors, and to Mary? Why couldn't she have stayed in

Melbourne? Sam shook her head. There was no point thinking like that. Charlie was home, so she'd just have to make the best of it.

Sam had been waiting every day for Drew to drop round and casually sling his arm around Charlie, for him to rekindle their relationship, but so far it hadn't happened. Her sister seemed equally uninterested. But then Charlie wasn't well, and would still be angry with Drew, surely, for his betrayal. Sam might just be seeing what she wanted to see. She hadn't found the nerve so far to ask Charlie outright.

Sam was in over her head. Confused, unsure, living in a torment of duty versus desire. She couldn't go on like this. It was time to confront Charlie with her own feelings, and try to gauge just how much Drew still meant to her sister.

Sam had told Charlie that she was deferring her commerce course. Her sister had been touchingly pleased by the news. So had Mary. Even Sam's father hadn't seemed to mind. 'It's your decision, Sammy,' he'd said. 'That university isn't going anywhere.' She resisted the possibility that he just didn't care. Wasn't he sending her money? It was partly guilt money, she knew that. Dad had flown straight back to Dubai from France, but then *away* was his default setting. She was used to it, and the allowance was helping keep Brumby's Run afloat. That, and the payments going into Charlie's bank account from her mystery benefactor.

Her mother hadn't been so easy to convince. Faith had stayed on in Europe after the initial month that she'd originally planned to be away. She'd taken Mamie and her arthritis to the Mediterranean for the duration of the northern winter. When Sam broke the news about her gap year, Faith had cried and argued and threatened. 'I'm coming straight home to talk some sense into you.'

'You can't change my mind,' Sam had said, gritting her teeth. 'Don't bother coming unless you bring Pharaoh too.' Her mind was made up. There would be no leaving Brumby's Run, no leaving Charlie – no leaving Drew. He'd risked a lot the night he hijacked Whirlwind. It was crazy and dangerous, and he'd done it just the same. It was an act of love, she knew that, and Sam loved him in return.

Sam's mobile rang. It was Mary. 'Sweetie, how are you? How's Charlie?'

'Fine,' said Sam cautiously. 'We're both fine.' She never quite knew what to expect from Mary's phone calls.

'Can you put Charlie on?'

Sam thought quickly. Charlie was off riding alone in the mountains, but she couldn't tell Mary that. 'She's outside somewhere. I'll get her to ring you, shall I?'

'Outside? She's not overdoing it, is she? The doctor said she should take it easy.'

Tell her yourself, Sam wanted to say. I'm not your daughter's keeper. But instead she just asked 'When are you coming home?'

Mary launched into a list of what sounded suspiciously like excuses. '. . . so, it won't be until Carlos gets the car fixed. Will that be all right? Can you girls manage a while longer?' Sam toyed with the idea of saying, no, they couldn't. Would it make any difference?

Sam was beginning to see that Charlie was right about Mary. She'd been a devoted mother during the crisis, no doubt about that, but had lost focus pretty quickly once Charlie was on the mend. 'Mum was on her best behaviour at the hospital,' Charlie had said. 'Trying to impress you. She can never keep up the Mother Mary act for long. Once there's a man involved, I come second. Always did. Maybe it's an abandonment complex because my dad ran out on her. She always hangs on to blokes too tight.'

'We can manage, Mary,' said Sam. 'We can manage just fine. Talk soon.' Psychoanalysing her birth mother was all very interesting, but there was a dinner to cook. With Mary acting so flaky, it was probably just as well that she stayed away. Mothers were such problem creatures.

Sam gave Condor a piece of cheese, chased him out the back door, and put on one of Charlie's Sara Storer CDs. She'd become a fan of Storer's sweet, country sound, with a subtle steel in the lyrics.

Sam looked in the fridge. She'd make something simple and tasty, like warm chicken salad, with wild blackberries and fresh cream for afterwards. And maybe buttery garlic bread. She needed to fatten Charlie up, and fortunately her culinary skills had advanced a long way from boiled eggs and toast. They'd been her staple back home in Melbourne on the rare occasion she prepared a meal for herself. Faith had a chef, but Sam dared not tell Charlie, or she'd never hear the end of it.

Sam pulled chicken strips out to defrost and set about chopping fresh greens and slicing the French loaf. Time ticked by. Still no Charlie. Sam made garlic butter, all the while glancing at the door. Strands of anxiety wadded to a ball in her stomach. Where on earth was her sister?

CHAPTER 32

It was after seven before the back door slammed and Charlie limped in. 'Whatever happened to you?' asked Sam. 'Did you have a fall?' Charlie shook her head, but she looked worn out, covered in mud, with grazed elbows and a sunburned face. Sam fetched disinfectant and tissues, and began dabbing at the broken skin on Charlie's skinny arms.

'Ow!' she pulled away.

Sam persisted, taking Charlie's elbow gently in her left hand, and cleaning it with her right. 'You have to be careful about infection,' she said, 'or you'll end up right back in that Melbourne hospital.' Might not be such a bad thing, thought Sam uncharitably. 'Where have you been anyway?'

'Up in the wetlands, below the Snake Creek watershed.' Charlie pulled an exercise book from her backpack. 'Some idiot has let cattle into the park. They've destroyed Corroboree Bog, and probably all the others besides.' Her voice quivered with exhaustion, or emotion, or both.

Charlie opened the notebook and began to read. '*Damage ranges from flattened vegetation, numerous cow pats, large patches of bare ground, trampled and dislodged plants.*' She looked up. 'A lot of the sphagnum moss was shrivelled and dead.' She went on reading. '*Cattle have caused serious erosion, making tracks that connect and drain ponds. Half of the bog is completely dry. These drainage channels can spread the water-borne spores of Chytrid fungus.* That's the fungus killing off frogs worldwide, and do you know the worst thing?' Sam shook her head, feeling sick. 'I only found two frogs up there – one dead and the other injured. It'll probably die too. There should have been dozens.' Charlie's voice raised a frantic notch. 'These are spotted tree frogs I'm talking about. Protected frogs, critically endangered.'

'Whose notes are those?'

'Mine.'

Sam barely believed her. 'They sound very … technical.'

'Do they?' Charlie's downcast face brightened with pride. 'When the mobile library was in Currajong, I always used to read the Department of Environment field observations. I tried to copy their recording style, their terminology. I've got oodles of notes, starting from when I was eight — a ten-year ecological history of Balleroo National Park.'

Sam was stunned. She hadn't imagined that her sister had a scholarly side. Charlie had been hiding her light under a bushel.

Charlie's voice grew tremulous. 'I rode Tambo up there, and then this bull charged me, and then this ranger shot it, and then . . . ' She started to sob. 'Then I discovered the ruined bog.' Charlie slumped into a kitchen chair. Her sobs turned to all-out wails racking her frail frame.

'A bull? What on earth —?' Sam pulled up a chair and wrapped her arms around Charlie's shuddering shoulders. 'It's okay,' she murmured over and over, until her sister seemed spent.

'Do you know a bloke called Karl Richter?' asked Charlie. The sudden change in tack left Sam momentarily confused. She shook her head.

'His voice sounds a bit German or something,' said Charlie. Still nothing. 'You didn't have your clothes on.' Sam felt her jaw drop. The day in the mountains when they caught the brumbies. The snake in the pool. How did Charlie know about that?

'You mean that park ranger?'

Charlie nodded. 'He's the one who shot the bull and saved my life. He thought I was you, and said that at least I had my clothes on this time.' She looked like she was expecting an explanation. Sam didn't know quite where to start, but told the story as best she could, leaving out the bit where Karl said she looked fetching in her underwear. 'I can see how that happened,' said Charlie when she'd finished. 'I wondered if people might get us mixed up. Did it happen much?'

This was it, the perfect segue. This was the time to explain how everybody in Currajong thought she was Charlie. Sam got up, poured her sister an orange juice, took a deep breath and began. This time she left nothing out of the story. She took hold of Charlie's hands and told her about how it had started with an innocent mistake, of how shy and embarrassed she'd been in the beginning, of how awkward and difficult it was to challenge people's assumptions. Sam dropped Charlie's hands and walked to the window, as if out there she might find more courage. When she turned back around, her sister's eyes were wide. Sam averted her gaze, hung her head and told Charlie about how she'd got used to playing the part. Of how wonderful it was to feel accepted by the tight-knit Currajong community, of how she'd relished the solid sense of belonging. Of how she felt like she'd come home.

Charlie listened in silence. When Sam ran out of words, she hesitantly lifted her eyes to Charlie's. Her sister's face had sort of crumpled, fallen in on itself, blurred. It was horrible. Sam rushed to kneel before her sister and held her hands again. Charlie gulped, like she might choke. 'Didn't anybody notice it wasn't me?' she said, her voice wavering.

'Oh, yes.' Sam tried to reassure her. 'Of course.'

'Who?'

Sam almost lied, then thought better of it. There'd been too much lying already. 'Spike,' she said. 'And Drew, of course.'

'Who else?' Sam didn't speak. 'Who else?' said Charlie, her voice angry now, demanding. Sam cringed. Her sister's pain was palpable. 'I grew up in Currajong,' said Charlie. 'You? You've been to France,

America, England – all around the world. But do you know what?' Sam shook her head. 'Before I got sick, before I went to Melbourne, I'd never been farther than Wodonga in my entire life. Not bloody once.' She rested her scrunched-up face in her hands for a moment. 'How do you think it feels, to realise that after a lifetime lived in this town, nobody even knows who I am? To realise that I'm completely interchangeable with the first damned stranger who waltzes into Currajong and looks a bit like me?'

Sam felt like she'd been struck. She rose from her knees and sank into the chair beside Charlie. There was a rap at the door and Drew walked in, followed by Bess, wagging her tail. Charlie hit him with both barrels. 'No one in this town knows who I am, do they Drew? I could have died and nobody would have even noticed.'

Bess whimpered and backed out the door. Drew gave Sam a look of thorough approval. 'You finally fessed up then.'

'Yes, she did,' said Charlie, her voice full of venom. 'My dear, loving sister finally fessed up. It wasn't enough that she hit the jackpot the day she was born and went off to live with a mega-rich family. It wasn't enough that I had cancer and she didn't. No, she had to come here, scavenge through what was left of my life, and pick the eyes out of that as well.'

'You asked me to come . . .' began Sam.

Charlie turned on her. 'I didn't ask you to play some bloody masquerade. What am I supposed to do now? I can't show my face in town. I'll be completely humiliated.'

'Hang on, Charlie,' said Drew. 'Don't be so hard on your sister. You two are dead ringers. Even I was fooled at first, and nobody knows you better than me.'

Charlie stood up and pointed an accusing finger at Sam. 'You said that he knew you weren't me.'

'He did,' Sam said, silently cursing Drew for his candour. 'After a few minutes, he did.'

Charlie collapsed back in her chair. She looked completely defeated. Sam didn't imagine this was the sort of incident-free recovery Professor Sung had in mind for her sister. Sam moved to hug her, to try to comfort her, but Charlie's accusing eyes stopped her in her tracks. Sam hugged Bess instead, glad of the unconditional affection shining in the big dog's eyes. It was the *damned stranger* comment that had hurt the most. Was that how Charlie thought of her? It was true enough, though. They barely knew each other. In Charlie's shoes, she'd be just as wild. If only Sam hadn't let the charade drag on for so long. Well, it was over now, and the whole town would soon discover what a fraud she was. There was no way around it.

Sam felt faint. She hurried down the hall to the bathroom and dragged a wet washer over her face. Red, sore-looking eyes looked back at her from the mirror. She perched on the edge of the ancient claw bath, head in hands. What would Charlie say if she knew Sam was in love with Drew? Sam bit her lip. She could just hear Charlie shouting that Sam had stolen her boyfriend, along with everything else. And the awful thing was, it was true. However she cared to spin it to herself, no matter how innocently it had all begun – the facts were the facts.

Impassioned voices sounded from the kitchen. A horrible thought hit her. What if Charlie didn't want her to stay any more? The thought of leaving Brumby's Run made Sam sick with grief. She wouldn't do it. She flat-out wouldn't do it. This land was her heritage as much as Charlie's, and Sam didn't intend to give up an inch of it without a fight.

The argument still raged in the kitchen. She could hear every word.

'You're an ungrateful bitch, Chaz,' said Drew. 'You always were.' His harsh words were tempered by the tone of their delivery - mockingly affectionate. 'Us letting your stock into the park was all that saved those poor buggers from starving to death. Anyway, they're back home now. Safe and sound and growing fat as butter.'

'It's too late,' said Charlie. 'The damage is done. It'll take years for those wetlands to recover — that's if they ever do.'

'What about your precious brumbies?' said Drew. 'I don't suppose they cause any damage, do they? I'm meant to let your cattle starve, but it's fine, apparently, for feral horses to trample all over the park.' It was a fair point, but Charlie ignored it.

'If my cattle were starving, it was because your father had the run of our best land,' she said angrily. 'I saw one of my cows today, with a scrubber bull above the bog. Stupid me, thought she must have escaped. I never thought you'd deliberately put cattle into Balleroo, Drew. How could you do that? It's a park, not a bloody paddock!' Her voice rose an octave. 'And my sister? Did she know about this?'

Sam went cold, knowing only too well Drew and his damned honesty.

'Absolutely,' said Drew. Of course he did. 'Sam helped me muster them in there. She did a fabulous job too,' he added, 'for a city girl.'

Why did Drew have to go and say that for? He was always so reckless with his words, so completely lacking in discretion. Sam heaved a big sigh. No, he was unfailingly truthful, that was all. Pity some of that honesty hadn't rubbed off on her. If she'd confessed to letting the cattle out in the first place, there'd have been no surprises for him to spring on Charlie.

'I should sue!' Charlie was yelling now. 'You had no lease any more. Why the hell didn't you just get your cattle off my land when I told you to?'

'It was actually your sister who told me to,' he reminded her, cool as a cucumber. 'And I had them out within a week. But the state *your* cows were in? They didn't have another week.' Everything sounded so reasonable, the way he explained it. 'Chaz.' His tone had changed to coaxing and kind. 'You should be thanking me instead of going off your nut. Did you bother to read the original lease contract?'

'No, why?' asked Charlie, still on the defensive, but sounding less sure of herself.

'Well, let me give you a little lesson in the law. Mary didn't have to sign any renewal. Dad was entitled to keep his cattle on Brumby's Run, keep on paying rent and still be a lawful tenant, because there's a thing called a periodic tenancy. It automatically renews itself each month, unless one of the parties gives notice.'

'Sam gave notice.'

'She's not a party to the agreement,' said Drew. 'She can't give notice. Neither can you – only Mary can. If anybody's going to sue for breach of contract, it's Dad.'

That choice piece of information provoked Charlie into a torrent of shouted insults. Drew returned fire with a few of his own. Bess whined and pushed her wet nose into the palm of Sam's hand. 'Well, girl,' she whispered, fondling the dog's big head. 'Time to face the music.'

CHAPTER 33

Charlie lay down on a soft bed of everlastings in order to better examine the bizarre fungus. With seven scarlet arms, it certainly earned its name of the common starfish fungus. She wrinkled her nose and held her breath. It may have been beautiful, but *Aseroe rubra* was a member of the stinkhorn family and smelled of rotten flesh. Flies crawled around its glistening red heart, unwittingly collecting spores. Charlie took a few photos and made some notes.

In the week since Sam's stunning confession, Charlie had taken to going bush every day. Out here it didn't matter a jot what the townsfolk believed. It didn't matter a jot what any human being on the face of the earth believed. This grand wilderness was indifferent to the petty concerns of man. She stood up and stroked Whirlwind's shoulder. 'Time to go.'

The mare lifted her head for a moment from the sweet patch of snowgrass, then went on grazing. Charlie took hold of a handful of mane and swung onto her back. Whirlwind hardly seemed to notice. Charlie gently pressed her heels to her side. 'I said time to go.'

The mare tossed up her own heels in play and set off through the trees, trotting back along the creek, then down the hill towards the yards of Brumby's Run. Jarrang trumpeted a greeting to his daughter.

Whirlwind picked up speed, cantering straight for the hay shed. When they swept inside, Charlie jumped off into a pile of loose hay. Whirlwind lay down beside her and rolled. Then she stood up, shook herself, and snatched a big mouthful of oaten hay from right under Charlie.

'Cheeky thing.' Charlie tried without success to tug the hay away from the mare. Whirlwind chastised her with a shove of her nose, then settled down to feed, pawing occasionally to reach the grain that had slipped through the stalks. Charlie helped her for a while, searching out tasty seed heads and offering them to the mare's whiffling lips. When the mare lost interest, Charlie lay back in the fragrant hay bed, pulled her new smart phone from her pocket, and read over the messages from Karl.

After the sexy ranger had saved her life, he'd been sending her texts. Charlie had seven of them now, one for each day since they met. They contained fascinating accounts of his daily work in Balleroo. Each one finished with an obscure frog-themed joke that she didn't always fully understand. *What is the first book tadpoles read at school? Metamorphosis by Kafka*, or *Two frogs were sitting on Robinson Crusoe's back. One frog said, 'I have to go now, but we'll meet again on Friday.'*

Charlie reread the latest message, the one that finished with the silly cartoon instead of a joke; the one that had left her in no doubt about Karl's intentions. A man without a shirt was sitting on an examination table. The doctor was frowning and pointing to a screen that displayed two images, side by side. The first was labelled *Normal Sperm*. It showed lots of tadpole-like sperm swimming around. The second image was labelled *Your Sperm*. Here the sperm had developed into little frogs, and the doctor's response — *I take it there hasn't been any sex for a while?* Could there ever be a more charming pick-up line? Charlie closed her eyes.

She'd never imagined somebody like Karl would come along, somebody who so completely shared her love of the natural world. It was clear from his texts that he understood the vital role each living thing played in the ecology of the national park. He valued spiders and ants. He could not contain his excitement upon discovering a colony of southern forest bats. And, of course, there was his adorable passion for the Balleroo bogs. Karl had another highly desirable quality. He was an outsider. Right now, everyone belonging to Currajong was in her sights.

Charlie hated knowing that the town had mistaken Sam for her. She loathed the incestuous little community; the community that had failed her so badly. What Sam saw as some idyllic Shangri-La was really a suffocating hole full of ignorant, close-minded people who didn't give a damn. Well who cared? She didn't need them.

Charlie drifted off to sleep in the hay, dreaming of the tantalising possibilities of Karl Richter. She woke an hour later with Whirlwind snorting affectionately in her face. She really was an excellent companion. The mare knew how to just let her be. Sam, on the other hand, fussed and worried about her all the time: about her health, her diet, her mood. And she kept on apologising – for everything. She apologised for putting the cattle into the park. She apologised for digging up Mum's mint patch, mistaking it for weeds. She apologised for impersonating Charlie all over Currajong. Sam couldn't be in the same room with her at the moment without being sorry for something. It was annoying.

Charlie stroked Whirlwind's velvet muzzle. To give Sam credit, she did keep trying to put things right. 'We'll go around town, the two of us,' she'd offered, again and again. 'I'll explain to everybody who I really am.' But Charlie wasn't ready for that ordeal. She'd made Sam promise to let the status quo stand, at least for now. Stuff the town. Maybe she'd wait until her hair grew back, style it like Sam's, and just step back into her own life with nobody the wiser.

Flicka called from her paddock, with a *why aren't you paying me any attention?* sort of neigh. The mare was due to foal any day now. Her belly had dropped, her udder was full, and milk squirted from her waxed-up teats whenever she walked. Better go check in on her, give her a brush and a good feed. Whirlwind followed Charlie into the yard for a bucket of oats. The girl rubbed the mare's little horns for luck and closed the gate.

The first time she'd brushed Whirlwind's flowing forelock, Charlie had made the remarkable discovery of the two tiny horns. She could think of no rational explanation for them. Perhaps the old stories about magical brumbies were true after all? The protrusions were about three centimetres long, and dark grey, exactly like horn buds on a five-month-old calf. Charlie was dying to tell Sam, but if she did, she'd also have to admit that she'd been handling Whirlwind, and that might start an argument. Her sister could wait a bit longer for that startling piece of information.

Sam was already cooking dinner when her sister came in. Charlie's attention was fixed firmly on the screen of her phone and her cheeks were aflame. When she looked up, she was positively glowing with pleasure.

'You look pretty happy about something,' said Sam, reluctant to interrogate Charlie, but curious nonetheless.

Charlie raised an eyebrow and shot her sister a cheeky grin. 'You could say that.'

'Well, don't keep me in suspense?'

'Might as well tell you,' said Charlie. 'I don't like keeping secrets from my sister.'

Sam looked suitably contrite, and Charlie nodded approval. 'It's another text from Karl.' She looked in the oven, then washed up at the sink. 'You know, that new park ranger? We're going to hook up.'

Sam felt her face flush with hope, and a question burned in her mind. This was her chance. Come on girl, she told herself. Are you going to wait forever? 'How will Drew feel about that?' she ventured.

Charlie snorted with laughter. 'Drew? What's he got to do with it?' Sam was lost for words. Had she really had it so wrong for so long? Charlie looked suddenly shrewd. 'Speaking of Drew, it's pretty clear he's keen,' she said. 'Can't take his eyes off you.'

Sam met her sister's gaze, her expectant brown eyes, and wanted to deny everything. What sort of person was she? Just come clean, for goodness sake. 'I didn't know about you and Drew when it started,' she said. 'I really didn't.' This wasn't going well. She was sounding so defensive. 'Drew never said anything.' No, don't blame Drew — just tell the truth and apologise. 'I'm sorry, Charlie. I'm in love with Drew. You can't help who you fall in love with, can you?'

There, she'd said it. Sam's heart heaved in her chest and sticky tears ran down her face. It was hard to gauge Charlie's expression through blurry eyes. She took a deep, staggered breath; more of a sob, really. She should have done this long ago.

Charlie stood up and walked over to the kitchen bench. She plucked a big wad of tissues from the box, came back over and pulled her chair around so they faced each other. With utmost tenderness, Charlie dabbed tears from Sam's eyes, and wiped her cheeks. 'Sam,' she said softly. 'Why did you think I'd mind?'

'He was yours, wasn't he? Just like everything else here in Currajong.' She heard the cry in her voice. Great, now she was snivelling like a baby. 'It's like you said, I did take over your life. If you hate me, that's fair enough. Thanks to me you're stuck in this house, and you can't face anybody. I didn't have the courage to tell you that I wanted your boyfriend as well.'

Sam's eyes were streaming. For a long time Charlie didn't respond. Then she wiped Sam's face again, harder this time. Ow, that hurt.

'What a bitch,' Charlie said at last. 'You thought Drew was my boyfriend?' Sam nodded, a hot rush of shame burning her cheeks. 'And then you fell in love with him, and pretended to my face that nothing was going on?'

'Nothing was going on,' insisted Sam, but her sister wasn't listening.

'You're a piece of work, you know that?' Charlie hung her head. 'Have you slept with him?'

'Yes,' admitted Sam, knowing how it must sound. 'But only once.' Had she really said that? What was he? A car she'd taken for a test drive?

Charlie burst out laughing. 'I had you pegged as a self-righteous, sanctimonious miss goody two-shoes. Drew told me how you'd gone around town paying our bills, making things right. Everybody loves you, he said. That pissed me right off. And now I find out that you're actually a sneaky, slutty little coward, just like me.' Sam held her breath. 'And I bloody love you for it,' said Charlie with a broad smile.

'You do?' Her sister wasn't making any sense.

'Don't get me wrong,' said Charlie. 'If it was true about me and Drew, I'd be seriously bummed, but luckily for you, it isn't.'

'But Drew admitted it. He said Mary hated you two being together.'

'She did,' said Charlie. 'But that was ages ago. Drew hasn't been my main squeeze since I cheated on him with Spike.'

That last item of information required further scrutiny, but not now. 'That's not what you said on the phone,' protested Sam. 'You said that you and Drew were tight, remember? You said he was your boyfriend.'

'Maybe I was on too many meds,' said Charlie, dismissively. 'Maybe you misunderstood.'

'I didn't misunderstand anything.' Sam cringed at the pleading tone in her voice, but she couldn't stop herself. 'I've been sick with guilt over this.'

'Aww … poor, hard-done-by Sam,' said Charlie, pushing the corners of her mouth down into a clown frown. Did Sam deserve to be mocked? Probably. 'Here's some advice. A sure-fire way to avoid all that sickening guilt. Don't sneak around with your sister's boyfriend in the first place.'

'Drew wasn't your boyfriend. You just said that,' said Sam, before groaning at the stupid circularity of her own logic. May as well make Charlie's next point for her. It would save time. 'But I thought he was.'

'Exactly,' said Charlie with a smug smile. 'I'm the forgiving type. One more apology should do it. That will make one million and one.'

Charlie had outfoxed her and Sam was glad about it. 'I'm sorry.'

'Good,' said Charlie, with a satisfied nod. 'I'll accept that. Drew's not my type, anyway. I've gone off cowboys and found me an intellectual instead.'

You had to hand it to her sister. She'd barely left the house, and she'd still managed to find a man. Charlie reached for Sam's phone where it lay on the table. She picked it up, and offered it to Sam.

'Call him,' said Charlie. 'I'll clear out and check on Flicka ... give you some space.'

Drew sat at the table in the kitchen, solemn-faced while Sam told her story; how she'd fallen for him, and pulled away because of a stupid misunderstanding — and how her feelings had never, ever changed. He listened in that intense, considered way he had, without interrupting. Finally she ran out of breath. Sam studied his face as if seeing it for the first time. His perfect nose, flared now with emotion. His penetrating green eyes, full of tenderness. His broad suntanned face and square chin, smudged with grease.

Still Drew was silent. Did she need to start all over again? Maybe she'd made no sense at all. One thing was certain; Sam was willing to explain herself a thousand times over if it would make him understand. But as she opened her mouth to speak, Drew stood up. Without a word he rounded the table and kissed her, long and deep and slow. She rose to meet him, throwing herself into his arms. Drew's hunger for her pulsed as strong as ever, and she laughed with the sheer delight of his response.

When they parted there was puzzlement as well as joy in Drew's expression. 'You sure did read me wrong,' he said, shaking his head. 'Why didn't you just ask me straight out?' She struggled to answer, struggled to find the right words to explain her monumental lack of faith in him. He shushed her and laid a forefinger across her lips. 'It doesn't matter. You were being loyal to your sister. There's no shame in that.'

'Bravo, bravo!' cried Charlie, applauding loudly. Neither of them had noticed her come in. They'd been lost in a world of their own. 'This is all very touching,' said Charlie, 'but Flicka's gone down. That foal's made up its mind to come.' Everybody scrambled out the door into the dusk. Sam had not witnessed the miracle of a birth before. It was to be a night of marvels.

CHAPTER 34

Sam took a moment, on waking, to recall the momentous happenings of the previous night. She stretched and yawned, reaching for where Drew should have lain beside her in the bed. It was an unpleasant jolt to find herself alone. Then the fullness of last night's events returned, and she knew exactly where he'd be — up at the yards with Flicka and her newborn colt.

Sam pulled on T-shirt and jeans, feeling like the cat that ate the cream. She tiptoed down the hall to the kitchen, trying not to wake Charlie. They'd all had quite a night, and for a number of reasons, nobody had had enough sleep. Sam yawned, put on the kettle and cut up some carrots for Flicka. She made two cups of tea, one for her and one for Drew, and took them outside.

One for Drew. The significance of simply making Drew a morning cup of tea gave her goose-bumps. After last night there'd be no more guilt, no more divided loyalties. Their love was finally out in the open, free of misunderstandings, and best of all, it was graced with Charlie's approval. The safe arrival of Flicka's foal felt like a final blessing on their happiness.

'Good morning, Bess.' The dog smiled and thumped her tail on the dusty porch. 'Coming to see the baby?' Bess barked assent and followed her up to the yards.

'He's gorgeous,' said Sam. 'Absolutely gorgeous.'

'Yep,' said Drew, from his perch on the yard rail. 'He sure is something to brag about.' Flicka stood guard over a foal so perfectly formed, so finely chiselled, he didn't look real. His coat was a pretty silvery grey that Drew assured her would shed out to deepest black.

Sam held up a mug. 'Brought you some tea.'

'I can't believe he's a black. A direct throwback to Abbey,' said Drew, shaking his head. 'I have a beautiful black colt with a double Abbey cross in his pedigree. Do you know how hard it is to get your hands on a horse like that?'

'Correction,' said Sam. 'I have a black colt with a double Abbey cross.'

Drew jumped down from the fence and pulled her in for a kiss. 'You'll spill the tea,' she said. He took both mugs from her and balanced them on a post. Then he picked her up and spun her around and around until she was dizzy with laughter.

'Correction,' he said, retrieving his tea. '*We* have a beautiful black colt with a double Abbey cross.' The foal nickered on cue.

Sam steadied herself against a rail until she could no longer hear her heartbeat. 'I don't know who this Abbey is,' she said. 'What's so special about him?'

He looked like he didn't believe her. 'Everybody knows Abbey. He's a legend.'

She shook her head. 'Sorry, no.'

'By Radiant? Going way back to Radium?'

She shook her head again. 'Still nothing.'

'Crikey, Sam. This is important stuff. What do they teach you in Melbourne?' He looked so completely perturbed, Sam turned away to hide her smile.

'Tell me, then.'

'Abbey is a stock horse foundation sire. Big and black, born in 1955 up in New South Wales, in a stall behind the Willawarrin pub. I've been there. There's a photo of me standing outside.'

'You've been there?'

Drew looked embarrassed. How utterly charming. 'Kind of a pilgrimage, I guess.' He pointed to the foal. 'When I first laid eyes on that little bloke, I thought to myself, I bet that's exactly what Abbey looked like when he was born.' How she loved seeing him all fired up like this, brimming with enthusiasm, impatient to dive headfirst into the future – their shared future. 'You know, they almost cut Abbey as a yearling?' he said. 'Can you imagine that?'

'Cut?'

'Gelded. His dam and sire were both by Radium II, half brother and sister. They thought he was too inbred. Thank Christ they changed their mind. That horse won the Taree campdraft at just eighteen months old.' Drew slid through the rails and stroked the foal, an expression of immense pride on his face. 'Abbey won twenty-three campdrafts with the legendary Harry Ball in the saddle. The pair couldn't be beat, and Harry worshipped that horse.' The foal sucked at Drew's shirt and he let it chew his fingers.

'That's a lovely story,' said Sam.

'Tragic ending, though. Harry's on the Pacific Highway, coming back from the Warwick Rodeo with Abbey, when there's a terrible accident. Harry's killed. As a tribute to her husband, Harry's wife decides nobody will ever ride Abbey again. She sends him over to Theo Hill at Comara Station. That stallion went on to found the finest stock horse bloodline in Australia.' Drew knelt down. The foal sniffed his face and he blew softly into its nose. 'And to think Abbey blood runs through this bloke's veins, eh? It's a fair dinkum miracle.'

There was no doubt about it. Sam did have a rival for Drew's affection, but it wasn't Charlie. Drew was in love with the little colt. Sam smiled as he gave the foal a great hug and Flicka whinnied her disapproval. The mare gathered the baby up with her nose and urged him away. He obediently turned tail and buried his nose beneath his mother's flank for a feed, tail wagging merrily.

Sam finished her tea. 'I have to go to work.'

Drew spun her around and kissed her comprehensively. 'I'm going to hang around here for a bit,' he said. 'Try that imprinting stuff you were talking about.'

Last night Sam had told him about Dr Robert Miller's theory for imprinting foals. It was all about bonding with humans in the brief window of time straight after birth. Such foals began to see humans as fellow horses instead of predators. The deep trust they established in their handler often lead to miraculous training results. Sam smiled. She'd handed Drew the perfect excuse to spend all day with the new colt. Flicka laid back her ears as Drew tried to hijack the foal again.

Sam fed her the carrots. 'You'd think he'd done all the work himself, wouldn't you?' she said to the mare, before heading for the car.

Phoenix's piercing neigh greeted her as she came in sight of the showground. He knew her car. At first Bushy had put it down to coincidence, but he agreed now that the colt recognised the blue beetle, and even responded to its engine noise coming up the track. Sam parked and went to say hello to Phoenix. The young stallion performed excited pirouettes as she approached, and accepted the apple she offered with a regal nod of his head. Flicka's newborn foal was adorable, true – but no horse could replace the special place Phoenix held in Sam's heart.

Sam headed for Bushy's *kitchen*, the narrow porch between the horse wash bays and his room. She needed a big mug of his strong, sweet tea, and a plate piled high with hot buttered toast, chock-full of fat raisins. A sugar hit might chase away her weariness.

Sam told him about the foal, but instead of being excited, Bushy was uncharacteristically quiet. He stirred the tea and handed her a steaming mug, as his deep-set eyes searched her face. 'I'm glad you've got a little 'un at home. That fella's going to teach you a lot.' A faint smile. 'That's if Drew ever lets you near him.'

Sam grinned. 'He's head over heels, all right.'

Phoenix burst into a series of commanding neighs. 'How do you reckon that golden colt's been going?' asked Bushy.

'Phoenix? He's fabulous, doesn't put a foot wrong. Soft mouth, good transitions, great laterals. Awesome stop. He's good to catch and float. Opens and closes gates. Stands for the farrier. You can even crack a whip off him.'

'You're a fair hand with that whip these days.' Sam nodded, curious. She knew Bushy. He was gearing up to saying something important. Bushy finished a mouthful of toast. 'How'd you like to take Phoenix home?' he said. 'That horse could use some bush work.'

'Really?' Sam could hardly believe her good fortune. 'I can take him home to Brumby's Run?'

'That you can. Ryan suggested it himself, just this morning.' Sam's smile grew larger. This was truly wonderful news, so why did Bushy look so gloomy? 'You're to finish Phoenix for his new owner,' he said, gazing into his tea.

Sam's smile faltered. She couldn't make sense of Bushy's words. 'New owner?'

'I'm afraid that colt's been sold.'

Anger and panic formed a heavy stone in Sam's stomach. 'Unsell him then,' she said swiftly. 'I'll buy him, whatever the cost.'

Bushy shook his head sadly. 'Can't be done. Apparently the buyer's promised Ryan a major sponsorship. He can't afford to welch on the deal.'

No. It was impossible — impossible to contemplate that this could happen to her again. Sam reeled from the kitchen and pelted to the yard where Phoenix pranced about, impatient for his morning feed. The colt was heartbreakingly beautiful, haloed in morning sunshine, framed by the majesty of Maroong Mountain. But Sam's eyes were brimful of tears and she couldn't see him anymore. All she saw was the formless shape of her own loss.

CHAPTER 35

The tail end of a bad dream slipped away, and Charlie woke up, knuckling sleep from her eyes. What a relief. This wasn't her hospital bed and she wasn't ill again. This was her own room at Brumby's . . . and someone was knocking on the door. She pulled on her clothes and ran down the hall. It was Karl.

The three weeks since she'd met Karl had been the most fascinating and rewarding weeks of her life. Nearly every day now, Karl swung by and collected her on his way up to Balleroo. He was conducting a field review on the impact of the grazing trial, and Charlie was helping him. She didn't know what was more exciting. Being involved in a serious scientific research program, or spending hours on end with Karl. With each day they spent together, Charlie felt more drawn to the quirky, sexy ranger.

She opened the door to Karl, offered him a dazzling smile, and grabbed her bag from the porch.

It had started with the texts. Then one morning Charlie had woken to the sound of a car coming up the track, had crept down the hall and peered out the bathroom window. A government vehicle and a khaki-clad figure stood in the drive : Karl.

Charlie stepped into jeans, leaving off her belt for once, letting them sit low on her hips. She gave a little shimmy. The mirror told her she looked good – no longer skeletal, but slim and healthy. The knock came at the door again. This time she opened it, to find Karl standing there, holding a cardboard box. He'd combed his sandy-blond hair and slicked it neatly back in an obvious effort to be presentable. With his boyish features, pressed khaki uniform and polished boots, Karl looked like an overgrown boy scout. Charlie almost expected a three-fingered salute and an admonition to be prepared. She tried to restrain herself, she really did, but laughter crept around her edges and spilt from her seams.

Karl looked perplexed, unhappy even. That wasn't what she wanted. Charlie slapped her hand resolutely over her mouth.

'Miss Kelly?' He inspected her face. 'It is Charlie Kelly this time? You have not transformed into another?'

'No, it's me. Charlie.'

He proffered the box. It looked heavy. 'For you.' She gestured for him to come in, and he put it down on the kitchen table. 'Open it.'

Inside were copies of government field notes for Balleroo, dating back to the nineteen fifties. Endangered species reports, flora and fauna surveys, bog water quality assessments, frog population counts. Charlie couldn't believe her eyes. It was a veritable treasure trove. 'Where did these come from?'

'The Department of Environment Library. I made copies.'

Charlie flipped through volume after precious volume. 'It must have taken forever.'

'It took some time, yes.' His eyes locked onto hers. 'Do you like them?'

'No.' His face fell. 'I *love* them.' She moved closer and pressed her lips against his cheek, sliding them at the last minute from his cheek to his mouth. He quivered and returned the kiss.

Then Drew had pushed in through the fly-wire door with impeccably bad timing. 'What's going on here?'

Karl seemed wary. Charlie introduced the men, then pulled Drew out the door. 'Haven't you got some cows to chase or something?'

Drew had put on his hat. 'Are you okay?'

'Of course I am. Now nick off, will you?'

'Your boyfriend?' Karl had asked her after Drew left. Charlie shook her head and Karl had smiled. 'Very good. May I see you tomorrow?'

'Yes Karl,' Charlie had said solemnly. 'You may.'

CHAPTER 36

Sam rose at first light to put the kettle on. The first week of April, and there was already a nip in the early morning air. Fog had crept down from the range overnight. Outside the window, trees loomed grey and amorphous in swirls of mist. Sam prayed it would clear to the sunny day promised by the forecast.

Charlie emerged from the hallway, pyjama-clad and yawning. The physical change in her sister these past six weeks had been nothing short of remarkable. She seemed taller. Her body had filled out, in spite of Sam's limited recipe range, and Charlie's own laziness in the kitchen. Her limbs, once skinny sticks, had grown ripe and smooth. Muscles were starting to define her upper arms and calves, rounding out the knobbly bits. Her sister no longer peered at the world through gaunt hollows. Clear amber eyes gazed from an angelic face, its heart shape enhanced by a newly defined widow's peak. Charlie's hairline curved back from the dark triangle in a way identical to Sam's own, exaggerating their resemblance. It was kind of flattering to think that people had mistaken her for this gorgeous girl. 'When are they supposed to get here, again?' asked Charlie, slipping bread into the toaster.

'Ten o'clock, and Drew will be over at nine to help saddle up. Is

Topsy's gear back up at the yards?' Charlie nodded. 'It's a miracle you found a crupper. That pony's got no wither at all. I lay awake half the night imagining the saddle, and the girl too, slipping straight over his head on the way home.'

Charlie applied slabs of butter and lashings of honey to the toast, then popped another round on. You couldn't fill her up lately.

'I'm still concerned about time,' said Sam. 'A twelve-year-old could slow us down more than we bargained for. Are you sure that track down to the creek isn't too steep for a child? I'll die if she falls off.' Sam started going through papers on the table. 'Where are those *waiver of liability* forms? Oh good, here they are. I wonder if we've got enough spares? People could make mistakes. Would it be enough for them to initial the correction, do you think? Or should we give them a completely new form? I think a new form, don't you, just to be on the safe side?'

Charlie plonked down tea and toast in front of Sam. 'Will you chill already?' She rolled her eyes and put still more bread into the toaster. 'It's only five people. We can do this standing on our heads.' Then she yawned and stuffed her mouth with honey toast.

Sam pressed a hand over her eyes and squinted them tight shut. Her sister was absolutely right. She needed to relax – although not quite as much as Charlie, perhaps. Charlie appeared to have gone back to sleep, hunched over her tea cup. Which was pretty remarkable, really, considering what a momentous day it was. Today, *Brumby's Run High Country Trails* welcomed its very first customers.

They'd put a test advertisement in the Currajong Gazette — *The majestic mountains of north-eastern Victoria abound with fascinating wildlife, ancient forests and stunning views. We offer rides through the heart of the high country. Explore spectacular Balleroo National Park. Visit historic huts, ride through unspoiled wilderness and breathe pure mountain air. An unforgettable horse-riding experience. Knowledgeable guides and horses to suit all abilities.*

Their target market wasn't locals, of course, but tourists. City slickers after an authentic bush experience. But for now it seemed sensible just to dip their toes in the water – run a few rides and see if they worked. If all went well, they'd launch an internet advertising campaign in the spring.

Charlie and Drew had done a good job planning the course of today's ride. It wound its way through the lush creek flats of Brumby's Run up to the national park entrance, where Drew had built an imposing bush-timber gateway. Then the track struck out through scattered candlebarks and peppermint gums growing close to the cliff face. It offered sweeping views across the range, all the way down to where Currajong nestled like a toy town beside the Merri River.

They passed several lookout points where riders and horses would have a chance to catch their breath, and allow any slowcoaches to catch up. The forest leg of the ride gave opportunities for spotting kangaroos, echidnas and perhaps even a rare brush-tailed rock wallaby or two. Near the end of the first hour, they would ford Snake Creek and stop for photos at scenic Bluff Falls. Platypus could usually be spotted in the ferny pools below the cascade, and eagles often soared above the escarpment. Then it would be just about time to head for home.

Their first clients were locals from nearby Tallangala, experienced riders all, and a perfect group for a test run. Sam had chosen their horses with great care: the smallest skewbald pony for the girl, the two creamy brumbies for the older aunts, and the pair of flaxen-maned taffies for the mother and father. Sam would ride Tara, a sensible brown mare. Charlie, of course, would ride Tambo, and Drew was coming along on Clancy.

They'd groomed the horses to within an inch of their lives. Their coats gleamed. Their manes lay combed and smooth. Even their hoofs were oiled and freshly trimmed. 'We're not off to the royal show,' Charlie had said, but she still seemed pleased at how well the horses scrubbed up, especially Tambo. She even helped Sam clean and polish the old tack that had been thrown in as a package deal with the Mitchell string.

There was something marvellously therapeutic about the process; sitting together in the kitchen, watching the ancient leather soak up warm oil applied with paint brushes — past differences forgotten. A final buff up with saddle soap completed the procedure. Bridles that looked like they'd never been cleaned in their life hung shining and supple. Buckles and bits gleamed. Saddles that had been covered in green grime came up almost like new.

Sam had been so looking forward to today; couldn't wait to show off their beautiful new horses and equipment. But now the day had actually arrived, nerves were getting the better of her.

'Would you go into town for more milk?' she asked Charlie. 'We mightn't have enough if they all want coffee.'

'We've got plenty of milk,' said Charlie, in the sort of tone one might use to reassure an anxious child. 'They'd need to drink about five mugs each for us to run out. And anyway, I don't go to town.'

'That's ridiculous,' said Sam. 'You can't just never go into Curra-jong again.'

'Why not?' Charlie licked honey from her fingers 'I've managed so far. Don't blame me. If you hadn't decided to steal my life, I wouldn't have to hide out here at Brumby's.'

Sam sighed and nodded. 'If that's what you want . . . and I suppose you're right about the milk.' She put the forms into a plastic sleeve and grabbed her hat from the hook near the door. 'I'm going up to feed the horses.'

Sam emerged into the chilly morning, wrapped her coat tight around her and looked skywards. Streamers of pastel blue showed beyond the mist, and a wan sun seemed determined to break through. Good, the day promised to be fine. A volley of neighs greeted her on her way up the hill, and Phoenix reared and boxed the air. Even the prospect of losing him wasn't enough to spoil her happiness today. Sam was firmly in denial on that score, and determined to believe in miracles.

She smiled and broke into a small dance, finishing with a twirl and curtsey as she reached the yards. A row of curious heads were lined up all along the rails. Jarrang snorted and turned his back on her fool-ishness. She laughed and plucked a sprig from a fragrant native mint bush that was blooming beside the yards. She buried her nose in its snowy-white flowers. They really were very beautiful, like tiny orchids. Trumpet-shaped, with splotches of colour – purple, red and yellow. She breathed in deep lungfuls of perfumed air, held the tiny bouquet aloft and bowed to her watchful, prick-eared audience. It would be impossible at that moment to feel any happier.

Sam took hold of the wheelbarrow and headed for the shed. Soon all the horses were happily munching their hay – all except for Whirlwind. She sulked in the yard next to Jarrang's, refusing to touch her food while Sam was watching. 'You're just like Charlie,' Sam scolded as she poured a measure of oats into the mare's feed bin. 'You'll bite your nose off to spite your face.'

After feeding up, Sam went to the little room beside the hay shed that was to serve as their office. She stacked the liability-waiver forms neatly on the desk, and tested the mobile eftpos machine. She picked up a business card and read it out aloud. *Brumby's Run High Country Trails. Horses to suit all riders. Proprietors Charlie Kelly and Sam Carmichael.* They were partners now, practically and legally.

Drew arrived at quarter to ten, and Sam and Charlie were ready for him. Horses brushed and saddled, forms waiting to be signed, helmets lined up on a bench. Sam had brought the portable butane cooker up to the office, and a bright new kettle was on the boil. Milk in an ice box, mugs and spoons in a row, shortbread biscuits for afterwards.

Charlie was trotting Topsy up and down the drive so he wouldn't be too fresh. 'Don't get him all sweaty,' yelled Sam.

Bess was barking now and Sam could hear a car. How exciting! Their first ever clients had arrived. She walked down to meet them, resisting the impulse to run. A pretty blonde child was hugging a happy Bess around the neck.

'Welcome to Brumby's Run,' Sam said, smiling. Everybody introduced themselves. Sam kept repeating their names in her head, to ensure she'd remember. The blonde girl was Meg Morgan. Her even blonder mother was Sue. Craig, her handsome father, reminded Sam of somebody, but she wasn't sure who. The two older aunties were Tracey and Mel. Five people wasn't too hard. How well would she manage with more?

'Are there brumbies?' asked Meg, eyes shining with expectation.

Sue hushed her. 'Don't mind Meg,' she said. 'My daughter's obsessed with those *Silver Brumby* books. I told her there wouldn't be real brumbies.'

'Oh, but there are,' said Sam, doing a quick mental calculation. Jarrang, Phoenix and Tambo. Whirlwind, the two creamies, and Flicka's newborn colt. 'We have seven brumbies,' she said. 'Two stallions, four mares and a foal.'

Meg exploded in questions, and Sam answered them as best she could. 'Can I ride one?' the girl asked eagerly as they walked up the hill to the yards.

'I actually had a lovely pony picked out for you.'

'Can't I ride a brumby,' begged Meg. 'Please?'

'My daughter's an excellent rider,' said Craig, ruffling the girl's hair. 'She's done five years of pony club, and has outgrown her Welsh Mountain pony. In fact we're looking around to buy something bigger. It would be a real thrill for Meg to ride a brumby.'

Sam considered her options. This was proving to be more difficult than she'd imagined. Their first clients hadn't even mounted, and already things weren't going according to plan. She compared the temperaments of the two creamies. They were equally quiet, especially if allowed to follow along in the middle of the string. Gemma was a little friendlier, perhaps more affectionate than Golden. Sam excused herself and went to talk to the others.

'The kid'll be fine on Gemma,' said Charlie.

'But we had the aunties on the brumbies.' Sam didn't like sudden changes of plan. 'Ruby might be too flighty, and the black mare, Jet? She likes the lead way too much. She wouldn't suit the aunties at all.'

'Simple,' said Charlie. 'Put an auntie on Tara, and you ride Phoenix instead.'

Sam considered her sister's suggestion. She hadn't ridden the golden colt out with the other horses before, but it was either that, or disappoint both the girl and her parents. 'Right, I'll get him ready. You guys have them sign the forms, and don't forget to offer them coffee, and ask them if they need the mounting block , and . . . ' But Drew and Charlie had already walked off, talking and laughing with the clients.

To say that Phoenix was keen would have been a monumental understatement. He trembled all over while Sam gave him a swift brush down. He neighed wildly while she saddled and bridled him. Then he danced down to meet the other riders. There was an audible gasp from the girl, and admiring glances all round.

'He's the most beautiful horse in the world,' sighed Meg. As if he understood, Phoenix redoubled his efforts to show off. All colts were full of themselves, but this was ridiculous. He frisked about so, that it took all Sam's skill just to mount. It was a bit like riding a pogo stick. He pranced and capered, seemed to hang suspended in space between strides, striking heroic poses in silhouette. He arched his neck and flirted with the mares, impressing everybody except his rider. Sam wrestled with the reins, trying without much success to make him pay attention.

They all set off up the hill. The plan was for Charlie and Drew to go up front, as they knew the way better than Sam did. If Charlie got too tired, she could simply go home. Sam would go last in line and keep an eye on the slower riders. At first Phoenix objected to the arrangement, tossing his head and jogging to try to overtake the leaders. But soon his herding instincts kicked in. Within a wild mob, the oldest mare travels at the front of the group and the stallion at the rear. By driving the mares ahead of him, he ensures that none stray, and they're less likely to be stolen by other males.

Phoenix enthusiastically threw himself into the role of mob stallion. He drove the group forward by running alongside the creamy mares in front of him, urging them on if they dawdled. Gemma and Golden had been raised in a wild brumby herd, and fell quickly in line with his demands. It was really very useful. The mares were a bit on the lazy side, and the bossy colt was saving their riders from having to constantly kick them on.

Golden stopped abruptly and ducked her head for a mouthful of grass. Phoenix snaked his head at her, swinging it from side to side like a threatening cobra and flattening his ears. The mare moved smartly forward.

'However did you teach him that?' asked Mel. Or was it Tracey? Sam had already gotten the aunties mixed up. 'You must be a wonderful trainer. I can't wait to tell my friend about you. She's wanting a horse for her daughter. I'll get her to give you a ring.'

Sam almost admitted to the woman that Phoenix had taken it upon himself to keep the group together. That Sam doubted she could stop him, even if she tried. But instead she just smiled and took the credit. 'Brumbies are highly intelligent and trainable,' she said. 'They make excellent saddle horses.'

'Well you've certainly sold us,' said the smiling auntie, and they all took off up the hill at a gentle canter.

The ride was a terrific success. Nobody fell off, for starters. Meg had no problems handling Gemma; in fact, all the horses behaved them-selves beautifully. And it wasn't only the horses. At the lookouts, eagles wheeled overhead on cue. In the forest, wallabies bounded by. Echidnas waddled across the path and they spotted a koala and her baby up a tree. It was neither too hot nor too cold. A light breeze kept the flies at bay and Charlie didn't get too tired.

The falls were a big hit, offering plenty of photo opportunities, and a pair of obliging platypus playing in a shady pool. Phoenix seemed determined to go for a swim, barging into the shallows, scattering diamonds of spray with his forefeet. Sam pushed him on with all her might, but Phoenix wasn't listening. Any minute now he'd roll in the stream and make a complete fool of her. Just as his legs buckled, Drew was at her side, taking the colt's reins and urging him from the water. Then he was gone, cantering off with the panache of a movie hero and the easy grace of a man born in the saddle. Sam sighed with pleasure. To think that dashing man was in love with her.

They left the falls precisely at eleven-thirty as scheduled, and thanks in no small part to Phoenix, arrived back at the yards on time. Sam had enjoyed herself more than anybody, and couldn't quite believe that she was about to be paid for the privilege. Meg helped Drew and Sam unsaddle the horses, while Charlie handed around coffee and biscuits.

'Brumbies are awesome,' the girl announced, as they turned Phoenix out. 'Can I see the others?' Meg was looking past the hay shed, to where Jarrang and Whirlwind stood in adjoining yards. 'Are they brumbies too?' Sam nodded. 'Can I have a look?' asked Meg. 'Please?'

Sam hesitated, but the girl's enthusiasm was infectious. 'Come on, then.' She indicated for the girl to follow her. 'Just don't get too close. They're still quite wild.'

Jarrang barely deigned to notice them, but Whirlwind rushed the fence with her ears pinned. Meg took a few steps backwards. 'I told you not to get too close.' Sam laid a protective hand on the girl's arm.

'What's her name?'

'Whirlwind.'

'She doesn't look like a brumby.' Meg moved forward again. The girl seemed unfazed by the mare's aggression, and had an appraising eye that belied her youth. 'She's too big, for one thing.'

Sam agreed. Whirlwind was tall for a brumby. Undoubtedly Jarrang had sired her – they had the same presence, the same white stripes on their hoofs. But it was clear that none of the mares in Jarrang's captured herd were Whirlwind's dam. 'Whether she looks it or not, that mare was wild-caught just a few months ago.'

'I love her mane,' said Meg. 'It looks like it's been crimped. I could brush it all day.' Sam nodded. Whirlwind really did have an incredible amount of mane. But there was something odd about it, now that she looked closely. It was no longer snarled and tangled. Instead it lay in silky waves. The mare's tail, too, fell in a full, luxurious curtain to her dappled hocks.

'Do you know who she looks like?' Meg didn't wait for Sam to answer. 'Gandalf's horse in the Lord of the Rings movies. Shadowfax was magical – Gandalf's partner, not his servant. Whirlwind looks just like Shadowfax.'

Charlie strolled over and caught the tail end of the conversation. 'She does, doesn't she?'

'Don't ask me how,' said Sam, who was a fan of those movies. They'd showcased so many beautiful horses, and she'd read quite a bit about their equine stars. 'Shadowfax was played by a sixteen year old Andalusian Stallion named Domero,' she told Meg. 'He was trained to work at liberty, responding to off camera cues.'

'He was awesome,' said Meg with a dreamy smile.

Sam nodded. 'Yes, he was.'

'Can I pat Whirlwind?' asked Meg.

Sam was about to warn the girl away when her sister interrupted. 'Sure thing, kid.' Charlie slid through the rails and pressed her cheek against the mare's neck. 'Come on in.'

Meg opened the gate before a horrified Sam had the presence of mind to stop her. The child held out her hand. Whirlwind arched her neck, elegant ears angled forward and her eyes kind, accepting Meg's fingers on her mane with a gracious nod of her head. There was a certain import, a holiness about the interaction, that was evident to both horse and human.

'Shadowfax could understand the speech of men,' Meg told Charlie, whispering as if she was in the presence of royalty. 'He was fearless and faster than any other horse in Middle Earth. Nobody could ride him except for Gandalf. He would accept neither bridle or saddle, and carried Gandalf only by his own choice.'

'What?' said Charlie, 'like this?' She grasped a handful of mane and casually swung herself onto Whirlwind's broad back. The mare twisted her neck and snuffled Charlie's leg.

'Come out now, Meg,' said Sam, in a low voice, her heart thudding hard. With one last pat, Meg slipped back through the gate. Sam resisted the impulse to seize the girl and hug her tight to her chest. Should she be furious with Charlie, or in awe of her dazzling horsemanship? Sam understood now. Charlie was in a league of her own. Still, if her sister ever got out of that yard alive, Sam might kill her herself.

Meg sparkled with a kind of intense joy, chattering on about how much she'd loved the day. Her prattle blurred into white noise. 'Get off now, Charlie,' said Sam, trying to keep her voice calm. 'I think she's had enough.'

'No, wait,' Meg was saying. 'Wait!' The girl was pulling at Sam's sleeve now. 'My uncle's here. I want to show him how Charlie can ride Whirlwind without a saddle or bridle.'

Sam looked towards the main yards and her skin crawled with fear. Spike Morgan was lounging against a rail. This girl beside her with the shining eyes? This must be Spike's niece. What a fool she was, not to have made the connection. He'd recognise the stolen mare in a second. Bushy had altered her brand, but the new scar was still fresh, the deceit still apparent. They'd let a twelve-year-old child go into a yard with the horse that had killed Spike's best friend, not two months ago. It would be the end of the road for their business. There'd be charges of negligence and of theft . . . and it would be the end of the road for Whirlwind. Sam fought for breath.

'Uncle Spike,' yelled Meg, and ran off towards him.

Charlie started at the sound of Spike's name, and gave Sam a shocked glance. Her apprehension was shared by Whirlwind, who reared. Charlie leaned low over her neck and clung to her mane, becoming part of the beautiful mare. 'Open the gate,' she said urgently. Sam shook her head and began to protest, but her voice only came in strangled gasps. 'Just do it!' hissed Charlie. Sam said a prayer, opened the gate and closed her eyes.

CHAPTER 37

Whirlwind cantered calmly up the hill, with Charlie securely aboard. Sam's breath still came in shallow spurts, but with every second that passed, her hands unclenched a little. Unbelievably, it looked like they were going to be all right.

The mare had stunning movement. Extended and elevated, cadenced and harmonious. Sam imagined for one moment how her gait would wow judges in the dressage arena. Whirlwind and Charlie gained the brow of the hill, just as Meg arrived with Uncle Spike in tow.

'Afternoon, princess,' he said, with a cocky lift of an eyebrow.

Ever since the fateful buckjump competition, Sam had gone to extraordinary lengths to avoid Spike. He'd not pursued her. Perhaps because he'd lost the bet, the deal that they'd go on a date if Spike was crowned King of the Mountain. Drew had claimed that honour.

Of course, this was a ridiculously simplistic take on things. Spike would have to be a very concrete thinker indeed to believe a relationship could be governed by the same sort of rules as a poker game, and she could be picked up like the kitty. But for whatever reason, until now he'd stayed away.

Meg pointed up the hill, to where Whirlwind's grey rump was vanishing into the trees. 'Did you see her?' she asked her uncle.

'Too far away,' said Spike. Meg's face fell. 'Cheer up,' he said. 'There are other brumbies, aren't there?' He tickled her and made her laugh. 'Show me them instead.'

Sam sized him up, and saw no sign that he'd recognised the mare. Charlie's courage and presence of mind had undoubtedly saved Whirlwind's life.

Meg grabbed Spike's arm and pulled him away to look at the new foal. Sam waited until they'd moved off, then ran over to where Drew was saddling Clancy. 'What are we going to do?'

'I'll find her,' he whispered, and took off up the mountain. Breathe, Sam told herself. Just breathe. There was still a lot to do – take the money, for a start. Hand around coffee and biscuits, collect some feedback.

'You've quite a fan in my daughter,' said Sue, as they watched Meg drag Spike over to see Phoenix. Sam smiled at the compliment and invited her into the office. Sue took out her credit card and slipped it into the reader. It whirred and clicked, and a few seconds later Sam was handing over a receipt for the very first payment to Brumby Trails. It wasn't a lot - petty cash from her father's perspective. But for some reason it felt like she'd made a million dollars. It must be true what they said about appreciating things more if you worked for them.

Sam was suddenly ashamed to think of how often she'd taken money for granted. Not this time though. This time she'd earned it. Holding that humble credit card docket felt as good as acing her final exams, or being selected in the A team for the state dressage squad. No, it wasn't like that at all. It was ten times better.

The whistling kettle brought her back to earth 'Coffee?' Sam asked.

Sue nodded and took a shortbread. 'You really have got the perfect setup here,' she said. 'Now, which brumbies are for sale? Meg has her heart set on a filly, freshly broken. She's keen to train a horse from scratch.' For a moment Sam didn't follow. 'And that stunning palomino colt,' said Sue. 'How much is his stud fee? I'm retiring my barrel racing mare and would like to put her in foal.' Sam didn't know what to say. Sue misinterpreted her silence. 'Don't say he's already fully booked for next season?' She sounded so disappointed. 'I like your buckskin stallion too. He's beautiful, but I'm afraid I've fallen in love with the palomino.'

Think quickly now. Her first instinct was to say no, to explain that there were no horses for sale, no stallions at stud. But this woman was handing them a potential new income stream on a plate. Bushy had half a dozen young brumbies, green broke, but going well under saddle. And how she'd love to see a foal by Phoenix. Sam's head told her that Phoenix wouldn't even be here in spring, but her heart refused to believe it. 'I do have some young stock,' Sam said cautiously. 'But wouldn't Meg be better off with an older, fully schooled horse? It's not a great idea for two youngsters to be learning on their own.'

'I couldn't agree more,' said Sue, nodding. 'That's why I want Meg to have lessons. We'll leave her new horse at Brumby's Run on agistment, and I'll drive her here three times a week after school.' Sue dipped the biscuit in her coffee. 'Oh, and on weekends. What do you charge for a full day? Do you have some sort of school-holiday program? Meg might like to bring her friends along.'

'We can do that,' said Sam, trying to sound bright and confident. Trying not to show how overwhelmed she really was. She needed to talk to Charlie. However Charlie was off in the bush somewhere, riding an unbroken man-killer without saddle or bridle. So much for the promises she'd made to Mary about not letting Charlie overdo it, about keeping her safe.

'Good,' said Sue. 'I won't have a look at your sale horses right now, if you don't mind.' Thank goodness for that. There weren't any sale horses. 'I'll come back on my own later. We're wanting to surprise Meg.' Sue took a card from her purse. 'Here's my contact details. Why don't you just text me the price and particulars?' She scribbled on the back and handed over the card.

Sam looked at the list written there. Stud fees. Lesson fees. Agistment fees. This was too good to be true. 'Meg is interested in high-school riding. You don't happen to know of a local coach, do you? It's all barrel racing and campdrafting around here.'

'I'm a level one NCAS dressage coach,' said Sam, 'if that's any help.'

'That sounds marvellous.' Sue looked impressed. 'What does it mean, exactly?'

'It's a certification through the Equestrian Federation of Australia national coaching scheme. It means I'm qualified to teach beginners through to elementary level. I used to help coach the juniors of the state dressage squad.'

'Good heavens, you are a find!' Sue was absolutely beaming. 'There's a group of girls at the Tallangala Pony Club who are dead keen on dressage. Just wait until they hear I've found them a coach.'

Craig and the aunties came in for cups of coffee, laughing and joking and saying how much they'd enjoyed their ride. Sam took a second look at Craig. Although older and heavier, the resemblance to his brother Spike was obvious now. If only she'd picked it earlier. Sue kept up a steady stream of chatter, aimed mainly at her husband, talking up the idea of buying Meg a brumby. Sam imagined Sue normally got her way.

'We'll be in touch,' said Sue, as they rose to leave. 'Don't forget to text me.' Sam waved Sue's card gaily about, to show she'd remember. Sue glanced around and dropped her voice to a stage whisper. 'I'd like photos of your available horses, maybe a little bit about them – and the price, of course. I presume they're all registered in the brumby stud book, or whatever it is you call it?'

Sam nodded. As far as she knew, all Bushy's horses were eligible for listing with the Brumby Association. She could hurry it through if she had to.

'Perfect.' Sue took one last biscuit. 'We'd best get going.'

They all crowded out the door. Meg was describing the finer points of natural-horsemanship training to her uncle. Spike lit up a smoke and slouched against the rails. Buckjumping was as far from natural horsemanship as you could imagine. But then there'd been his impressive performance in the Bareback Challenge, cantering perfect circles without saddle or bridle, revving that silly chainsaw. He knew a thing or two about communicating with his mount. Sam took a good look at Spike. Objectively, he was gorgeous, but she was immune to his charms. Drew had it all over him. Spike sauntered over, and winked at her. 'You've done a top job, princess. Those horses look a million dollars.'

Sam gave him a smile of genuine gratitude, though she doubted he'd be so generous if he knew about Whirlwind. She said goodbye, and the group moved off to their cars, Meg bouncing about like an excited labrador puppy. Sam stood and watched until she was certain they'd all gone, then felt in her pocket. Where was her phone? It suddenly rang from the office, and she dashed to retrieve it. Drew. He'd found Charlie and she was fine. Was it safe to come home? Right, they wouldn't be long. Sam let out a deep breath, made herself a strong coffee and sat down to wait.

No rational explanation existed for what she was seeing. Charlie and Drew, companionably cantering their horses down the hill. Whirlwind stood like a rock while Charlie slipped off her back, and then the mare followed – followed – her sister into the yard.

Charlie started to groom her. Sam tiptoed to the rails and watched Whirlwind lean into the body brush, the way Pharaoh used to do. She blinked away the sharp sting of tears, wanting to berate her sister for forging this secret alliance behind her back. For making a fool of her. Then she thought of Drew. Charlie had no monopoly on secret alliances.

Sam started to say, 'You've got some explaining to do,' but stopped herself. It was exactly that kind of preachy attitude that had caused problems between them in the first place. No wonder Charlie hadn't been straight with her. So instead she said, 'It all went so well. The Morgans were thrilled.'

'Did they pay?' asked Charlie. Sam nodded. Her sister looked exhausted, completely done in, but completely happy at the same time. She waved Sam into the yard. Cautiously Sam ducked through the rails and approached the mare. Whirlwind showed no fear, no hostility. She allowed Sam to stroke her shoulder, her neck, her cheek. Miracles really did happen.

'Here, what do you make of this?' said Charlie, tugging at Whirlwind's flowing grey forelock. 'I've been dying to show you.' The mare obligingly lowered her head. Unbelievable.

Charlie took hold of Sam's hand and placed it under the forelock. What on earth? Beneath Sam's fingers were two bony bulges, like baby horns. Sam looked at her sister askance. Charlie grinned. 'Cool, isn't it? She actually is a demon horse.'

Sam had a closer look. No doubt about it — a pair of tiny horns grew from Whirlwind's forehead. Sam guessed the rodeo men wouldn't have noticed them. You'd have to lift her forelock first.

'This is amazing,' said Sam. A thought struck her from left field. 'She doesn't have warts under her tail, does she?'

'How did you know?' said Charlie. 'You can't see them unless you're right up close.' Sam ignored the reminder that, until now, she hadn't been able to get anywhere near the mare. Sure enough, there was a cluster of little warts at the base of her tail. It was beginning to make outlandish sense. Whirlwind's height and strength, her luxuriant mane and tail, her magnificent charisma.

'There is a breed of horned horse,' said Sam, slowly. 'Very rare, though. Impossibly rare.'

'Get out!' said Charlie.

'It's true. They're called Carthusian Andalusians. The most ancient equine stud book in the world. All descended from one grey foundation stallion, Esclavo. He had little horns and warts under his tail. Monks protected his bloodlines for hundreds of years. Esclavo was said to be the perfect horse; perfect in conformation and perfect in temperament. My dressage coach says Carthusians are the finest high-school mounts ever known.'

'Are there any left?' asked Charlie.

'Some,' said Sam. 'They're bred at a special stud farm owned by the Spanish government. Not much chance of running into one on Maroong Mountain though.'

'So these Carthusian horses,' said Drew. 'They're Andalusians, you said?'

Sam nodded. 'The oldest, purest strain of all.'

'But Jarrang is Whirlwind's father,' said Charlie. 'The same striped hoofs. That's no coincidence.'

'No, it's not,' said Drew. He'd been listening to their conversation with a thoughtful look on his face. 'Jarrang's her sire all right. A more interesting question is, who's her dam?' He ducked through the rails and headed for the hay shed. Sam chased after him, followed by Charlie.

'You know something, don't you?' said Sam.

'I might.' Drew was gathering biscuits of hay. 'But don't you think the horses deserve a feed first?'

They distributed the hay. It seemed to take forever. When they'd finished, the trio sat outside the office with the last of the coffee and biscuits.

'So?' asked Sam.

'There's a place that breeds those Andalusians over at Jindabyne. El Soldado Stud or something like that . . . Don Campbell's joint. A few years back they lost a filly. Real special she was, apparently. Imported all the way from Spain.'

'When you say lost, you mean what? Died?'

'No, I mean just what I said. Lost – or stolen more like it. Some mad brumby stallion came down and kicked the slip rails out of her yard during the night.'

They all sat for a bit without speaking. Sam guessed they were all thinking the same thing. That lost Andalusian filly was Whirlwind's mother. 'Did she have horns and warts under her tail?' asked Sam.

'How should I know?' said Drew, swigging his coffee. 'But if I were you, I'd be finding out.'

Late afternoon ambled through to evening. 'When will dinner be ready?' Charlie eyed the oven hungrily.

'Not for ages.' Sam slapped some cheese on a piece of bread and pushed it across the table to her sister, the events of the day still spinning in her head. 'Think we can really do this?'

'Hell, yeah!' said Charlie. 'Our own brumby stud. They'll be the next big fashion. We've already got the makings of a great herd. First we get Jarrang and Phoenix into the stud book.' Sam's heart lurched. She hadn't told her sister that the colt had been sold. 'And there's Whirlwind and the two creamies. In the meantime, we buy in some started brumbies from Bushy, school them a bit more and sell them as heritage horses.' Charlie was buzzing with excitement and energy. It was impossible to believe this was the shadow of a girl she'd first met in the hospital, all those months ago. 'We'll offer the Coalition an overflow sanctuary for freshly caught horses in return for being able to train up and sell some youngsters. We'll run the herd up near the park boundary and give brumby-spotting tours. Oh, and take in horses for training, charge agistment for them. We'll make a bloody fortune.'

'And what will we do in our spare time?' asked Sam, trying to keep a straight face.

'Don't,' said Charlie, giving her a playful punch. 'We can do it. You just watch us.'

CHAPTER 38

Charlie watched Karl's face as they drove through the gate into Balleroo National Park, studying his profile. She liked the way his lightly tanned skin blended with his head of sandy blond hair. Sun had bleached the tips, giving him highlights, like a male model might have in a magazine. Karl took his eyes off the road and turned to smile at her. Those compelling slate-grey eyes contrasted with his fair complexion. He looked like he could read her mind.

She'd fallen hard for Karl. The man was in a class of his own, a different breed. There was the physical attraction, of course, but it was more than that. She loved the sexy hint of an accent in his voice, the clipped consonants and oddly formal rhythm of his speech. It conjured up images of exotic places and faraway lands. But Karl's most desirable quality — and she surprised herself with this one — was his mind.

Charlie had never met an environmentalist before. People generally considered her fascination with Balleroo curious at best, mad at worst. In school she was labelled a greenie, and suffered open hostility from kids whose families had been run off the alpine cattle leases they'd held for generations. She'd learned to hide her opinions.

She didn't have to hide anything from Karl. Miracle of miracles, he actually shared her views. For Charlie, discovering that a kindred spirit existed in her world was like discovering she wasn't the last person alive after a nuclear holocaust. Karl had done a university course in environmental science. He'd even won some sort of Young Conservationist of the Year prize in his last job on the New South Wales north coast. The award, apparently, was for dramatically reversing species decline, and increasing local support for grey-headed flying fruit bat colonies. 'You can't achieve good ecological outcomes,' he said, 'without bringing the community along with you.' Consensus conservation, he called it.

'You'll never get consensus in Currajong,' said Charlie.

Karl didn't share this view. He was an optimist. 'There are plenty of people like us,' he said, as they slowed to allow a kangaroo and her half-grown joey to bound across the road.

'Not around here,' argued Charlie. 'Alpine grazing's been going on for over a hundred years. It's a cultural thing. People say cattle reduce fuel for bushfires. They say they eat the weeds.'

'Not everybody.' Karl swerved to avoid a deep pothole. 'Some people say they spread the weeds.'

'The cattlemen don't, and they're the ones who count.'

'You'd be surprised.' Karl tossed her a pamphlet - the newsletter of an organisation called *The Ecological Farmers Network*.

'What's this mob on about, then?' asked Charlie.

'It's a progressive association of farmers, all sorts, cattle producers as well. They support environmental programs, especially those that protect biodiversity.' He turned off the road and headed up a corrugated fire trail. 'You know Ray Hardy? Runs cattle out at Jackson's Track?' Charlie nodded. 'He's a member. And Julie Wilson from the berry farm, and Frank Jones from Claremont Wines. Frank wants to do trips into Balleroo – combine them with fine dining and accommodation. He doesn't want cow pats all over the park. And there's Balleroo Bees, promoting alpine wildflower honey. And John Brooks from the trout farm. I could go on,' he said. 'They're all jumping on board.'

But Charlie would not be convinced. 'It won't be enough.'

'Do you know what I think?' said Karl. Charlie shook her head. He pulled the car over and trained his serious grey eyes upon her. 'I think you've got a chip on your shoulder. I think it's been there for a very long time and ...' He pointed to a tall candlebark. 'I think it's about the size of that tree.'

'As big as that?' She tried to laugh off his remark and failed. Instead her voice was small, barely recognisable. Where was her usual smart comeback when she needed it? Karl leaned over, took her face in steady hands, and kissed her with infinite care. It wasn't just a kiss. It was an article of faith, a reassurance, even a dare. A dare to let it all go, to heave the heavy chip away and walk lightly once more on the earth. A pledge that he would see her through, if she had courage enough to take the risk. The kiss of a man with a woman, not a boy with a girl, and it literally took her breath away. Karl stroked her cheek. There was something deeply intimate and reassuring about the caress.

'Are we good to go?' he asked. She nodded and he returned his hands to the wheel. She missed his touch already. The jeep continued up the mountain, turned left at a fork in the track and stopped abruptly. Dozens of red-and-white Herefords dotted the slope, cows with well-grown calves, ready for weaning.

'It's just like at the other sites,' he said, snatching up a notebook. 'Not a radio collar in sight.' They'd spent the last week tracking down the four hundred head Bill had put into the park. Their movements were meant to be monitored with GPS collars. So far, Karl and Charlie had not found one single beast fitted with a tracking device.

'What happens now?' asked Charlie.

Karl kissed her again, a brief, triumphant kiss this time. 'We have enough evidence,' he said, patting his camera. 'Let's shut this trial down.'

CHAPTER 39

'Y ou ready?' asked Charlie.

'Ready as I'll ever be.' This wasn't true. Sam felt like a deer in the spotlights. Today was the day she'd decided to come clean with the town. It was a natural progression. For months now, a bulldozer of truth had inexorably ploughed its way through her life, tearing down each lie. The charade Sam had acted out for the people of Currajong would be the final falsehood to fall.

Charlie parked the car outside the general store. Marjorie first. She was known for her big heart. 'What if she hates me for it?' Sam cringed at the pathetic tone of her voice.

'Too bad,' said Charlie. 'Just do it.'

'Right.' Sam took a second to steel herself to the task ahead. She waited until there were no customers in the shop, then braved the door.

'Charlie,' said Marjorie. She stopped cleaning the glass refrigerator doors and put down her spray bottle. 'What can I do for you?'

'Do you have a minute?' asked Sam.

Marjorie looked around at the empty shop. 'It sure looks that way.'

'I've got something to tell you.' Marjorie's gentle face softened.

'This probably sounds ridiculous, but … I'm not really Charlie. I've been pretending. To you, to everybody.'

Marjorie put on her most sympathetic smile. 'I know, love. I know.'

Sam had her next sentence ready to go, her mouth running ahead of her brain, trying to get the humiliation over with. 'My name is Samantha—' Sam stopped short. She must have misheard. 'You know?'

Marjorie leaned over and patted her hand. 'Yes, dear.'

'Since when?' It was almost a demand.

'Since the beginning. Would you like tea? Or coffee perhaps?' Marjorie put on the kettle. 'I only have instant, I'm afraid.'

'I don't understand,' said Sam. 'Why didn't you say something?'

'I didn't like to pry. I supposed you had your reasons, and you'd tell me in your own time — when you were ready. I've lived in this town all my life, dear. Most of us have. We all knew about Mary's babies and the terrible choice she had to make.' Marjorie walked to the front door and flipped the sign to *Closed*. 'You're very different from your sister. I guessed right away. I've been worried about Charlie. Such a kind girl, that one. Always came by to help me load up the deliveries of a Friday, because of my back. Is she okay?'

'Yes,' said Sam. 'Yes, she is. Would you like to see her? She's out in the car.'

'Well, bring her in, for goodness sake!' said Marjorie.

Sam went out to the car. 'Have you done it?' asked Charlie. Sam nodded. 'What happened?'

'Marjorie wants to see you.' Charlie looked scared stiff. 'Come on,' said Sam. 'It's going to be fine.' They pushed their way through the door together.

'Charlie.' Marjorie beamed and enfolded her in a motherly embrace. 'Welcome home.'

It was the same thing all over town. Wherever they went, people confessed that they already knew. 'Course I did,' said George at the produce store, with a gruff laugh. 'The new *not quite right* Charlie didn't have a clue. Our Charlie wouldn't have been silly enough to buy that damn Showstopper horse feed, when you can mix your own for half the price. Or buy a rubber mallet to drive in steel fence posts. Or ask if you could buy fencing wire by the metre.'

Sam felt her cheeks burn. 'Why didn't you say?'

'Wasn't any of my business, was it?' he said. 'I could see you were a good kid, and you must've had your reasons. I was just happy to know that other little baby of Mary's was okay; happy to know she'd finally come home to Currajong.'

Even Harry from the garage had known. 'You may be a loud-mouth bitch, Charlie, but I've got to hand it to you – you know your way around an engine better than my best apprentice. This one?' He gestured to Sam with a toss of his head. 'Wouldn't know a carburettor from a head gasket.' He wiped his greasy black hands on a rag. 'What's your name again?'

'Samantha. Or Sam. Call me Sam.'

Harry looked at her like she'd gone mad. 'I'd just as soon go on calling you Charlie,' he said, putting his head back under the bonnet. 'Seeing as I'm used to it.'

It was an extraordinary thing. Like the collective consciousness of the town had quietly chosen to embrace Sam for who she was, regard-less of names or labels. They'd accepted her on face value, not in place of Charlie, but in addition to Charlie. 'Come on,' said Sam. 'We've got one last visit to make.'

Sam and Charlie stood together in Bushy's kitchen. He regarded them with no hint of surprise. So he knew too. 'Let's have a cuppa.' His face cracked into a smile. They sat down on plastic chairs around a card table, while Bushy switched on the electric kettle. He took a cigarette from a metal tin, fetched three chipped mugs from hooks on the wall, and added sugar and coffee. 'Run out of milk, I'm afraid.'

'Bushy,' asked Sam. 'That very first day, did you—?'

'Oh, I knew all right.' He lit his cigarette and coughed twice. 'I'm no fool.' Charlie let out a whoop of laughter and Sam wanted to strangle her. 'You wasn't bad with them horses. You made a fair fist of it.' He blew a smoke ring and grinned, like he'd just heard a very funny joke. 'But you weren't no Charlie.'

'I don't understand,' said Sam in confusion. 'You'd never even met my sister.'

'Didn't have to.' He turned to Charlie. 'You've got a quite a reputation, young lady.'

Charlie bristled, instantly on the defensive. 'Do you think I give a rat's?'

'The finest young rider and trainer ever turned out of the district. That's the reputation I'm talking about.'

Charlie's jaw dropped. 'People actually say that?'

'My word, they do.' The humming kettle began to whistle. He flicked off the switch. 'And if you'd stop making so much noise yourself, you might be able to hear them.'

'Outside,' ordered Sam. Condor cocked his head and flew onto the kitchen table instead, scattering her papers to the floor. Sam didn't scold him. She hadn't been able to concentrate anyway. Her thoughts kept returning to the extraordinary events of yesterday. Sam gave the big black bird a crust and chased him out the back door. Then she gathered the forms from the floor and put them aside, giving up the pretence of doing paperwork. Sam was in no mood for quarterly income estimates and insurance policies. Instead she put on Kasey Chambers' latest album and gazed out the window to the luminous, blue mountains beyond.

Everything was perfect. At last there were no more secrets, no more misunderstandings or half-truths. Today was the first day of a new, authentic life here in Currajong. She had Charlie's confidence and affection. She had the unconditional acceptance of the town. And best of all, she had Drew's love. Sam felt capable of anything.

Phoenix's imperious neigh sounded from the yard, reminding Sam that everything wasn't perfect after all. Ryan had put the young stallion through his paces during the week, and pronounced him ready to go to his new owner. That wasn't going to happen, not if she could help it. What she needed was a plan. Maybe Dad could help? Outbid the buyer, make Ryan an offer he couldn't refuse? The sound of wheels on gravel distracted Sam from her reverie. Maybe it was Drew? If they put their heads together, they were bound to come up with a solution.

'Hello? Anybody home?' Sam froze. Faith was the last person on earth that Sam expected to walk into the kitchen.

'Mum, what on earth are you doing here?' Faith approached Sam with outstretched arms and enfolded her in a hug. For one lovely, fleeting moment, Sam was excited to see her mother. She had so much to tell her, so much to show her. Such a lot to brag about. But in almost the same instant images of Pharaoh crowded into her mind, hardening her heart. Sam pulled away. She hadn't forgiven her mother, not by a long shot.

'Darling, I told you I was coming.' Sam looked blank. 'On the phone . . . from Saint Tropez?'

'I didn't think you were serious,' said Sam. 'I told you not to.'

'Nonsense, Samantha. Surely I can visit my own daughter?'

Sam marshalled up a hundred responses in her head – clever ones, bitter ones, sarcastic ones – but couldn't blurt out a single line. 'Why didn't you ring first?' was the best she could manage.

Faith heaved a great sigh. 'I thought you might not agree to see me, Samantha.'

She was probably right. Sam stared at her mother, lost for words. Faith looked larger than life and utterly out of place in Brumby's little kitchen. You could tell she'd been in France. The French always over-dressed for everything. Whatever would Charlie make of her? Faith wore high heels, belted tailored trousers and a lavender blouse. Lavender for God's sake. The elegant ensemble was set off with a striped silk scarf and sparkling cluster earrings. Had Faith always looked so overdone? Or had Sam's own tastes been stripped bare in this remote place?

She wanted to run to her room, flee from this old life that was so unexpectedly catching up with her. Then a wild, hopeful thought struck her. 'You got Pharaoh back, didn't you? That why you're here.'

Faith's face fell. 'It's not possible, darling. I've tried my hardest. Pharaoh is not for sale.'

Sam was hollow with disappointment. 'I want you to go, Mum. I'm not ready to do this.'

'Not even a pot of tea?' asked Faith. 'I have . . . I have quite a lot to tell you.' She looked genuinely stricken at the prospect of having to leave.

Sam studied her mother's anxious, eager face and relented. 'Sit down, Mum.' Sam pulled out a chair at the kitchen table, half expecting her mother to turn up her nose at its cracked linoleum seat. But Faith nodded her thanks and sat down without complaint. Sam put on the kettle and sat down too. For a little while nobody spoke. 'You haven't told me what a dump this place is yet,' said Sam at last.

To Sam's surprise, Faith's eyes glistened with tears. She reached across the table and took Sam's hands tenderly in her own. 'I'm sorry about Pharaoh. That was so terribly, terribly wrong of me.' Her tone was unusually heartfelt. 'You may not believe this, Samantha, hurt as you are, but I miss him too. I will never stop trying to bring Pharaoh home.' Her mother's obvious contrition was very moving. Sam was confused, unsure of how to react. 'I do have something else to offer,' said Faith.

Sam cut her off. 'There's nothing else I want from you.'

Faith cast her an uncertain glance, then reached into her bag and produced a large, yellow envelope. 'For you, Samantha. Please, at least look at it.' Sam nearly pushed it back across the table unopened, but curiosity won out.

No, it couldn't be. At first she was too stunned to appreciate the significance of what she was reading. Registration papers declaring Phoenix to be a foundation sire of the Australian Brumby Studbook. She read on, not daring to believe. His owner was listed as Samantha Carmichael.

'Are you happy, darling?'

For a while Sam forgot how to speak. 'Oh yes,' she said, when she finally found her tongue. 'God, yes!'

'Then you must forgive me for Pharaoh,' said her mother. 'You simply must.'

This was classic Faith. Ordering forgiveness, like it was a new fragrance or something. But her mother's high-handedness could not detract from the pure joy of the occasion. 'Thank you,' said Sam, overwhelmed. 'I feel like I'm dreaming. How did you know about Phoenix?'

'Mary told me.'

Could Faith's visit become any more astonishing? 'But I thought you hated Mary?'

'We're very different people, that's true.' The kettle began its low whistle. 'But we share a powerful connection — you.' Sam turned off the kettle and sat back down. 'Samantha.' Her mother's tone became serious. 'I have some rather more difficult news for you.'

'What's wrong? Is Dad okay?'

Faith frowned. 'May I have some water?'

Impatiently Sam fetched her a glass. Through the kitchen window she saw Drew's ute pull up outside. She sat back down and fixed her eyes on Faith. 'Mum just tell me.' The tension became unbearable.

Faith took a sip, uttered a shuddering sigh and said at last, 'Your father and I . . . we've separated. We're getting a divorce.' The water in the glass rippled, betraying her unsteady arm.

'Oh, Mum, no,' Sam reached for her hand. 'What happened?'

'Your father has been unfaithful, Samantha. On more than one occasion it seems.' She shook her head sorrowfully. 'It's been a great trial for me.'

'Of course, Mum. Of course it has.' Sam squeezed her hand. 'We'll get through this together.'

'There's more,' said Faith. 'Much more. It's about … your father.'

'Mum, you already said that.'

Faith shook her head. 'I mean your real father, your biological father.'

Sam felt the blood rush to her head. The mysterious Robert Smith? Could she finally meet him? 'What have you found out? Do you know where he is? We think he's been sending money to Mary and Charlie ever since the transplant.'

'I don't doubt it.' Faith nodded as if it all made sense. 'He's a very wealthy man. A generous man as well.'

'So you know him?' Sam's hands were trembling.

'I do. We both know him, as a matter of fact.'

Faith seemed paralysed. A vile thought struck Sam. Bill Chandler - Bill was her father. Wealthy enough to be the secret benefactor. Living next door to Mary all these years. It had to be Bill. Thank God Drew was adopted. Otherwise, well, it didn't bear thinking about.

'Tell me the truth, Mum. I can take it.'

Sam steeled herself for the shocking confirmation, while Faith forced a smile. 'Your father is . . . well, he's your father and my husband — Victor Carmichael.'

Her mother's words made no sense. 'You mean Dad is really my dad?' Faith nodded. 'And Charlie's too?'

'It all came out in France,' said Faith. 'If you'd come, he'd have never confessed. He'd have been too ashamed. In any case, he told me the whole story ... and now I'm telling you.'

Sam opened her mouth to speak, but Faith raised her eyebrows. 'Please, Samantha, don't interrupt me. I may not be able to start again.'

Sam nodded and Faith gave her a grateful smile. 'It's almost twenty years ago now. Your father was a cabinet minister. He undertook a tour of the Upper Murray, supporting some conservative party candidate in a by-election campaign.' She took a deep breath and appeared to be composing herself. 'He met Mary somehow.' Faith gulped her water. 'She was a girl of seventeen. Your father was forty.' The words hung in the room like a bad smell. 'He behaved very badly, Samantha. In every way. He gave the girl ...' Faith looked suddenly shamefaced. 'He gave your mother a false name, but was careless with his phone number. When Mary discovered her pregnancy, she rang him and left messages. He ignored them. Can you imagine that? We'd been trying for years to have a child, and he ignores this poor pregnant girl. Mary rang him once a month until the babies . . . until you and Charlene were born. I suppose she was hoping he might help her, so she needn't relinquish one of her twins.'

'He didn't?'

'No, he didn't. Instead he did something monstrous. He organised to privately adopt one of the infants. It didn't matter which one, apparently. Your father wanted to give me a baby, you see. He knew how much I wanted one, and he loved me – in his own peculiar way. But he knew that I'd leave him if I discovered the truth.'

'So,' said Sam, reeling from the news. 'When I found out that I was adopted, he let me think he wasn't my real father, even though he was? Just so he didn't have to tell you the truth?'

'When he learned your sister was so terribly ill, the guilt was too much for him. He set up a generous monthly stipend for Charlie and Mary. He bought your sister a car. Our accountant raised the unexplained expenditure with me last week, and I confronted Victor.' Faith looked grim. 'There were other liaisons. My whole marriage has been a lie. The one thing real about it is you, Samantha, and so here we are.'

Sam's eyes filled with tears as she tried to take her mother's words in. How hurt Faith must feel. And how weird to learn her dad was, well, her dad. 'Is that everything?' she asked, suspecting more secrets.

'It's enough, don't you think?' Faith gave a shaky smile.

'So Dad really is my father, and he's Charlie's father too?'

Faith nodded. Sam slumped back into her chair. For the second time in months, her world had been utterly changed. Was nothing ever real?

Drew poked his head around the door. 'You two okay?'

Sam looked into his concerned face, into Faith's solicitous eyes. She thought of Charlie. How astonished she'd be by this news ... her news too. Whirlwind and Phoenix and the new foal —Sam's dream herd grazed peacefully in the shadow of Maroong Mountain. Who was she kidding? It didn't get more real than this.

CHAPTER 40

Sam fussed about the kitchen, rearranging scones on the plate, pretending to be busy. Charlie got off the phone, her face ashen. 'He wants to meet me.' She looked so unsure, like a scared rabbit. She looked about twelve.

'What do *you* want to do?' asked Sam. 'That's the important thing.'

'I haven't a clue,' said Charlie. 'Part of me hates him – a big part.' Sam nodded. She felt the same way. 'But part of me is dying of curiosity. You know our father, Sam. You always have. I want that chance.'

It had been a week since Faith dropped her bombshell. Sam was almost as confused as Charlie. Dad was flying home. He was sorry, he said. Wanted to make amends. Wanted his wife back. Wanted to make it right — for his daughters, for Faith, for Mary . . . but how to atone for a lifetime of deceit? Sam's own brief charade paled beside her father's cruel folly.

Drew and Bill walked in, voices raised. 'Abbey's a bloody good bloodline,' said Bill. 'I'll give you that, but breeding brumbies?' He snorted. 'You need your head read.'

'We already have two top stallions, Dad, with bookings for next year's stud season. And Sam's dressage training a first-cross Andalusian-brumby mare, caught straight out of the park. Reckons she'll get her to Grand Prix standard without any trouble at all.' He helped himself to a scone. 'Remember when El Soldado Ranch lost that imported mare a few years back?'

Bill nodded. 'Don was ropeable. That mare was some special strain? A Carpathian, I think he said. He paid a fortune for her.'

'A Carthusian,' corrected Drew. 'And that lost Carthusian is the dam of Sam's mare. Don's been out to confirm it – and get this, he offered to buy her. Imagine that. Don Campbell wanting to buy a brumby. Not a bad foundation mare to start out with, eh?'

'I'll be the judge of that,' grumbled Bill.

'Come up to the yards and see for yourself then,' said Drew. 'We'll keep the new colt here at Brumby's Run though.' He gave his father a friendly punch. 'You're not gelding this one, Dad.'

That night a storm raged over the mountain. Sam couldn't sleep. She slipped from bed without waking Drew, wrapped herself in the fluffy bathrobe that was a present from her mother, and tiptoed down the hall. She could hear Charlie's steady breathing as she passed her bedroom, Bess's soft snoring in her basket by the fire.

Sam pushed open the back door and stood until she had her night eyes. Things began to take shape in the gloom. Condor squawked from his perch on the verandah, ruffled his feathers and tucked his head back beneath his wing. The wind roared through the tree-tops. Shadows shifted and shook. Lightning cracked and lit up the scene for just an instant, giving Sam a snapshot of the sheds and yards and the wild dark forest beyond.

When Sam slipped off her robe, it felt like she was shedding more than her clothes. She walked naked into the rain. This was hers – all this power and beauty and terror. This was her home. The pain of loneliness was a vague memory that seemed to belong to somebody else. And as she whispered a small prayer to the spirit of Maroong Mountain, something told her that she need never be alone again.

ACKNOWLEDGEMENTS

Thank you to A.B. 'Banjo' Paterson, whose wonderful poem *Brumby's Run* inspired this story.

Thanks to the team at Pilyara Press, especially Kathryn Ledson, Kate Belle and Sydney Smith.

Thanks to Kathryn Massey, president of the Hunter Valley Brumby Association, for her tireless work on behalf of the magnificent wild horses of Australia.

And finally, thanks to my patient family for their love and support.

ABOUT THE AUTHOR

Bestselling Aussie Jennifer Scoullar writes page-turning fiction about the land, people and wildlife that she loves.

Scoullar is a lapsed lawyer who harbours a deep appreciation and respect for the natural world. She lives on a farm in Australia's southern Victorian ranges, and has ridden and bred horses all her life.

Her passion for animals and the bush is the catalyst for her best-selling books, which are all inspired by different landscapes.

Visit Jennifer's website to enter the monthly prize draw! If you enjoyed this book and have a moment or two, please leave an online rating or review. Reviews are of great help to authors.

www.jenniferscoullar.com

www.ingramcontent.com/pod-product-compliance
Lightning Source LLC
Chambersburg PA
CBHW032109180726
48284CB00002B/513